MIKE CAVALLARO's

NICO BRAVO

AND THE HOUND OF HADES

:01
First Second
NEW YORK

First Second

Copyright © 2019 by Mike Cavallaro

Published by First Second
First Second is an imprint of Roaring Brook Press, a division
of Holtzbrinck Publishing Holdings Limited Partnership
175 Fifth Avenue, New York, NY 10010

Don't miss your next favorite book from First Second! For the latest updates
go to firstsecondnewsletter.com and sign up for our enewsletter.

Library of Congress Control Number: 2018938076

Paperback ISBN: 978-1-62672-751-9
Hardcover ISBN: 978-1-250-19698-9

Our books may be purchased in bulk for promotional, educational, or business use.
Please contact your local bookseller or the Macmillan Corporate and Premium Sales Department at
(800) 221-7945 ext. 5442 or by email at MacmillanSpecialMarkets@macmillan.com.

First edition, 2019
Edited by Mark Siegel and Steve Behling
Book design by Rob Steen
Color by Gabrielle Gomez and Mike Cavallaro
Printed in China by 1010 Printing International Limited, North Point, Hong Kong

Written in fits and starts on whatever was handy, including scraps of paper, notepads, smartphones,
and laptops. The artwork was drawn digitally in Clip Studio on a MacBook Pro and a Cintiq 13HD,
lettered using Adobe Illustrator, and colored in Photoshop.

Paperback: 10 9 8 7 6 5 4 3 2 1
Hardcover: 10 9 8 7 6 5 4 3 2 1

TO BART

PART 1:
ROUND, LIKE A CUBE.

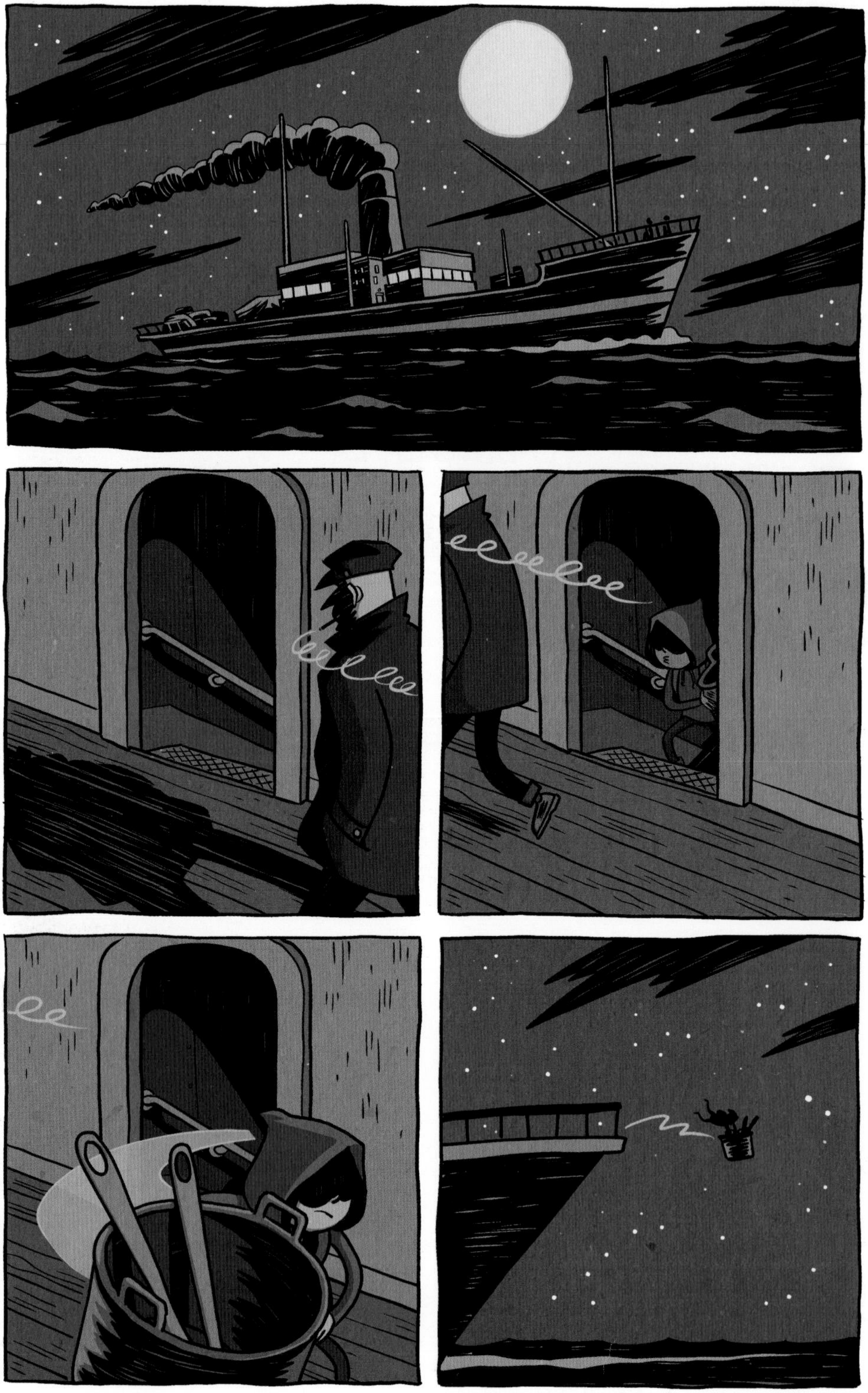

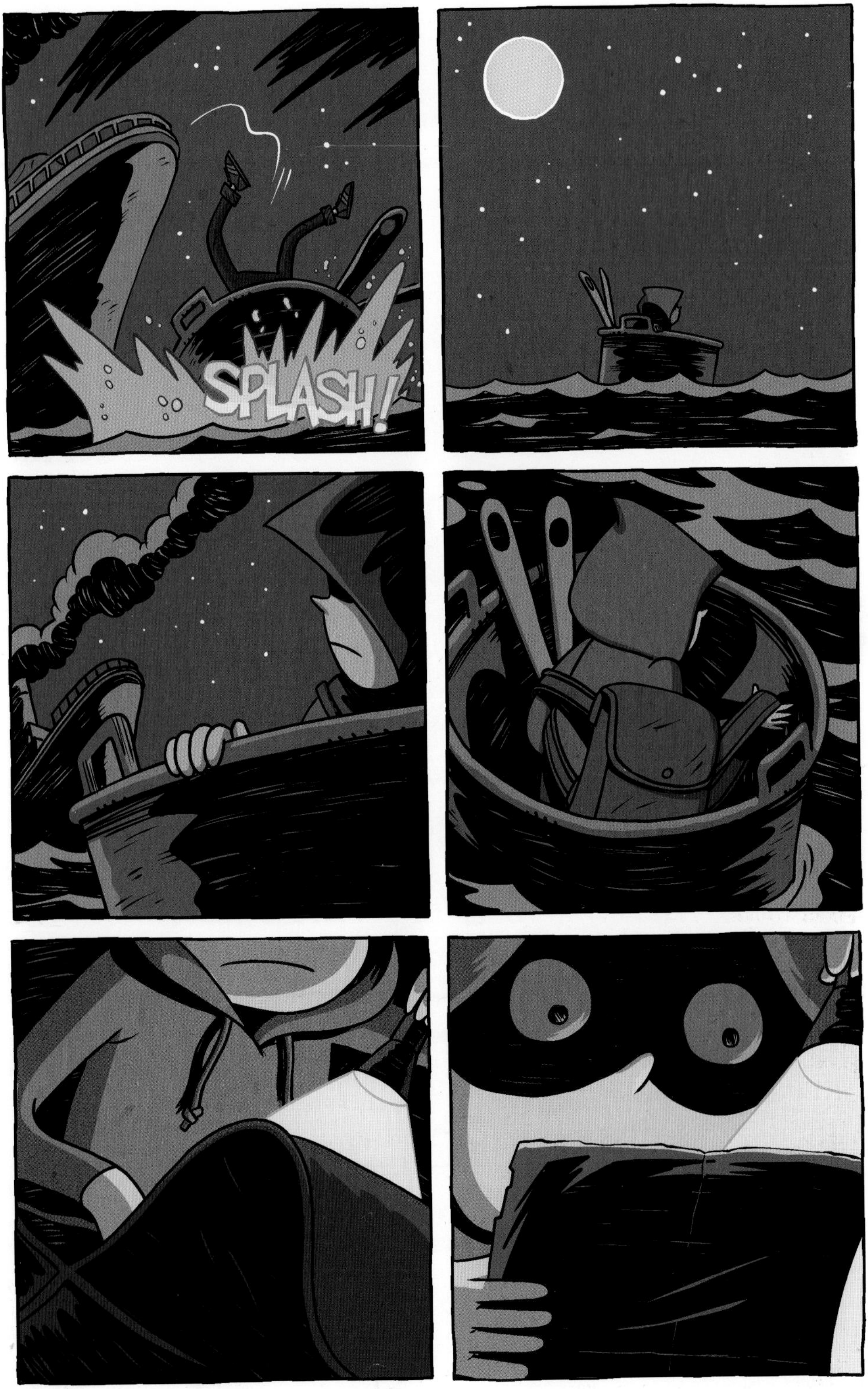
SPLASH!

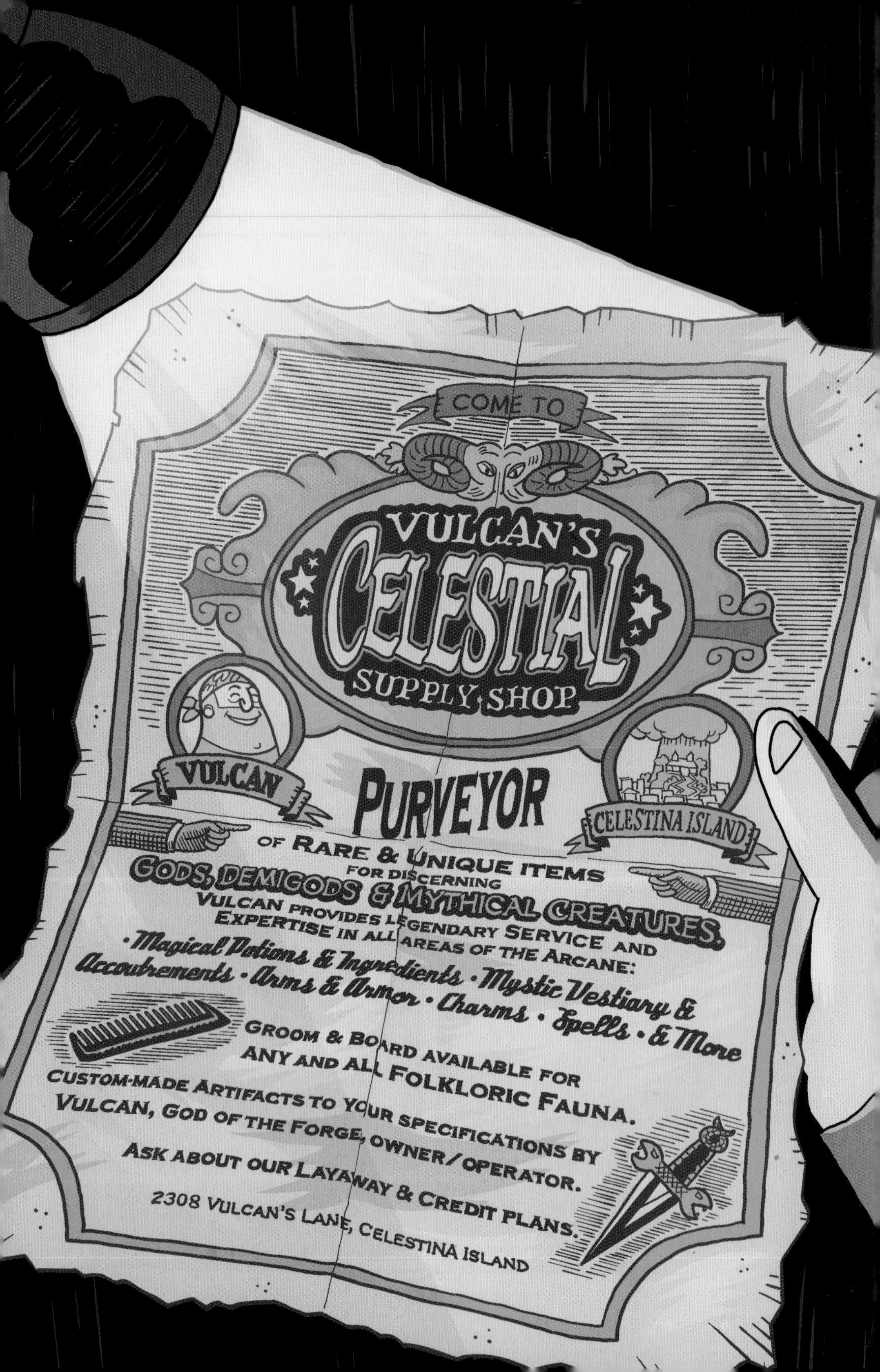
COME TO
VULCAN'S
CELESTIAL
SUPPLY SHOP
VULCAN
CELESTINA ISLAND
PURVEYOR
OF RARE & UNIQUE ITEMS
FOR DISCERNING
GODS, DEMIGODS & MYTHICAL CREATURES.
VULCAN PROVIDES LEGENDARY SERVICE AND
EXPERTISE IN ALL AREAS OF THE ARCANE:
• Magical Potions & Ingredients • Mystic Vestiary & Accoutrements • Arms & Armor • Charms • Spells • & More
GROOM & BOARD AVAILABLE FOR
ANY AND ALL FOLKLORIC FAUNA.
CUSTOM-MADE ARTIFACTS TO YOUR SPECIFICATIONS BY
VULCAN, GOD OF THE FORGE, OWNER/OPERATOR.
ASK ABOUT OUR LAYAWAY & CREDIT PLANS.
2308 VULCAN'S LANE, CELESTINA ISLAND

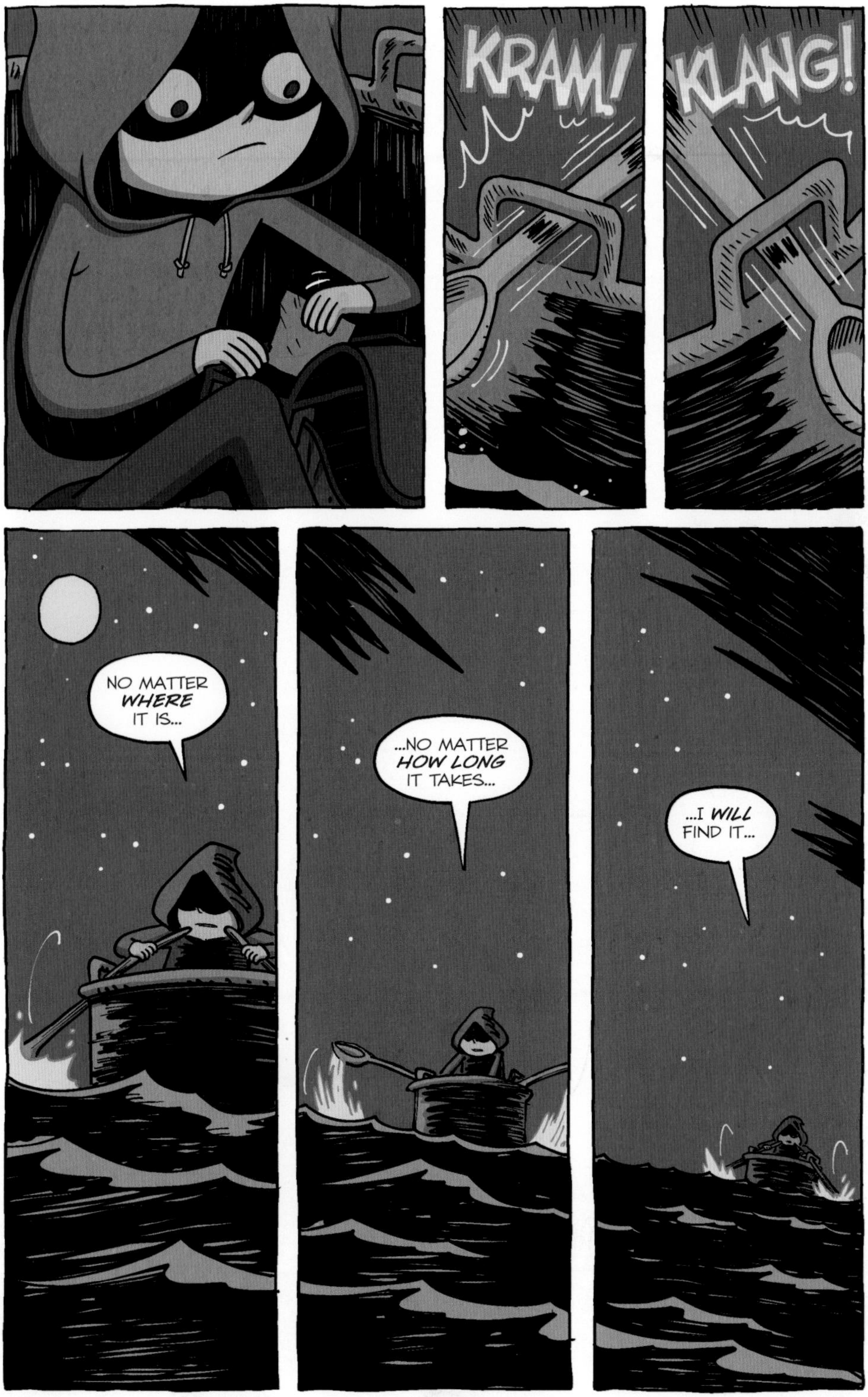

KRAM!
KLANG!
NO MATTER WHERE IT IS...
...NO MATTER HOW LONG IT TAKES...
...I WILL FIND IT...

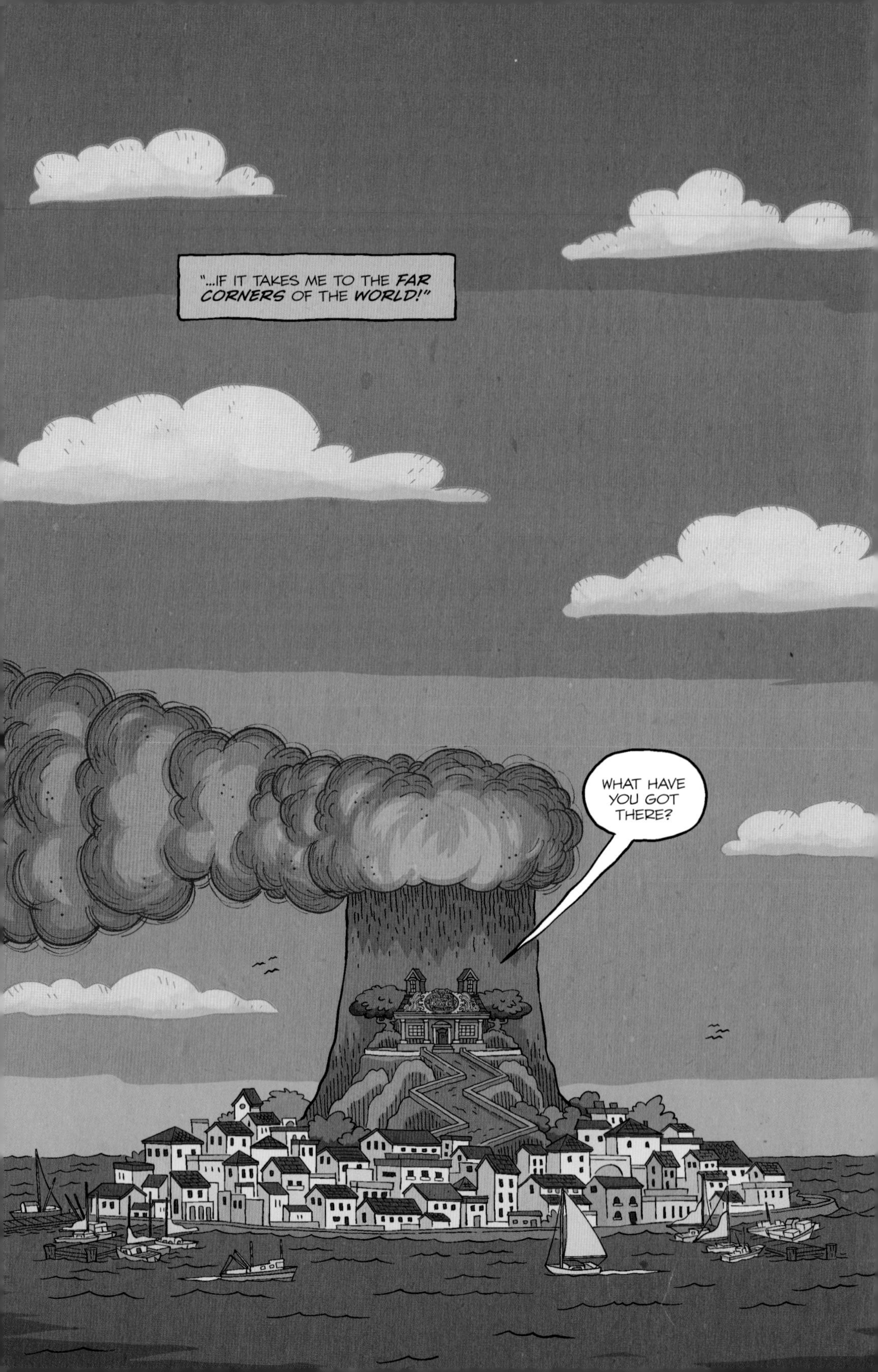
"...IF IT TAKES ME TO THE FAR CORNERS OF THE WORLD!"
WHAT HAVE YOU GOT THERE?

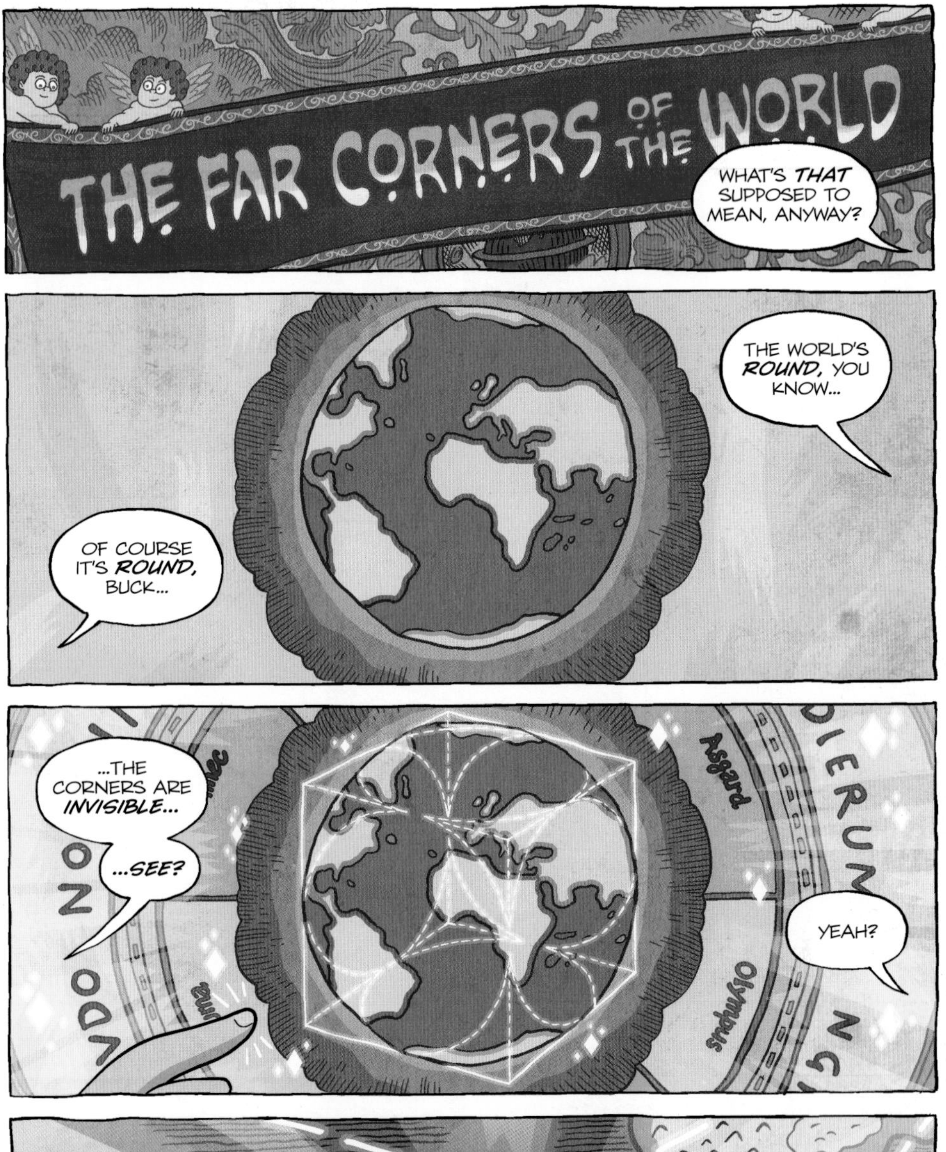
THE FAR CORNERS OF THE WORLD
WHAT'S ***THAT*** SUPPOSED TO MEAN, ANYWAY?
THE WORLD'S ***ROUND,*** YOU KNOW...
OF COURSE IT'S ***ROUND,*** BUCK...
...THE CORNERS ARE ***INVISIBLE...***
...SEE?
Asgard
YEAH?
YEAH. ACCORDING TO THIS, THERE'S ***EIGHT CORNERS*** AND WE LIVE RIGHT IN THE ***MIDDLE*** OF ONE...
Celestina Island
AND PEOPLE SAY ***I'M*** CRAZY...

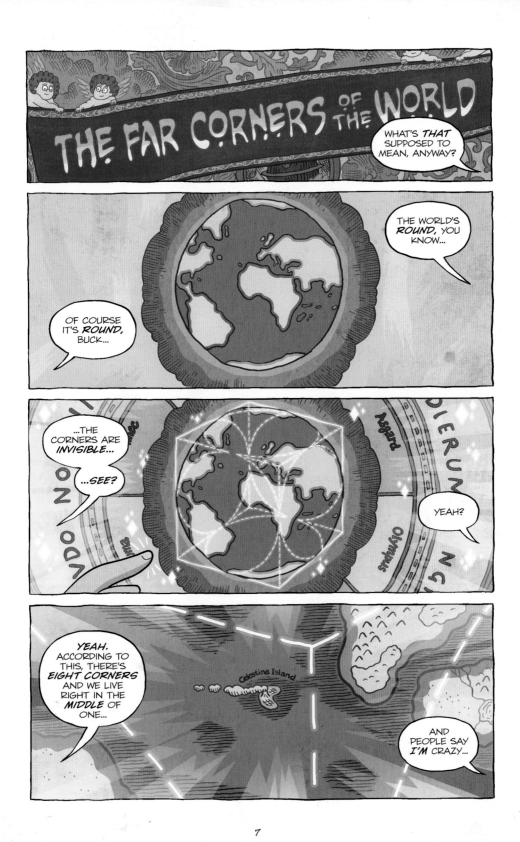

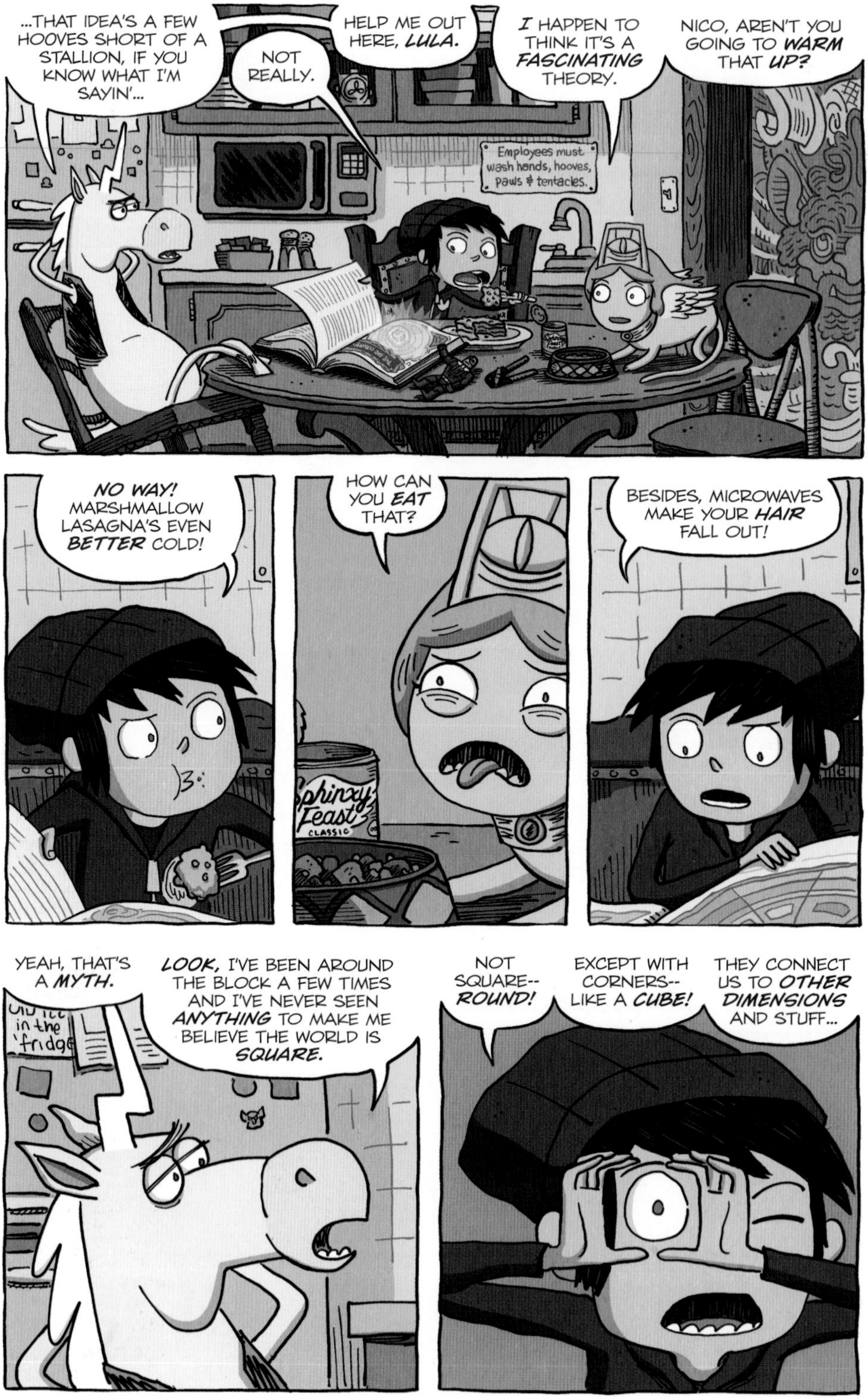
...THAT IDEA'S A FEW HOOVES SHORT OF A STALLION, IF YOU KNOW WHAT I'M SAYIN'...
NOT REALLY.
HELP ME OUT HERE, LULA.
I HAPPEN TO THINK IT'S A FASCINATING THEORY.
NICO, AREN'T YOU GOING TO WARM THAT UP?
Employees must wash hands, hooves, paws & tentacles.
NO WAY! MARSHMALLOW LASAGNA'S EVEN BETTER COLD!
HOW CAN YOU EAT THAT?
Sphinxy Feast CLASSIC
BESIDES, MICROWAVES MAKE YOUR HAIR FALL OUT!
YEAH, THAT'S A MYTH.
LOOK, I'VE BEEN AROUND THE BLOCK A FEW TIMES AND I'VE NEVER SEEN ANYTHING TO MAKE ME BELIEVE THE WORLD IS SQUARE.
NOT SQUARE-- ROUND!
EXCEPT WITH CORNERS-- LIKE A CUBE!
THEY CONNECT US TO OTHER DIMENSIONS AND STUFF...

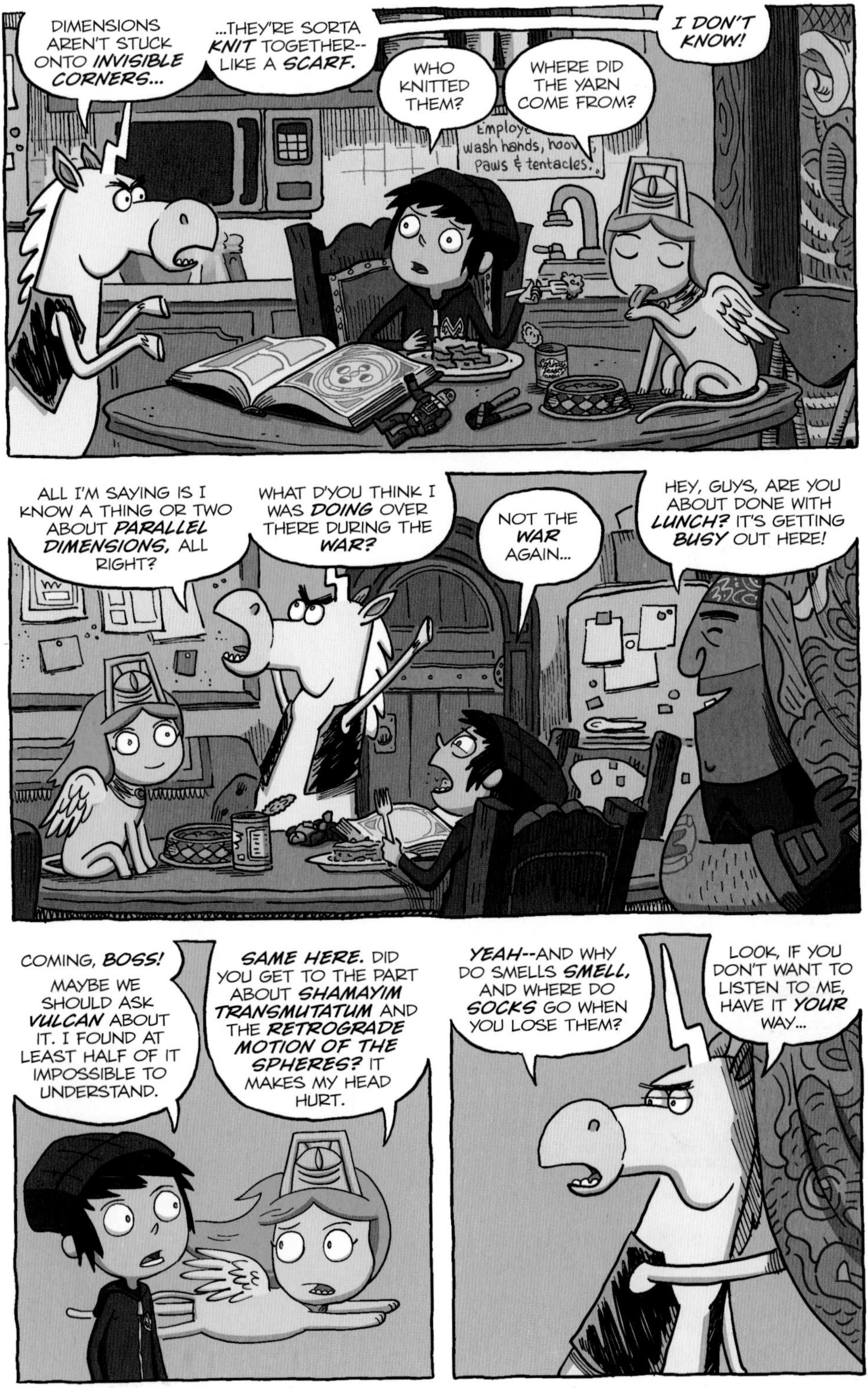
DIMENSIONS AREN'T STUCK ONTO INVISIBLE CORNERS...
...THEY'RE SORTA KNIT TOGETHER-- LIKE A SCARF.
WHO KNITTED THEM?
WHERE DID THE YARN COME FROM?
I DON'T KNOW!
Employe wash hands, hoov paws & tentacles.
ALL I'M SAYING IS I KNOW A THING OR TWO ABOUT PARALLEL DIMENSIONS, ALL RIGHT?
WHAT D'YOU THINK I WAS DOING OVER THERE DURING THE WAR?
NOT THE WAR AGAIN...
HEY, GUYS, ARE YOU ABOUT DONE WITH LUNCH? IT'S GETTING BUSY OUT HERE!
COMING, BOSS!
MAYBE WE SHOULD ASK VULCAN ABOUT IT. I FOUND AT LEAST HALF OF IT IMPOSSIBLE TO UNDERSTAND.
SAME HERE. DID YOU GET TO THE PART ABOUT SHAMAYIM TRANSMUTATUM AND THE RETROGRADE MOTION OF THE SPHERES? IT MAKES MY HEAD HURT.
YEAH--AND WHY DO SMELLS SMELL, AND WHERE DO SOCKS GO WHEN YOU LOSE THEM?
LOOK, IF YOU DON'T WANT TO LISTEN TO ME, HAVE IT YOUR WAY...

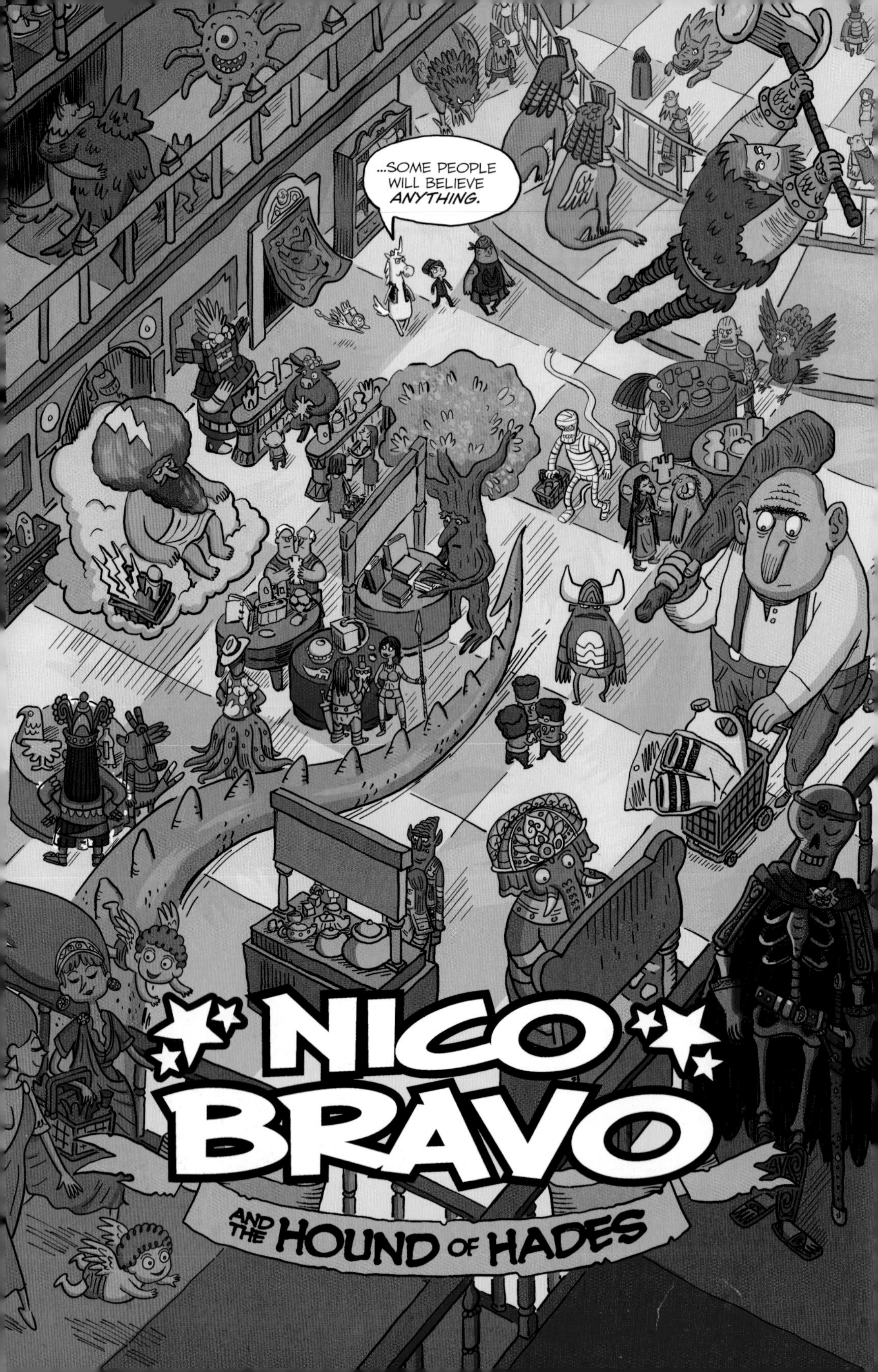
...SOME PEOPLE WILL BELIEVE *ANYTHING.*
NICO BRAVO
AND THE HOUND OF HADES

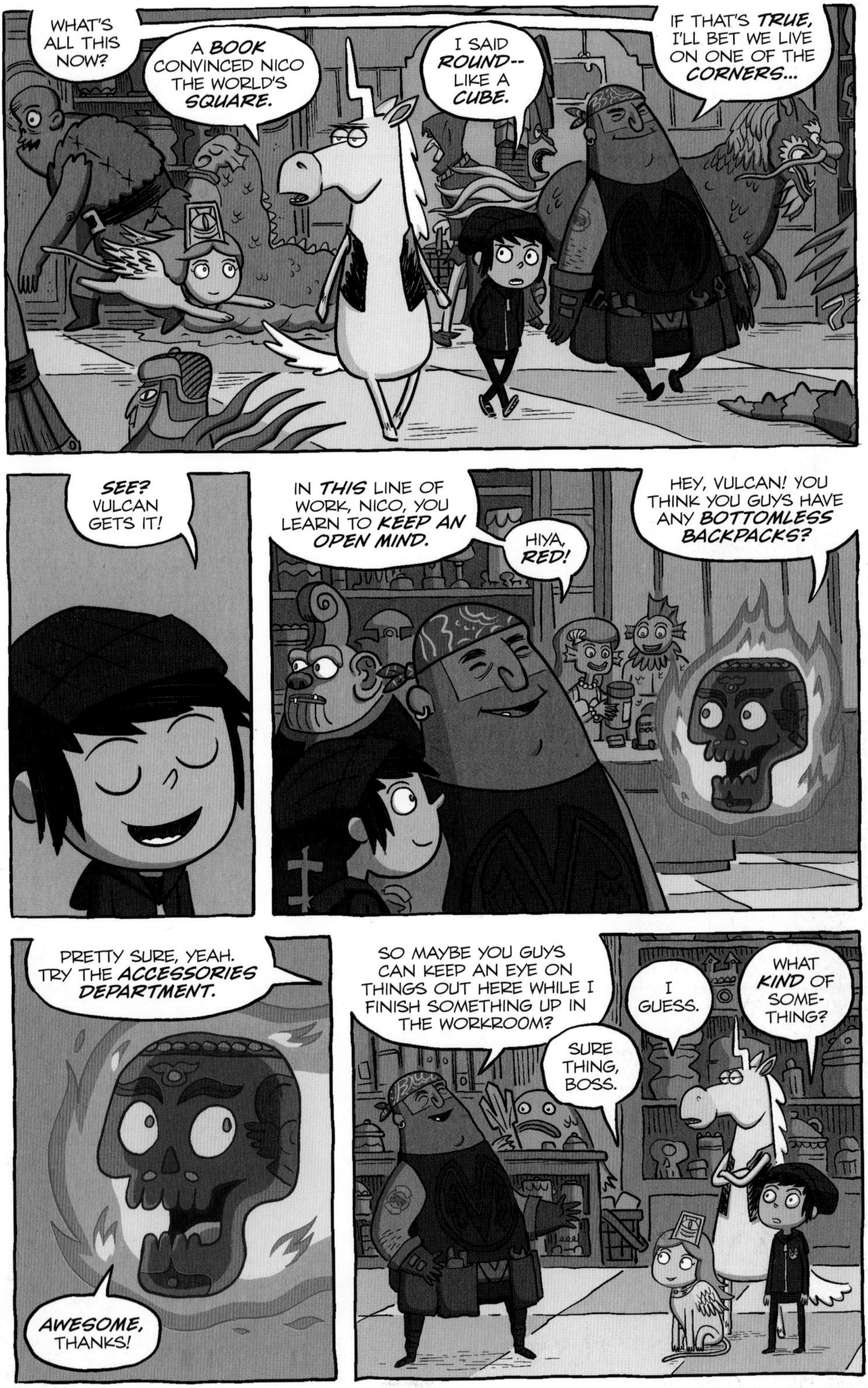
WHAT'S ALL THIS NOW?
A **BOOK** CONVINCED NICO THE WORLD'S **SQUARE.**
I SAID **ROUND--** LIKE A **CUBE.**
IF THAT'S **TRUE,** I'LL BET WE LIVE ON ONE OF THE **CORNERS...**
SEE? VULCAN GETS IT!
IN **THIS** LINE OF WORK, NICO, YOU LEARN TO **KEEP AN OPEN MIND.**
HIYA, **RED!**
HEY, VULCAN! YOU THINK YOU GUYS HAVE ANY **BOTTOMLESS BACKPACKS?**
PRETTY SURE, YEAH. TRY THE **ACCESSORIES DEPARTMENT.**
AWESOME, THANKS!
SO MAYBE YOU GUYS CAN KEEP AN EYE ON THINGS OUT HERE WHILE I FINISH SOMETHING UP IN THE WORKROOM?
SURE THING, BOSS.
I GUESS.
WHAT **KIND** OF SOME-THING?

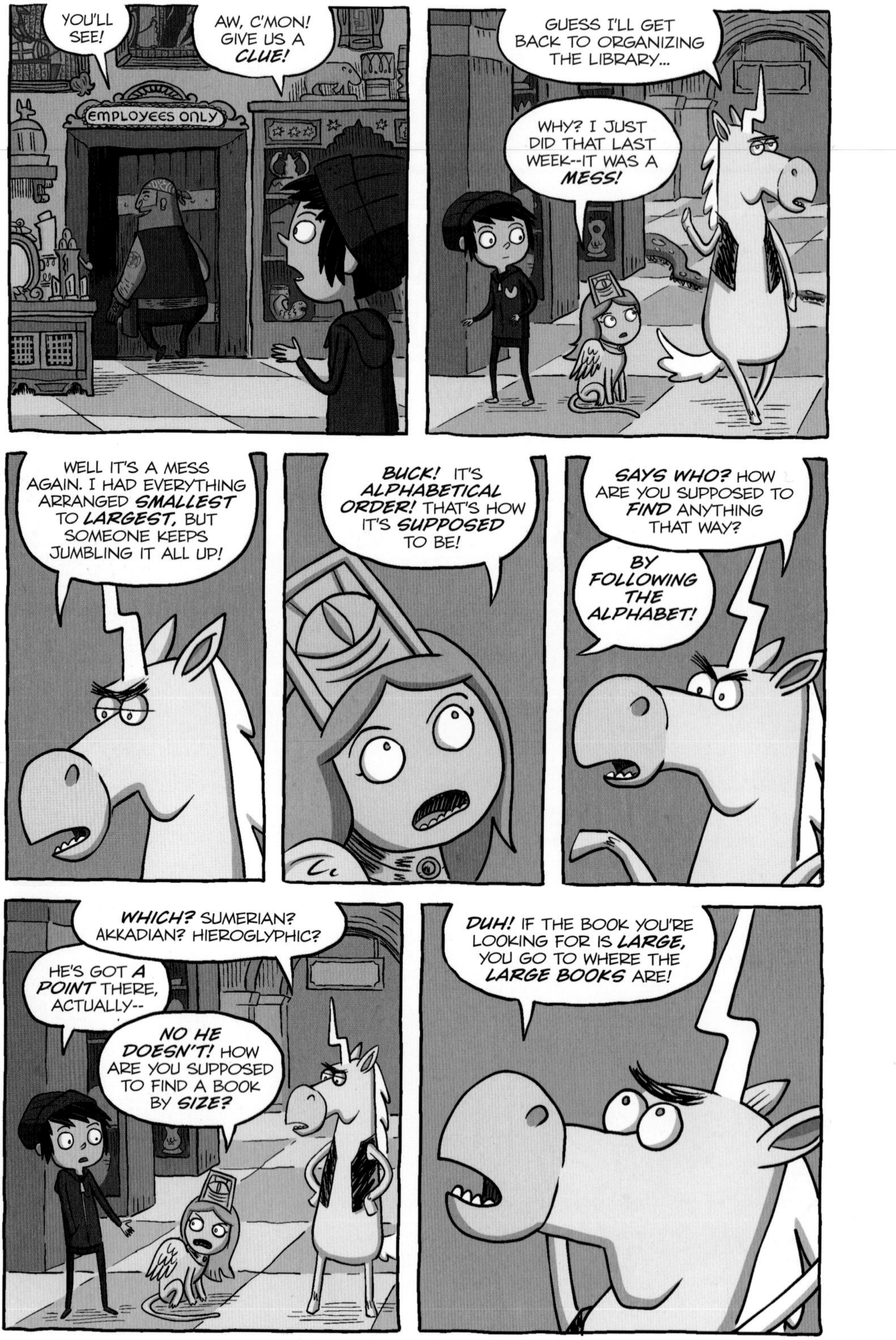
YOU'LL SEE!
AW, C'MON! GIVE US A CLUE!
EMPLOYEES ONLY
GUESS I'LL GET BACK TO ORGANIZING THE LIBRARY...
WHY? I JUST DID THAT LAST WEEK--IT WAS A MESS!
WELL IT'S A MESS AGAIN. I HAD EVERYTHING ARRANGED SMALLEST TO LARGEST, BUT SOMEONE KEEPS JUMBLING IT ALL UP!
BUCK! IT'S ALPHABETICAL ORDER! THAT'S HOW IT'S SUPPOSED TO BE!
SAYS WHO? HOW ARE YOU SUPPOSED TO FIND ANYTHING THAT WAY?
BY FOLLOWING THE ALPHABET!
WHICH? SUMERIAN? AKKADIAN? HIEROGLYPHIC?
HE'S GOT A POINT THERE, ACTUALLY--
NO HE DOESN'T! HOW ARE YOU SUPPOSED TO FIND A BOOK BY SIZE?
DUH! IF THE BOOK YOU'RE LOOKING FOR IS LARGE, YOU GO TO WHERE THE LARGE BOOKS ARE!

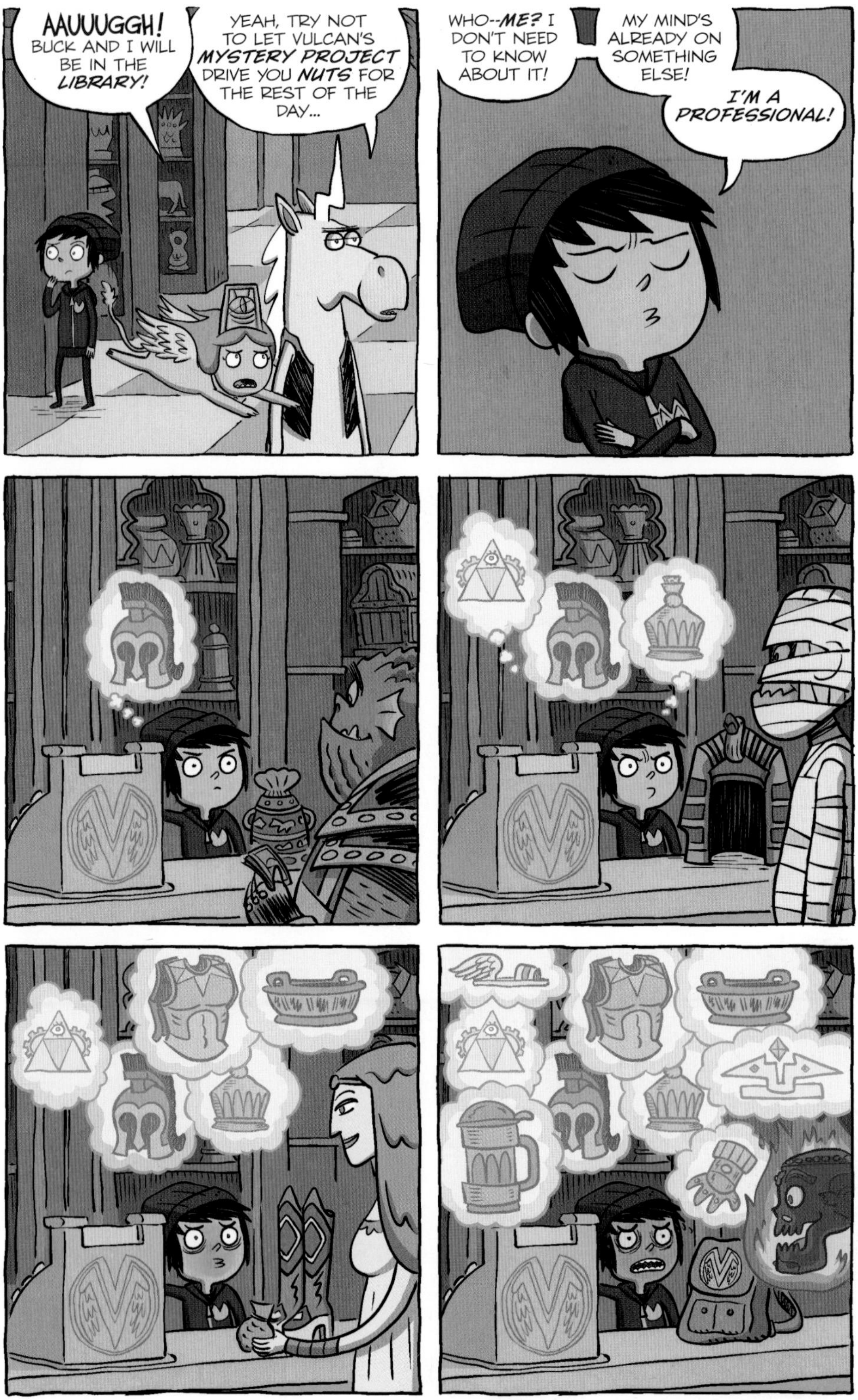
AAUUUGGH! BUCK AND I WILL BE IN THE LIBRARY!
YEAH, TRY NOT TO LET VULCAN'S MYSTERY PROJECT DRIVE YOU NUTS FOR THE REST OF THE DAY...
WHO--ME? I DON'T NEED TO KNOW ABOUT IT!
MY MIND'S ALREADY ON SOMETHING ELSE!
I'M A PROFESSIONAL!

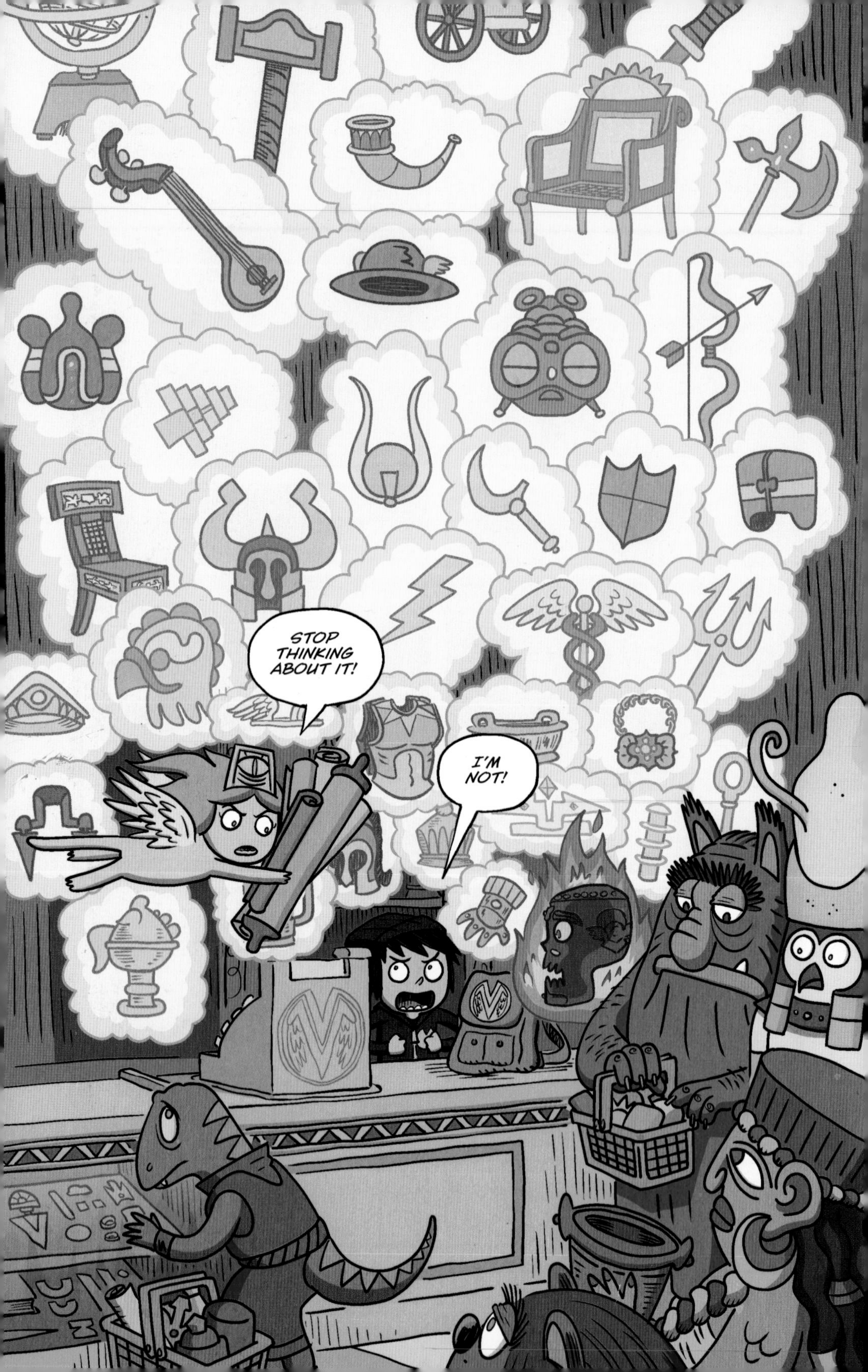
STOP THINKING ABOUT IT!
I'M NOT!

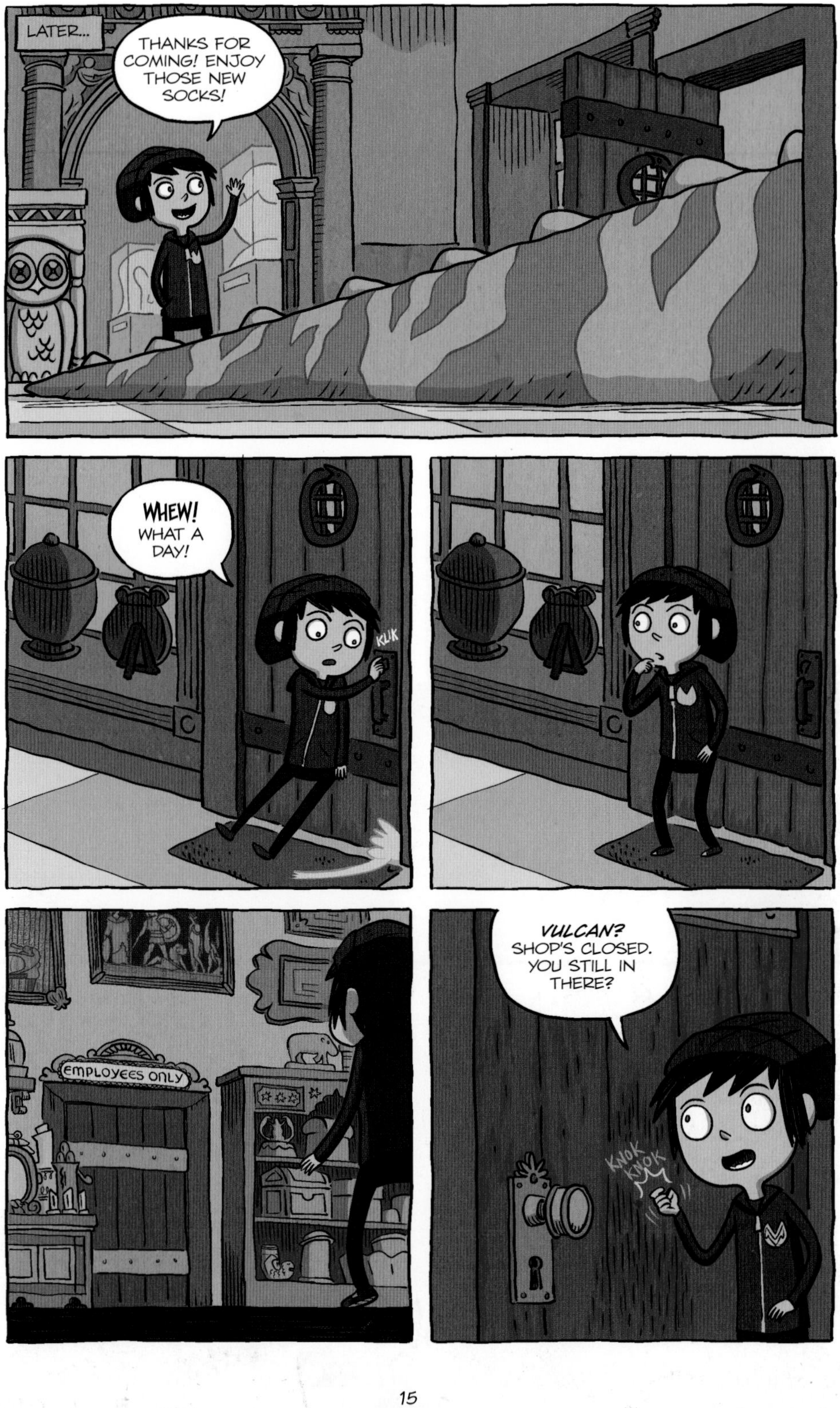
LATER...
THANKS FOR COMING! ENJOY THOSE NEW SOCKS!
WHEW! WHAT A DAY!
KLIK
EMPLOYEES ONLY
VULCAN? SHOP'S CLOSED. YOU STILL IN THERE?
KNOK KNOK

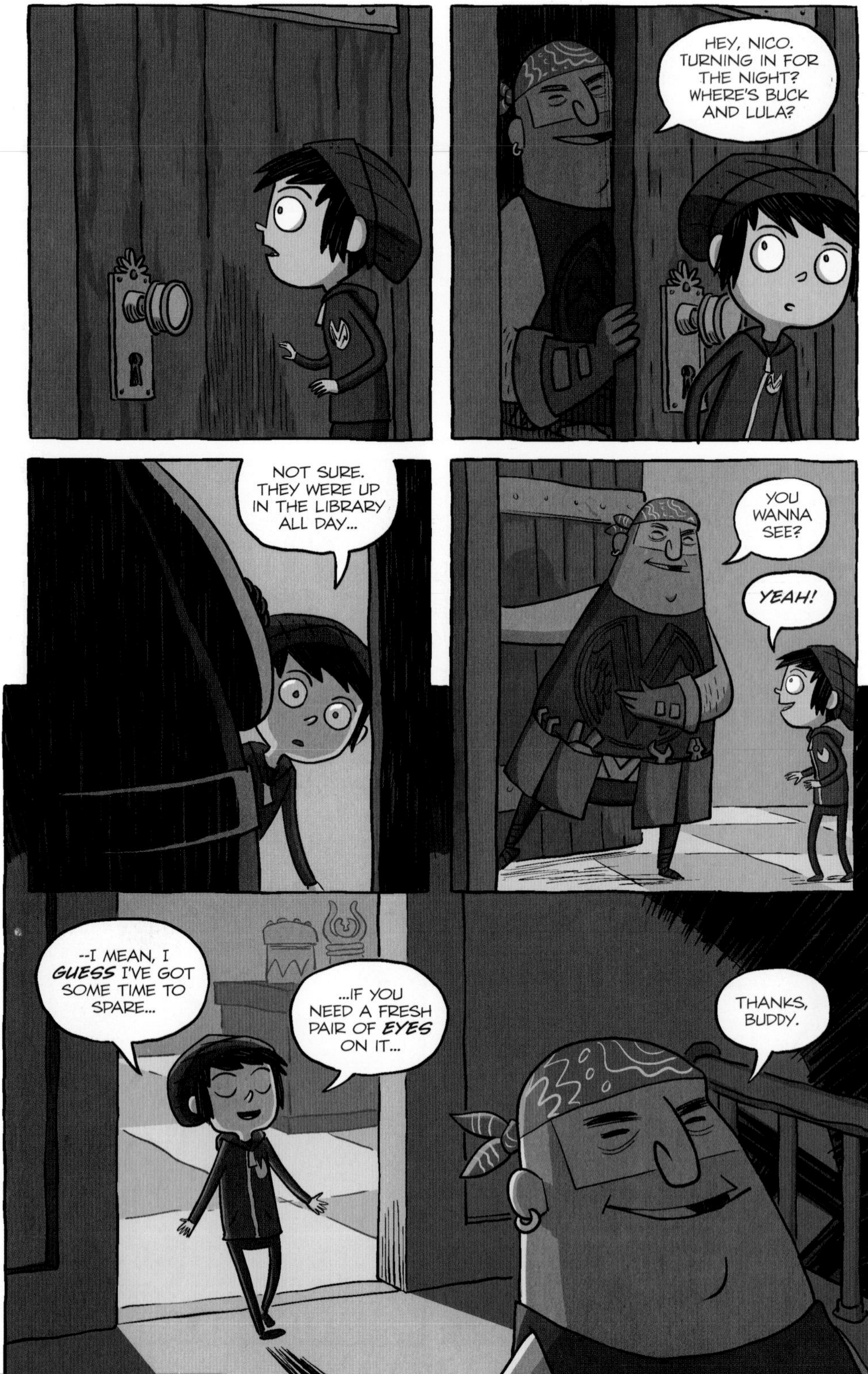
HEY, NICO. TURNING IN FOR THE NIGHT? WHERE'S BUCK AND LULA?
NOT SURE. THEY WERE UP IN THE LIBRARY ALL DAY...
YOU WANNA SEE?
YEAH!
--I MEAN, I GUESS I'VE GOT SOME TIME TO SPARE...
...IF YOU NEED A FRESH PAIR OF EYES ON IT...
THANKS, BUDDY.

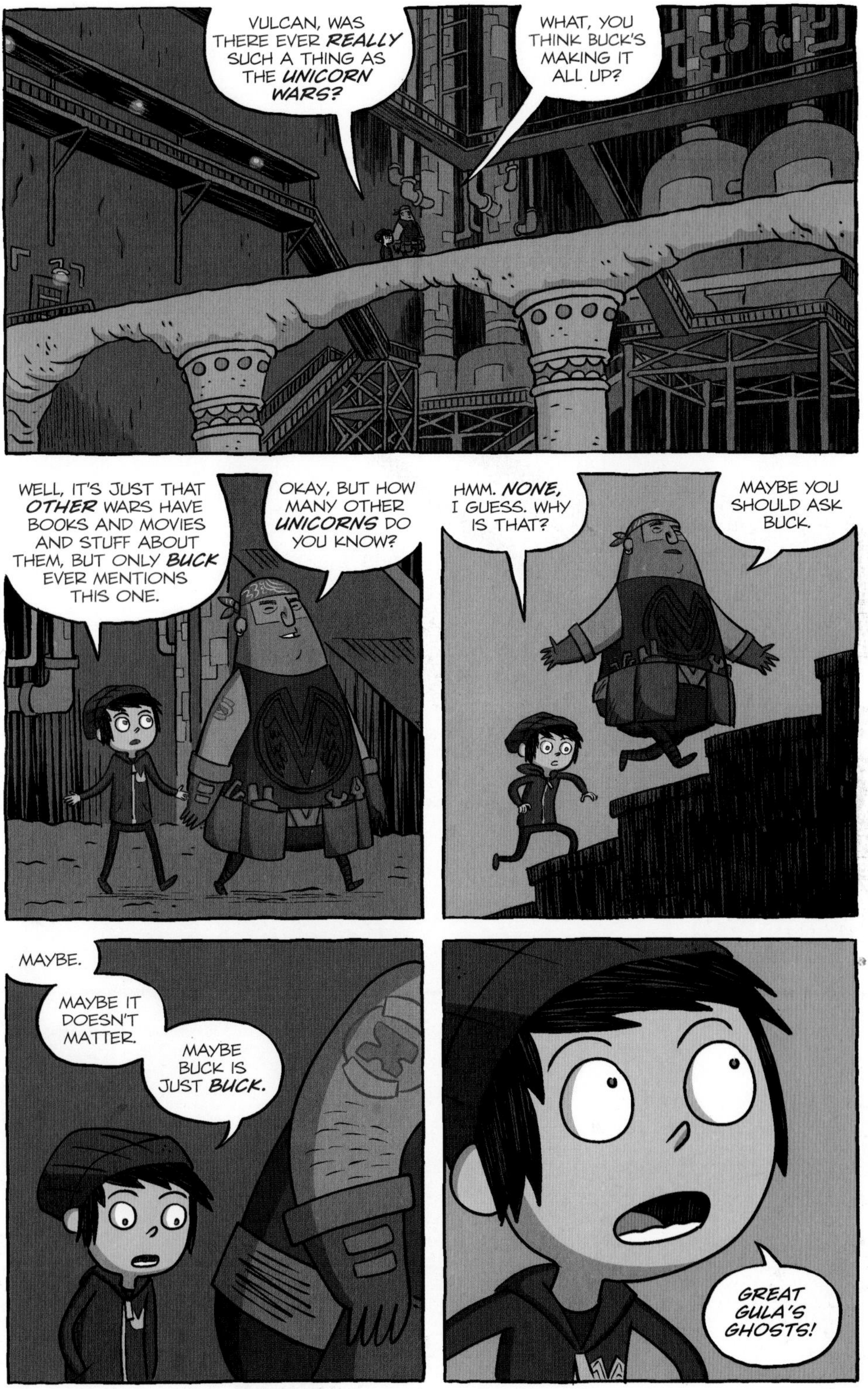
VULCAN, WAS THERE EVER REALLY SUCH A THING AS THE UNICORN WARS?
WHAT, YOU THINK BUCK'S MAKING IT ALL UP?
WELL, IT'S JUST THAT OTHER WARS HAVE BOOKS AND MOVIES AND STUFF ABOUT THEM, BUT ONLY BUCK EVER MENTIONS THIS ONE.
OKAY, BUT HOW MANY OTHER UNICORNS DO YOU KNOW?
HMM. NONE, I GUESS. WHY IS THAT?
MAYBE YOU SHOULD ASK BUCK.
MAYBE.
MAYBE IT DOESN'T MATTER.
MAYBE BUCK IS JUST BUCK.
GREAT GULA'S GHOSTS!

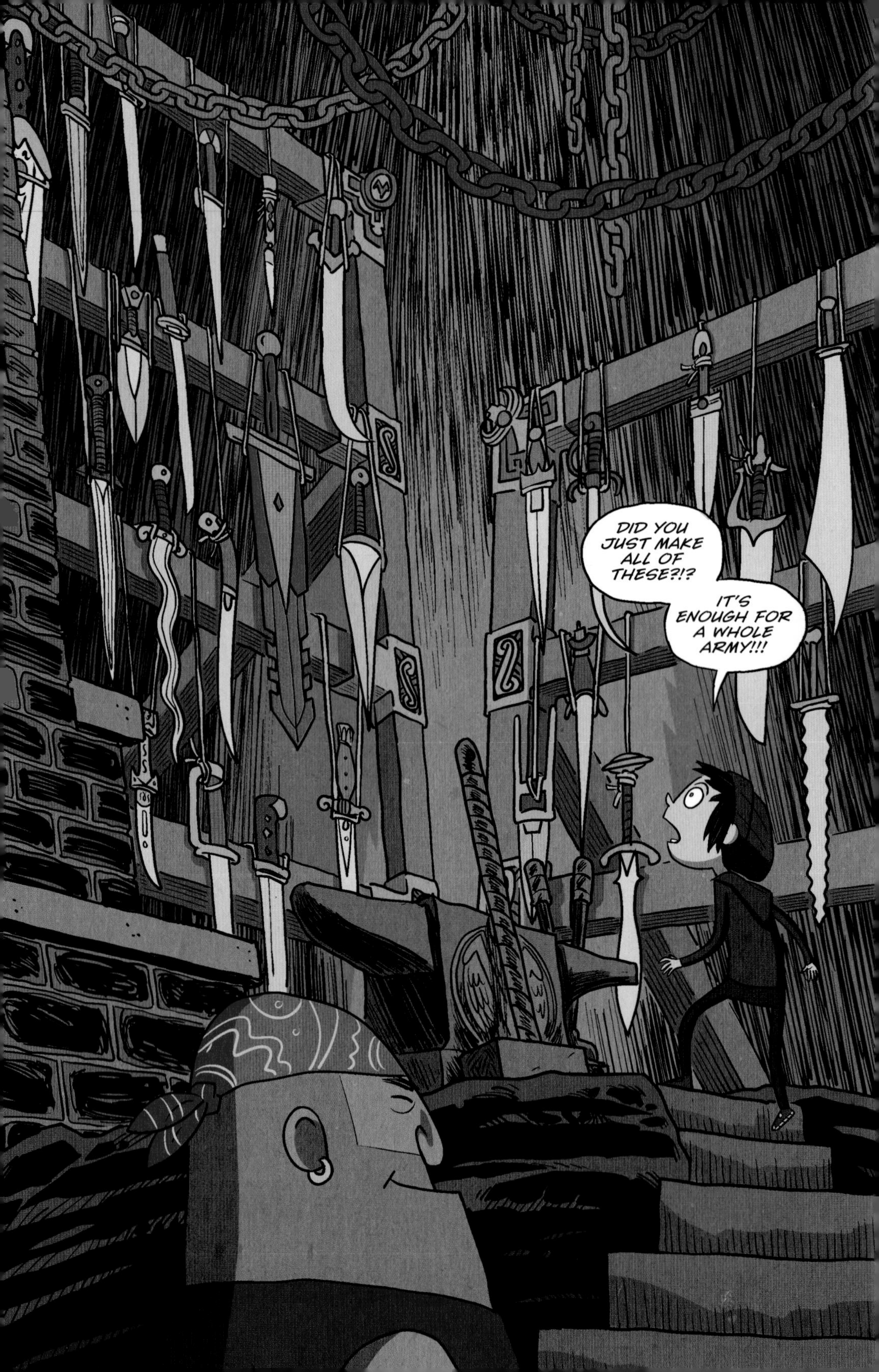
DID YOU JUST MAKE ALL OF THESE?!?
IT'S ENOUGH FOR A WHOLE ARMY!!!

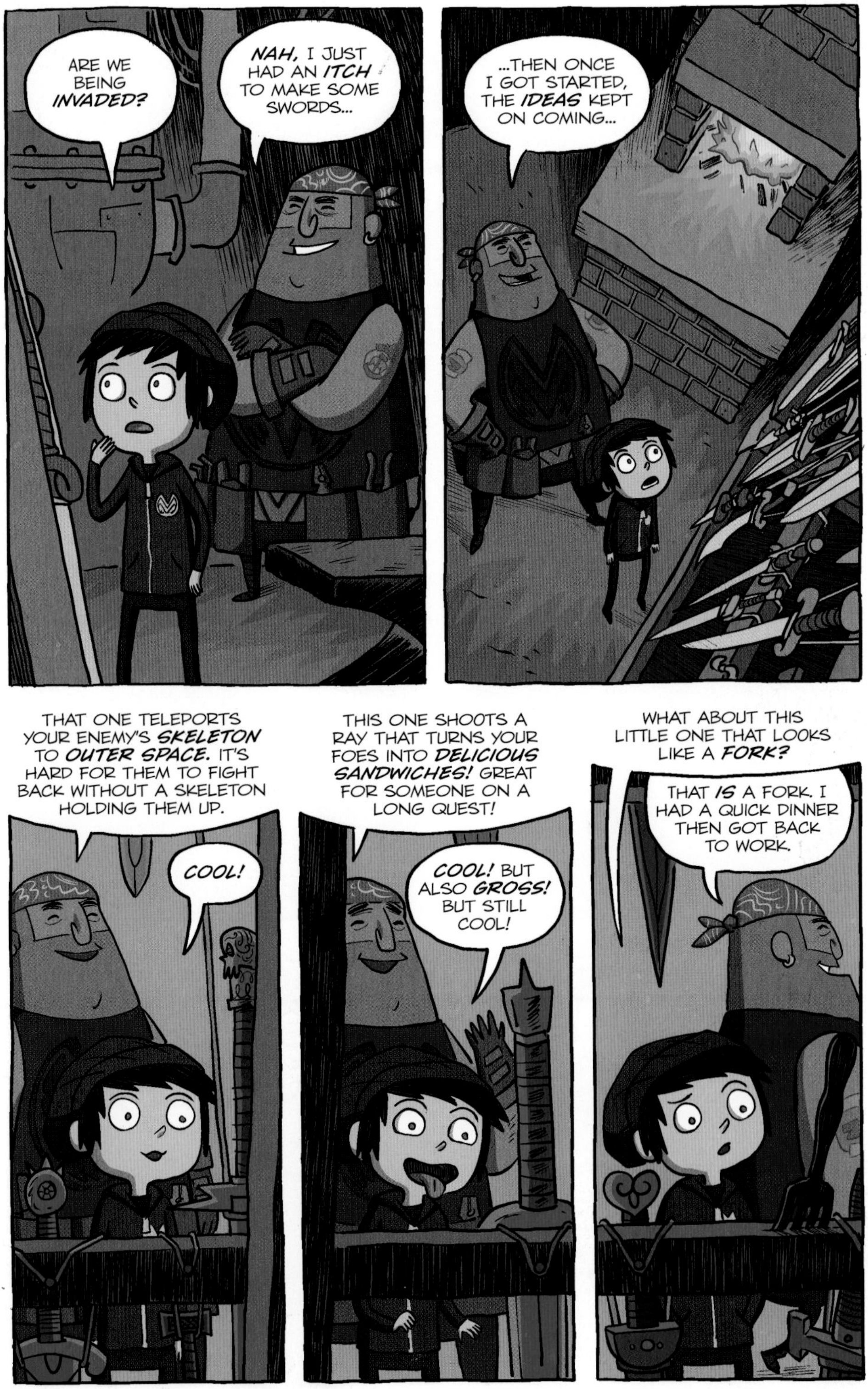
ARE WE BEING INVADED?
NAH, I JUST HAD AN ITCH TO MAKE SOME SWORDS...
...THEN ONCE I GOT STARTED, THE IDEAS KEPT ON COMING...
THAT ONE TELEPORTS YOUR ENEMY'S SKELETON TO OUTER SPACE. IT'S HARD FOR THEM TO FIGHT BACK WITHOUT A SKELETON HOLDING THEM UP.
COOL!
THIS ONE SHOOTS A RAY THAT TURNS YOUR FOES INTO DELICIOUS SANDWICHES! GREAT FOR SOMEONE ON A LONG QUEST!
COOL! BUT ALSO GROSS! BUT STILL COOL!
WHAT ABOUT THIS LITTLE ONE THAT LOOKS LIKE A FORK?
THAT IS A FORK. I HAD A QUICK DINNER THEN GOT BACK TO WORK.

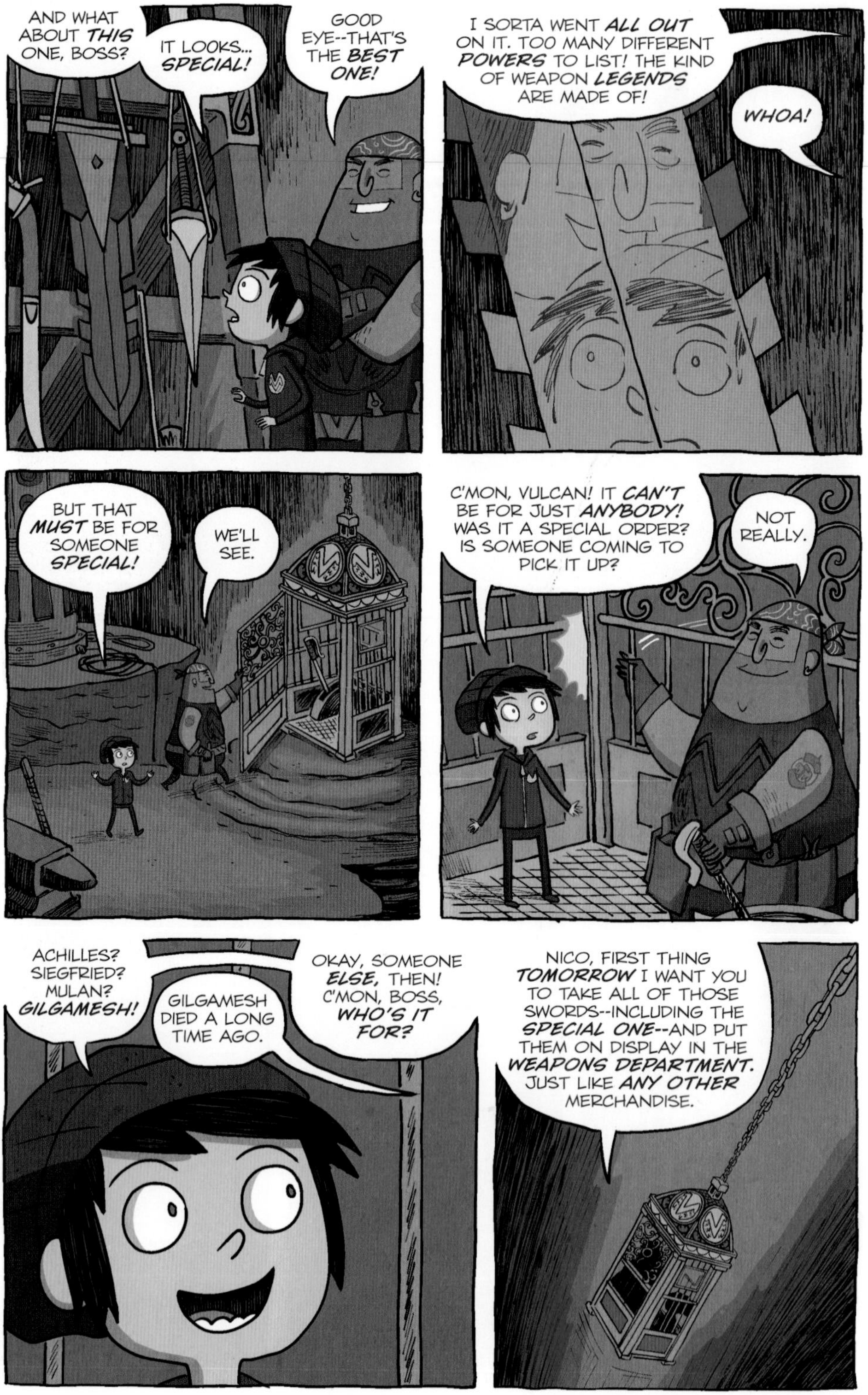
AND WHAT ABOUT THIS ONE, BOSS?
IT LOOKS... SPECIAL!
GOOD EYE--THAT'S THE BEST ONE!
I SORTA WENT ALL OUT ON IT. TOO MANY DIFFERENT POWERS TO LIST! THE KIND OF WEAPON LEGENDS ARE MADE OF!
WHOA!
BUT THAT MUST BE FOR SOMEONE SPECIAL!
WE'LL SEE.
C'MON, VULCAN! IT CAN'T BE FOR JUST ANYBODY! WAS IT A SPECIAL ORDER? IS SOMEONE COMING TO PICK IT UP?
NOT REALLY.
ACHILLES? SIEGFRIED? MULAN? GILGAMESH!
GILGAMESH DIED A LONG TIME AGO.
OKAY, SOMEONE ELSE, THEN! C'MON, BOSS, WHO'S IT FOR?
NICO, FIRST THING TOMORROW I WANT YOU TO TAKE ALL OF THOSE SWORDS--INCLUDING THE SPECIAL ONE--AND PUT THEM ON DISPLAY IN THE WEAPONS DEPARTMENT. JUST LIKE ANY OTHER MERCHANDISE.

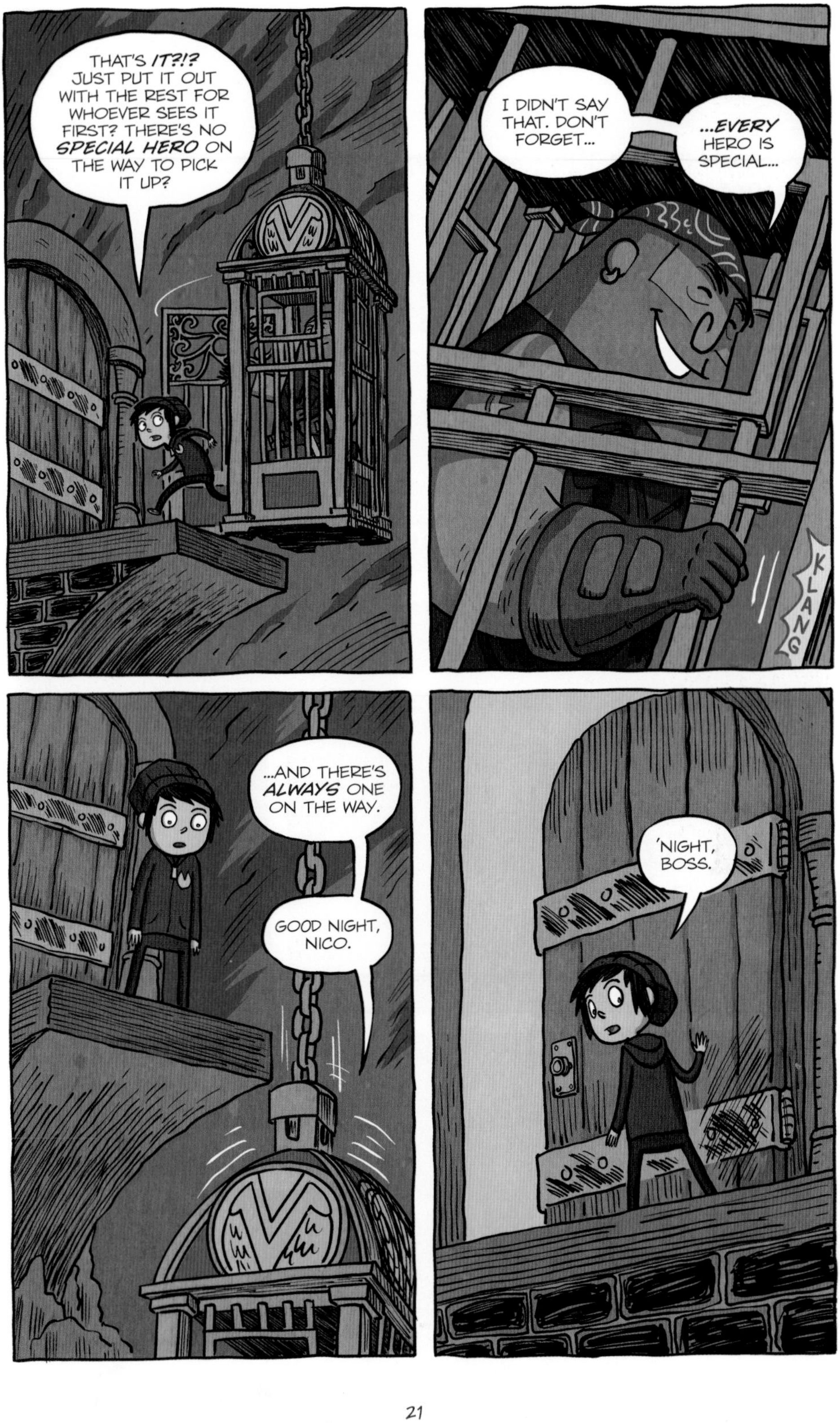
THAT'S *IT?!?* JUST PUT IT OUT WITH THE REST FOR WHOEVER SEES IT FIRST? THERE'S NO ***SPECIAL HERO*** ON THE WAY TO PICK IT UP?
I DIDN'T SAY THAT. DON'T FORGET...
...***EVERY*** HERO IS SPECIAL...
KLANG
...AND THERE'S ***ALWAYS*** ONE ON THE WAY.
GOOD NIGHT, NICO.
'NIGHT, BOSS.

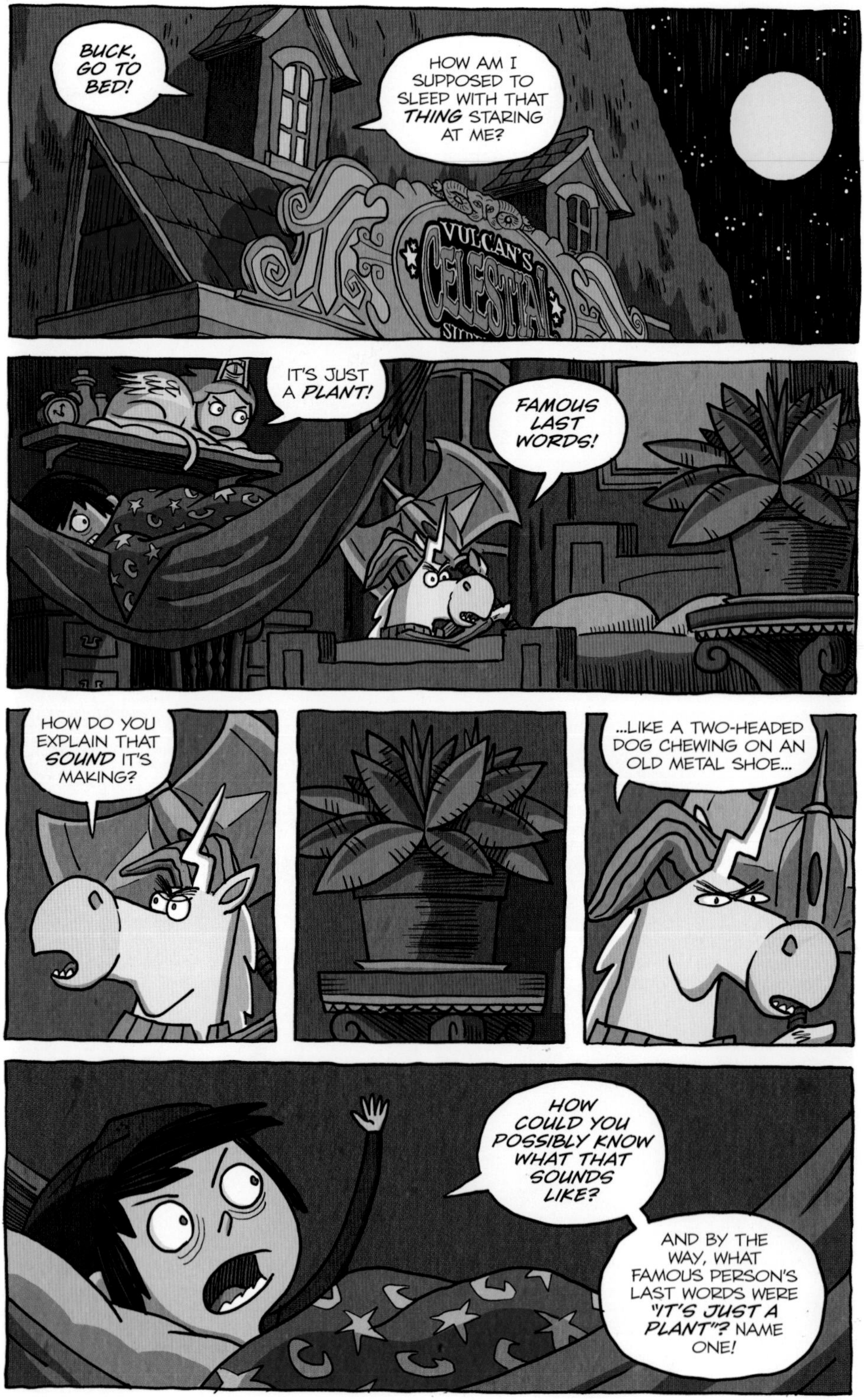
BUCK, GO TO BED!
HOW AM I SUPPOSED TO SLEEP WITH THAT *THING* STARING AT ME?
VULCAN'S CELESTIAL
IT'S JUST A *PLANT!*
FAMOUS LAST WORDS!
HOW DO YOU EXPLAIN THAT *SOUND* IT'S MAKING?
...LIKE A TWO-HEADED DOG CHEWING ON AN OLD METAL SHOE...
HOW COULD YOU POSSIBLY KNOW WHAT THAT SOUNDS LIKE?
AND BY THE WAY, WHAT FAMOUS PERSON'S LAST WORDS WERE *"IT'S JUST A PLANT"?* NAME ONE!

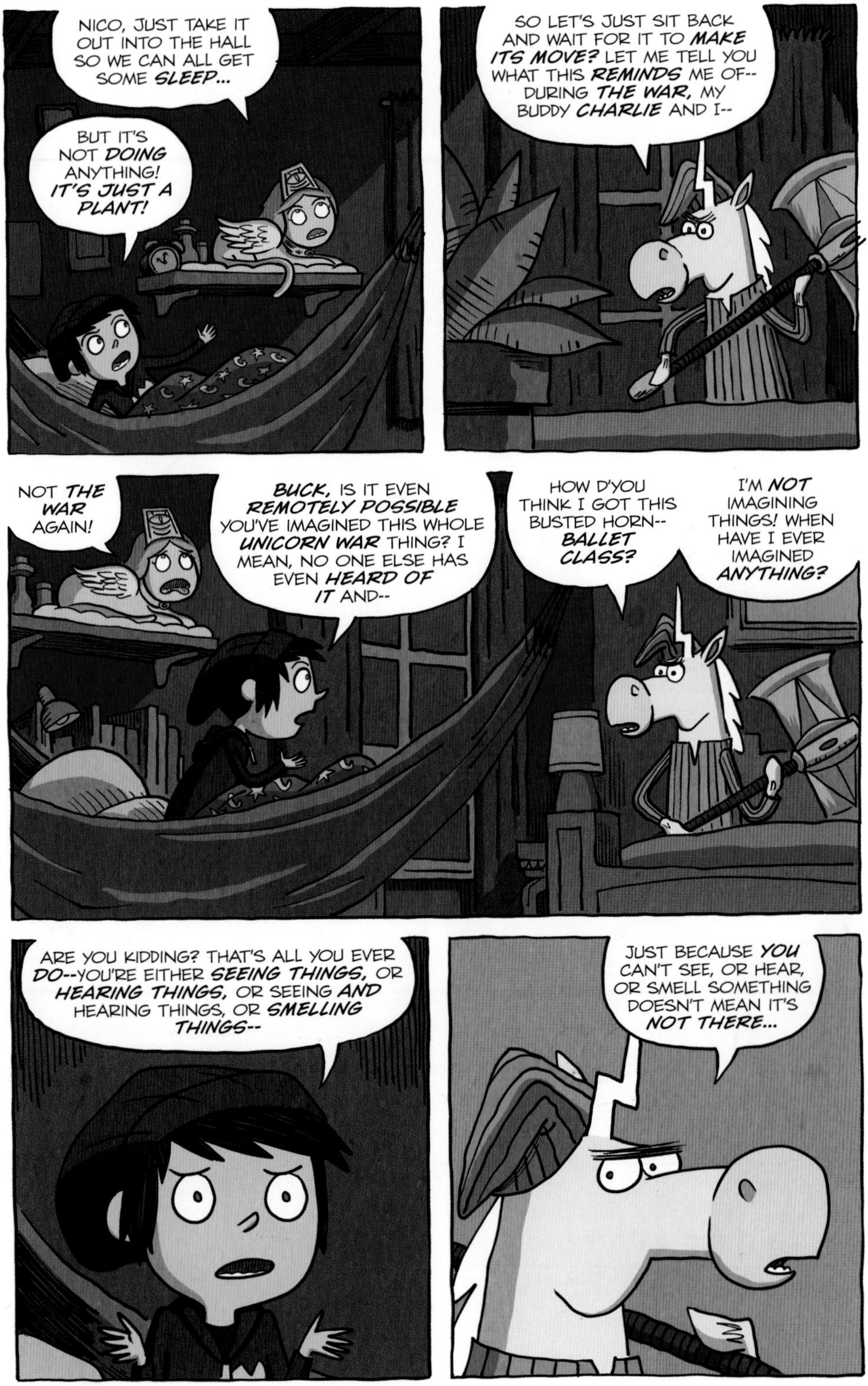

NICO, JUST TAKE IT OUT INTO THE HALL SO WE CAN ALL GET SOME SLEEP...
BUT IT'S NOT DOING ANYTHING! IT'S JUST A PLANT!
SO LET'S JUST SIT BACK AND WAIT FOR IT TO MAKE ITS MOVE? LET ME TELL YOU WHAT THIS REMINDS ME OF-- DURING THE WAR, MY BUDDY CHARLIE AND I--
NOT THE WAR AGAIN!
BUCK, IS IT EVEN REMOTELY POSSIBLE YOU'VE IMAGINED THIS WHOLE UNICORN WAR THING? I MEAN, NO ONE ELSE HAS EVEN HEARD OF IT AND--
HOW D'YOU THINK I GOT THIS BUSTED HORN-- BALLET CLASS?
I'M NOT IMAGINING THINGS! WHEN HAVE I EVER IMAGINED ANYTHING?
ARE YOU KIDDING? THAT'S ALL YOU EVER DO--YOU'RE EITHER SEEING THINGS, OR HEARING THINGS, OR SEEING AND HEARING THINGS, OR SMELLING THINGS--
JUST BECAUSE YOU CAN'T SEE, OR HEAR, OR SMELL SOMETHING DOESN'T MEAN IT'S NOT THERE...

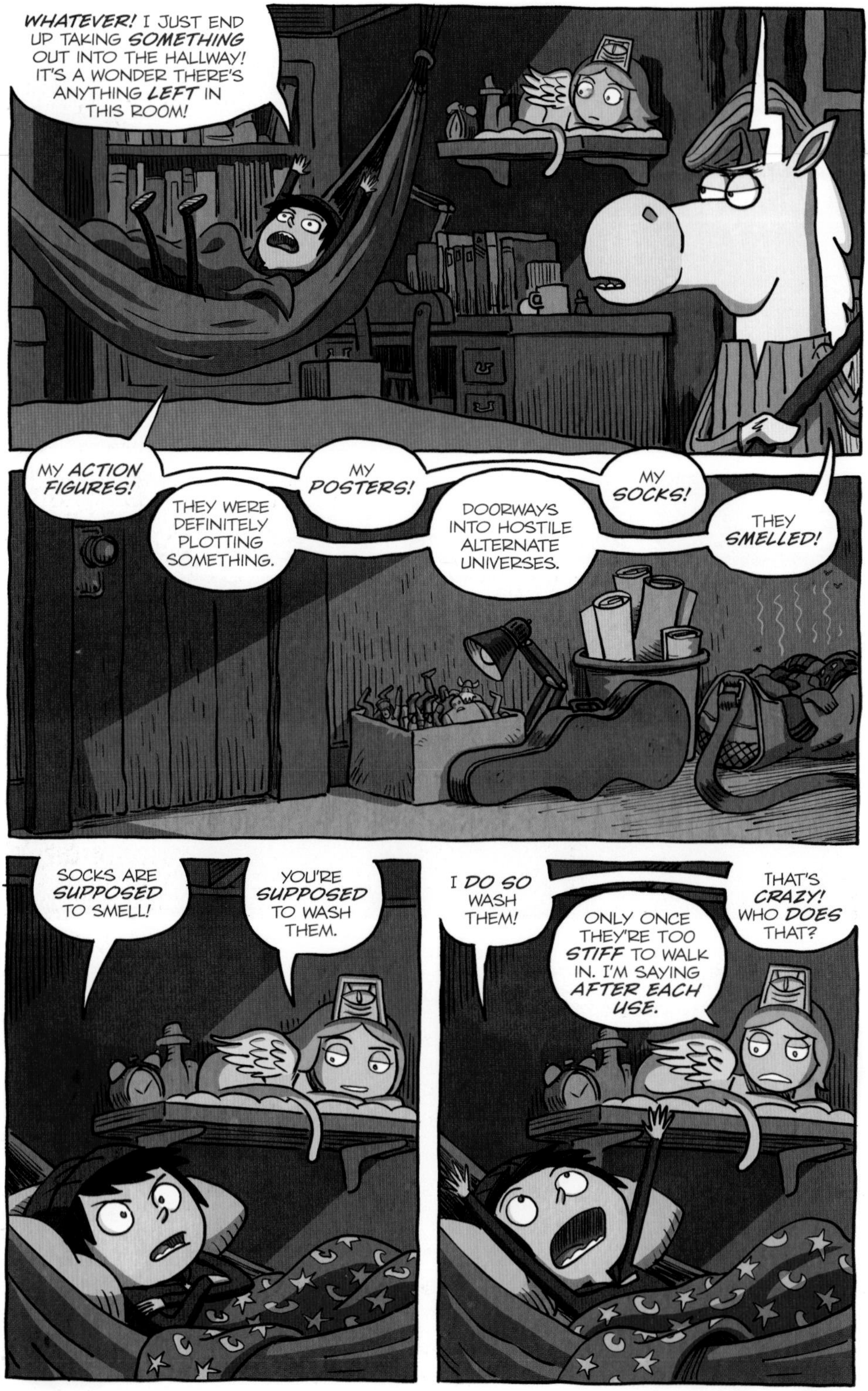
WHATEVER! I JUST END UP TAKING SOMETHING OUT INTO THE HALLWAY! IT'S A WONDER THERE'S ANYTHING LEFT IN THIS ROOM!
MY ACTION FIGURES!
THEY WERE DEFINITELY PLOTTING SOMETHING.
MY POSTERS!
DOORWAYS INTO HOSTILE ALTERNATE UNIVERSES.
MY SOCKS!
THEY SMELLED!
SOCKS ARE SUPPOSED TO SMELL!
YOU'RE SUPPOSED TO WASH THEM.
I DO SO WASH THEM!
ONLY ONCE THEY'RE TOO STIFF TO WALK IN. I'M SAYING AFTER EACH USE.
THAT'S CRAZY! WHO DOES THAT?

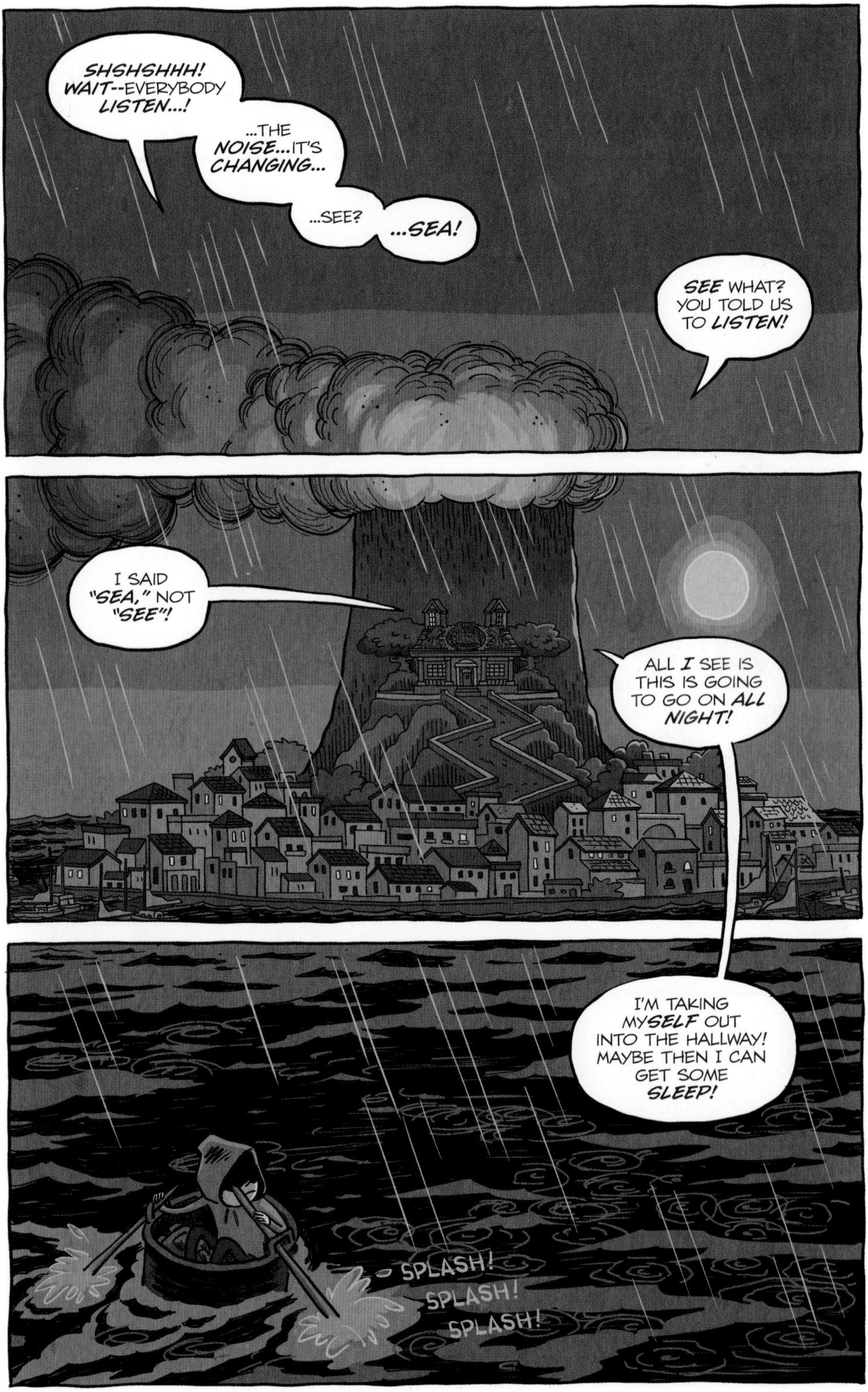
SHSHSHH! WAIT--EVERYBODY LISTEN...!
...THE NOISE...IT'S CHANGING...
...SEE?
...SEA!
SEE WHAT? YOU TOLD US TO LISTEN!
I SAID "SEA," NOT "SEE"!
ALL I SEE IS THIS IS GOING TO GO ON ALL NIGHT!
I'M TAKING MYSELF OUT INTO THE HALLWAY! MAYBE THEN I CAN GET SOME SLEEP!
SPLASH!
SPLASH!
SPLASH!

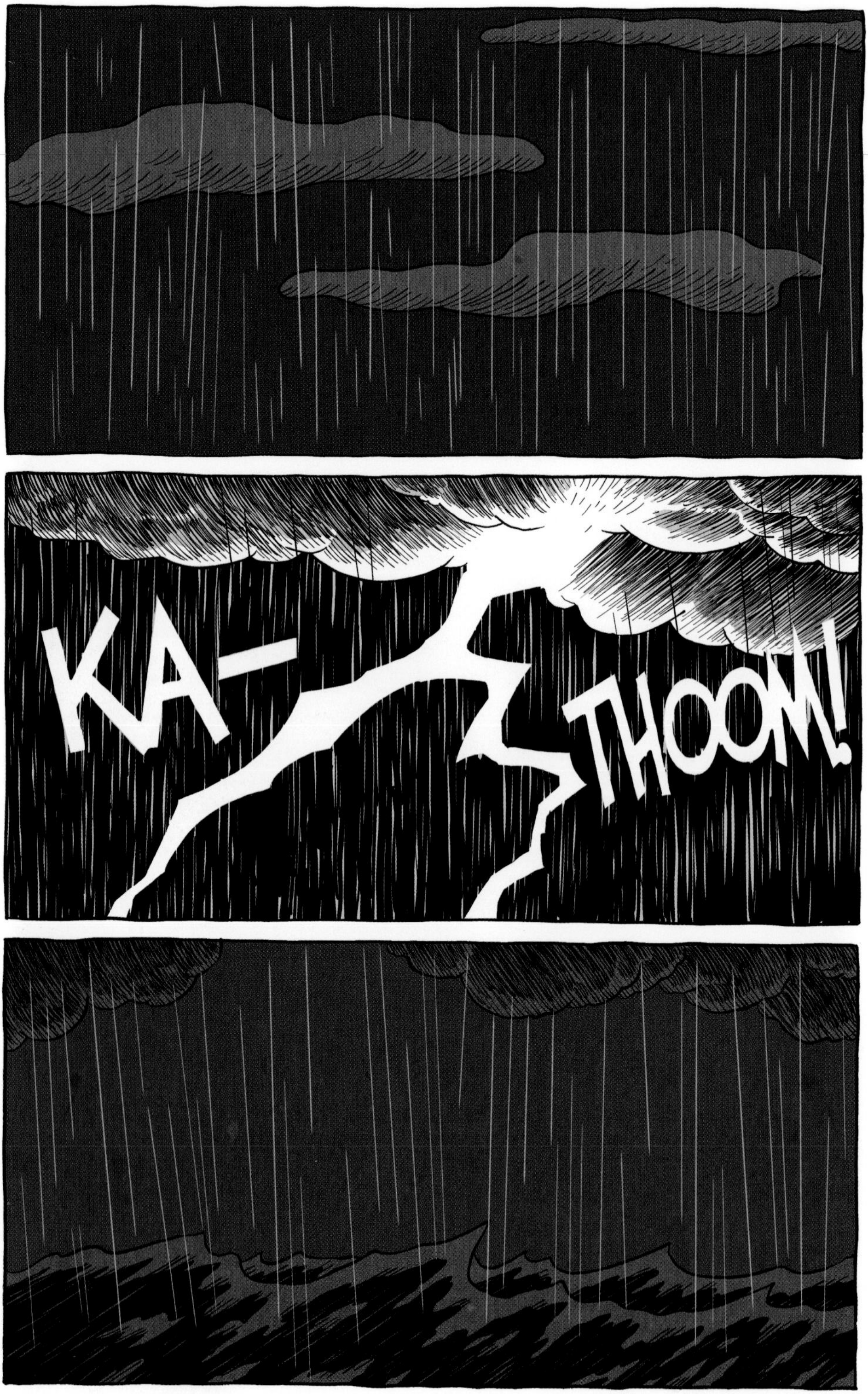
KA-
THOOM!

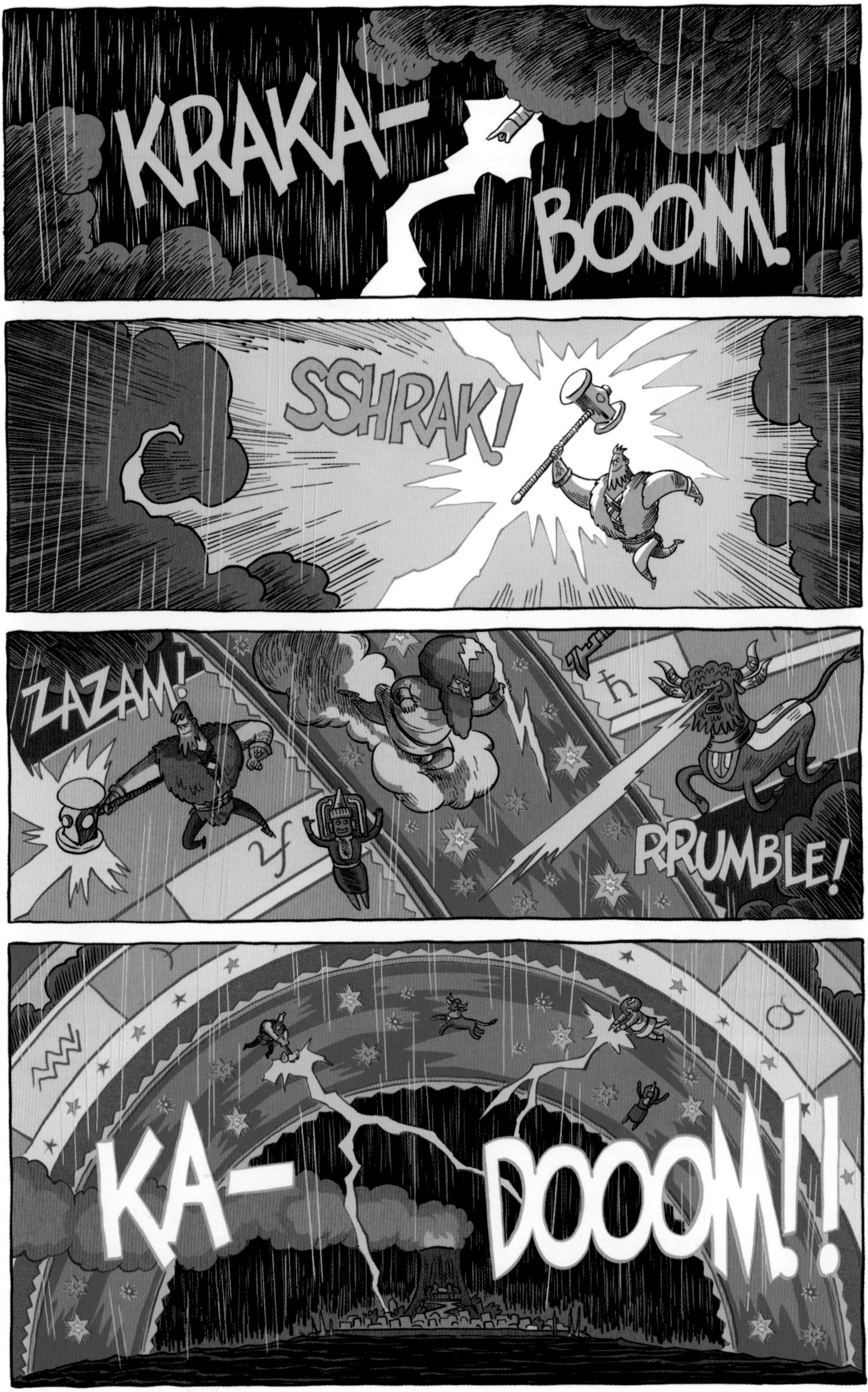
KRAKA-
BOOM!
SSHRAK!
ZAZAM!
RRUMBLE!
KA-
DOOOM!!

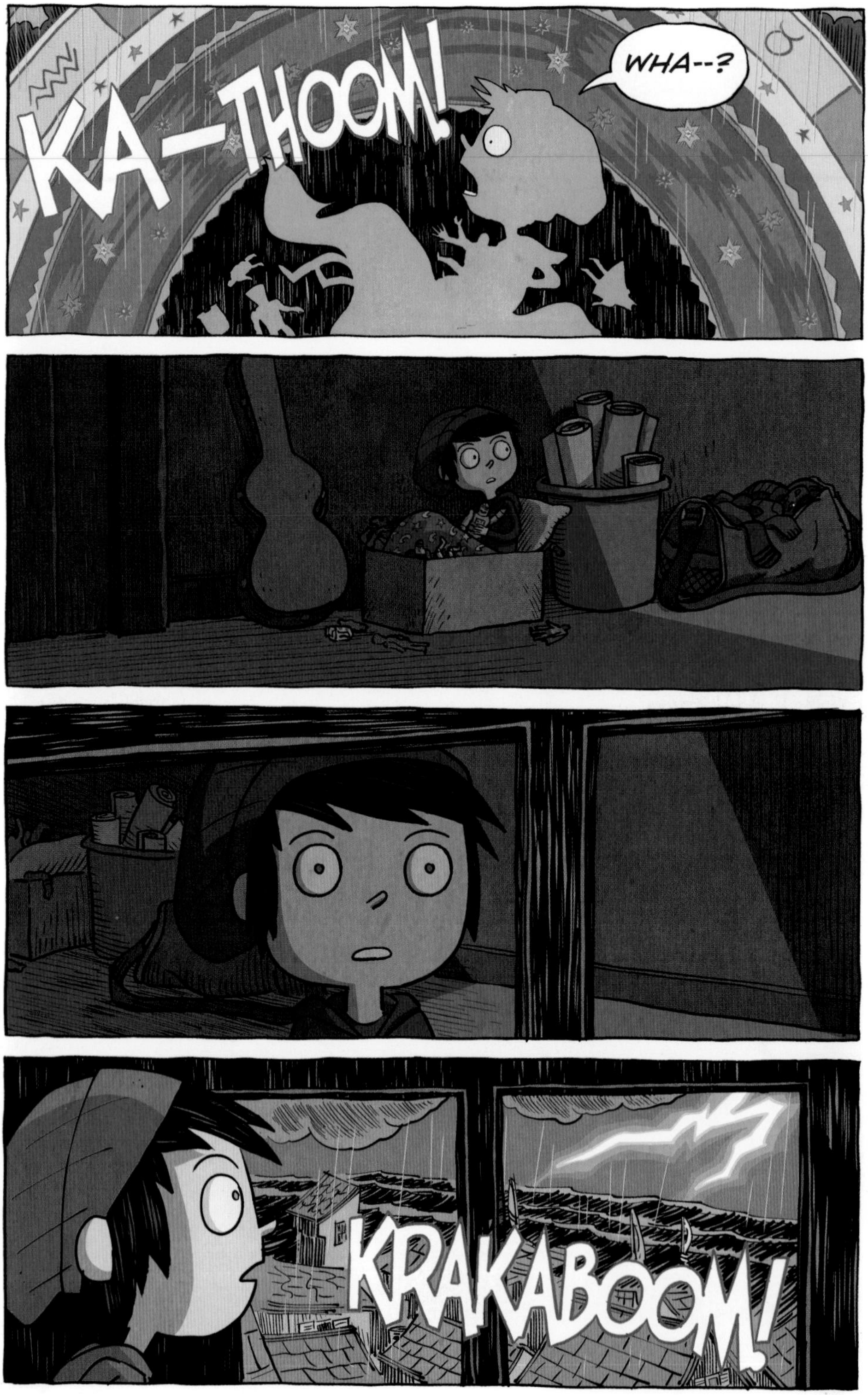
KA-THOOM!
WHA--?
KRAKABOOM!

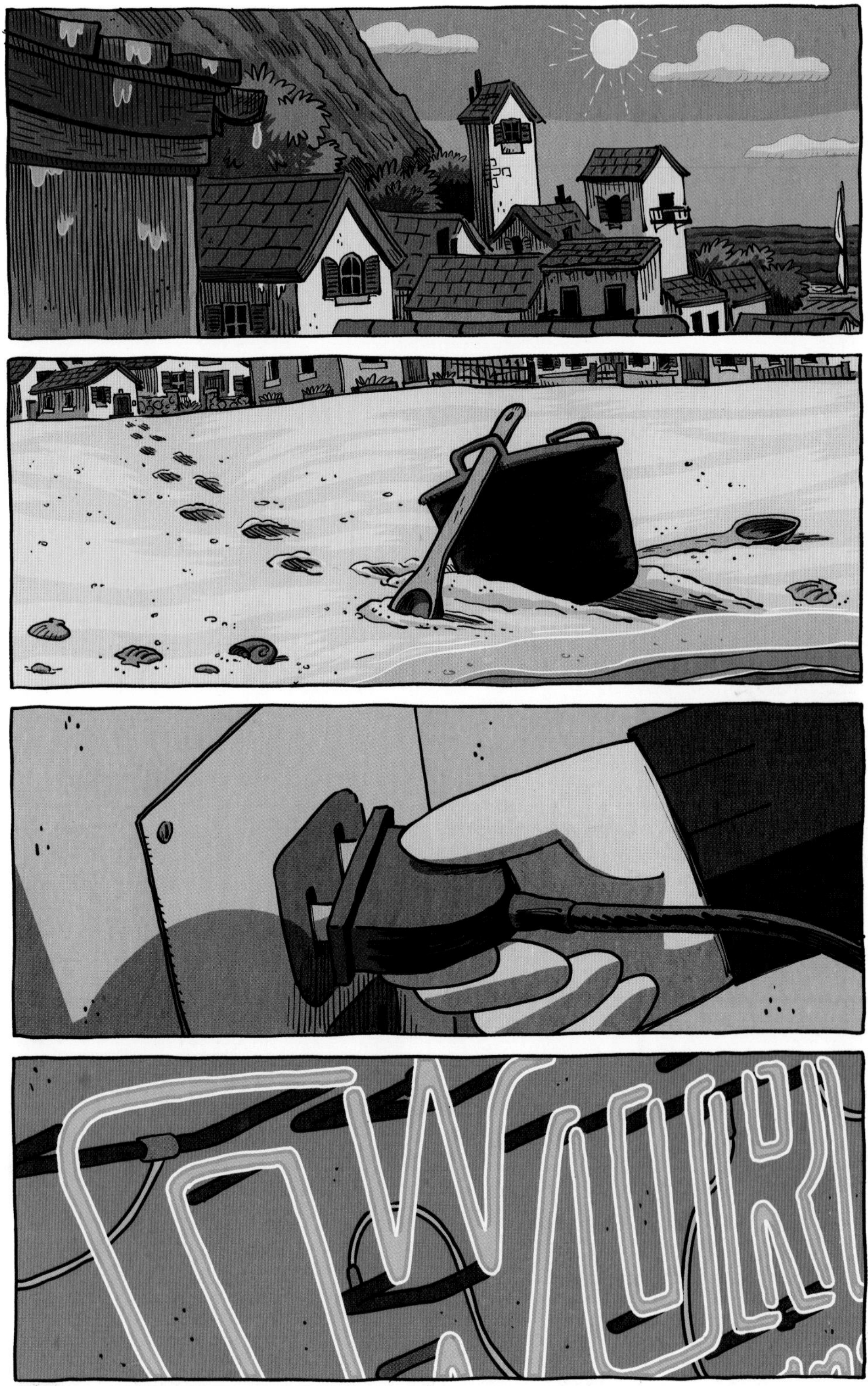

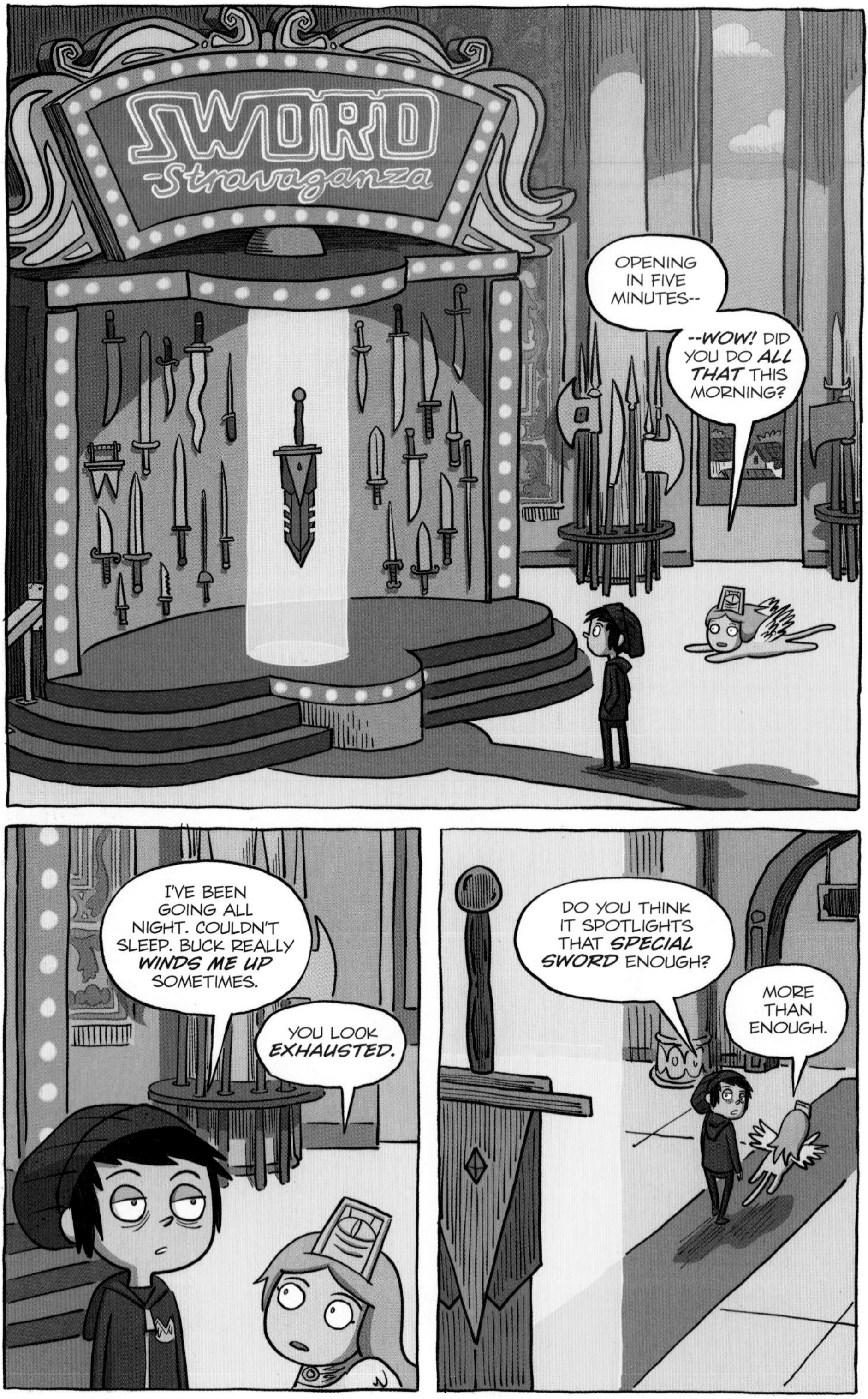
SWORD
-Stravaganza
OPENING IN FIVE MINUTES--
--**WOW!** DID YOU DO **ALL THAT** THIS MORNING?
I'VE BEEN GOING ALL NIGHT. COULDN'T SLEEP. BUCK REALLY **WINDS ME UP** SOMETIMES.
YOU LOOK **EXHAUSTED.**
DO YOU THINK IT SPOTLIGHTS THAT **SPECIAL SWORD** ENOUGH?
MORE THAN ENOUGH.

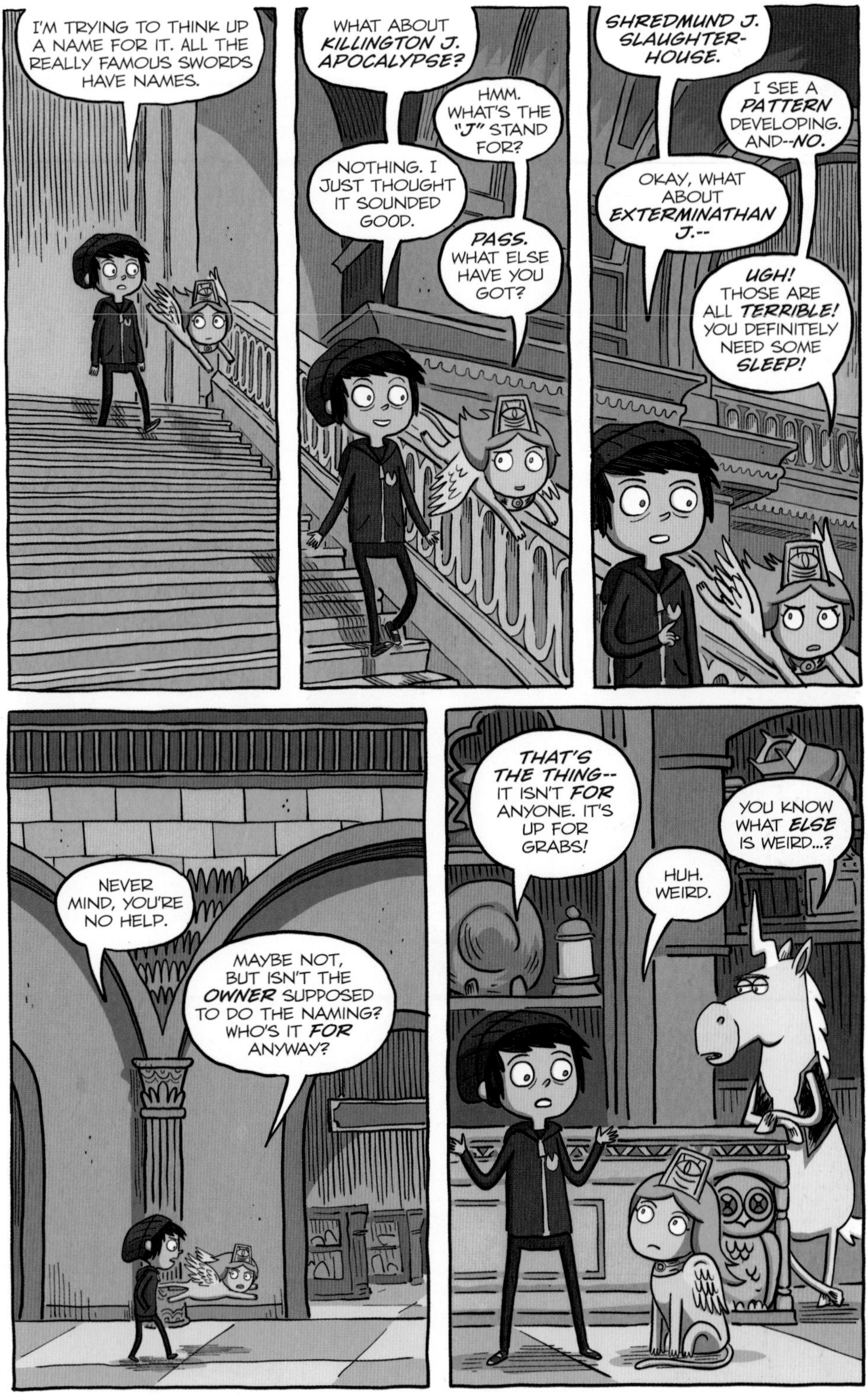
I'M TRYING TO THINK UP A NAME FOR IT. ALL THE REALLY FAMOUS SWORDS HAVE NAMES.
WHAT ABOUT KILLINGTON J. APOCALYPSE?
HMM. WHAT'S THE "J" STAND FOR?
NOTHING. I JUST THOUGHT IT SOUNDED GOOD.
PASS. WHAT ELSE HAVE YOU GOT?
SHREDMUND J. SLAUGHTER-HOUSE.
I SEE A PATTERN DEVELOPING. AND--NO.
OKAY, WHAT ABOUT EXTERMINATHAN J.--
UGH! THOSE ARE ALL TERRIBLE! YOU DEFINITELY NEED SOME SLEEP!
NEVER MIND, YOU'RE NO HELP.
MAYBE NOT, BUT ISN'T THE OWNER SUPPOSED TO DO THE NAMING? WHO'S IT FOR ANYWAY?
THAT'S THE THING-- IT ISN'T FOR ANYONE. IT'S UP FOR GRABS!
HUH. WEIRD.
YOU KNOW WHAT ELSE IS WEIRD...?

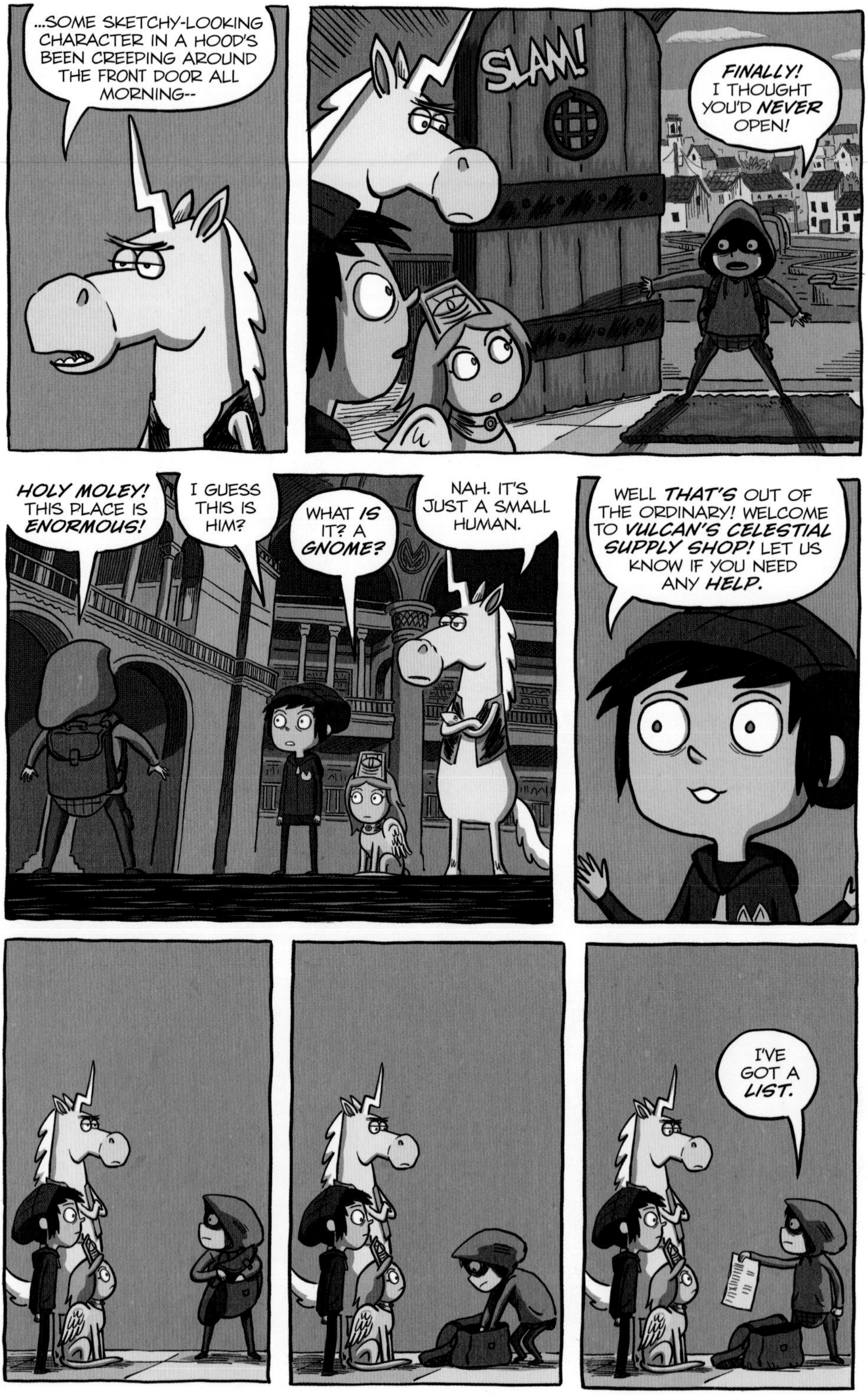
...SOME SKETCHY-LOOKING CHARACTER IN A HOOD'S BEEN CREEPING AROUND THE FRONT DOOR ALL MORNING--
SLAM!
FINALLY! I THOUGHT YOU'D NEVER OPEN!
HOLY MOLEY! THIS PLACE IS ENORMOUS!
I GUESS THIS IS HIM?
WHAT IS IT? A GNOME?
NAH. IT'S JUST A SMALL HUMAN.
WELL THAT'S OUT OF THE ORDINARY! WELCOME TO VULCAN'S CELESTIAL SUPPLY SHOP! LET US KNOW IF YOU NEED ANY HELP.
I'VE GOT A LIST.

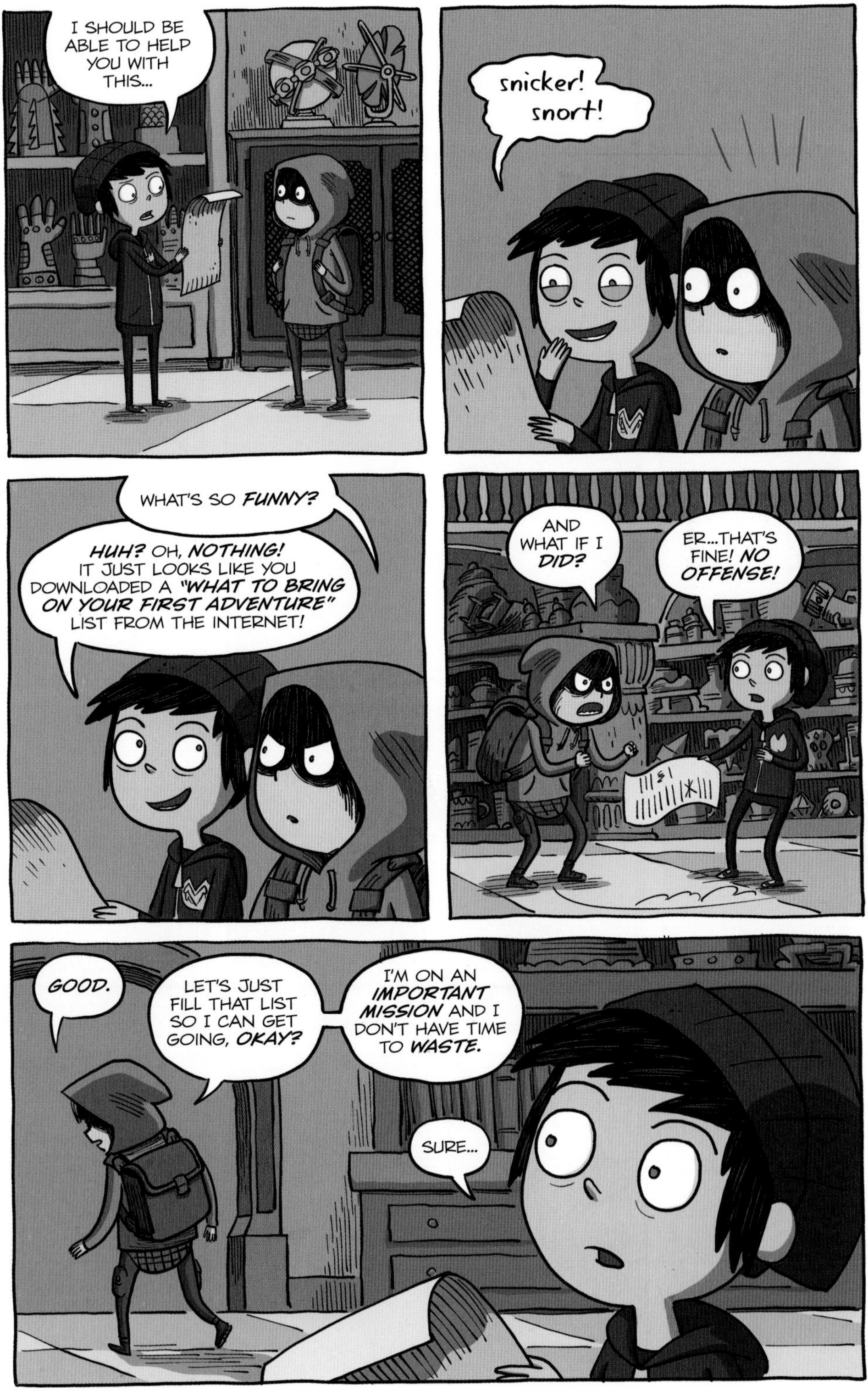
I SHOULD BE ABLE TO HELP YOU WITH THIS...
snicker! snort!
WHAT'S SO FUNNY?
HUH? OH, NOTHING! IT JUST LOOKS LIKE YOU DOWNLOADED A "WHAT TO BRING ON YOUR FIRST ADVENTURE" LIST FROM THE INTERNET!
AND WHAT IF I DID?
ER...THAT'S FINE! NO OFFENSE!
GOOD.
LET'S JUST FILL THAT LIST SO I CAN GET GOING, OKAY?
I'M ON AN IMPORTANT MISSION AND I DON'T HAVE TIME TO WASTE.
SURE...

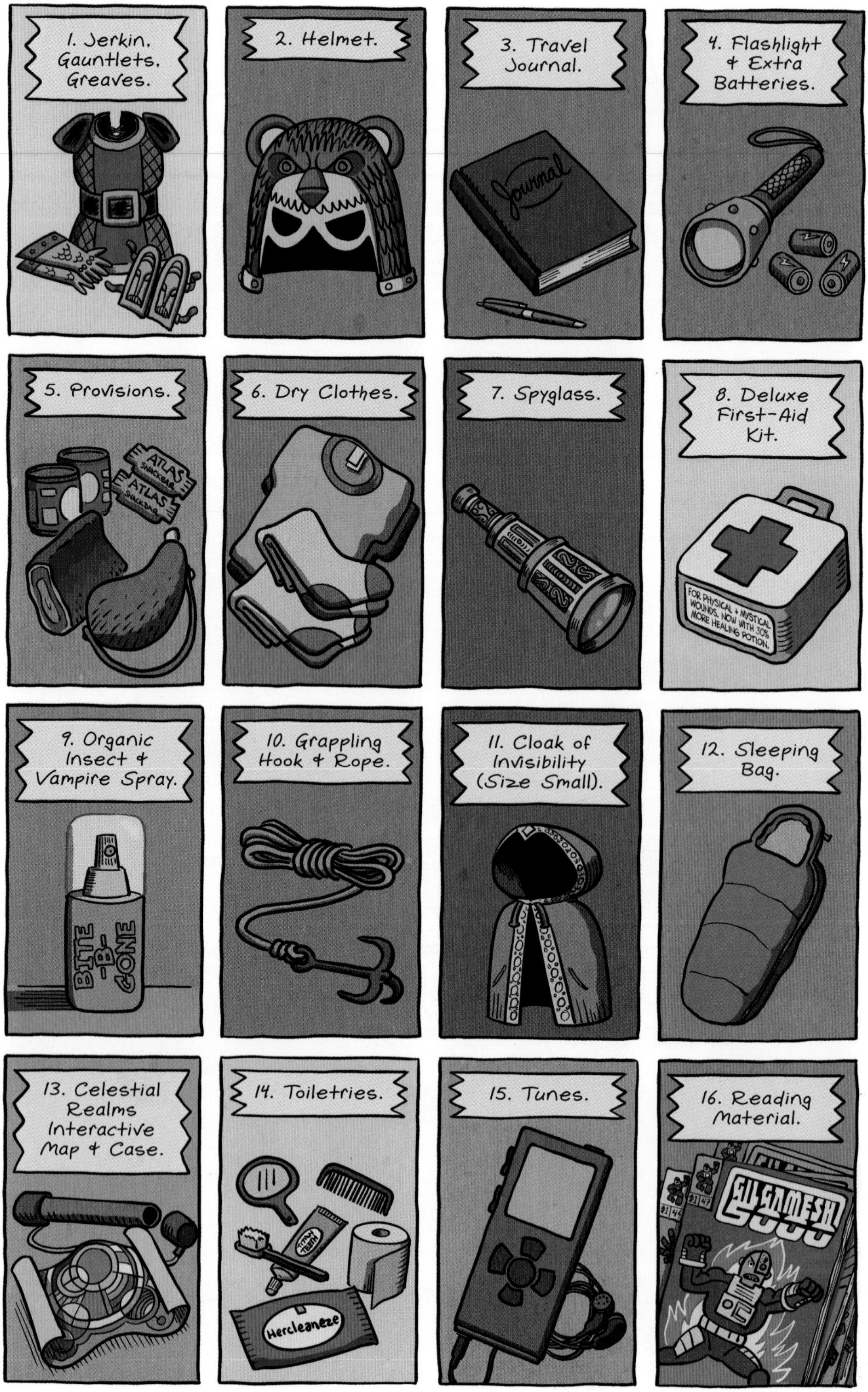
1. Jerkin, Gauntlets, Greaves.
2. Helmet.
3. Travel Journal.
Journal
4. Flashlight & Extra Batteries.
5. Provisions.
ATLAS SNACKBAR
ATLAS SNACKBAR
6. Dry Clothes.
7. Spyglass.
8. Deluxe First-Aid Kit.
FOR PHYSICAL + MYSTICAL WOUNDS. NOW WITH 30% MORE HEALING POTION.
9. Organic Insect & Vampire Spray.
BITE-B-GONE
10. Grappling Hook & Rope.
11. Cloak of Invisibility (Size Small).
12. Sleeping Bag.
13. Celestial Realms Interactive Map & Case.
14. Toiletries.
Hercleaneze
15. Tunes.
16. Reading Material.
GILGAMESH

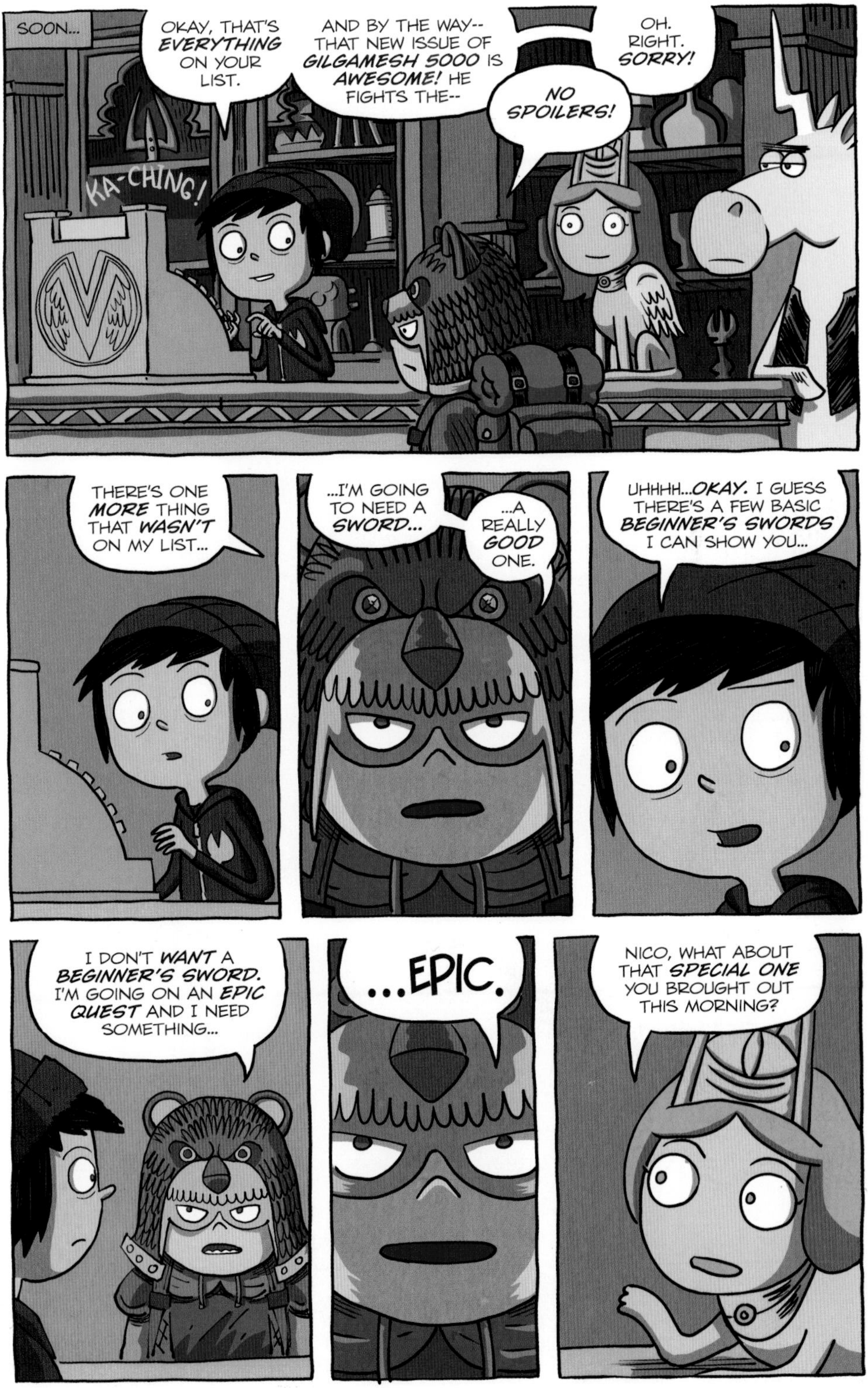
SOON...
OKAY, THAT'S EVERYTHING ON YOUR LIST.
KA-CHING!
AND BY THE WAY-- THAT NEW ISSUE OF GILGAMESH 5000 IS AWESOME! HE FIGHTS THE--
NO SPOILERS!
OH. RIGHT. SORRY!
THERE'S ONE MORE THING THAT WASN'T ON MY LIST...
...I'M GOING TO NEED A SWORD...
...A REALLY GOOD ONE.
UHHHH...OKAY. I GUESS THERE'S A FEW BASIC BEGINNER'S SWORDS I CAN SHOW YOU...
I DON'T WANT A BEGINNER'S SWORD. I'M GOING ON AN EPIC QUEST AND I NEED SOMETHING...
...EPIC.
NICO, WHAT ABOUT THAT SPECIAL ONE YOU BROUGHT OUT THIS MORNING?

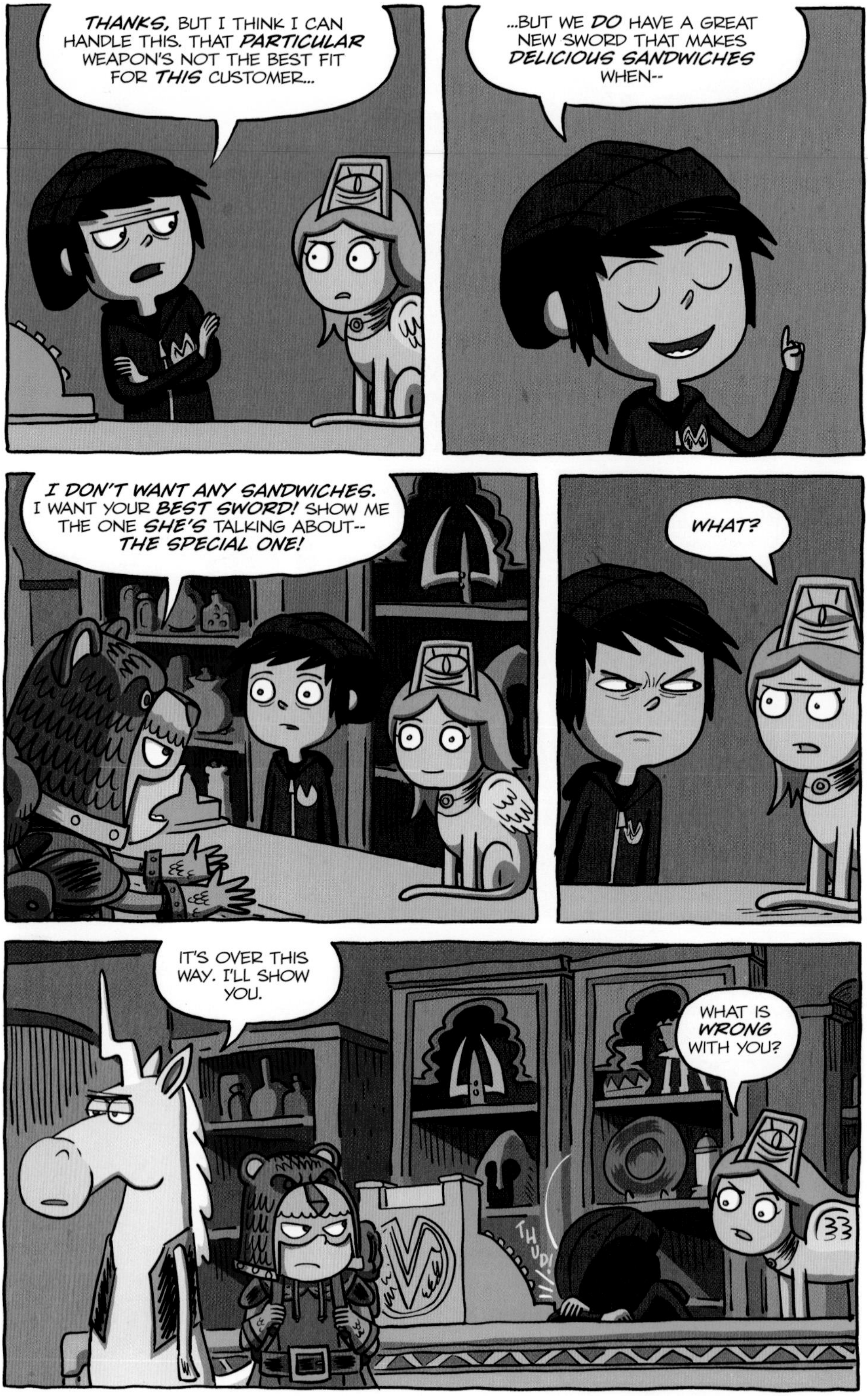
THANKS, BUT I THINK I CAN HANDLE THIS. THAT PARTICULAR WEAPON'S NOT THE BEST FIT FOR THIS CUSTOMER...
...BUT WE DO HAVE A GREAT NEW SWORD THAT MAKES DELICIOUS SANDWICHES WHEN--
I DON'T WANT ANY SANDWICHES. I WANT YOUR BEST SWORD! SHOW ME THE ONE SHE'S TALKING ABOUT-- THE SPECIAL ONE!
WHAT?
IT'S OVER THIS WAY. I'LL SHOW YOU.
WHAT IS WRONG WITH YOU?
THUD!

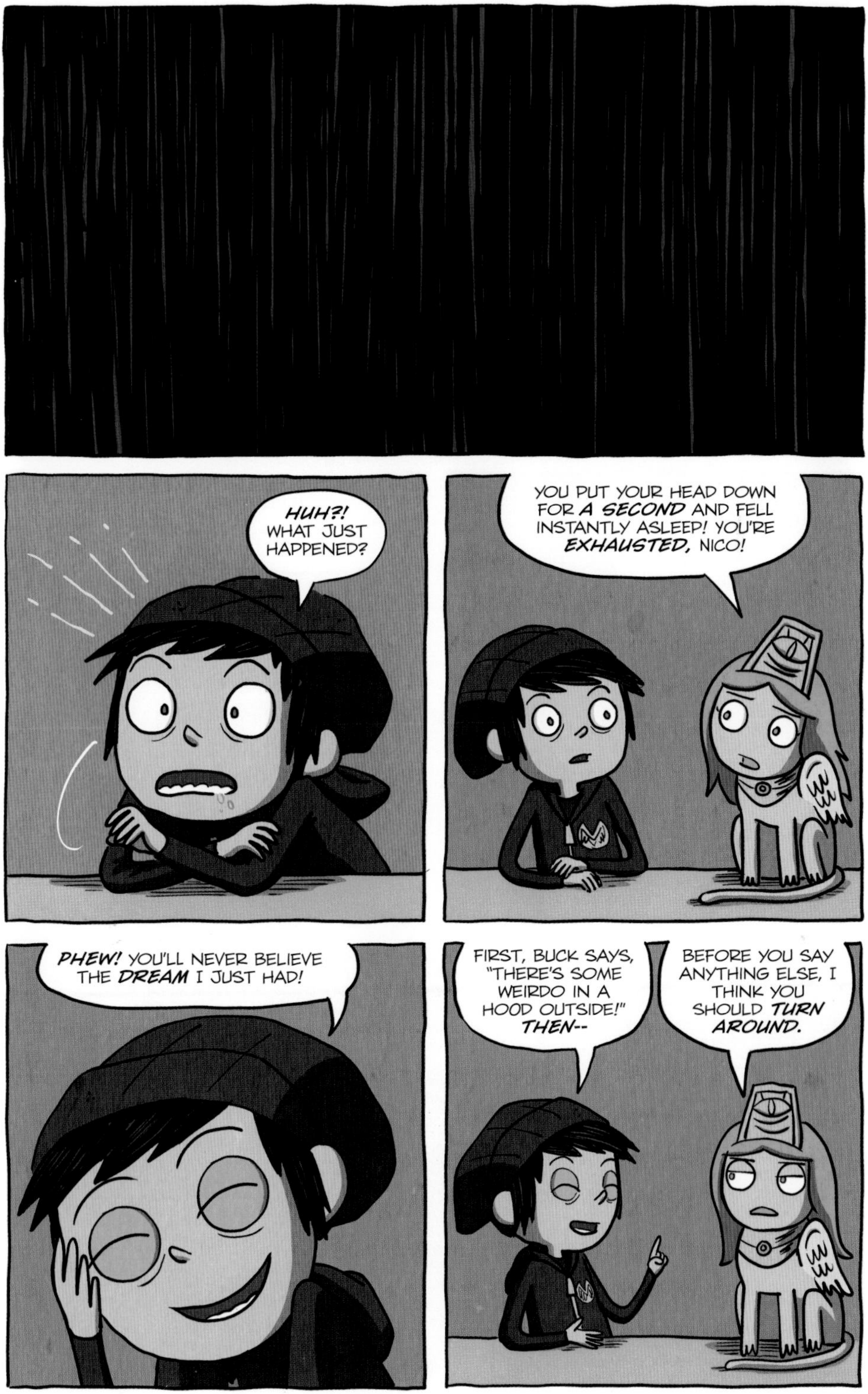
HUH?! WHAT JUST HAPPENED?
YOU PUT YOUR HEAD DOWN FOR A SECOND AND FELL INSTANTLY ASLEEP! YOU'RE EXHAUSTED, NICO!
PHEW! YOU'LL NEVER BELIEVE THE DREAM I JUST HAD!
FIRST, BUCK SAYS, "THERE'S SOME WEIRDO IN A HOOD OUTSIDE!" THEN--
BEFORE YOU SAY ANYTHING ELSE, I THINK YOU SHOULD TURN AROUND.

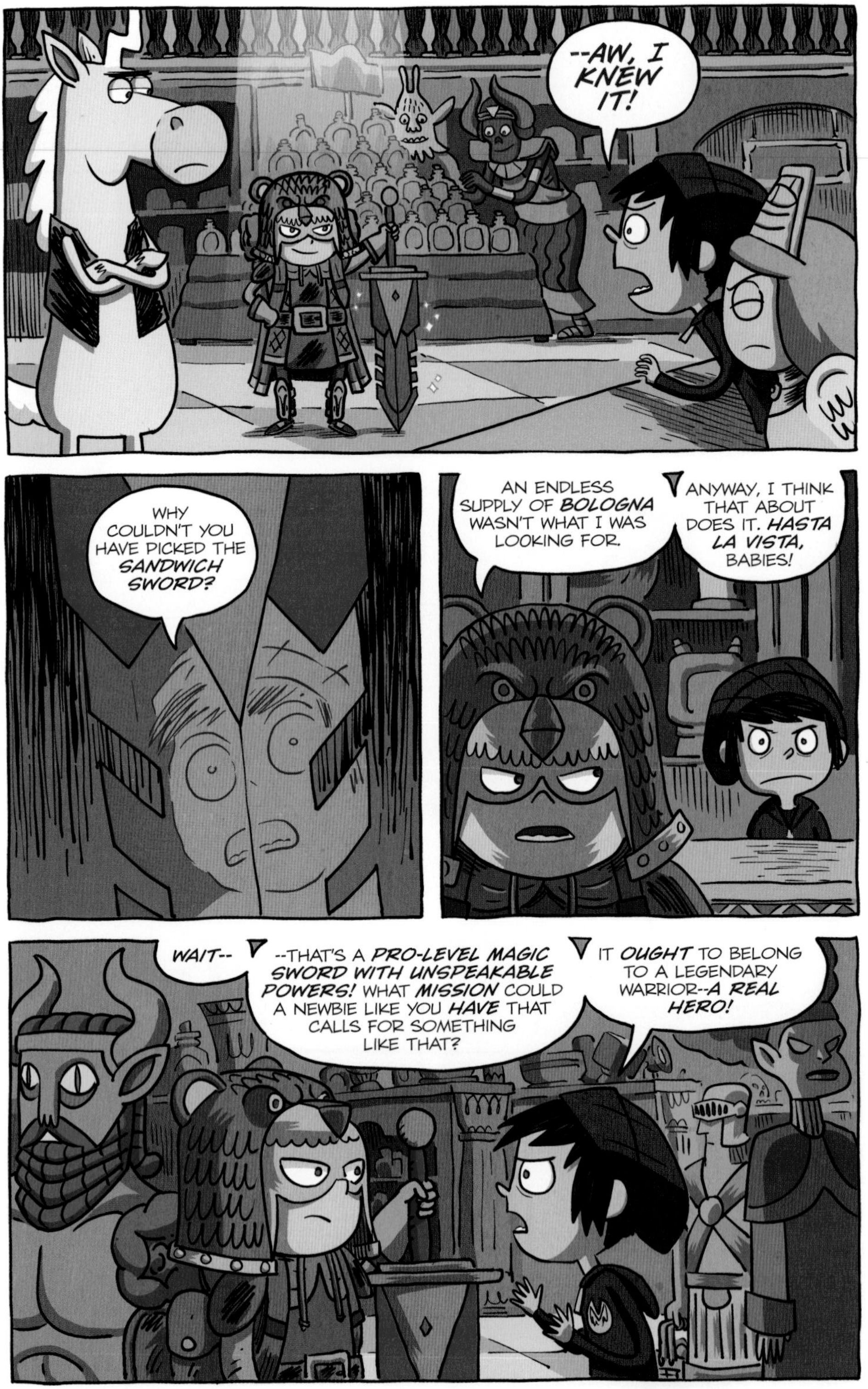
--AW, I KNEW IT!
WHY COULDN'T YOU HAVE PICKED THE SANDWICH SWORD?
AN ENDLESS SUPPLY OF BOLOGNA WASN'T WHAT I WAS LOOKING FOR.
ANYWAY, I THINK THAT ABOUT DOES IT. HASTA LA VISTA, BABIES!
WAIT--
--THAT'S A PRO-LEVEL MAGIC SWORD WITH UNSPEAKABLE POWERS! WHAT MISSION COULD A NEWBIE LIKE YOU HAVE THAT CALLS FOR SOMETHING LIKE THAT?
IT OUGHT TO BELONG TO A LEGENDARY WARRIOR--A REAL HERO!

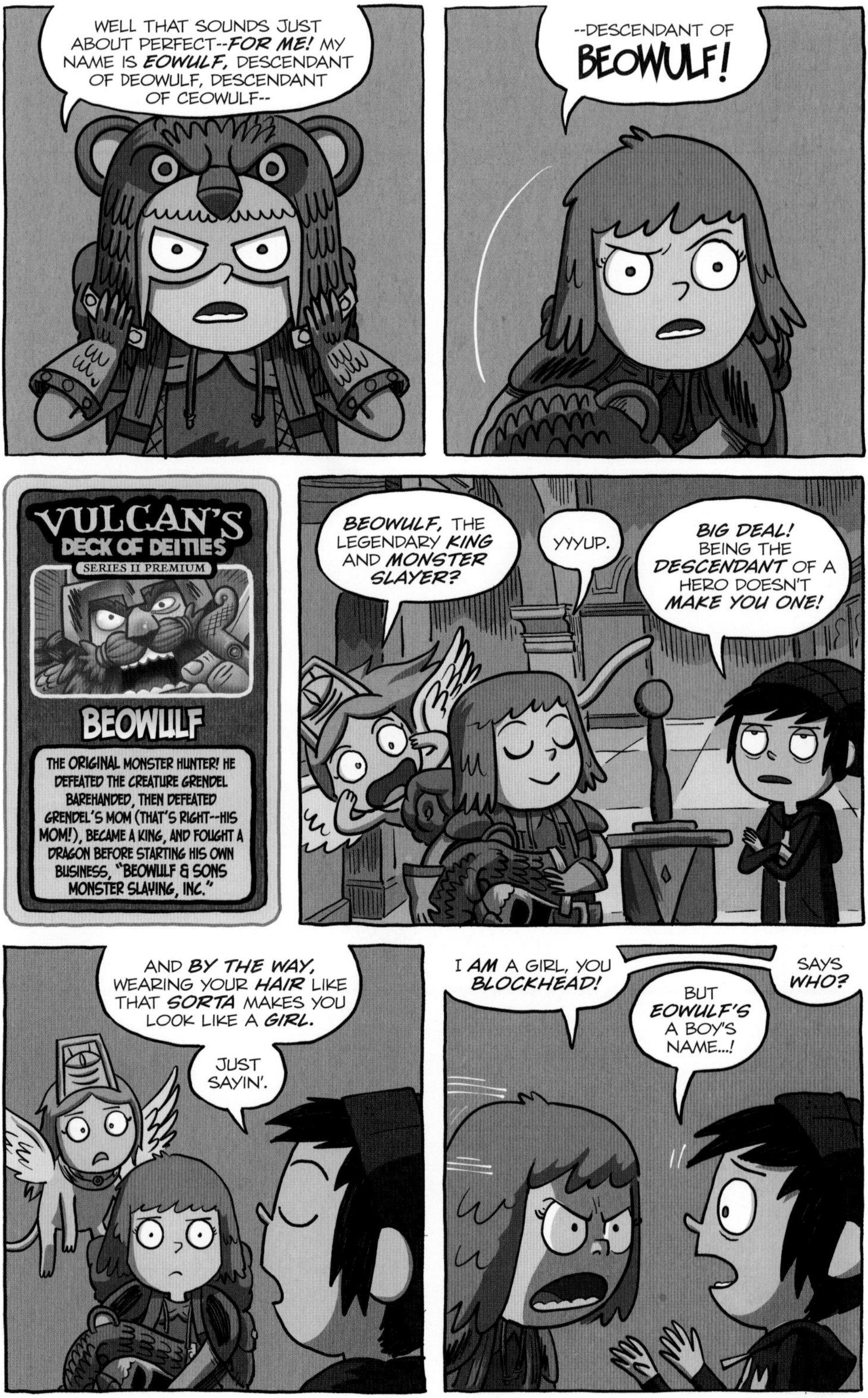
WELL THAT SOUNDS JUST ABOUT PERFECT--FOR ME! MY NAME IS EOWULF, DESCENDANT OF DEOWULF, DESCENDANT OF CEOWULF--
--DESCENDANT OF BEOWULF!
VULCAN'S DECK OF DEITIES
SERIES II PREMIUM
BEOWULF
THE ORIGINAL MONSTER HUNTER! HE DEFEATED THE CREATURE GRENDEL BAREHANDED, THEN DEFEATED GRENDEL'S MOM (THAT'S RIGHT--HIS MOM!), BECAME A KING, AND FOUGHT A DRAGON BEFORE STARTING HIS OWN BUSINESS, "BEOWULF & SONS MONSTER SLAYING, INC."
BEOWULF, THE LEGENDARY KING AND MONSTER SLAYER?
YYYUP.
BIG DEAL! BEING THE DESCENDANT OF A HERO DOESN'T MAKE YOU ONE!
AND BY THE WAY, WEARING YOUR HAIR LIKE THAT SORTA MAKES YOU LOOK LIKE A GIRL.
JUST SAYIN'.
I AM A GIRL, YOU BLOCKHEAD!
BUT EOWULF'S A BOY'S NAME...!
SAYS WHO?

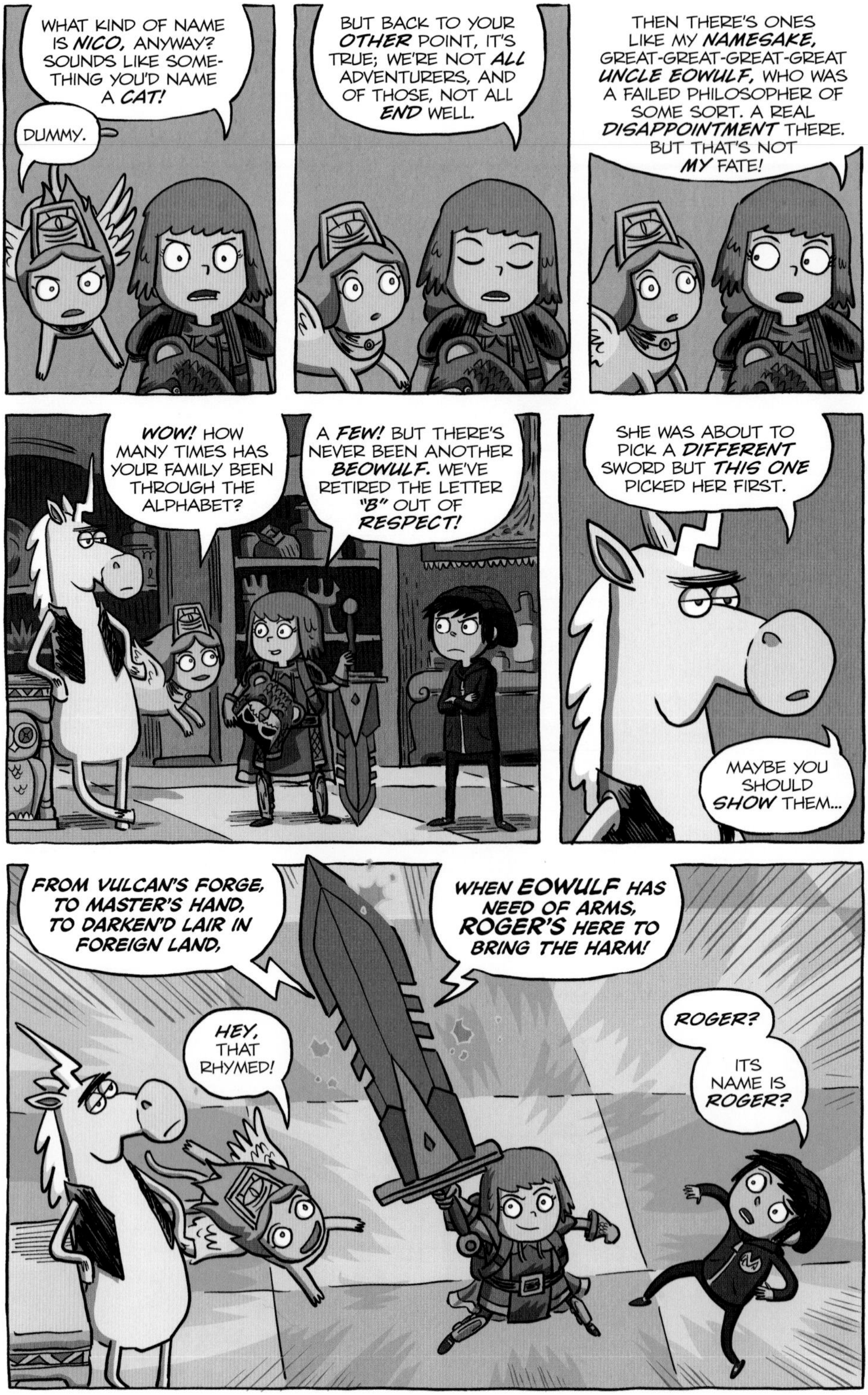
WHAT KIND OF NAME IS NICO, ANYWAY? SOUNDS LIKE SOME-THING YOU'D NAME A CAT!
DUMMY.
BUT BACK TO YOUR OTHER POINT, IT'S TRUE; WE'RE NOT ALL ADVENTURERS, AND OF THOSE, NOT ALL END WELL.
THEN THERE'S ONES LIKE MY NAMESAKE, GREAT-GREAT-GREAT-GREAT UNCLE EOWULF, WHO WAS A FAILED PHILOSOPHER OF SOME SORT. A REAL DISAPPOINTMENT THERE. BUT THAT'S NOT MY FATE!
WOW! HOW MANY TIMES HAS YOUR FAMILY BEEN THROUGH THE ALPHABET?
A FEW! BUT THERE'S NEVER BEEN ANOTHER BEOWULF. WE'VE RETIRED THE LETTER "B" OUT OF RESPECT!
SHE WAS ABOUT TO PICK A DIFFERENT SWORD BUT THIS ONE PICKED HER FIRST.
MAYBE YOU SHOULD SHOW THEM...
FROM VULCAN'S FORGE, TO MASTER'S HAND, TO DARKEN'D LAIR IN FOREIGN LAND,
WHEN EOWULF HAS NEED OF ARMS, ROGER'S HERE TO BRING THE HARM!
HEY, THAT RHYMED!
ROGER?
ITS NAME IS ROGER?

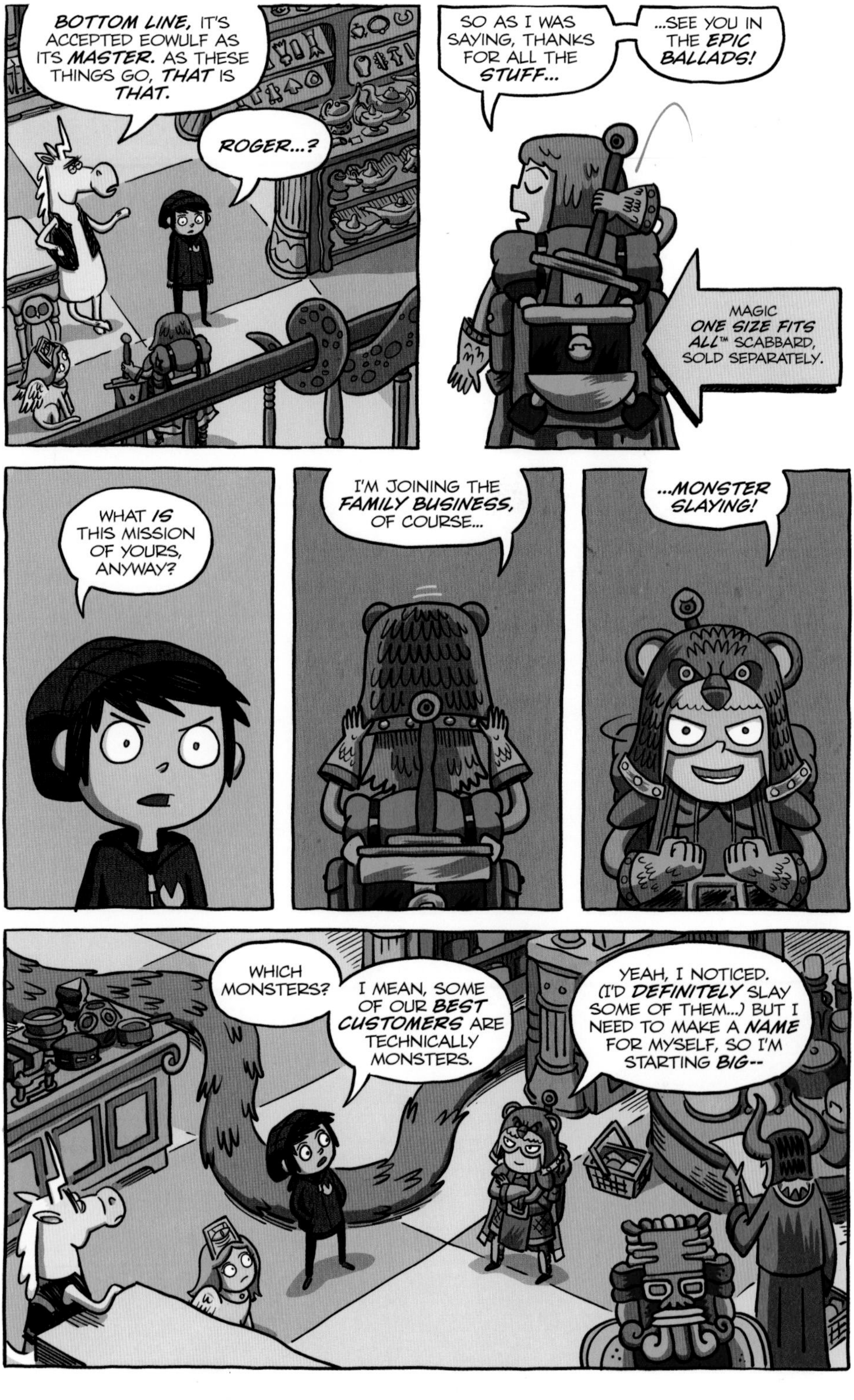
BOTTOM LINE, IT'S ACCEPTED EOWULF AS ITS MASTER. AS THESE THINGS GO, THAT IS THAT.
ROGER...?
SO AS I WAS SAYING, THANKS FOR ALL THE STUFF...
...SEE YOU IN THE EPIC BALLADS!
MAGIC ONE SIZE FITS ALL™ SCABBARD, SOLD SEPARATELY.
WHAT IS THIS MISSION OF YOURS, ANYWAY?
I'M JOINING THE FAMILY BUSINESS, OF COURSE...
...MONSTER SLAYING!
WHICH MONSTERS?
I MEAN, SOME OF OUR BEST CUSTOMERS ARE TECHNICALLY MONSTERS.
YEAH, I NOTICED. (I'D DEFINITELY SLAY SOME OF THEM...) BUT I NEED TO MAKE A NAME FOR MYSELF, SO I'M STARTING BIG--

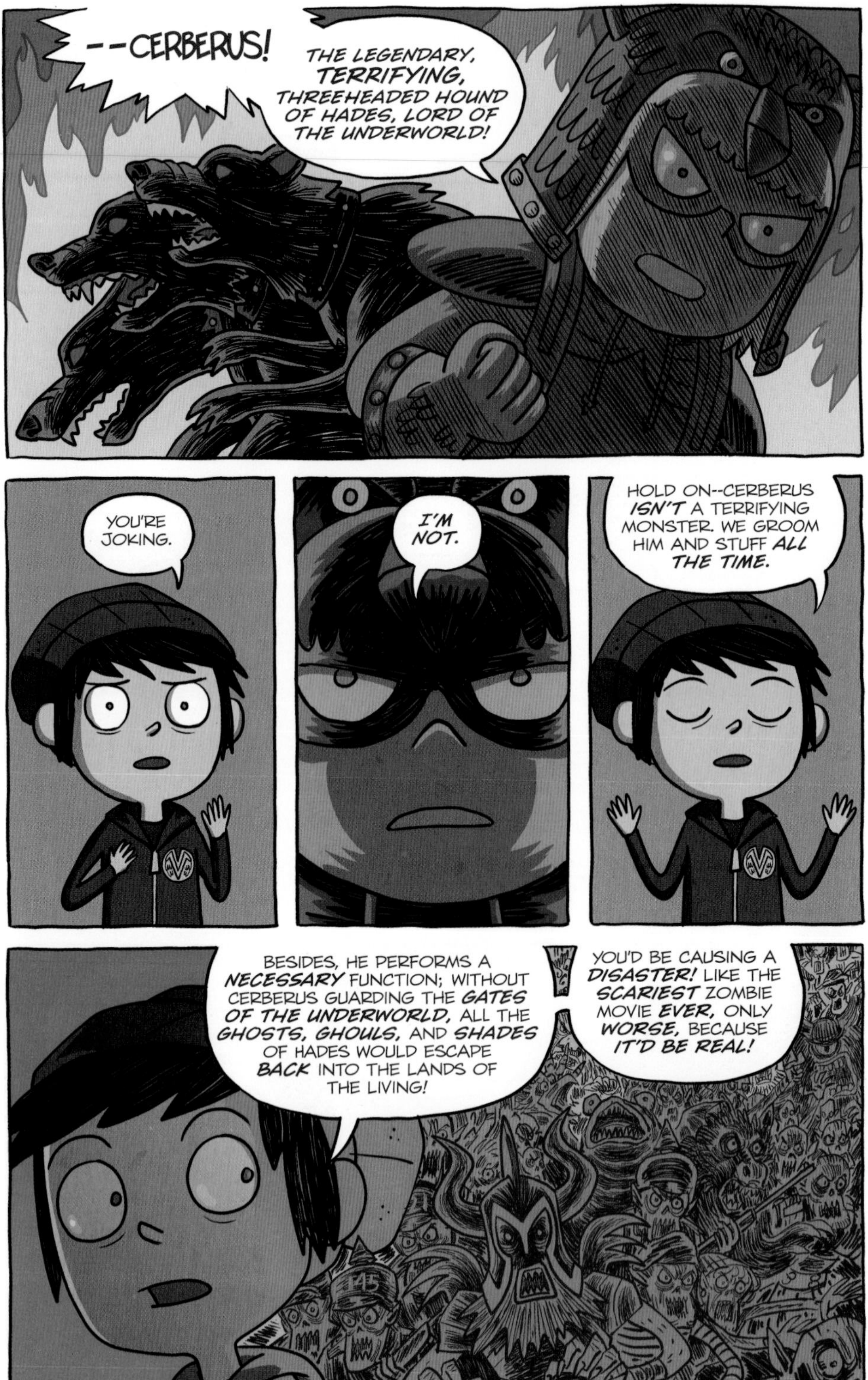
--CERBERUS!
THE LEGENDARY, TERRIFYING, THREEHEADED HOUND OF HADES, LORD OF THE UNDERWORLD!
YOU'RE JOKING.
I'M NOT.
HOLD ON--CERBERUS ISN'T A TERRIFYING MONSTER. WE GROOM HIM AND STUFF ALL THE TIME.
BESIDES, HE PERFORMS A NECESSARY FUNCTION; WITHOUT CERBERUS GUARDING THE GATES OF THE UNDERWORLD, ALL THE GHOSTS, GHOULS, AND SHADES OF HADES WOULD ESCAPE BACK INTO THE LANDS OF THE LIVING!
YOU'D BE CAUSING A DISASTER! LIKE THE SCARIEST ZOMBIE MOVIE EVER, ONLY WORSE, BECAUSE IT'D BE REAL!

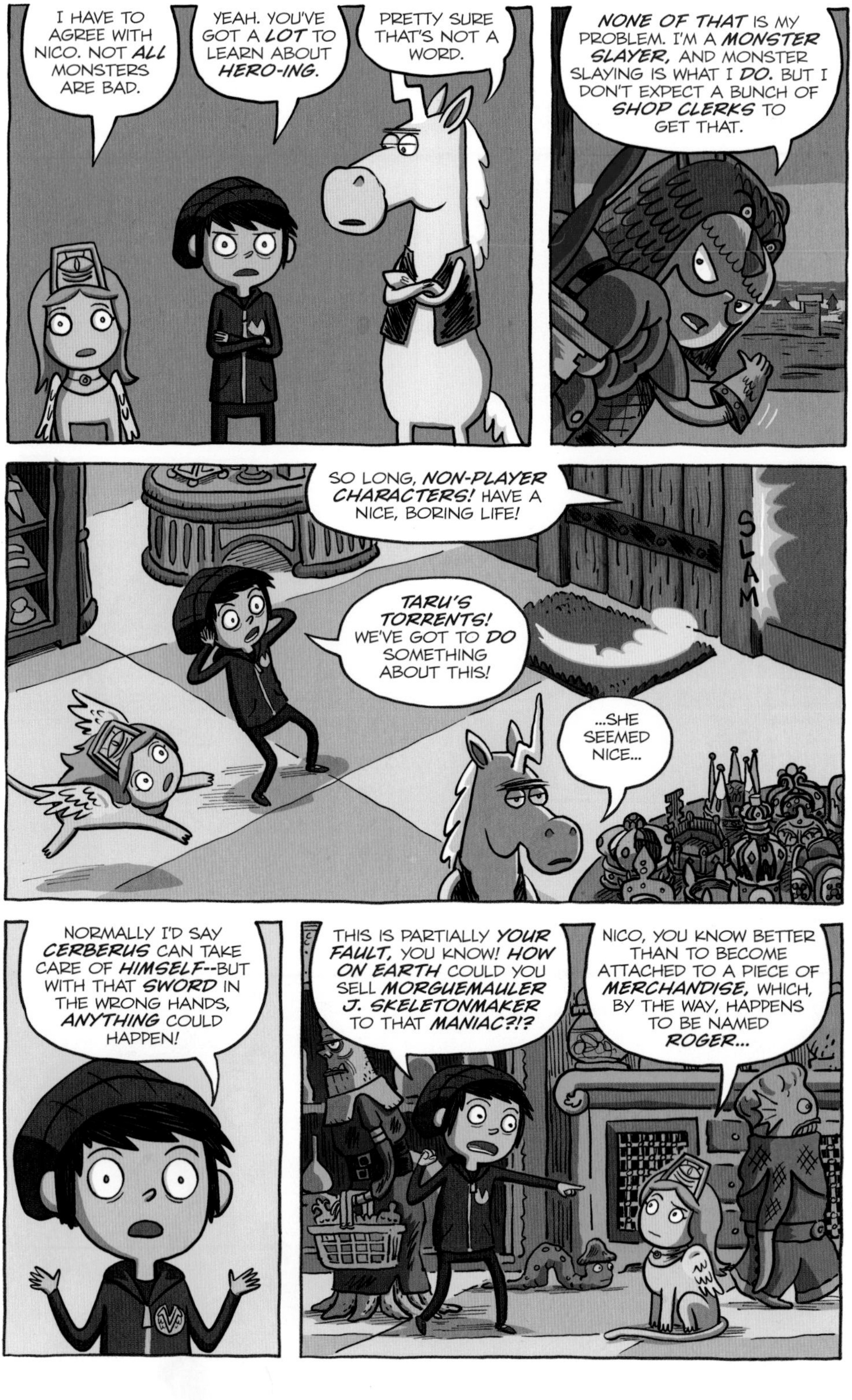
I HAVE TO AGREE WITH NICO. NOT ALL MONSTERS ARE BAD.
YEAH. YOU'VE GOT A LOT TO LEARN ABOUT HERO-ING.
PRETTY SURE THAT'S NOT A WORD.
NONE OF THAT IS MY PROBLEM. I'M A MONSTER SLAYER, AND MONSTER SLAYING IS WHAT I DO. BUT I DON'T EXPECT A BUNCH OF SHOP CLERKS TO GET THAT.
SO LONG, NON-PLAYER CHARACTERS! HAVE A NICE, BORING LIFE!
SLAM
TARU'S TORRENTS! WE'VE GOT TO DO SOMETHING ABOUT THIS!
...SHE SEEMED NICE...
NORMALLY I'D SAY CERBERUS CAN TAKE CARE OF HIMSELF--BUT WITH THAT SWORD IN THE WRONG HANDS, ANYTHING COULD HAPPEN!
THIS IS PARTIALLY YOUR FAULT, YOU KNOW! HOW ON EARTH COULD YOU SELL MORGUEMAULER J. SKELETONMAKER TO THAT MANIAC?!?
NICO, YOU KNOW BETTER THAN TO BECOME ATTACHED TO A PIECE OF MERCHANDISE, WHICH, BY THE WAY, HAPPENS TO BE NAMED ROGER...

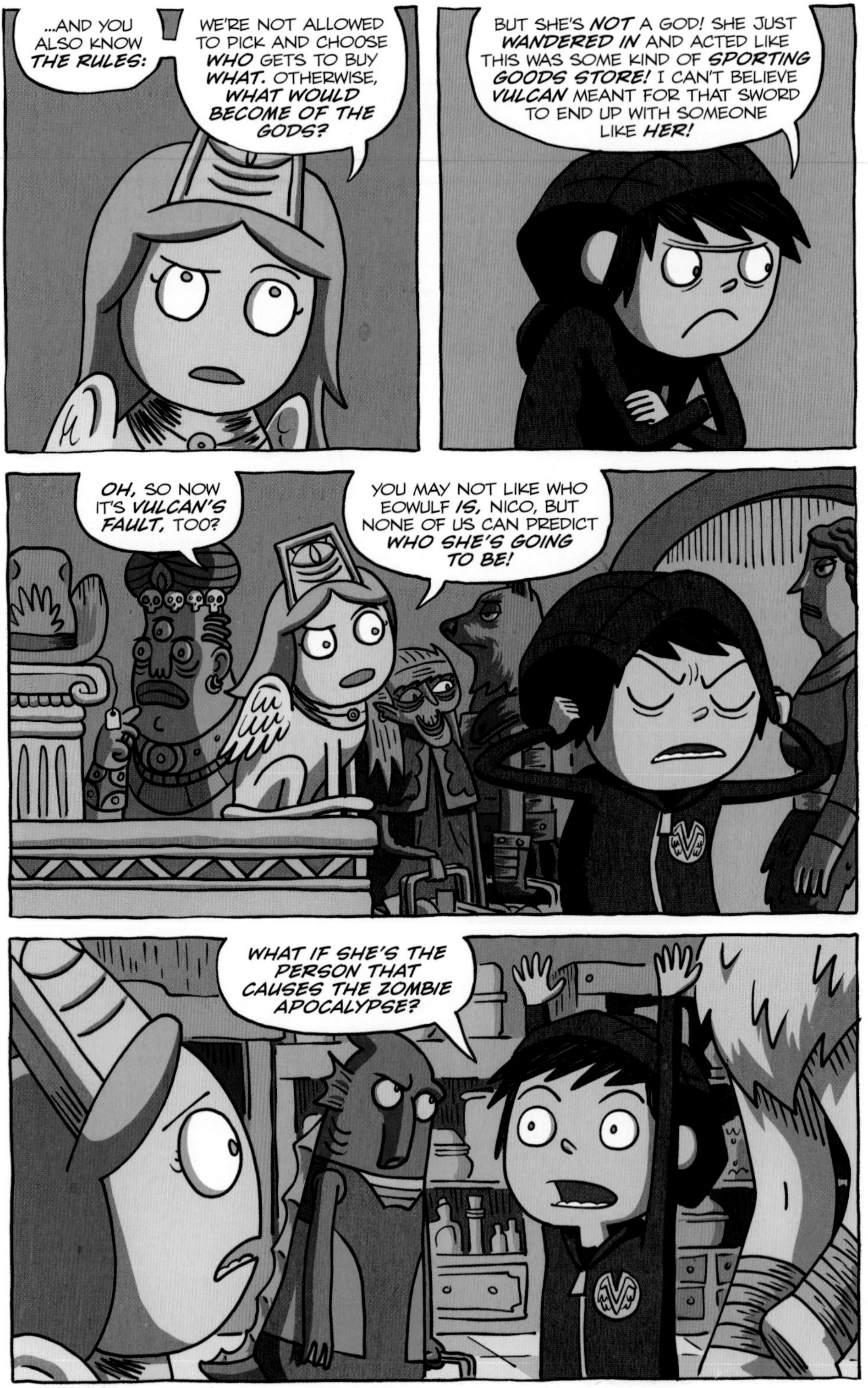
...AND YOU ALSO KNOW *THE RULES:*
WE'RE NOT ALLOWED TO PICK AND CHOOSE *WHO* GETS TO BUY *WHAT.* OTHERWISE, *WHAT WOULD BECOME OF THE GODS?*
BUT SHE'S *NOT* A GOD! SHE JUST *WANDERED IN* AND ACTED LIKE THIS WAS SOME KIND OF *SPORTING GOODS STORE!* I CAN'T BELIEVE *VULCAN* MEANT FOR THAT SWORD TO END UP WITH SOMEONE LIKE *HER!*
OH, SO NOW IT'S *VULCAN'S FAULT,* TOO?
YOU MAY NOT LIKE WHO EOWULF *IS,* NICO, BUT NONE OF US CAN PREDICT *WHO SHE'S GOING TO BE!*
WHAT IF SHE'S THE PERSON THAT CAUSES THE ZOMBIE APOCALYPSE?

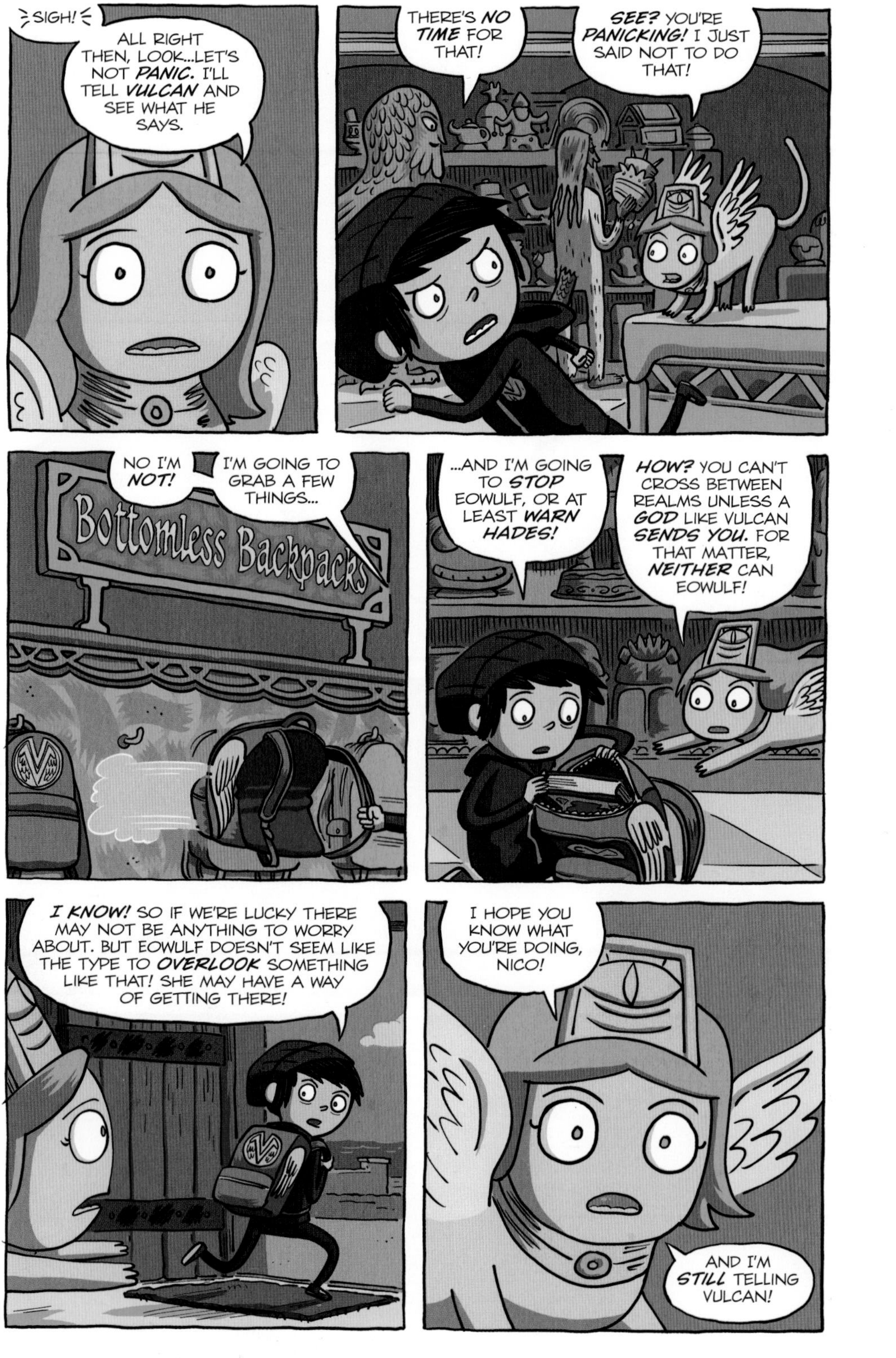
SIGH!
ALL RIGHT THEN, LOOK...LET'S NOT PANIC. I'LL TELL VULCAN AND SEE WHAT HE SAYS.
THERE'S NO TIME FOR THAT!
SEE? YOU'RE PANICKING! I JUST SAID NOT TO DO THAT!
NO I'M NOT!
I'M GOING TO GRAB A FEW THINGS...
Bottomless Backpacks
...AND I'M GOING TO STOP EOWULF, OR AT LEAST WARN HADES!
HOW? YOU CAN'T CROSS BETWEEN REALMS UNLESS A GOD LIKE VULCAN SENDS YOU. FOR THAT MATTER, NEITHER CAN EOWULF!
I KNOW! SO IF WE'RE LUCKY THERE MAY NOT BE ANYTHING TO WORRY ABOUT. BUT EOWULF DOESN'T SEEM LIKE THE TYPE TO OVERLOOK SOMETHING LIKE THAT! SHE MAY HAVE A WAY OF GETTING THERE!
I HOPE YOU KNOW WHAT YOU'RE DOING, NICO!
AND I'M STILL TELLING VULCAN!

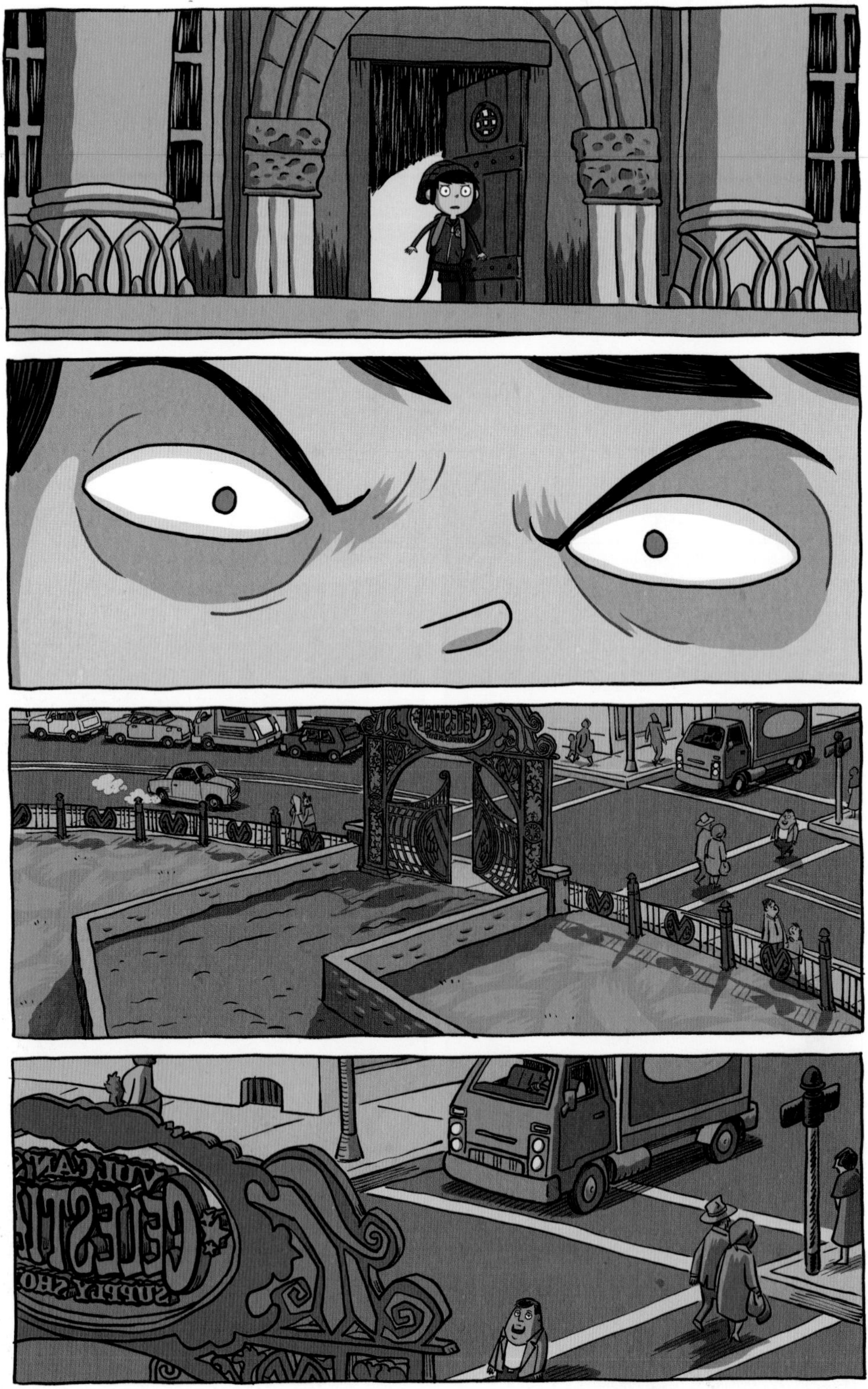

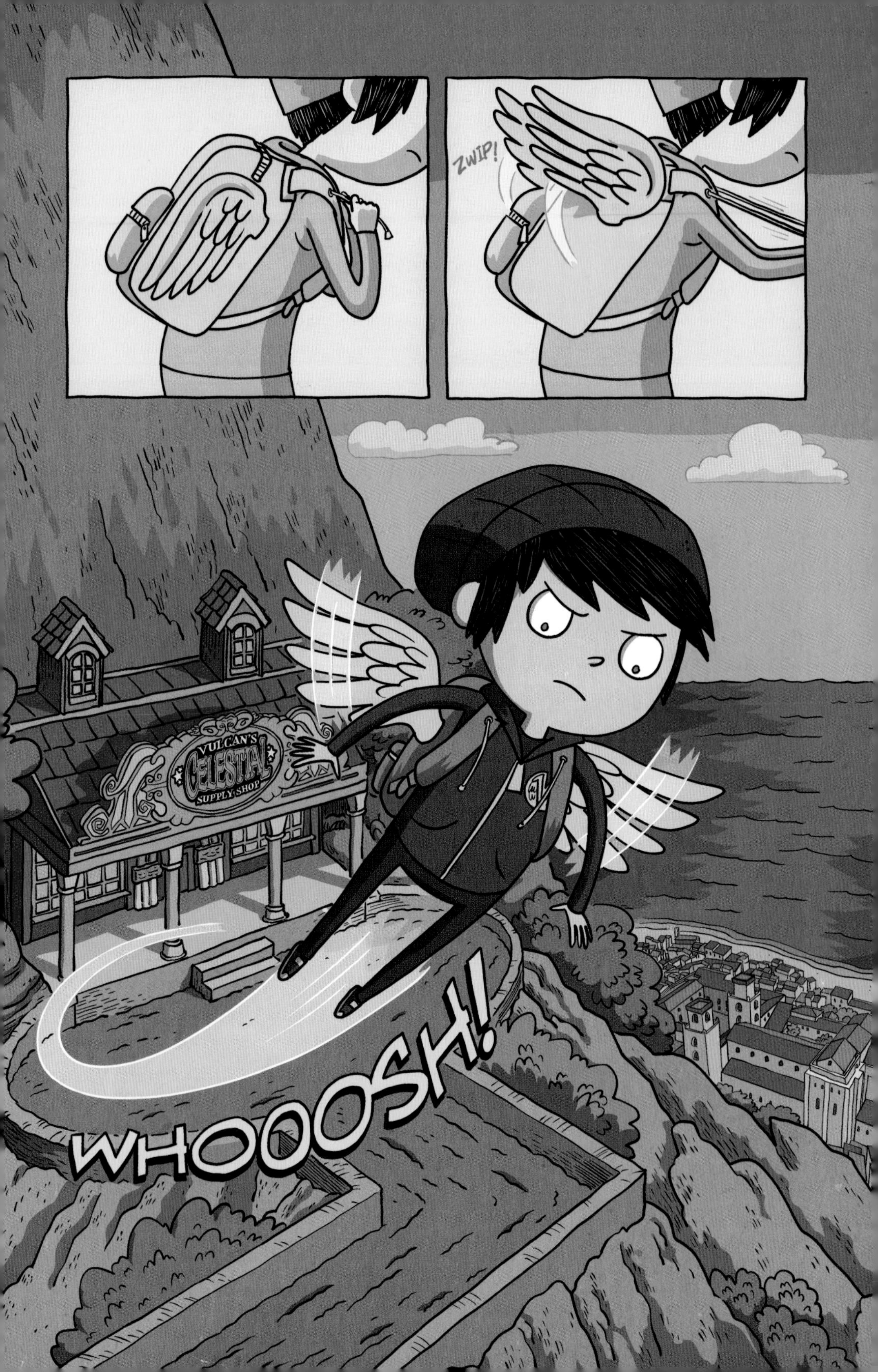
ZWIP!
VULCAN'S
CELESTIAL
SUPPLY SHOP
WHOOOOSH!

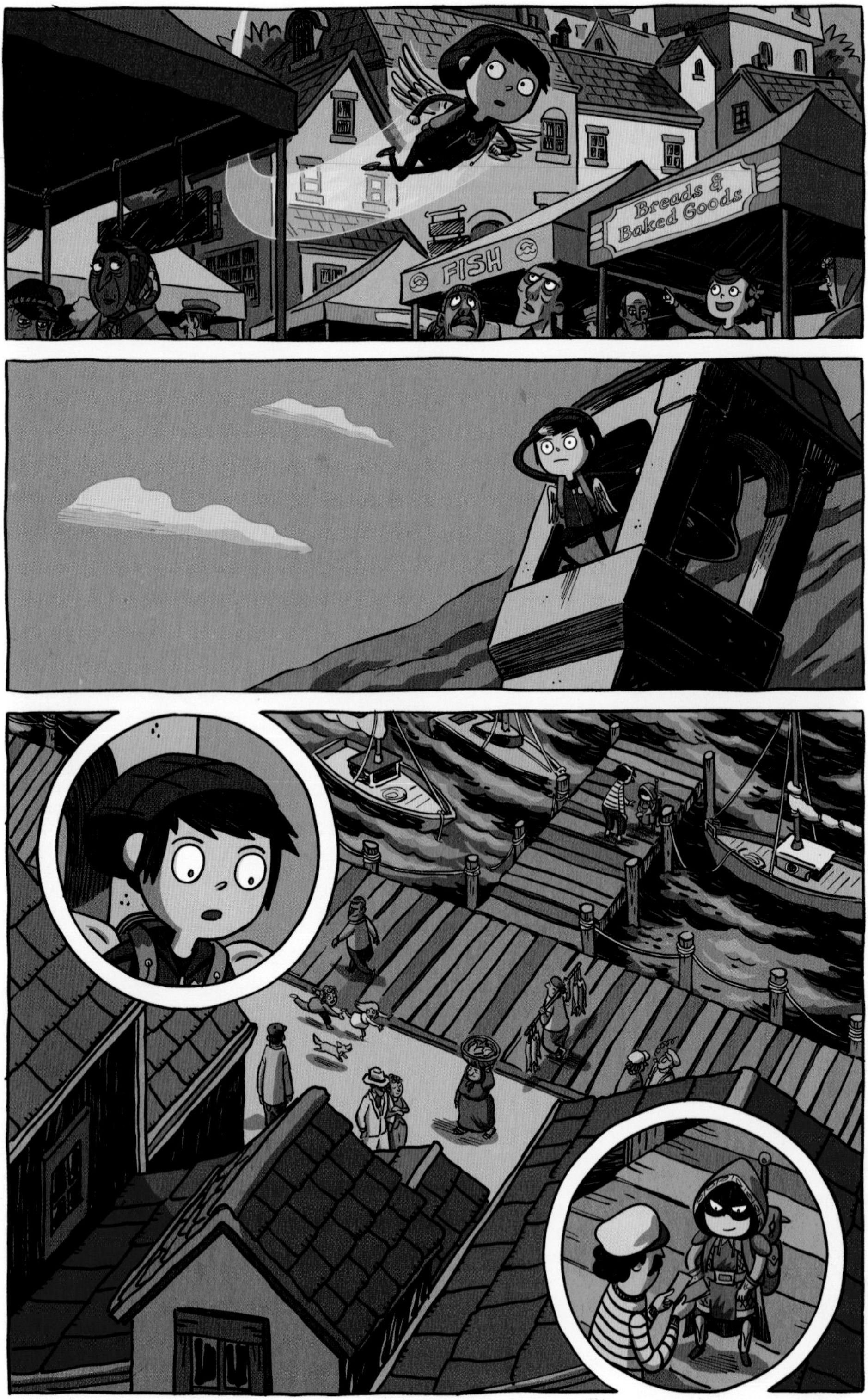
Breads &
Baked Goods
FISH

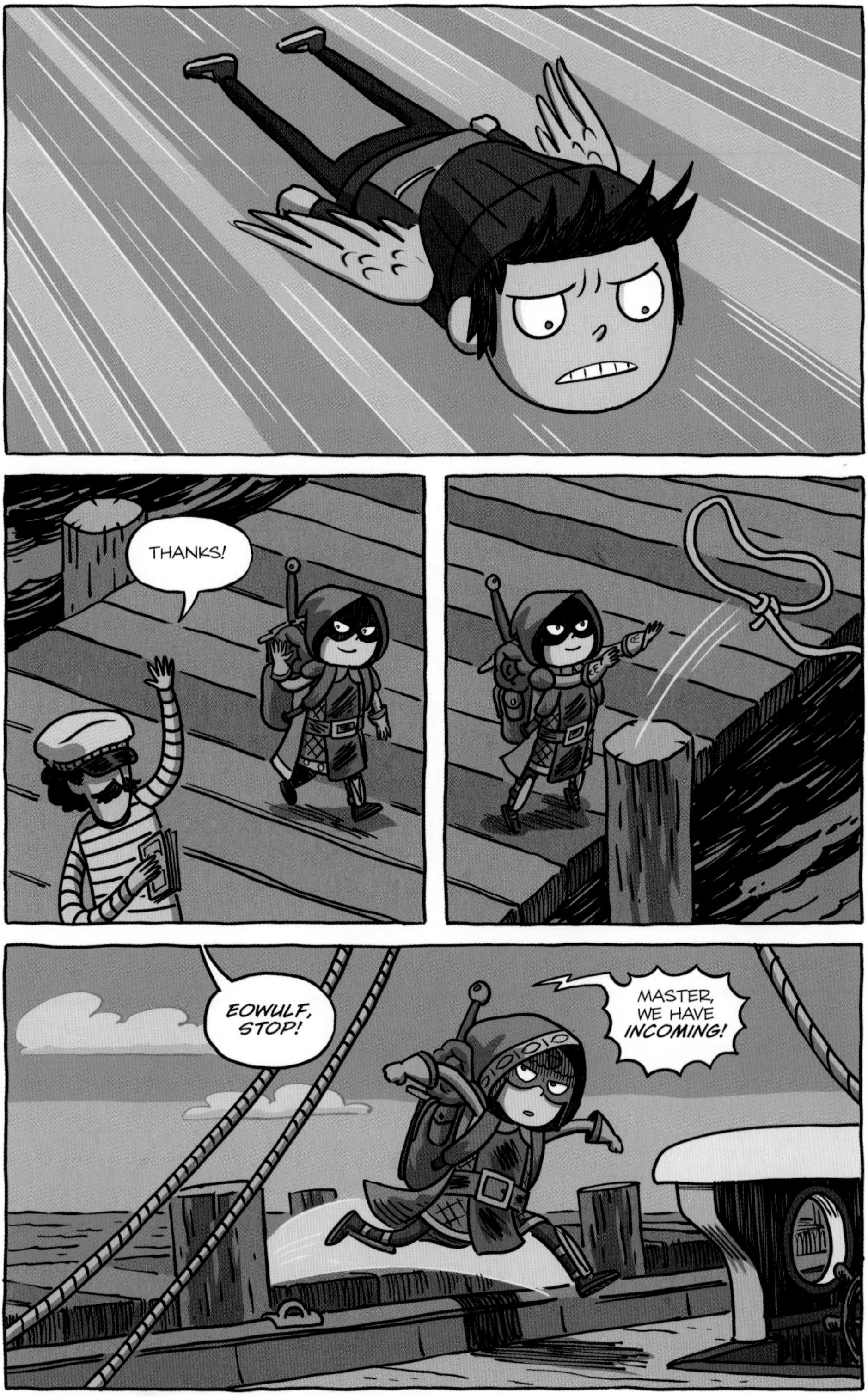
THANKS!
EOWULF, STOP!
MASTER, WE HAVE INCOMING!

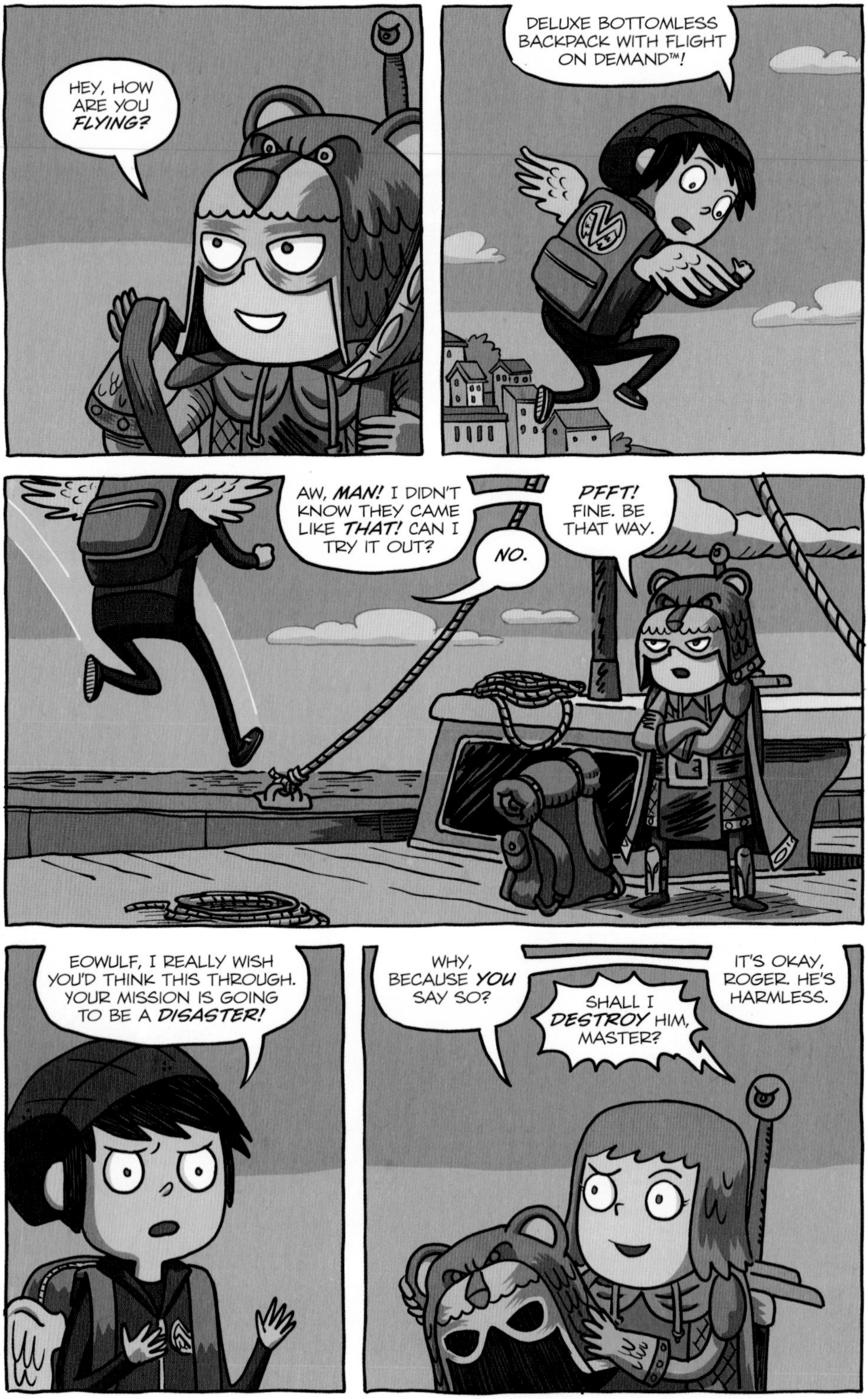
HEY, HOW ARE YOU *FLYING?*
DELUXE BOTTOMLESS BACKPACK WITH FLIGHT ON DEMAND™!
AW, *MAN!* I DIDN'T KNOW THEY CAME LIKE *THAT!* CAN I TRY IT OUT?
NO.
PFFT! FINE. BE THAT WAY.
EOWULF, I REALLY WISH YOU'D THINK THIS THROUGH. YOUR MISSION IS GOING TO BE A *DISASTER!*
WHY, BECAUSE *YOU* SAY SO?
SHALL I *DESTROY* HIM, MASTER?
IT'S OKAY, ROGER. HE'S HARMLESS.

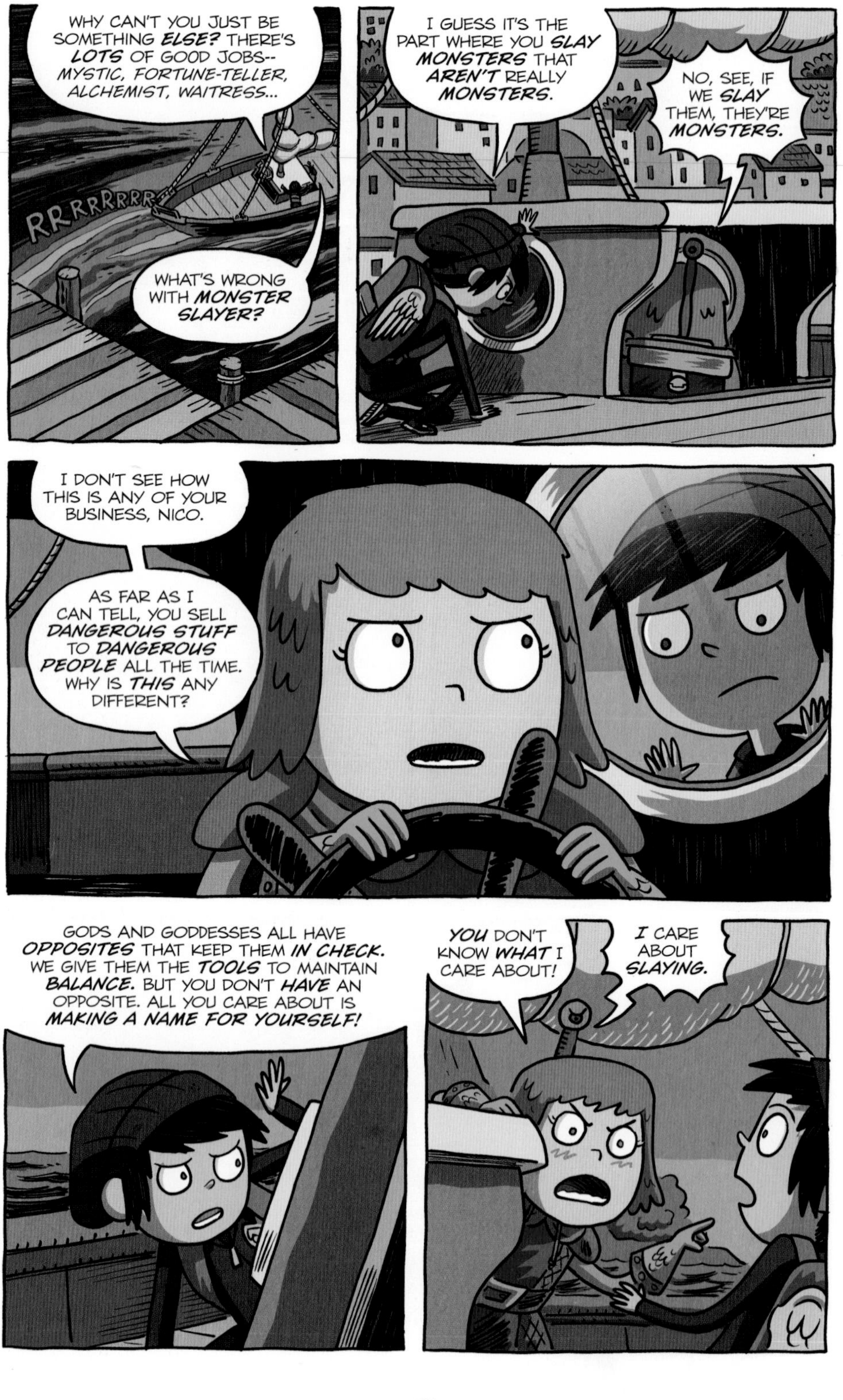
WHY CAN'T YOU JUST BE SOMETHING ELSE? THERE'S LOTS OF GOOD JOBS-- MYSTIC, FORTUNE-TELLER, ALCHEMIST, WAITRESS...
RRRRRRRRR
WHAT'S WRONG WITH MONSTER SLAYER?
I GUESS IT'S THE PART WHERE YOU SLAY MONSTERS THAT AREN'T REALLY MONSTERS.
NO, SEE, IF WE SLAY THEM, THEY'RE MONSTERS.
I DON'T SEE HOW THIS IS ANY OF YOUR BUSINESS, NICO.
AS FAR AS I CAN TELL, YOU SELL DANGEROUS STUFF TO DANGEROUS PEOPLE ALL THE TIME. WHY IS THIS ANY DIFFERENT?
GODS AND GODDESSES ALL HAVE OPPOSITES THAT KEEP THEM IN CHECK. WE GIVE THEM THE TOOLS TO MAINTAIN BALANCE. BUT YOU DON'T HAVE AN OPPOSITE. ALL YOU CARE ABOUT IS MAKING A NAME FOR YOURSELF!
YOU DON'T KNOW WHAT I CARE ABOUT!
I CARE ABOUT SLAYING.

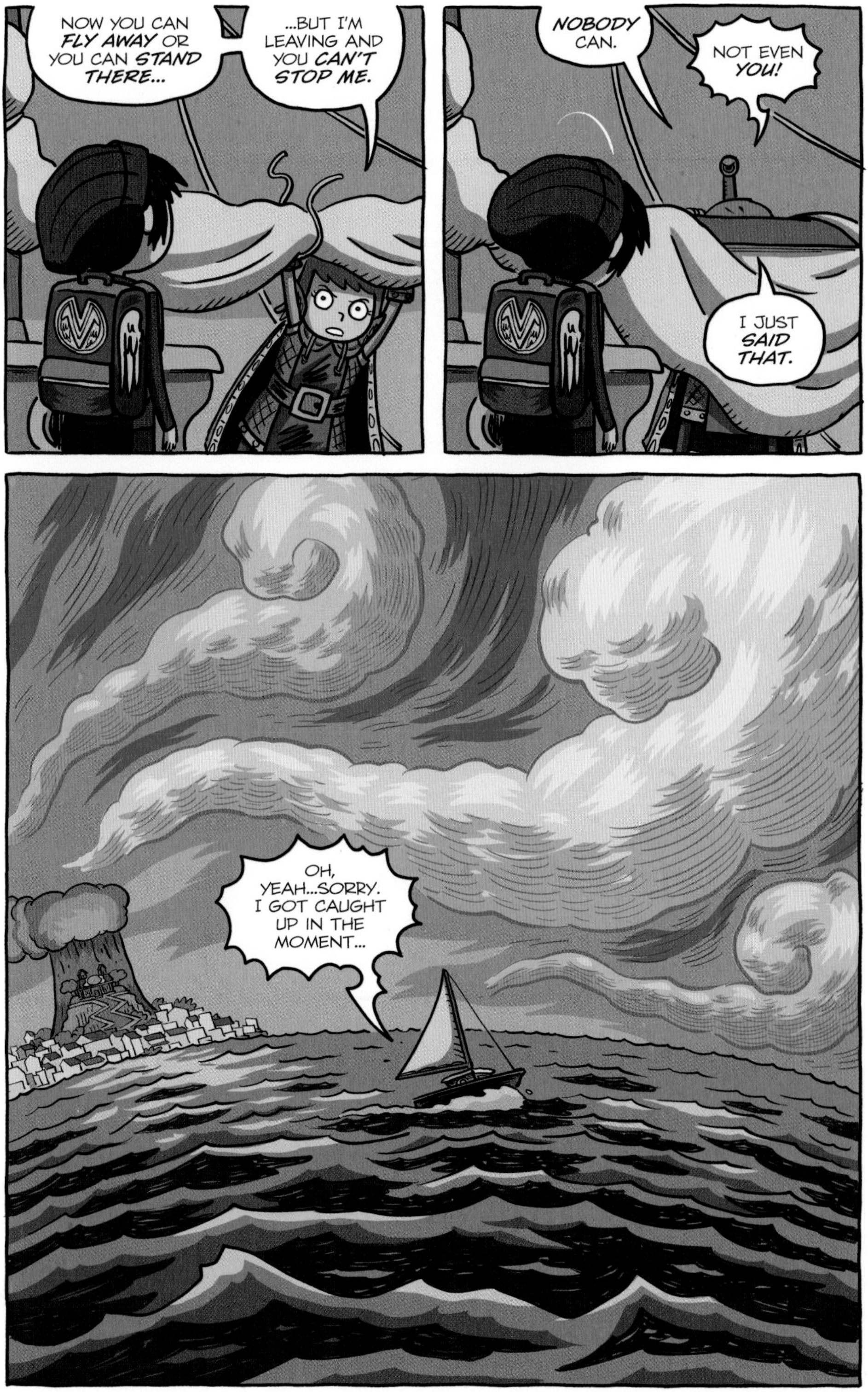
NOW YOU CAN FLY AWAY OR YOU CAN STAND THERE...
...BUT I'M LEAVING AND YOU CAN'T STOP ME.
NOBODY CAN.
NOT EVEN YOU!
I JUST SAID THAT.
OH, YEAH...SORRY. I GOT CAUGHT UP IN THE MOMENT...

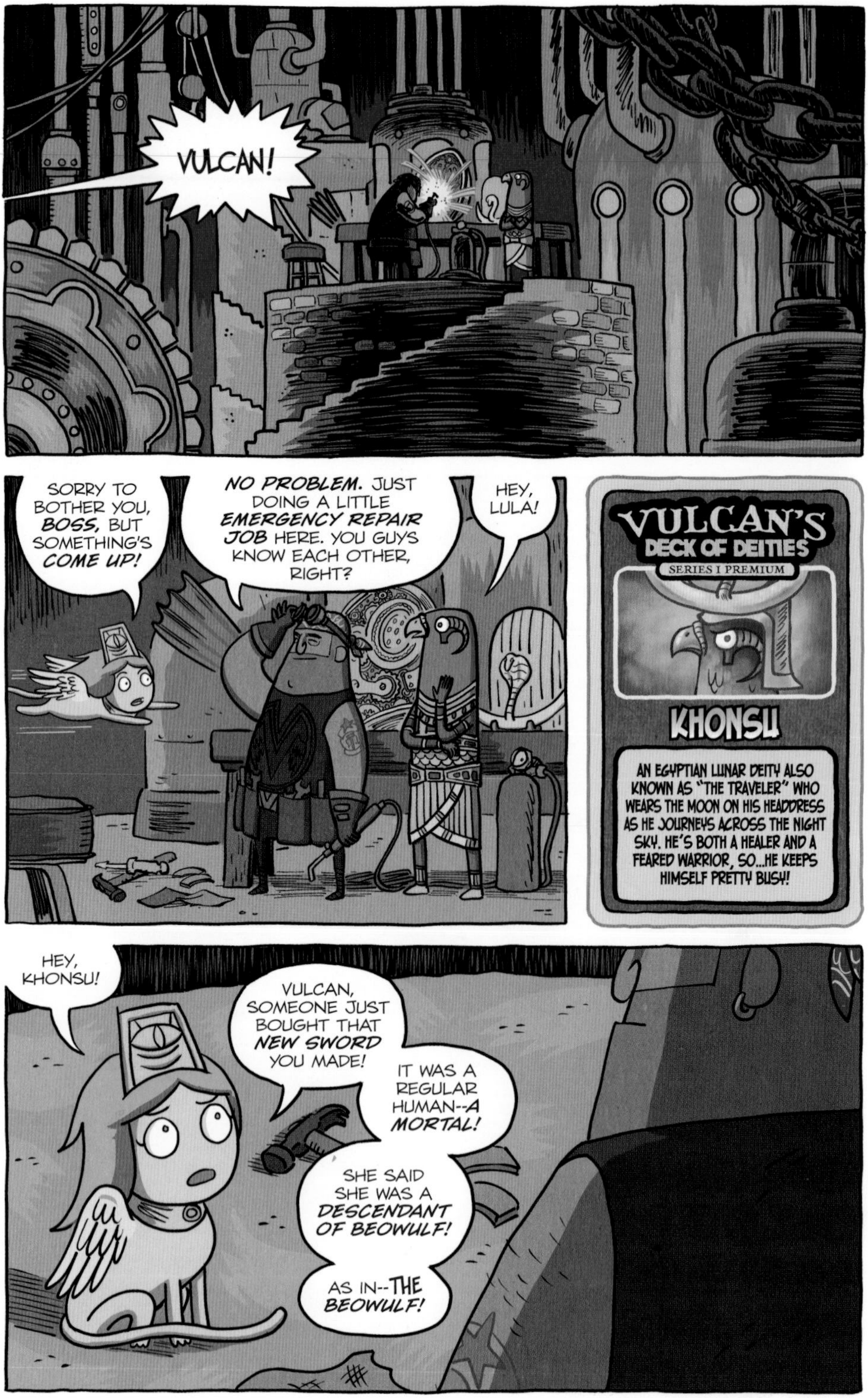
VULCAN!
SORRY TO BOTHER YOU, BOSS, BUT SOMETHING'S COME UP!
NO PROBLEM. JUST DOING A LITTLE EMERGENCY REPAIR JOB HERE. YOU GUYS KNOW EACH OTHER, RIGHT?
HEY, LULA!
VULCAN'S DECK OF DEITIES
SERIES I PREMIUM
KHONSU
AN EGYPTIAN LUNAR DEITY ALSO KNOWN AS "THE TRAVELER" WHO WEARS THE MOON ON HIS HEADDRESS AS HE JOURNEYS ACROSS THE NIGHT SKY. HE'S BOTH A HEALER AND A FEARED WARRIOR, SO...HE KEEPS HIMSELF PRETTY BUSY!
HEY, KHONSU!
VULCAN, SOMEONE JUST BOUGHT THAT NEW SWORD YOU MADE!
IT WAS A REGULAR HUMAN--A MORTAL!
SHE SAID SHE WAS A DESCENDANT OF BEOWULF!
AS IN--THE BEOWULF!

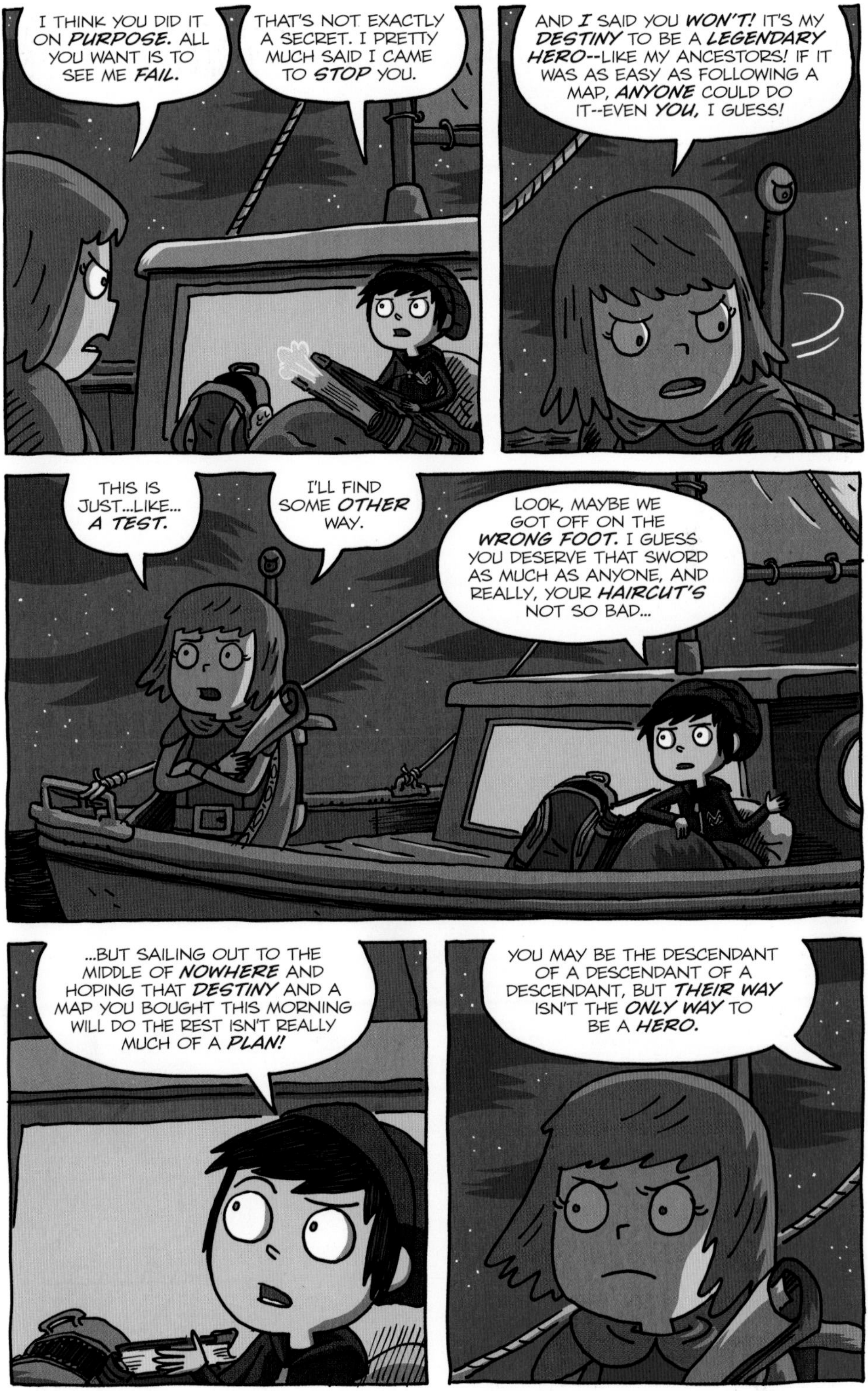

I THINK YOU DID IT ON PURPOSE. ALL YOU WANT IS TO SEE ME FAIL.
THAT'S NOT EXACTLY A SECRET. I PRETTY MUCH SAID I CAME TO STOP YOU.
AND I SAID YOU WON'T! IT'S MY DESTINY TO BE A LEGENDARY HERO--LIKE MY ANCESTORS! IF IT WAS AS EASY AS FOLLOWING A MAP, ANYONE COULD DO IT--EVEN YOU, I GUESS!
THIS IS JUST...LIKE... A TEST.
I'LL FIND SOME OTHER WAY.
LOOK, MAYBE WE GOT OFF ON THE WRONG FOOT. I GUESS YOU DESERVE THAT SWORD AS MUCH AS ANYONE, AND REALLY, YOUR HAIRCUT'S NOT SO BAD...
...BUT SAILING OUT TO THE MIDDLE OF NOWHERE AND HOPING THAT DESTINY AND A MAP YOU BOUGHT THIS MORNING WILL DO THE REST ISN'T REALLY MUCH OF A PLAN!
YOU MAY BE THE DESCENDANT OF A DESCENDANT OF A DESCENDANT, BUT THEIR WAY ISN'T THE ONLY WAY TO BE A HERO.

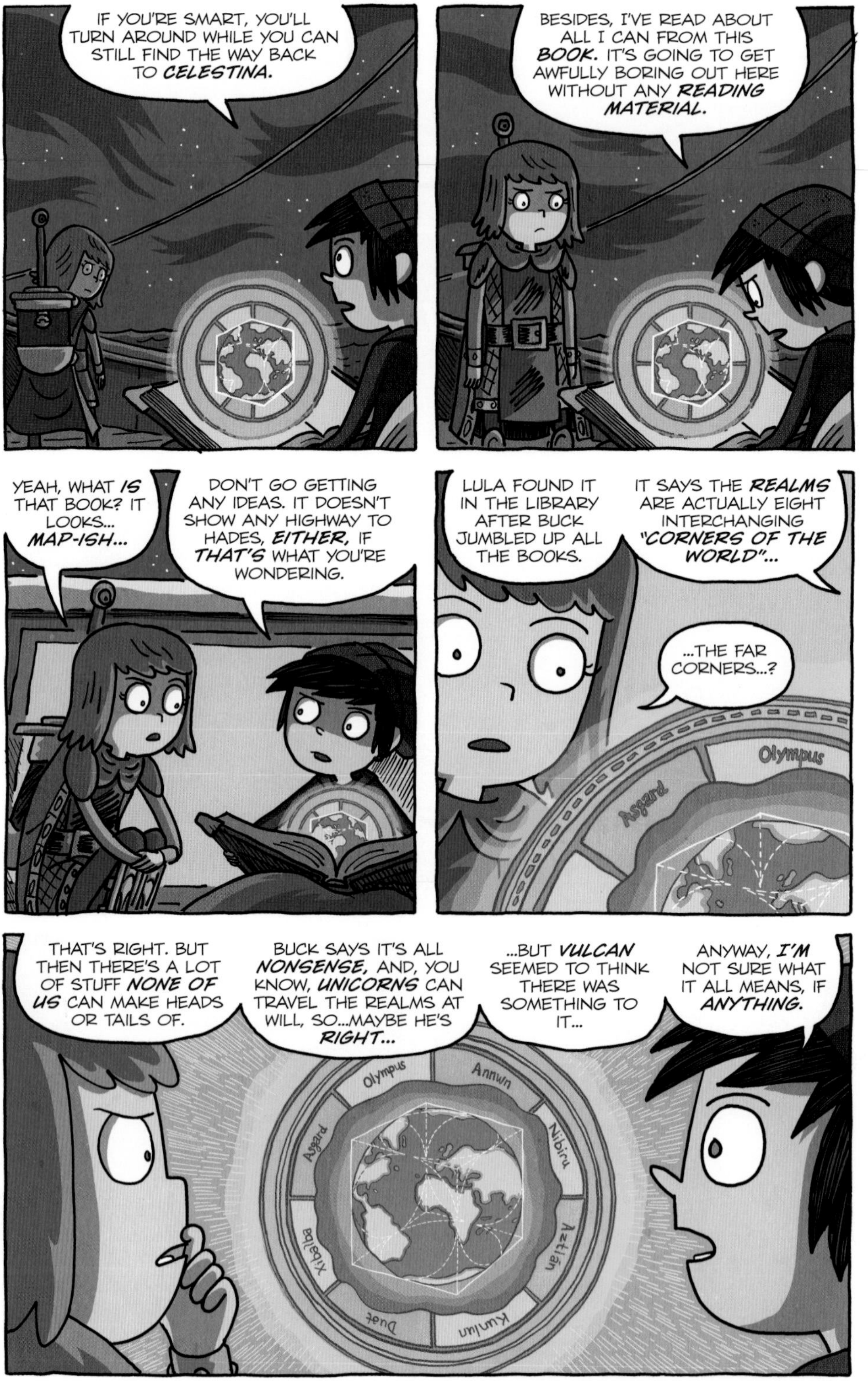
IF YOU'RE SMART, YOU'LL TURN AROUND WHILE YOU CAN STILL FIND THE WAY BACK TO CELESTINA.
BESIDES, I'VE READ ABOUT ALL I CAN FROM THIS BOOK. IT'S GOING TO GET AWFULLY BORING OUT HERE WITHOUT ANY READING MATERIAL.
YEAH, WHAT IS THAT BOOK? IT LOOKS... MAP-ISH...
DON'T GO GETTING ANY IDEAS. IT DOESN'T SHOW ANY HIGHWAY TO HADES, EITHER, IF THAT'S WHAT YOU'RE WONDERING.
LULA FOUND IT IN THE LIBRARY AFTER BUCK JUMBLED UP ALL THE BOOKS.
IT SAYS THE REALMS ARE ACTUALLY EIGHT INTERCHANGING "CORNERS OF THE WORLD"...
...THE FAR CORNERS...?
Olympus
Asgard
THAT'S RIGHT. BUT THEN THERE'S A LOT OF STUFF NONE OF US CAN MAKE HEADS OR TAILS OF.
BUCK SAYS IT'S ALL NONSENSE, AND, YOU KNOW, UNICORNS CAN TRAVEL THE REALMS AT WILL, SO...MAYBE HE'S RIGHT...
...BUT VULCAN SEEMED TO THINK THERE WAS SOMETHING TO IT...
ANYWAY, I'M NOT SURE WHAT IT ALL MEANS, IF ANYTHING.
Olympus
Annwn
Nibiru
Aztlán
Kunlun
Duat
Xibalba
Asgard

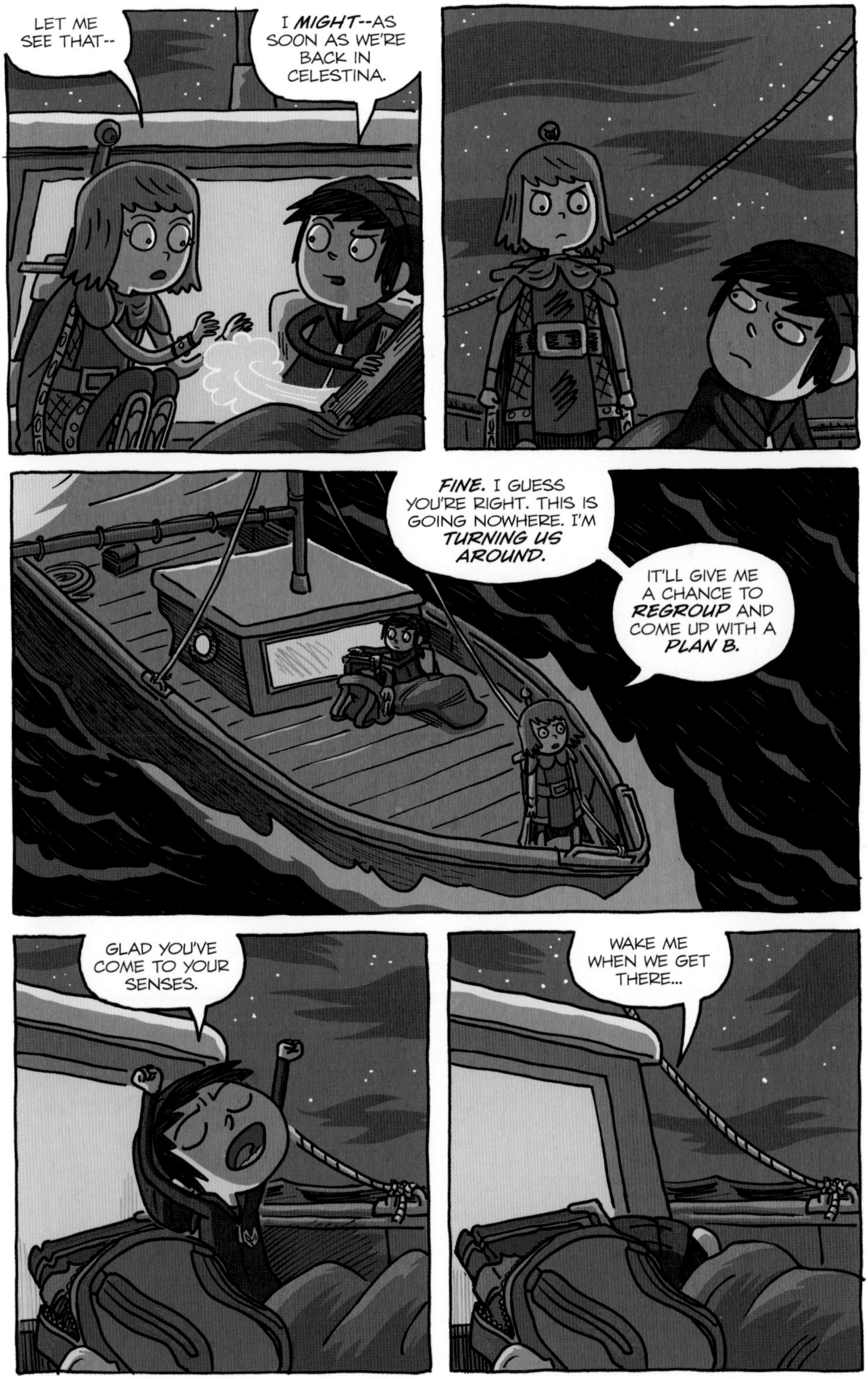
LET ME SEE THAT--
I *MIGHT*--AS SOON AS WE'RE BACK IN CELESTINA.
FINE. I GUESS YOU'RE RIGHT. THIS IS GOING NOWHERE. I'M *TURNING US AROUND.*
IT'LL GIVE ME A CHANCE TO *REGROUP* AND COME UP WITH A *PLAN B.*
GLAD YOU'VE COME TO YOUR SENSES.
WAKE ME WHEN WE GET THERE...

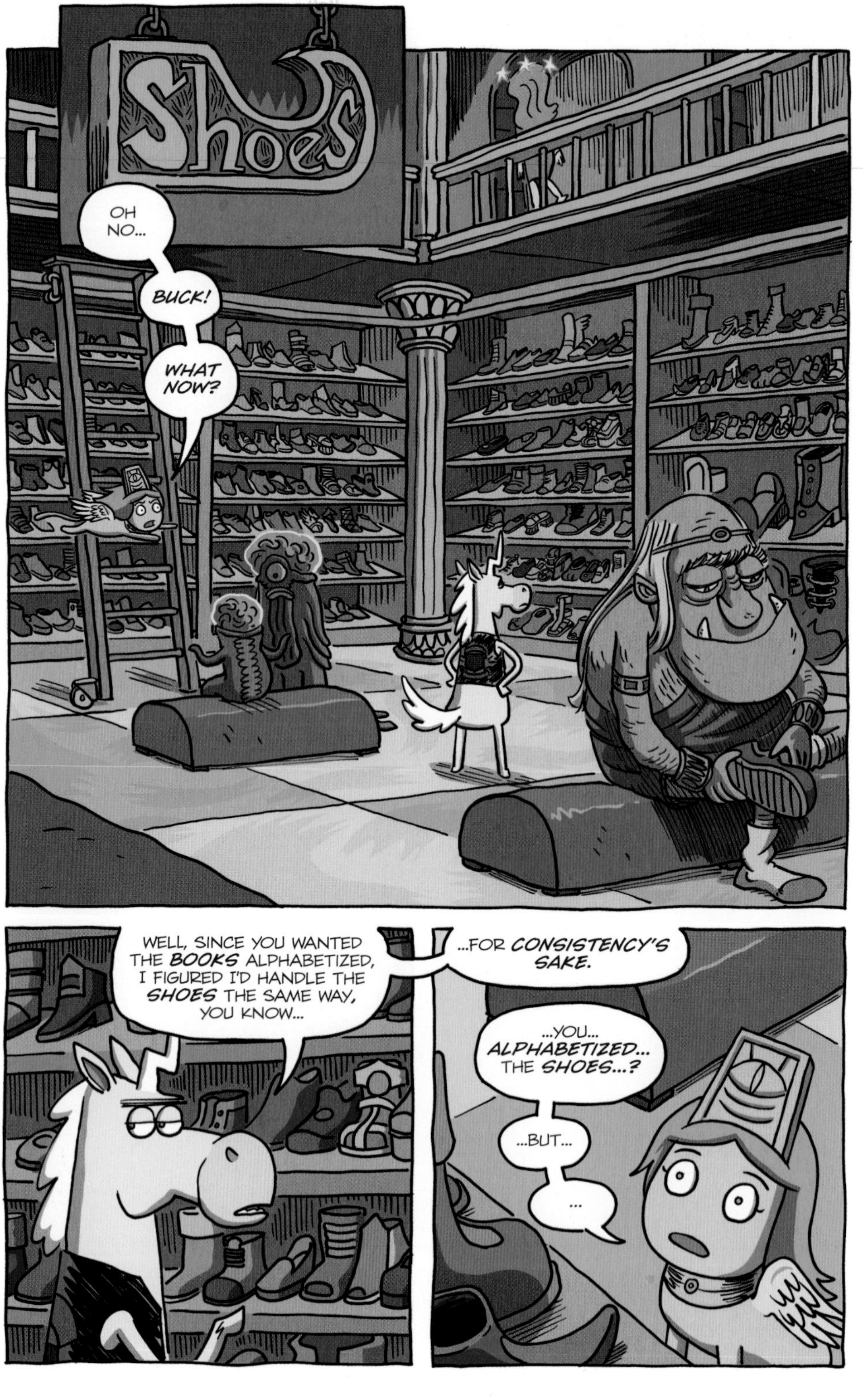
Shoes
OH NO...
BUCK!
WHAT NOW?
WELL, SINCE YOU WANTED THE BOOKS ALPHABETIZED, I FIGURED I'D HANDLE THE SHOES THE SAME WAY, YOU KNOW...
...FOR CONSISTENCY'S SAKE.
...YOU... ALPHABETIZED... THE SHOES...?
...BUT...
...

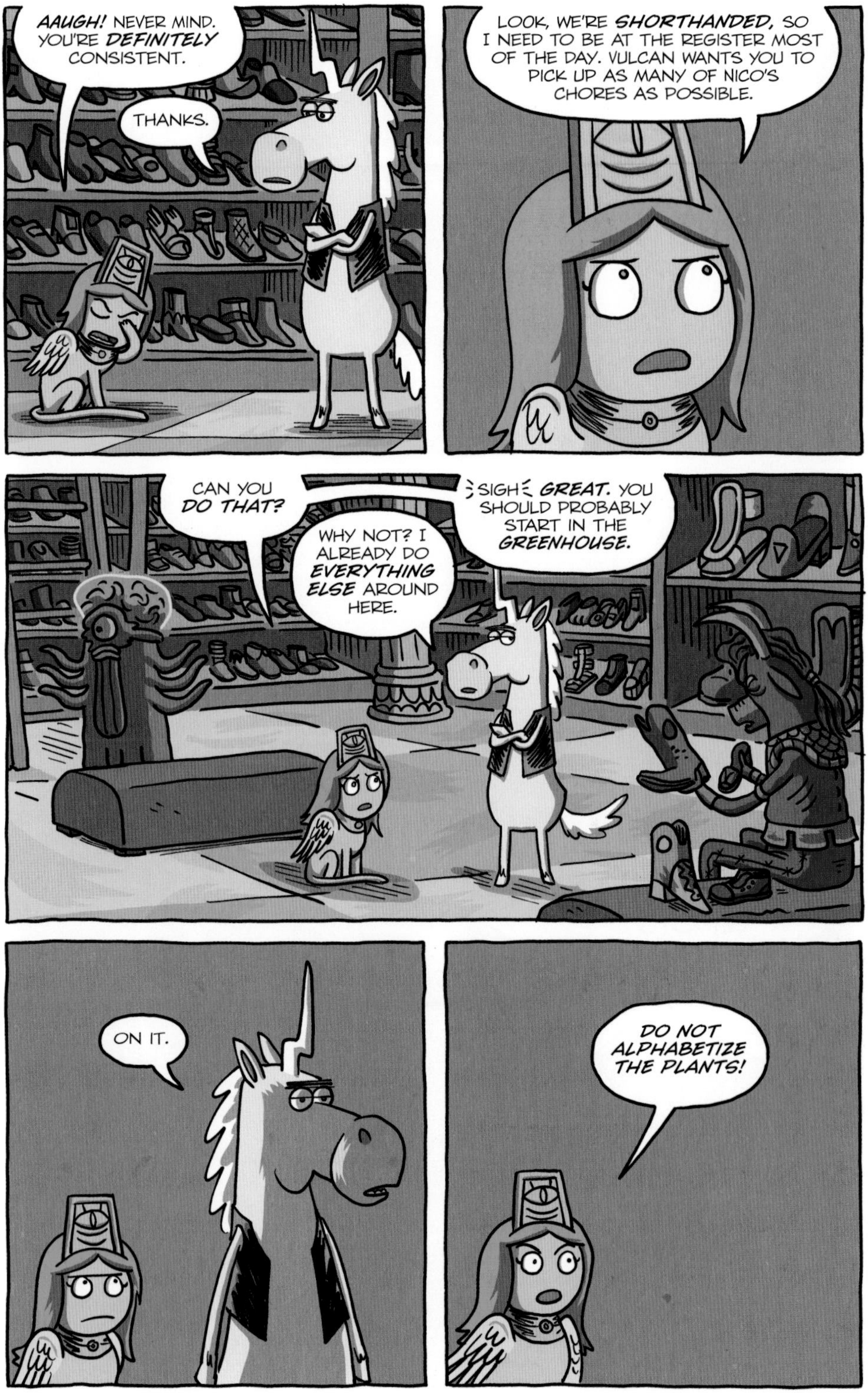
AAUGH! NEVER MIND. YOU'RE DEFINITELY CONSISTENT.
THANKS.
LOOK, WE'RE SHORTHANDED, SO I NEED TO BE AT THE REGISTER MOST OF THE DAY. VULCAN WANTS YOU TO PICK UP AS MANY OF NICO'S CHORES AS POSSIBLE.
CAN YOU DO THAT?
WHY NOT? I ALREADY DO EVERYTHING ELSE AROUND HERE.
SIGH GREAT. YOU SHOULD PROBABLY START IN THE GREENHOUSE.
ON IT.
DO NOT ALPHABETIZE THE PLANTS!

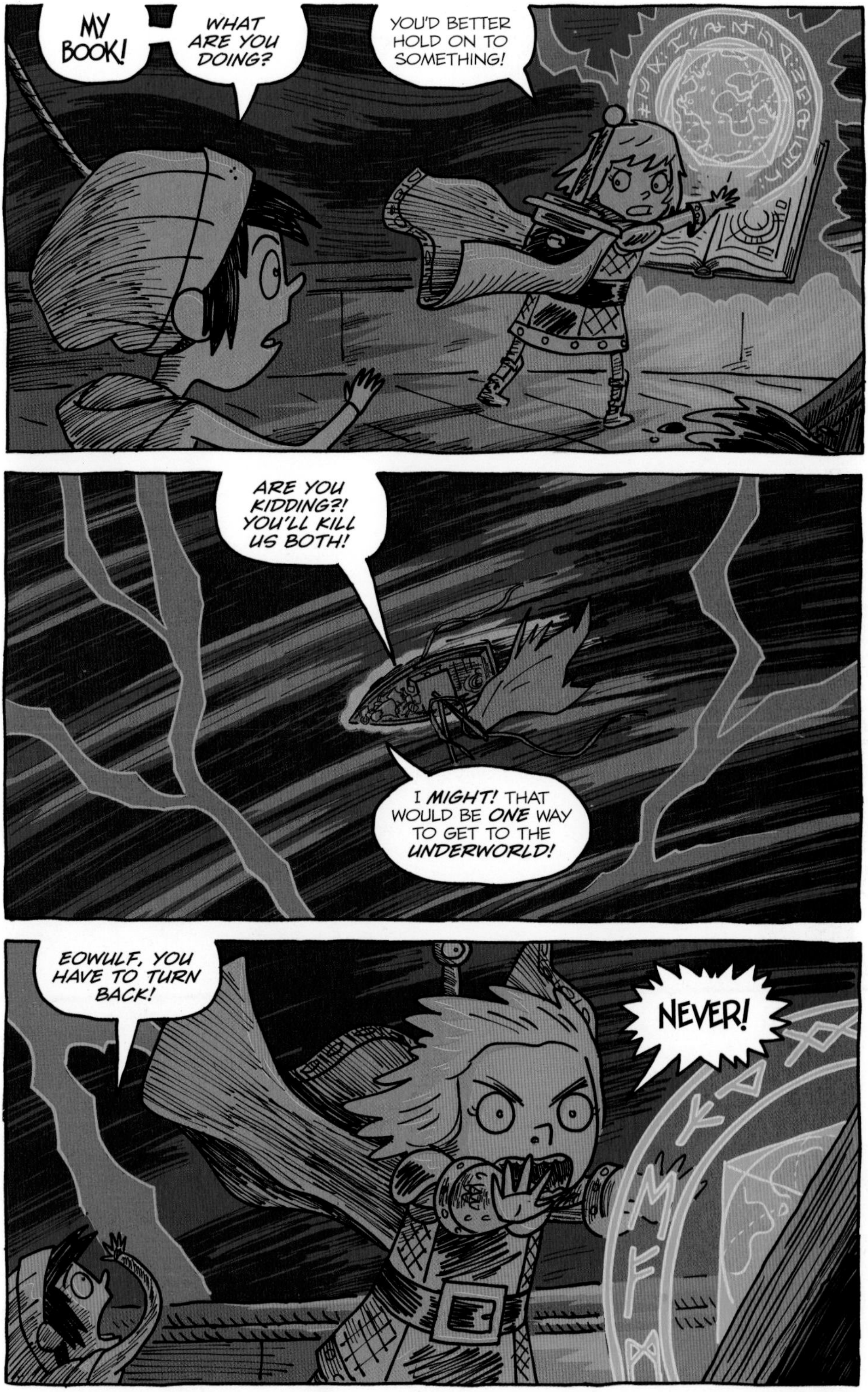
MY BOOK!
WHAT ARE YOU DOING?
YOU'D BETTER HOLD ON TO SOMETHING!
ARE YOU KIDDING?! YOU'LL KILL US BOTH!
I MIGHT! THAT WOULD BE ONE WAY TO GET TO THE UNDERWORLD!
EOWULF, YOU HAVE TO TURN BACK!
NEVER!

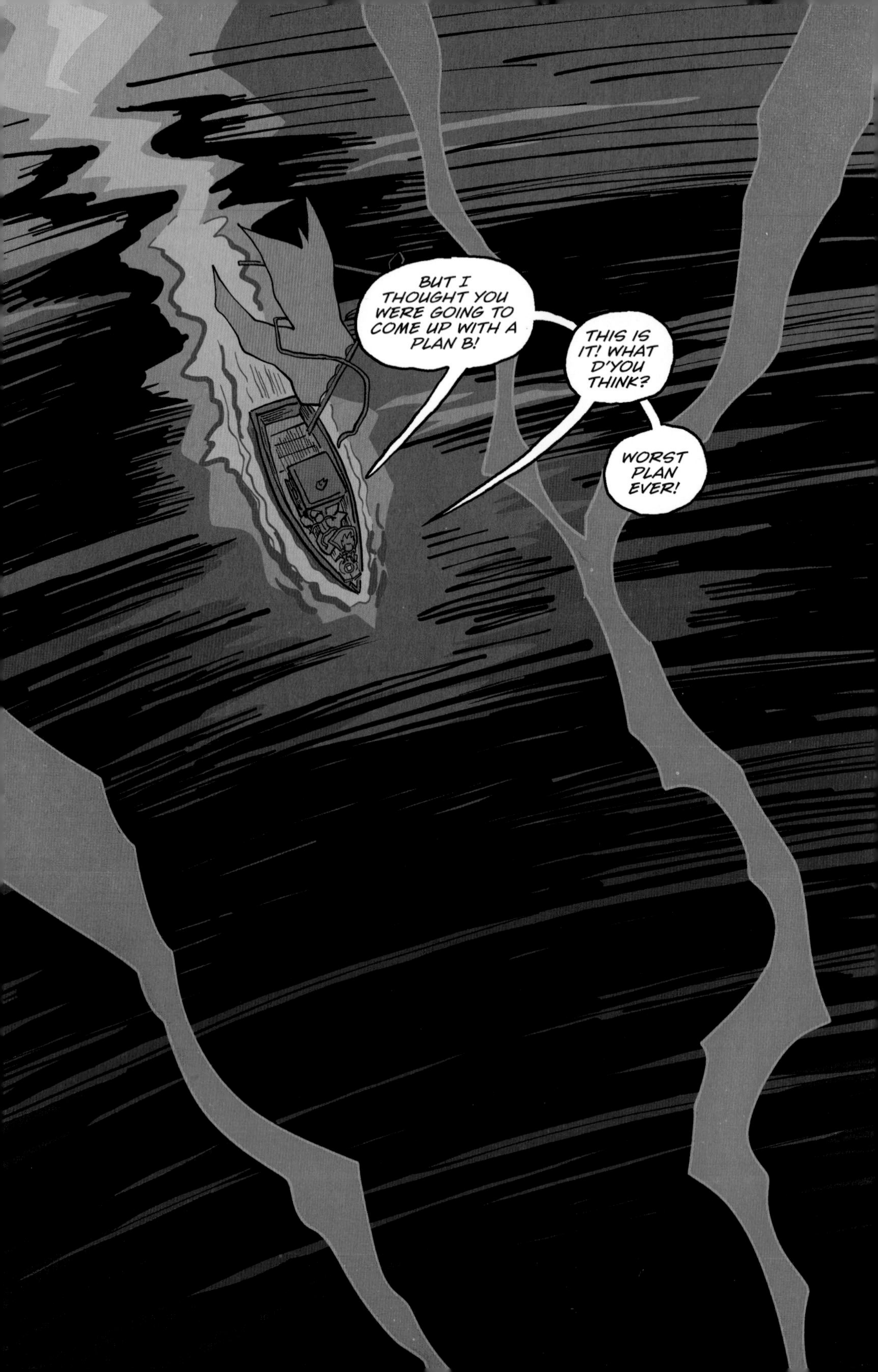
BUT I THOUGHT YOU WERE GOING TO COME UP WITH A PLAN B!
THIS IS IT! WHAT D'YOU THINK?
WORST PLAN EVER!

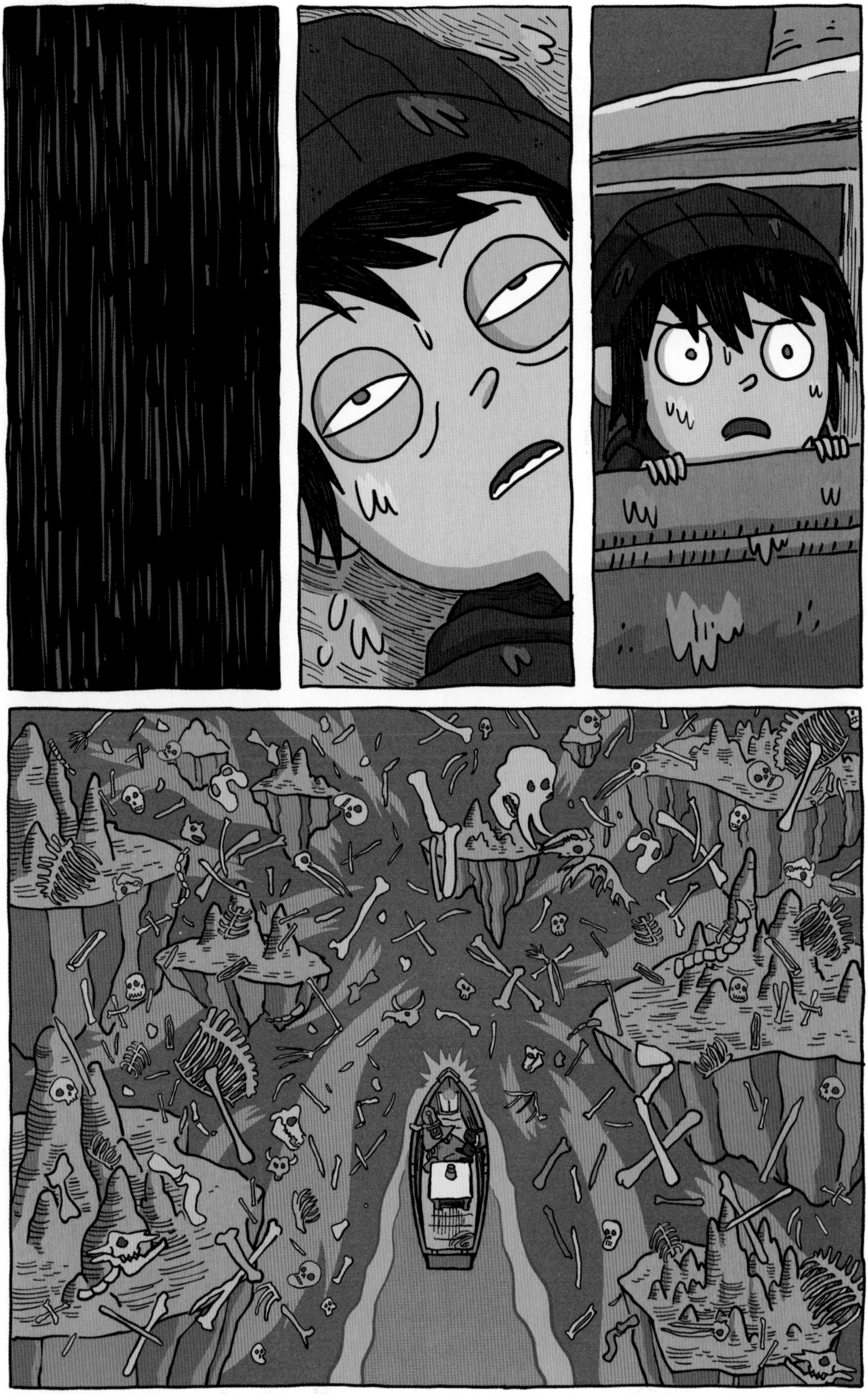

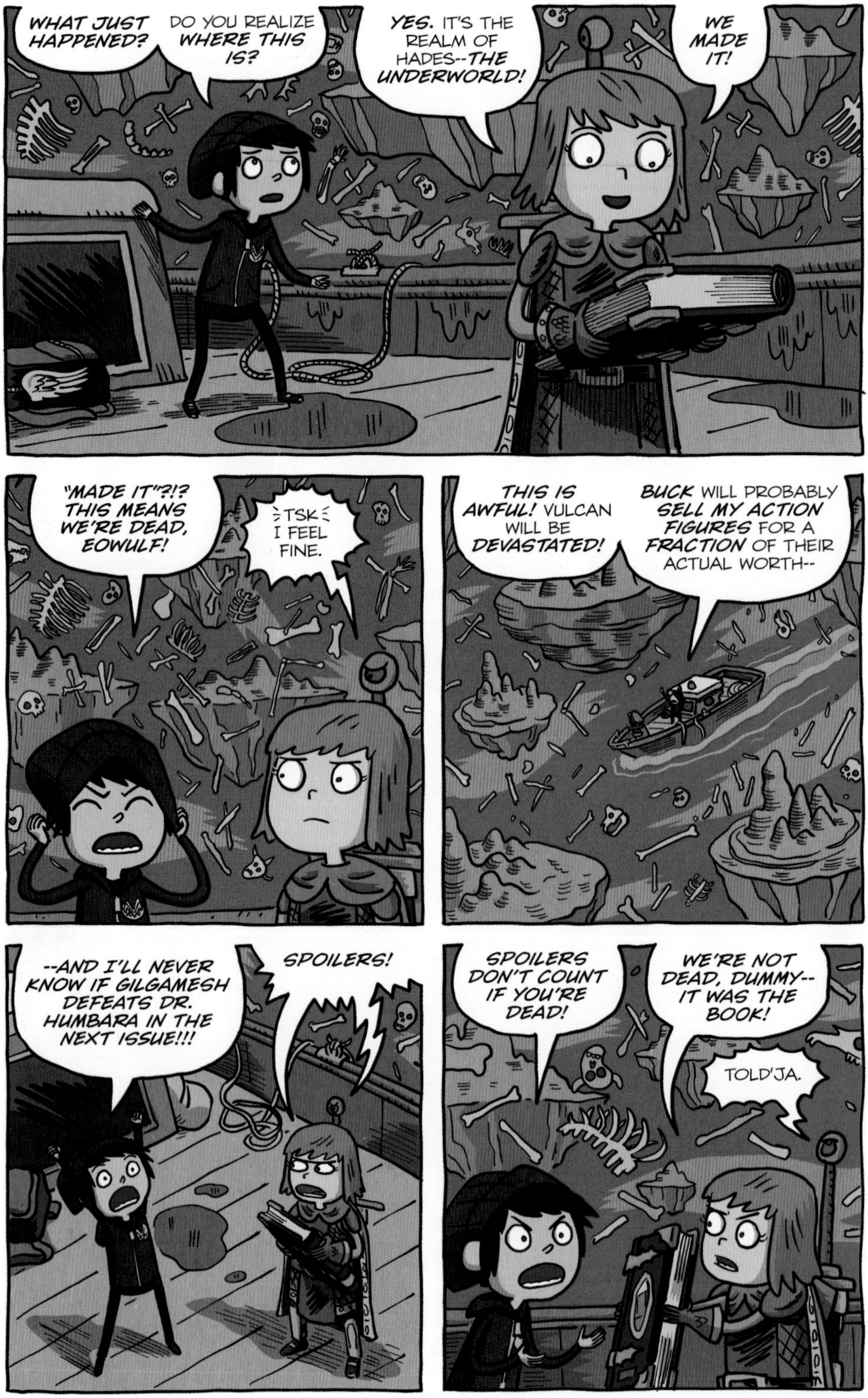
WHAT JUST HAPPENED?
DO YOU REALIZE WHERE THIS IS?
YES. IT'S THE REALM OF HADES--THE UNDERWORLD!
WE MADE IT!
"MADE IT"?!? THIS MEANS WE'RE DEAD, EOWULF!
TSK I FEEL FINE.
THIS IS AWFUL! VULCAN WILL BE DEVASTATED!
BUCK WILL PROBABLY SELL MY ACTION FIGURES FOR A FRACTION OF THEIR ACTUAL WORTH--
--AND I'LL NEVER KNOW IF GILGAMESH DEFEATS DR. HUMBARA IN THE NEXT ISSUE!!!
SPOILERS!
SPOILERS DON'T COUNT IF YOU'RE DEAD!
WE'RE NOT DEAD, DUMMY-- IT WAS THE BOOK!
TOLD'JA.

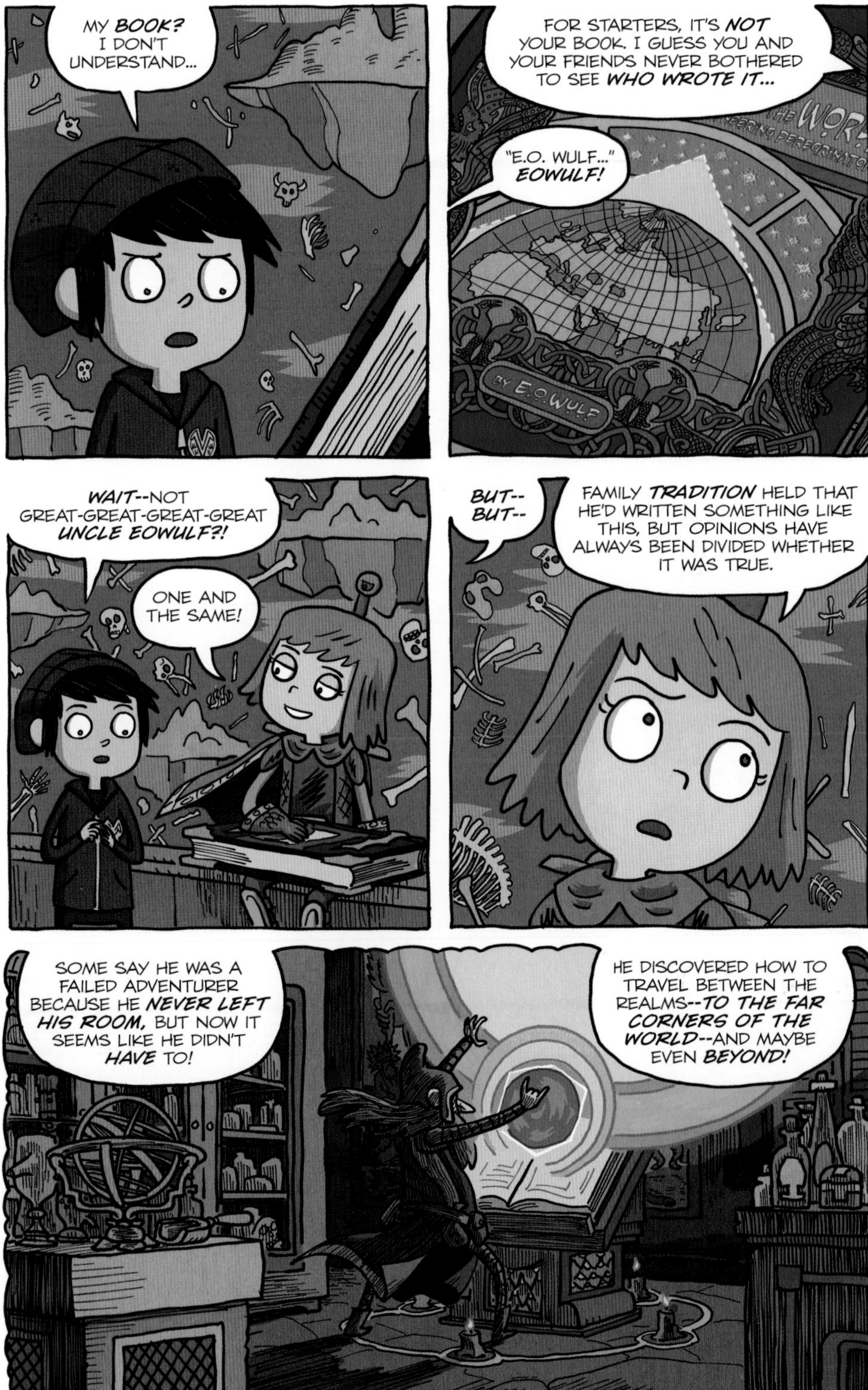
MY BOOK? I DON'T UNDERSTAND...
FOR STARTERS, IT'S NOT YOUR BOOK. I GUESS YOU AND YOUR FRIENDS NEVER BOTHERED TO SEE WHO WROTE IT...
"E.O. WULF..." EOWULF!
BY E.O.WULF
WAIT--NOT GREAT-GREAT-GREAT-GREAT UNCLE EOWULF?!
ONE AND THE SAME!
BUT-- BUT--
FAMILY TRADITION HELD THAT HE'D WRITTEN SOMETHING LIKE THIS, BUT OPINIONS HAVE ALWAYS BEEN DIVIDED WHETHER IT WAS TRUE.
SOME SAY HE WAS A FAILED ADVENTURER BECAUSE HE NEVER LEFT HIS ROOM, BUT NOW IT SEEMS LIKE HE DIDN'T HAVE TO!
HE DISCOVERED HOW TO TRAVEL BETWEEN THE REALMS--TO THE FAR CORNERS OF THE WORLD--AND MAYBE EVEN BEYOND!

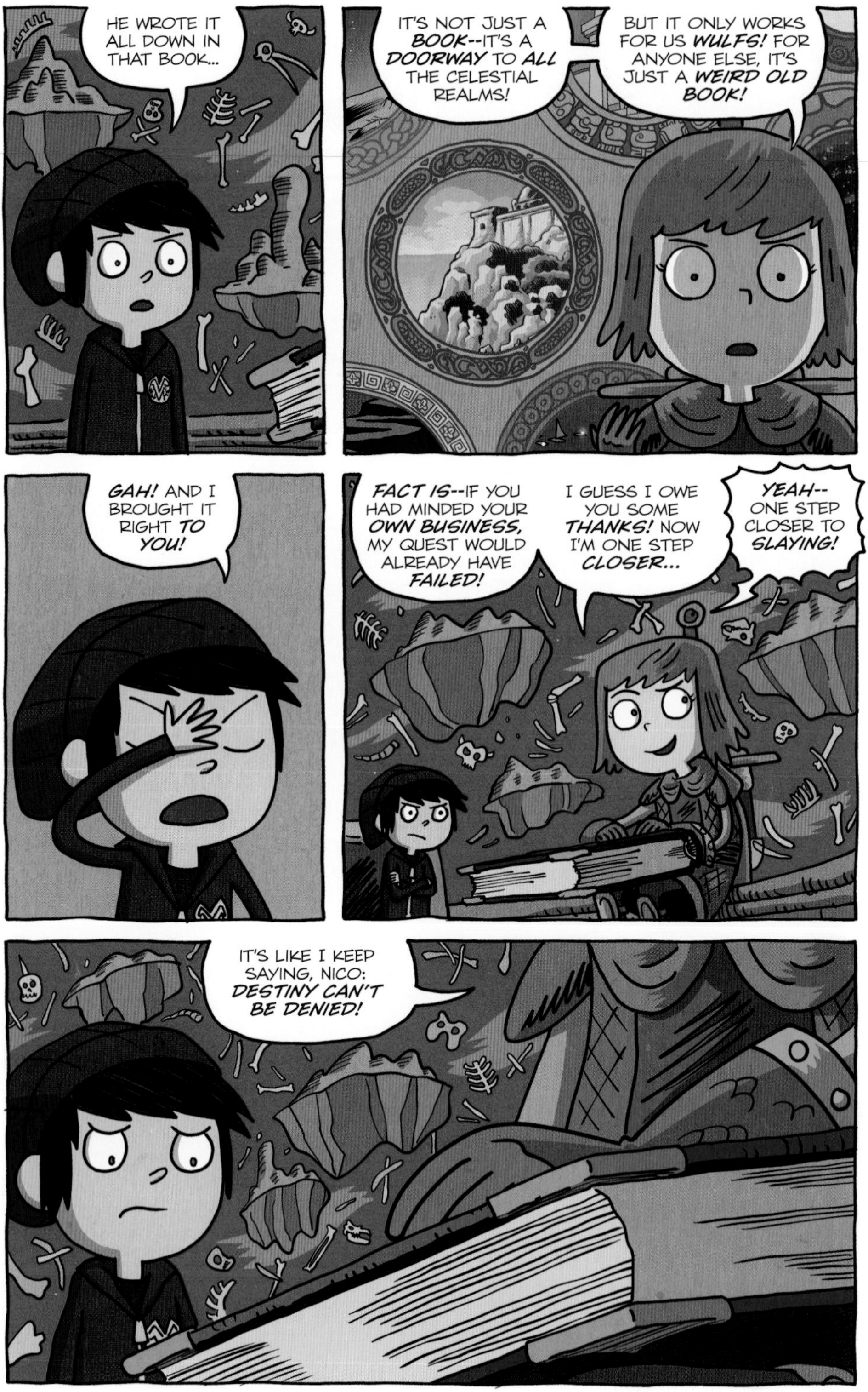
HE WROTE IT ALL DOWN IN THAT BOOK...
IT'S NOT JUST A BOOK--IT'S A DOORWAY TO ALL THE CELESTIAL REALMS!
BUT IT ONLY WORKS FOR US WULFS! FOR ANYONE ELSE, IT'S JUST A WEIRD OLD BOOK!
GAH! AND I BROUGHT IT RIGHT TO YOU!
FACT IS--IF YOU HAD MINDED YOUR OWN BUSINESS, MY QUEST WOULD ALREADY HAVE FAILED!
I GUESS I OWE YOU SOME THANKS! NOW I'M ONE STEP CLOSER...
YEAH--ONE STEP CLOSER TO SLAYING!
IT'S LIKE I KEEP SAYING, NICO: DESTINY CAN'T BE DENIED!

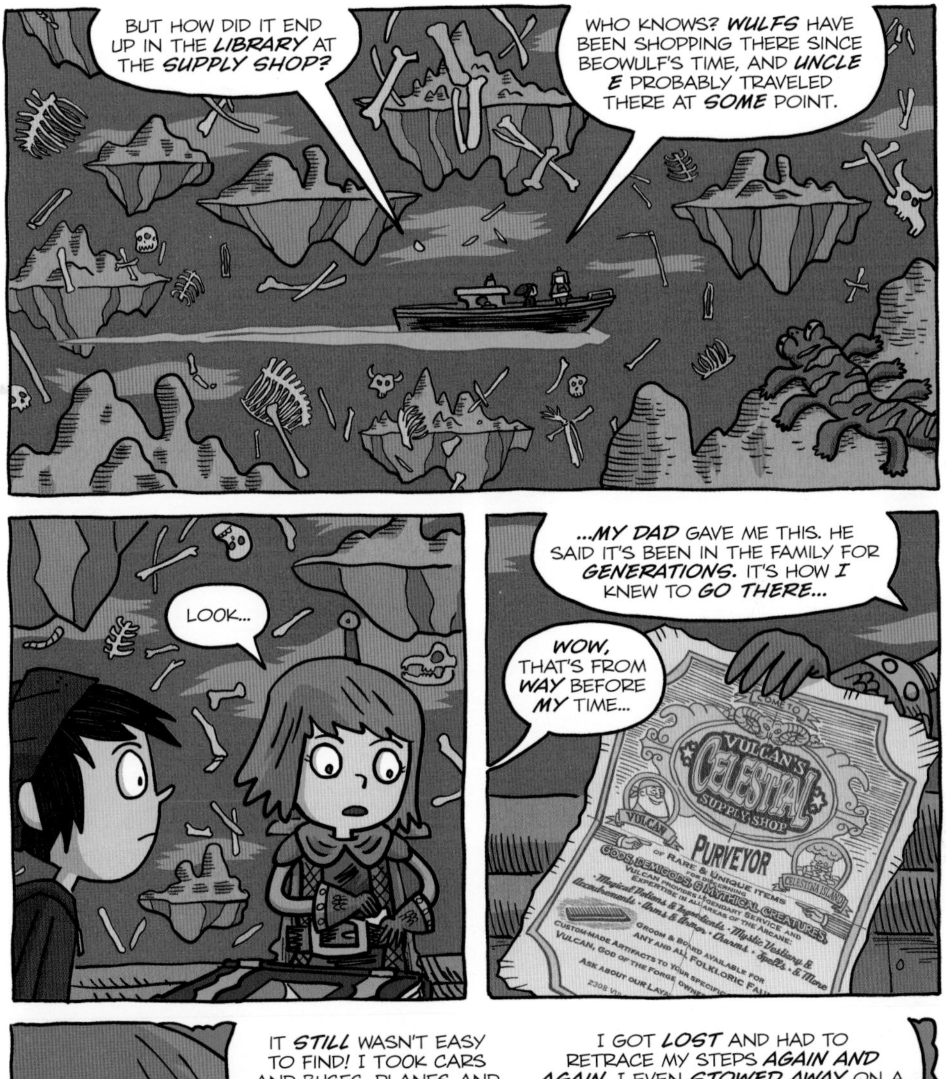
BUT HOW DID IT END UP IN THE LIBRARY AT THE SUPPLY SHOP?
WHO KNOWS? WULFS HAVE BEEN SHOPPING THERE SINCE BEOWULF'S TIME, AND UNCLE E PROBABLY TRAVELED THERE AT SOME POINT.
LOOK...
...MY DAD GAVE ME THIS. HE SAID IT'S BEEN IN THE FAMILY FOR GENERATIONS. IT'S HOW I KNEW TO GO THERE...
WOW, THAT'S FROM WAY BEFORE MY TIME...
COME TO
VULCAN'S CELESTIAL SUPPLY SHOP
PURVEYOR
OF RARE & UNIQUE ITEMS
GODS, DEMIGODS & MYTHICAL CREATURES
IT STILL WASN'T EASY TO FIND! I TOOK CARS AND BUSES, PLANES AND TRAINS, A FEW HORSES, AND A CAMEL.
I GOT LOST AND HAD TO RETRACE MY STEPS AGAIN AND AGAIN. I EVEN STOWED AWAY ON A TRAMP STEAMER, AND THEN ROWED TO THE ISLAND IN A BIG POT FROM THE GALLEY!
TAXI

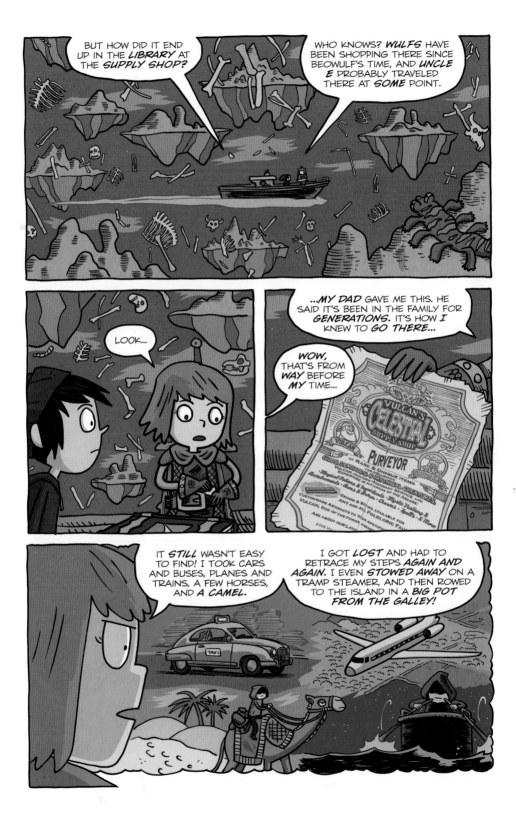

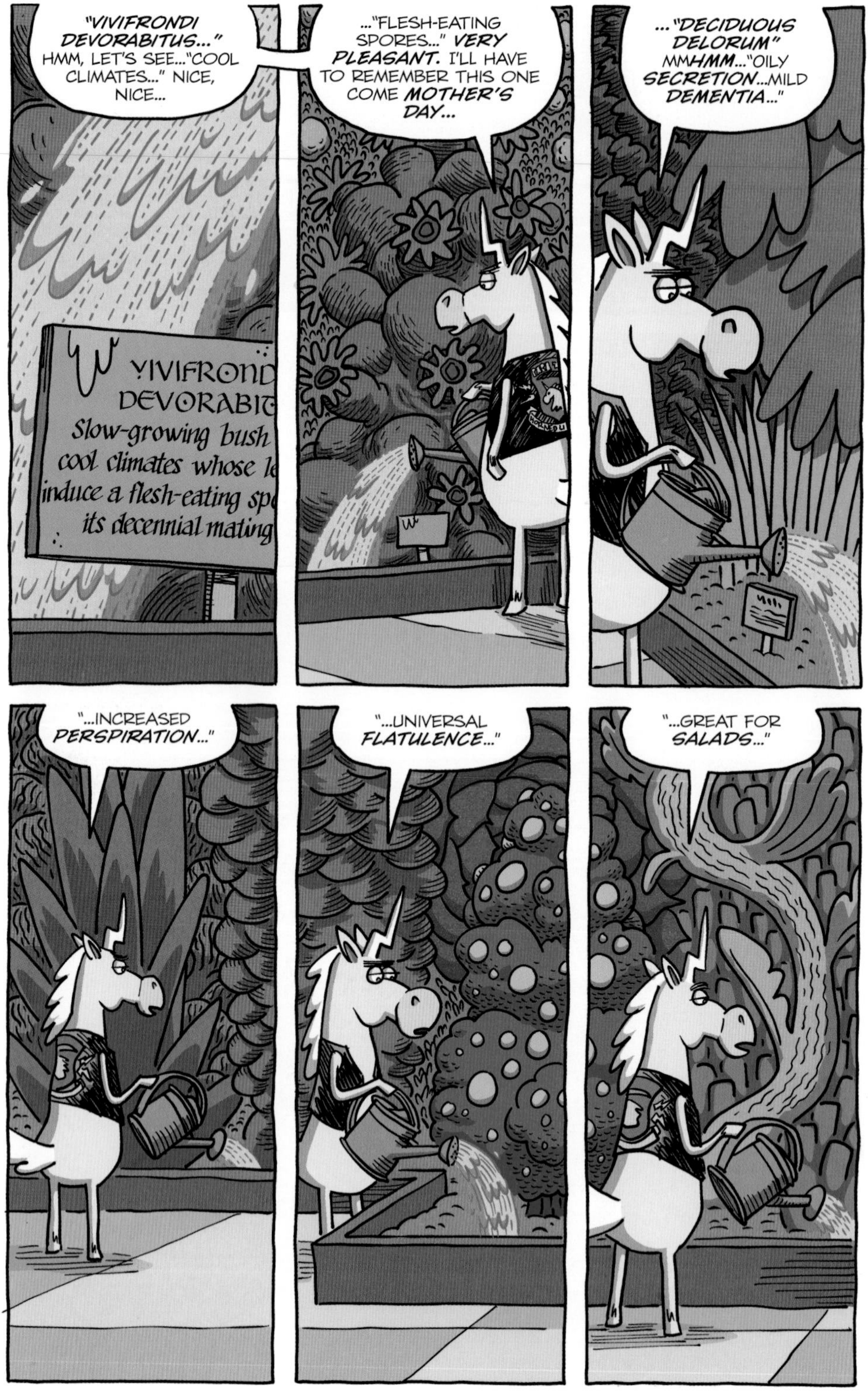
"VIVIFRONDI DEVORABITUS..." HMM, LET'S SEE..."COOL CLIMATES..." NICE, NICE...
...."FLESH-EATING SPORES..." VERY PLEASANT. I'LL HAVE TO REMEMBER THIS ONE COME MOTHER'S DAY...
..."DECIDUOUS DELORUM" MMHMM..."OILY SECRETION...MILD DEMENTIA..."
"...INCREASED PERSPIRATION..."
"...UNIVERSAL FLATULENCE..."
"...GREAT FOR SALADS..."

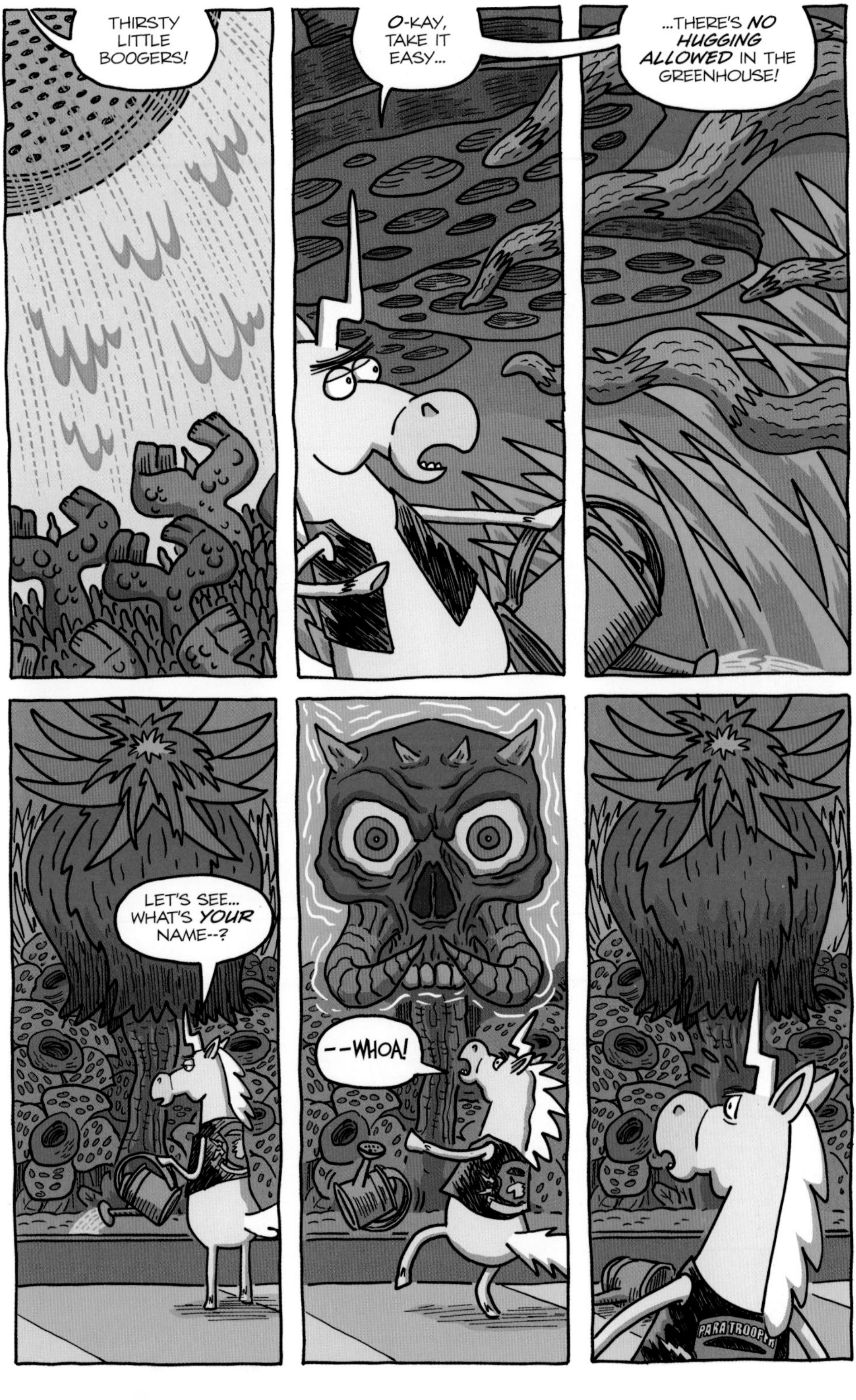
THIRSTY LITTLE BOOGERS!
O-KAY, TAKE IT EASY...
...THERE'S NO HUGGING ALLOWED IN THE GREENHOUSE!
LET'S SEE... WHAT'S YOUR NAME--?
--WHOA!
PARA TROOPER

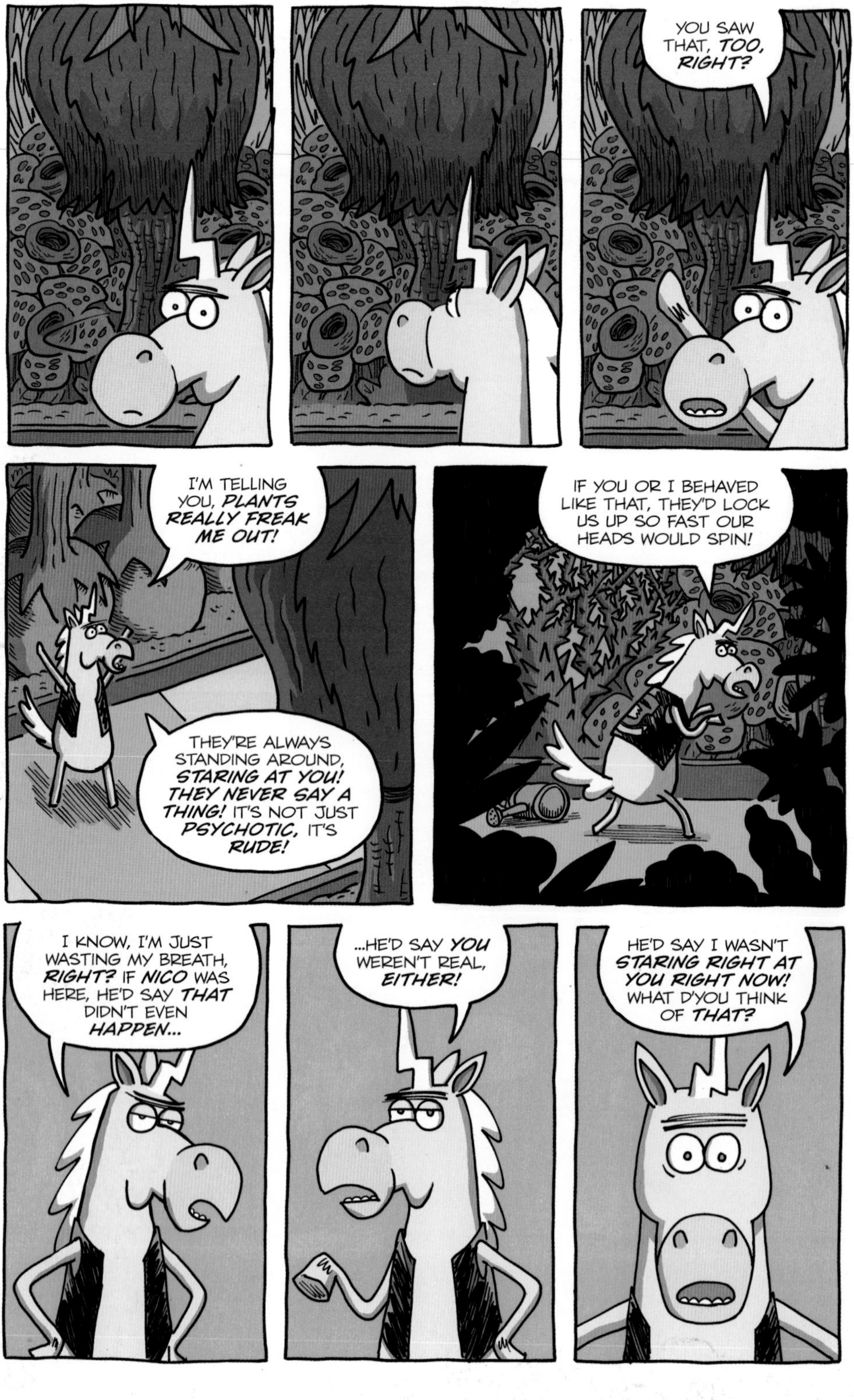
YOU SAW THAT, TOO, RIGHT?
I'M TELLING YOU, PLANTS REALLY FREAK ME OUT!
THEY'RE ALWAYS STANDING AROUND, STARING AT YOU! THEY NEVER SAY A THING! IT'S NOT JUST PSYCHOTIC, IT'S RUDE!
IF YOU OR I BEHAVED LIKE THAT, THEY'D LOCK US UP SO FAST OUR HEADS WOULD SPIN!
I KNOW, I'M JUST WASTING MY BREATH, RIGHT? IF NICO WAS HERE, HE'D SAY THAT DIDN'T EVEN HAPPEN...
...HE'D SAY YOU WEREN'T REAL, EITHER!
HE'D SAY I WASN'T STARING RIGHT AT YOU RIGHT NOW! WHAT D'YOU THINK OF THAT?

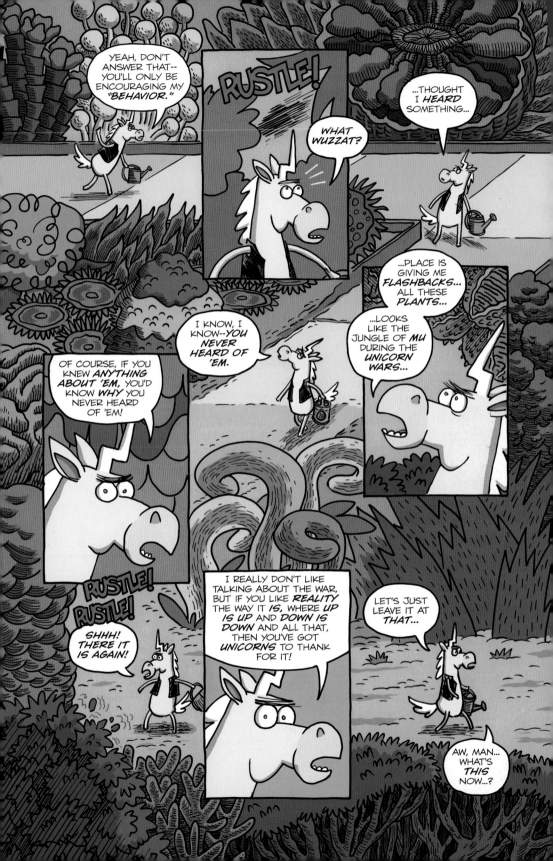

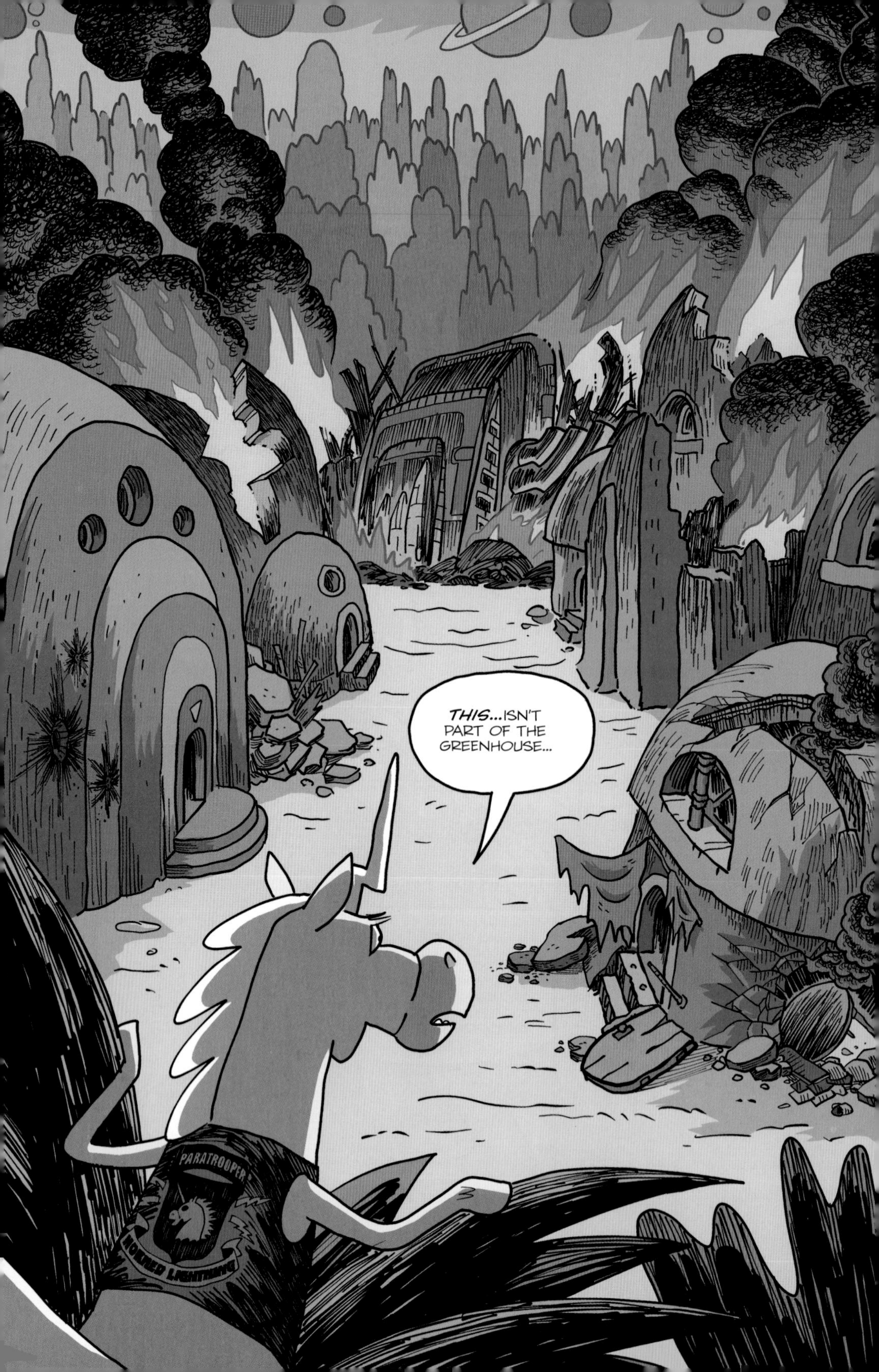
THIS...ISN'T PART OF THE GREENHOUSE...
PARATROOPER
HORNED LIGHTNING

PART 2:
KNIT
TOGETHER.

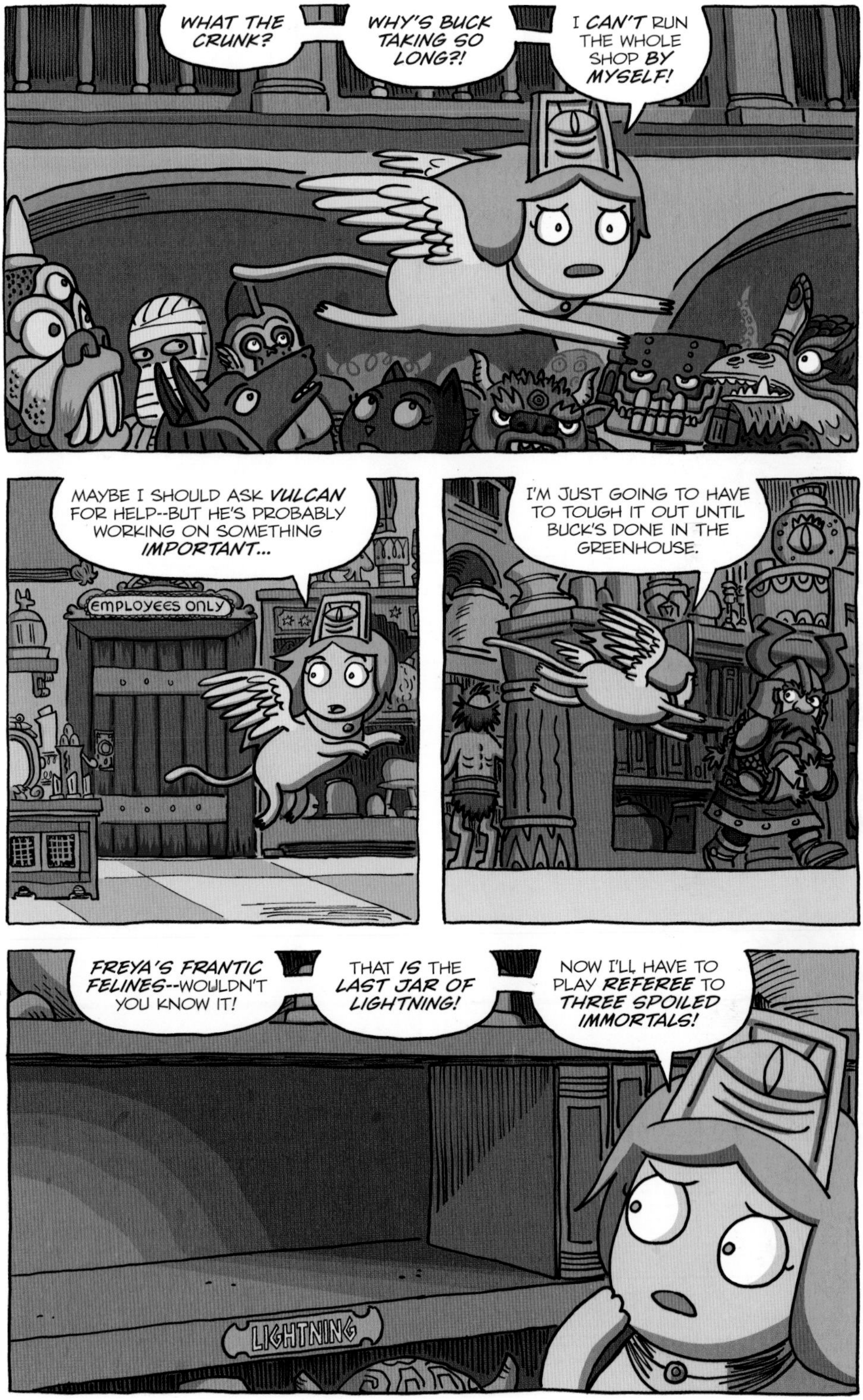
WHAT THE CRUNK?
WHY'S BUCK TAKING SO LONG?!
I CAN'T RUN THE WHOLE SHOP BY MYSELF!
MAYBE I SHOULD ASK VULCAN FOR HELP--BUT HE'S PROBABLY WORKING ON SOMETHING IMPORTANT...
EMPLOYEES ONLY
I'M JUST GOING TO HAVE TO TOUGH IT OUT UNTIL BUCK'S DONE IN THE GREENHOUSE.
FREYA'S FRANTIC FELINES--WOULDN'T YOU KNOW IT!
THAT IS THE LAST JAR OF LIGHTNING!
NOW I'LL HAVE TO PLAY REFEREE TO THREE SPOILED IMMORTALS!
LIGHTNING

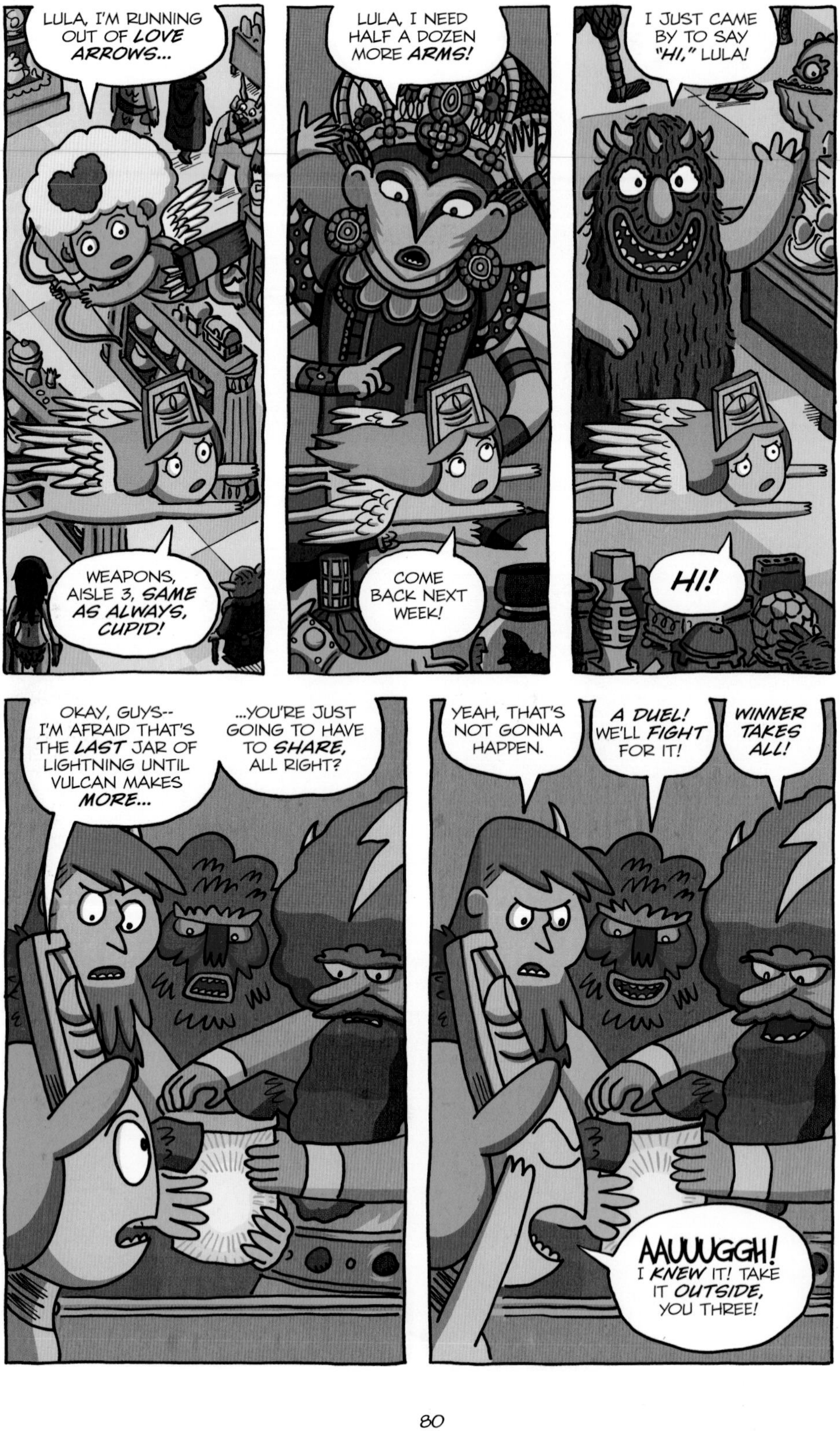
LULA, I'M RUNNING OUT OF LOVE ARROWS...
WEAPONS, AISLE 3, SAME AS ALWAYS, CUPID!
LULA, I NEED HALF A DOZEN MORE ARMS!
COME BACK NEXT WEEK!
I JUST CAME BY TO SAY "HI," LULA!
HI!
OKAY, GUYS-- I'M AFRAID THAT'S THE LAST JAR OF LIGHTNING UNTIL VULCAN MAKES MORE...
...YOU'RE JUST GOING TO HAVE TO SHARE, ALL RIGHT?
YEAH, THAT'S NOT GONNA HAPPEN.
A DUEL! WE'LL FIGHT FOR IT!
WINNER TAKES ALL!
AAUUUGGH! I KNEW IT! TAKE IT OUTSIDE, YOU THREE!

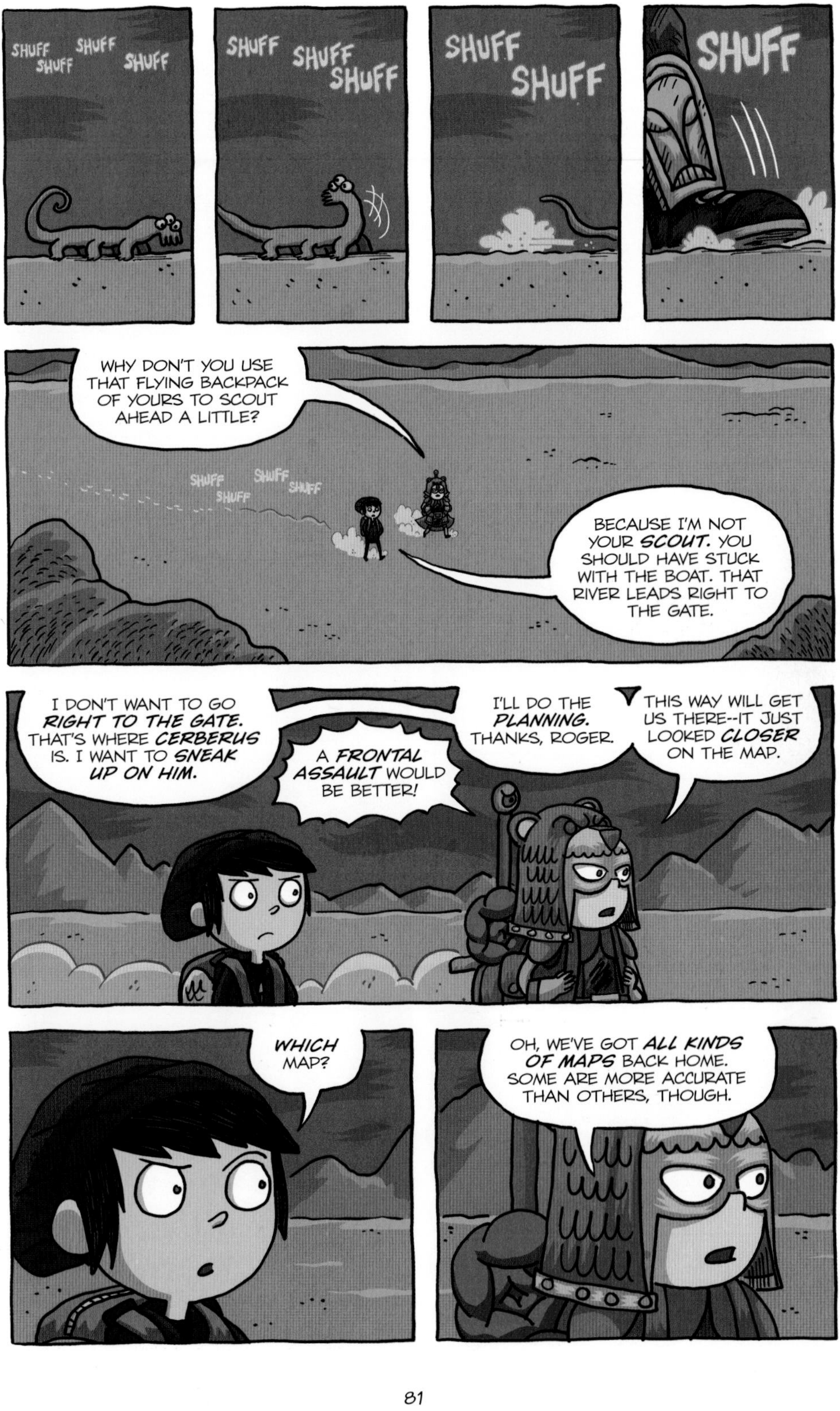
SHUFF SHUFF SHUFF SHUFF
SHUFF SHUFF SHUFF
SHUFF SHUFF
SHUFF
WHY DON'T YOU USE THAT FLYING BACKPACK OF YOURS TO SCOUT AHEAD A LITTLE?
SHUFF SHUFF SHUFF SHUFF
BECAUSE I'M NOT YOUR SCOUT. YOU SHOULD HAVE STUCK WITH THE BOAT. THAT RIVER LEADS RIGHT TO THE GATE.
I DON'T WANT TO GO RIGHT TO THE GATE. THAT'S WHERE CERBERUS IS. I WANT TO SNEAK UP ON HIM.
A FRONTAL ASSAULT WOULD BE BETTER!
I'LL DO THE PLANNING. THANKS, ROGER.
THIS WAY WILL GET US THERE--IT JUST LOOKED CLOSER ON THE MAP.
WHICH MAP?
OH, WE'VE GOT ALL KINDS OF MAPS BACK HOME. SOME ARE MORE ACCURATE THAN OTHERS, THOUGH.

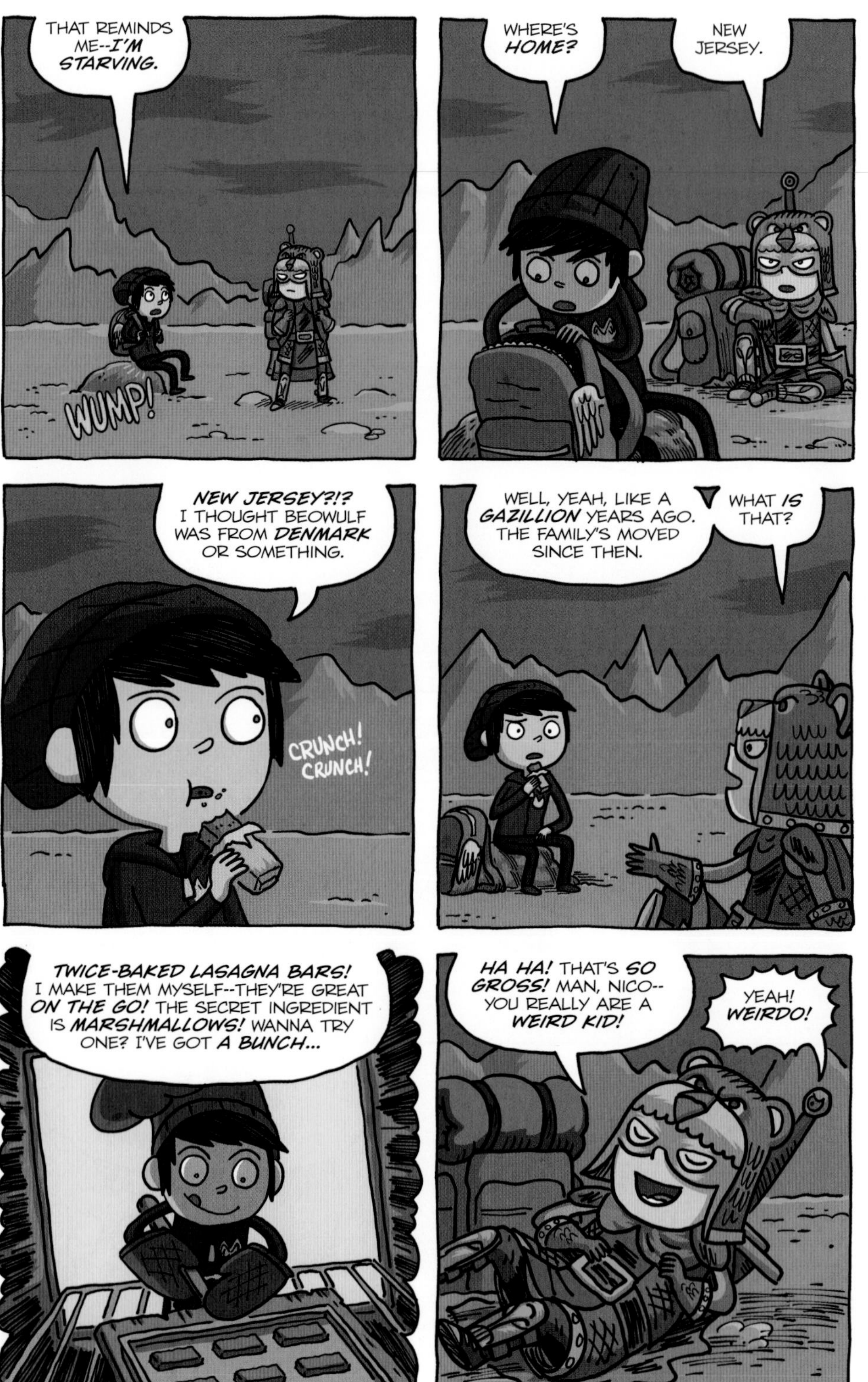
THAT REMINDS ME--I'M STARVING.
WUMP!
WHERE'S HOME?
NEW JERSEY.
NEW JERSEY?!? I THOUGHT BEOWULF WAS FROM DENMARK OR SOMETHING.
CRUNCH! CRUNCH!
WELL, YEAH, LIKE A GAZILLION YEARS AGO. THE FAMILY'S MOVED SINCE THEN.
WHAT IS THAT?
TWICE-BAKED LASAGNA BARS! I MAKE THEM MYSELF--THEY'RE GREAT ON THE GO! THE SECRET INGREDIENT IS MARSHMALLOWS! WANNA TRY ONE? I'VE GOT A BUNCH...
HA HA! THAT'S SO GROSS! MAN, NICO-- YOU REALLY ARE A WEIRD KID!
YEAH! WEIRDO!

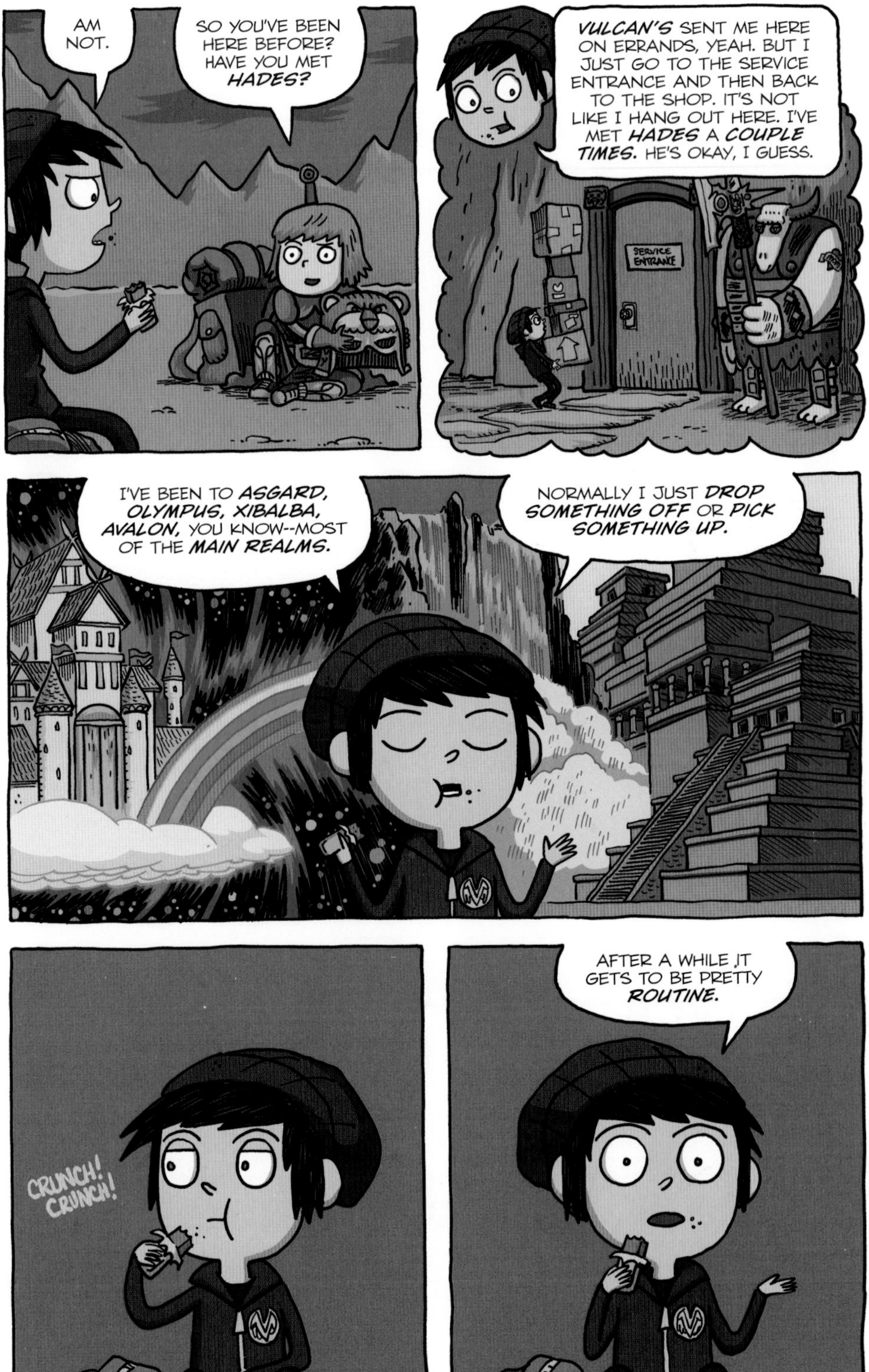
AM NOT.
SO YOU'VE BEEN HERE BEFORE? HAVE YOU MET HADES?
VULCAN'S SENT ME HERE ON ERRANDS, YEAH. BUT I JUST GO TO THE SERVICE ENTRANCE AND THEN BACK TO THE SHOP. IT'S NOT LIKE I HANG OUT HERE. I'VE MET HADES A COUPLE TIMES. HE'S OKAY, I GUESS.
SERVICE ENTRANCE
I'VE BEEN TO ASGARD, OLYMPUS, XIBALBA, AVALON, YOU KNOW--MOST OF THE MAIN REALMS.
NORMALLY I JUST DROP SOMETHING OFF OR PICK SOMETHING UP.
CRUNCH! CRUNCH!
AFTER A WHILE IT GETS TO BE PRETTY ROUTINE.

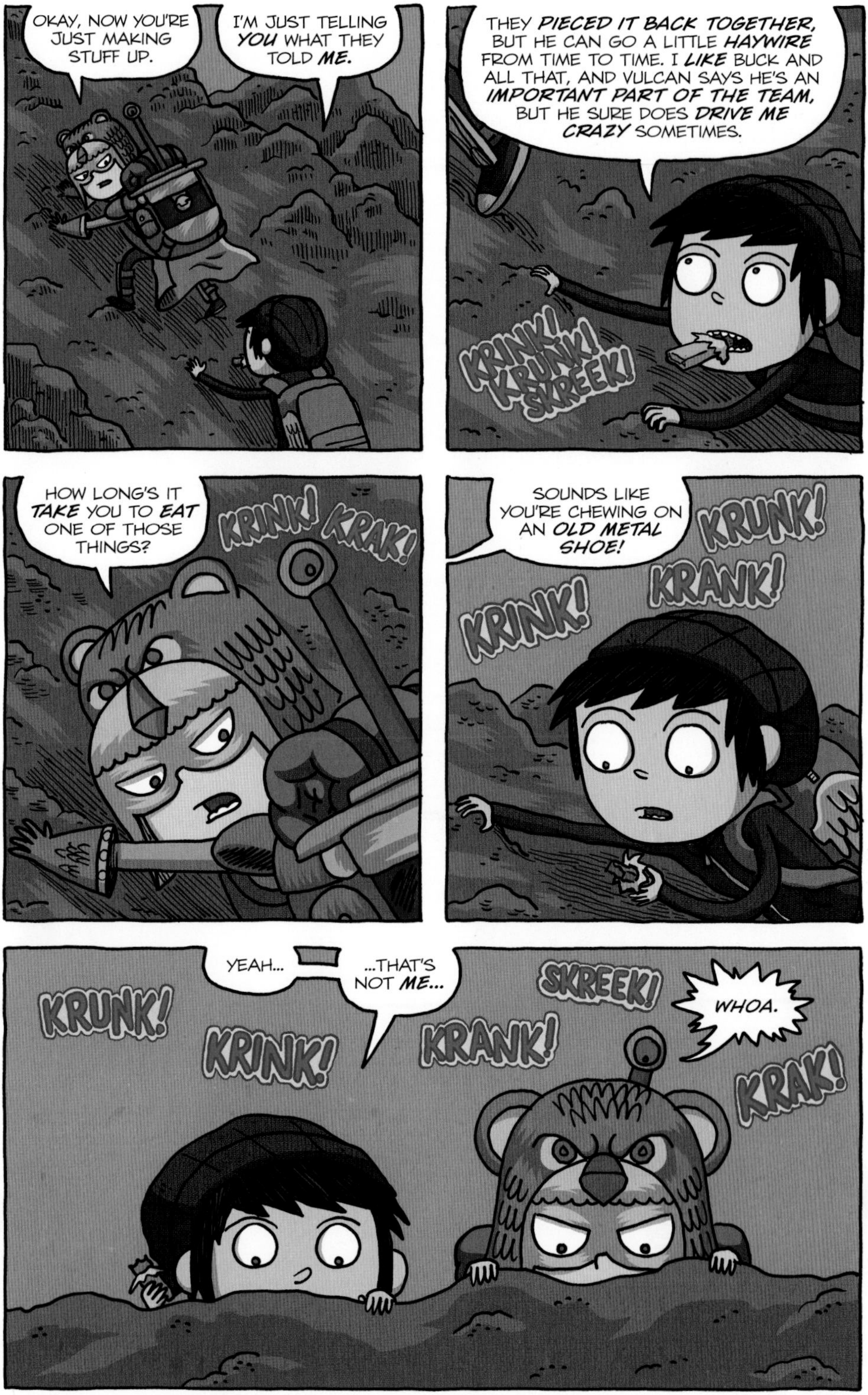
OKAY, NOW YOU'RE JUST MAKING STUFF UP.
I'M JUST TELLING *YOU* WHAT THEY TOLD *ME.*
THEY *PIECED IT BACK TOGETHER,* BUT HE CAN GO A LITTLE *HAYWIRE* FROM TIME TO TIME. I *LIKE* BUCK AND ALL THAT, AND VULCAN SAYS HE'S AN *IMPORTANT PART OF THE TEAM,* BUT HE SURE DOES *DRIVE ME CRAZY* SOMETIMES.
KRINK! KRUNK! SKREEK!
HOW LONG'S IT *TAKE* YOU TO *EAT* ONE OF THOSE THINGS?
KRINK! KRAK!
SOUNDS LIKE YOU'RE CHEWING ON AN *OLD METAL SHOE!*
KRUNK! KRANK! KRINK!
YEAH...
...THAT'S NOT *ME...*
KRUNK! KRINK! KRANK! SKREEK!
WHOA.
KRAK!

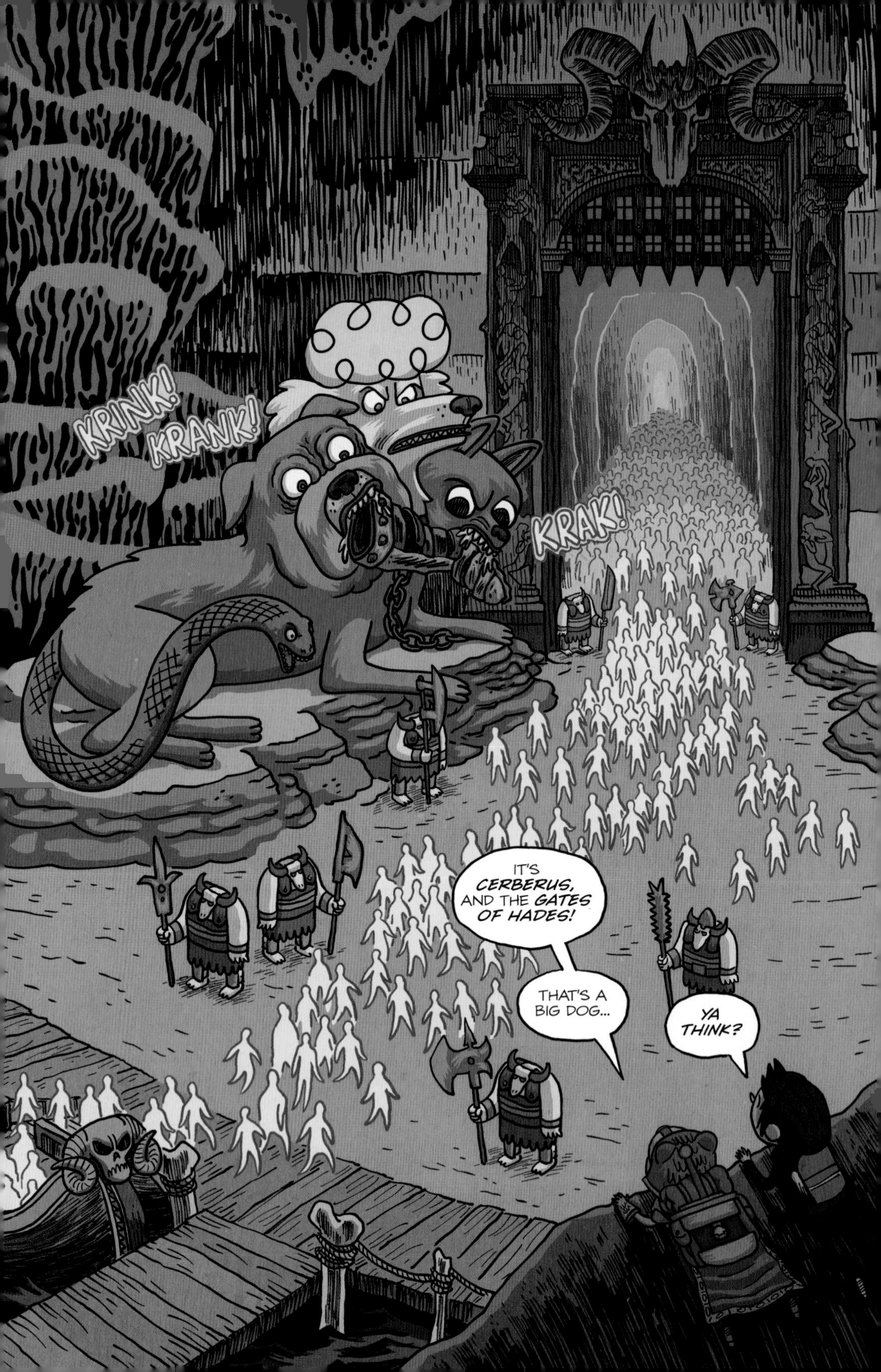
KRINK! KRANK!
KRAK!
IT'S CERBERUS, AND THE GATES OF HADES!
THAT'S A BIG DOG...
YA THINK?

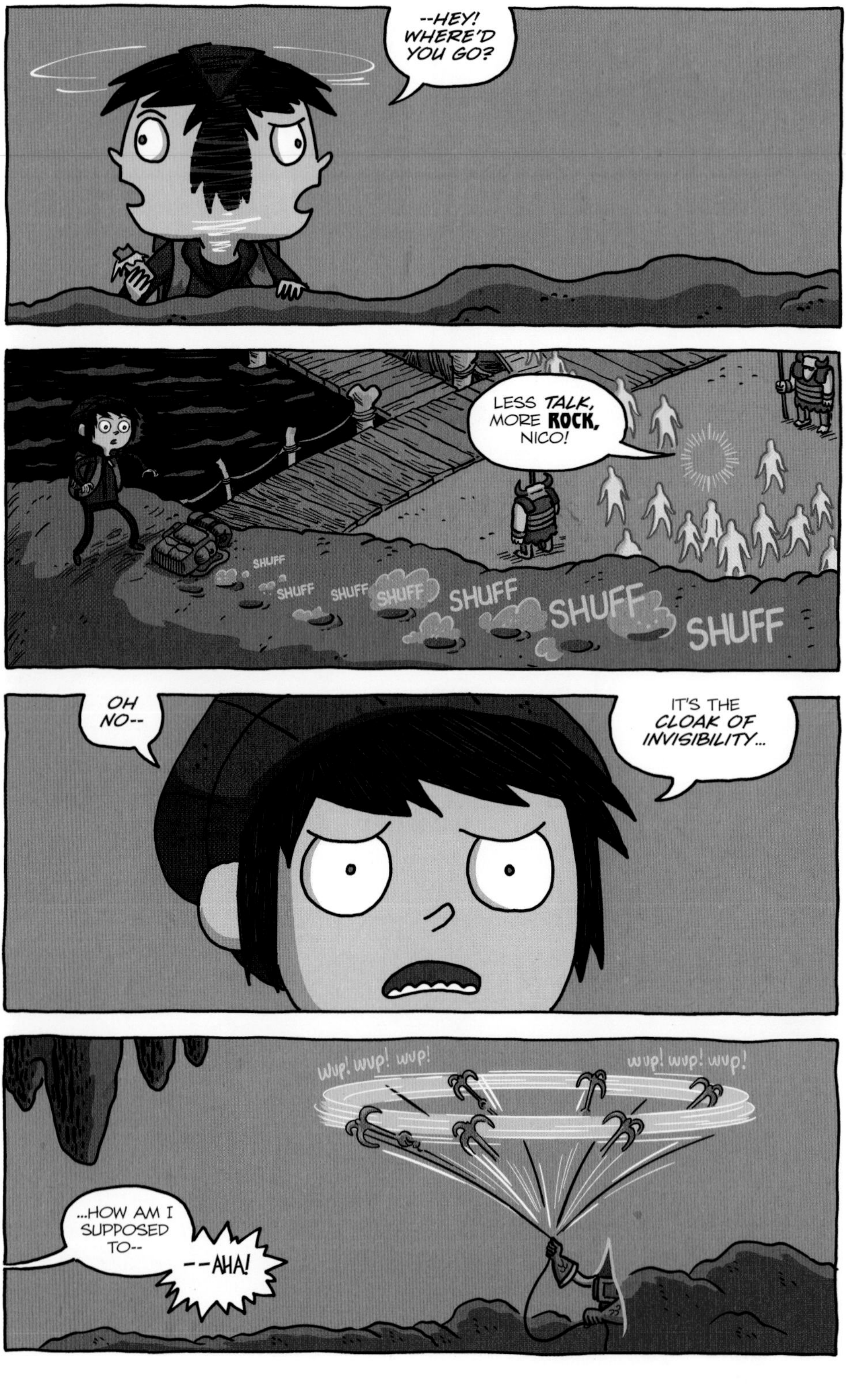

--HEY! WHERE'D YOU GO?
LESS TALK, MORE ROCK, NICO!
SHUFF SHUFF SHUFF SHUFF SHUFF SHUFF SHUFF
OH NO--
IT'S THE CLOAK OF INVISIBILITY...
wup! wup! wup!
wup! wup! wup!
...HOW AM I SUPPOSED TO--
--AHA!

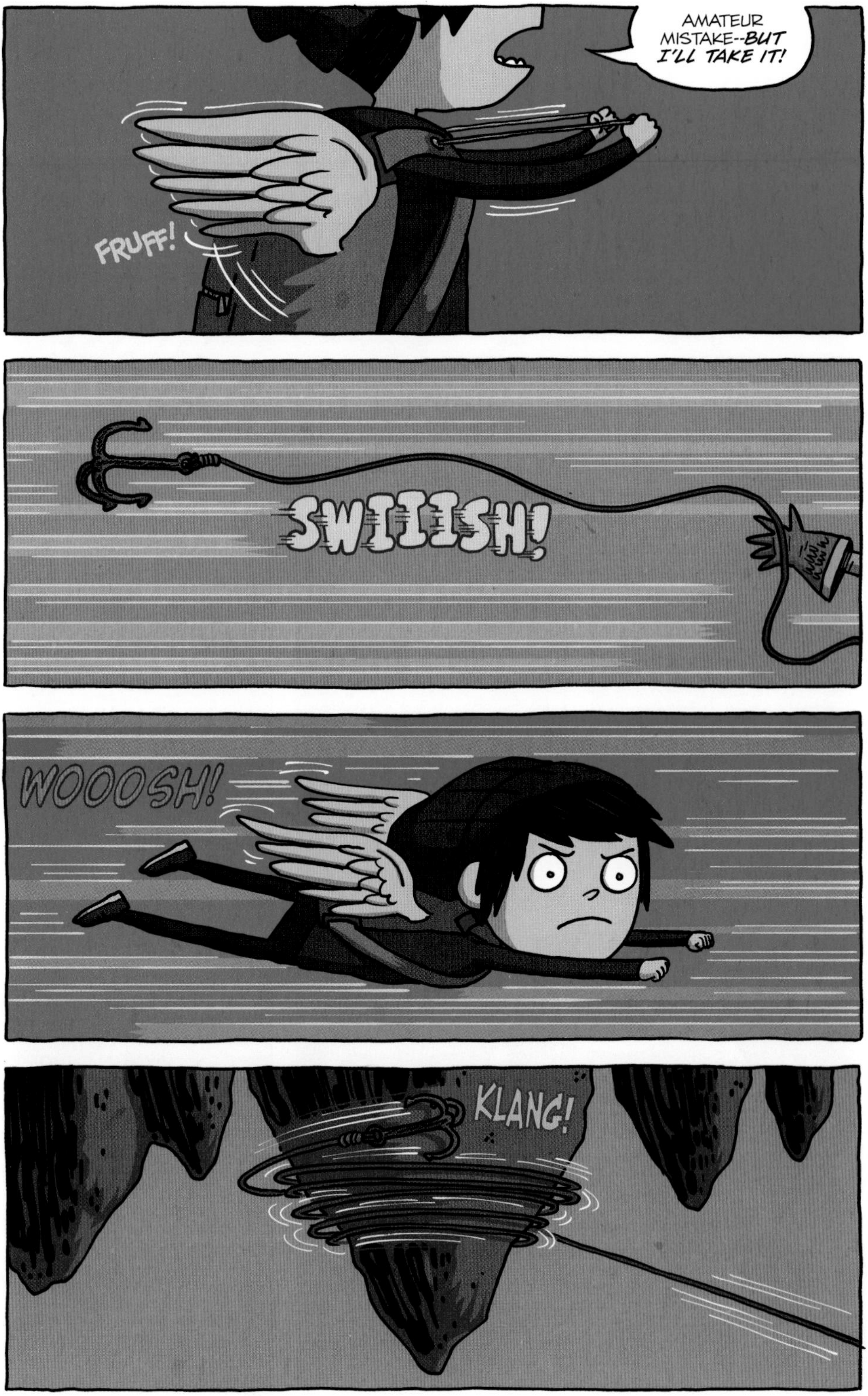
AMATEUR MISTAKE--BUT I'LL TAKE IT!
FRUFF!
SWIIISH!
WOOOSH!
KLANG!

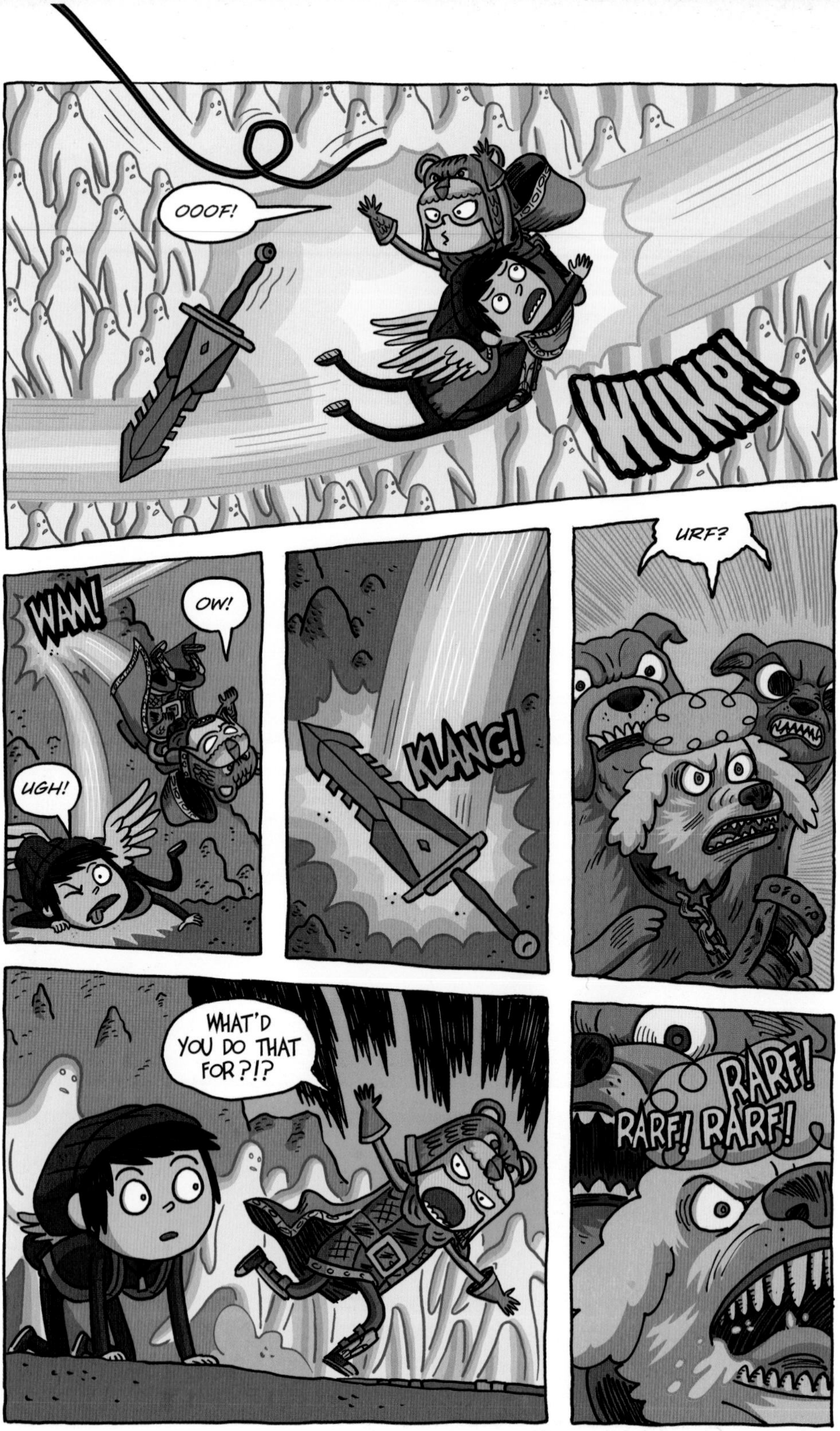
OOOF!
WUMP!
WAM!
OW!
UGH!
KLANG!
URF?
WHAT'D YOU DO THAT FOR?!?
RARF! RARF! RARF!

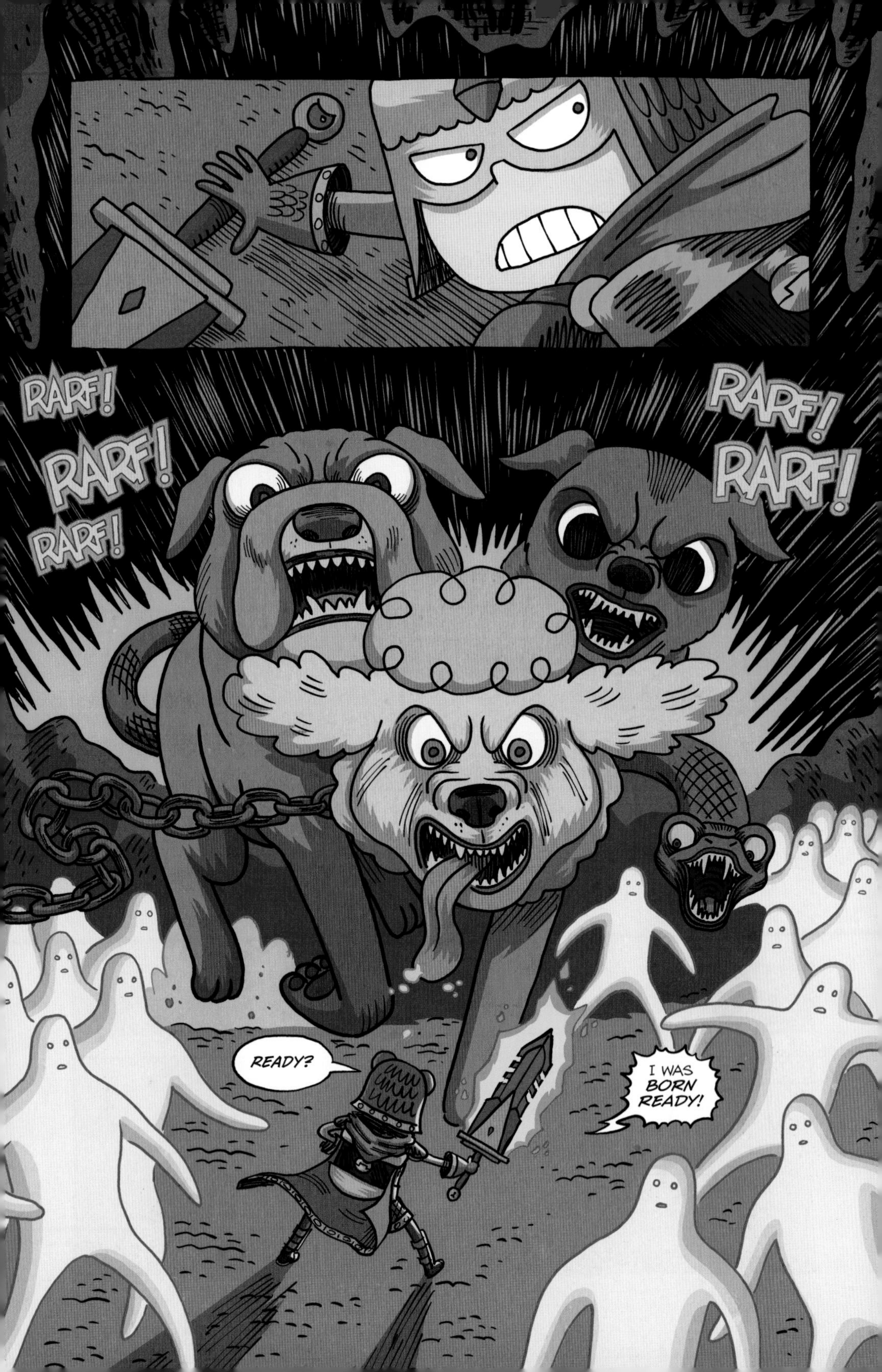
RARF!
RARF!
RARF!
RARF!
RARF!
READY?
I WAS BORN READY!

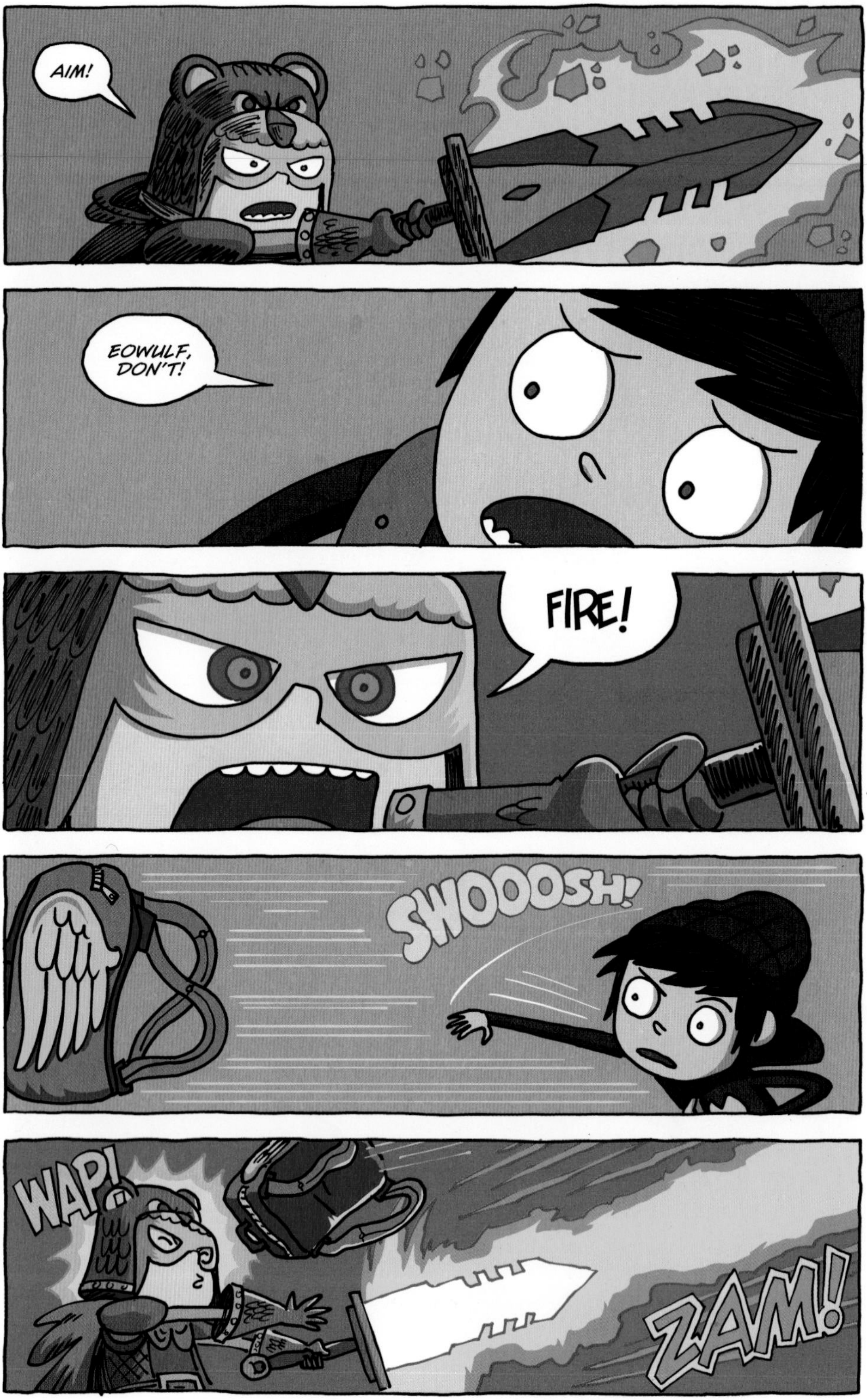
AIM!
EOWULF, DON'T!
FIRE!
SHOOOSH!
WAP!
ZAM!

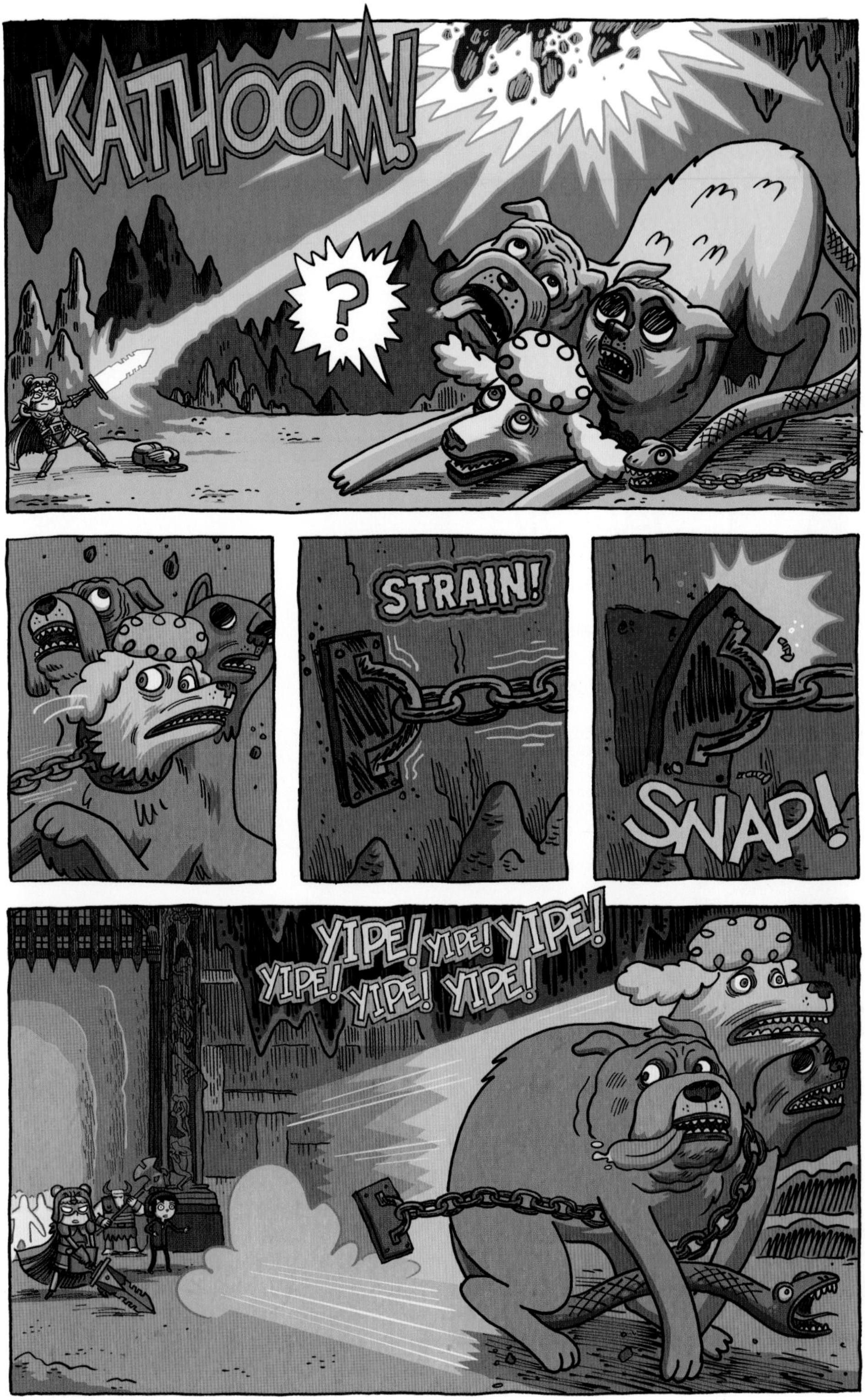
KATHOOM!
?
STRAIN!
SNAP!
YIPE! YIPE! YIPE!
YIPE! YIPE! YIPE!

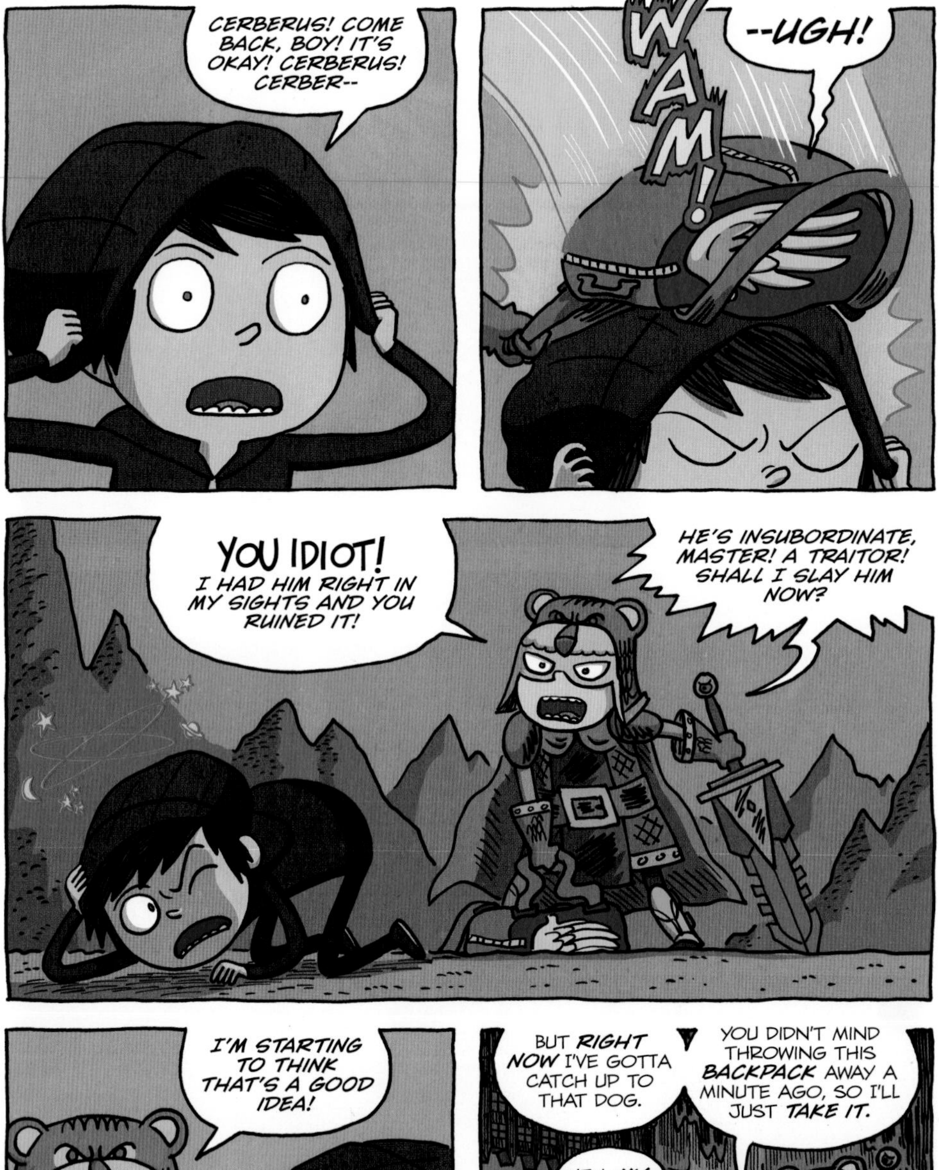
CERBERUS! COME BACK, BOY! IT'S OKAY! CERBERUS! CERBER--
WAM!
--UGH!
YOU IDIOT! I HAD HIM RIGHT IN MY SIGHTS AND YOU RUINED IT!
HE'S INSUBORDINATE, MASTER! A TRAITOR! SHALL I SLAY HIM NOW?
I'M STARTING TO THINK THAT'S A GOOD IDEA!
BUT RIGHT NOW I'VE GOTTA CATCH UP TO THAT DOG.
YOU DIDN'T MIND THROWING THIS BACKPACK AWAY A MINUTE AGO, SO I'LL JUST TAKE IT.
HEY, MY STUFF!

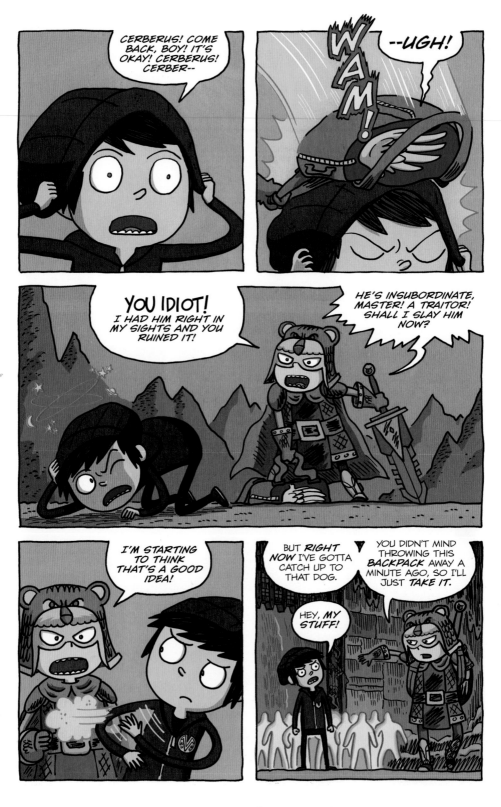

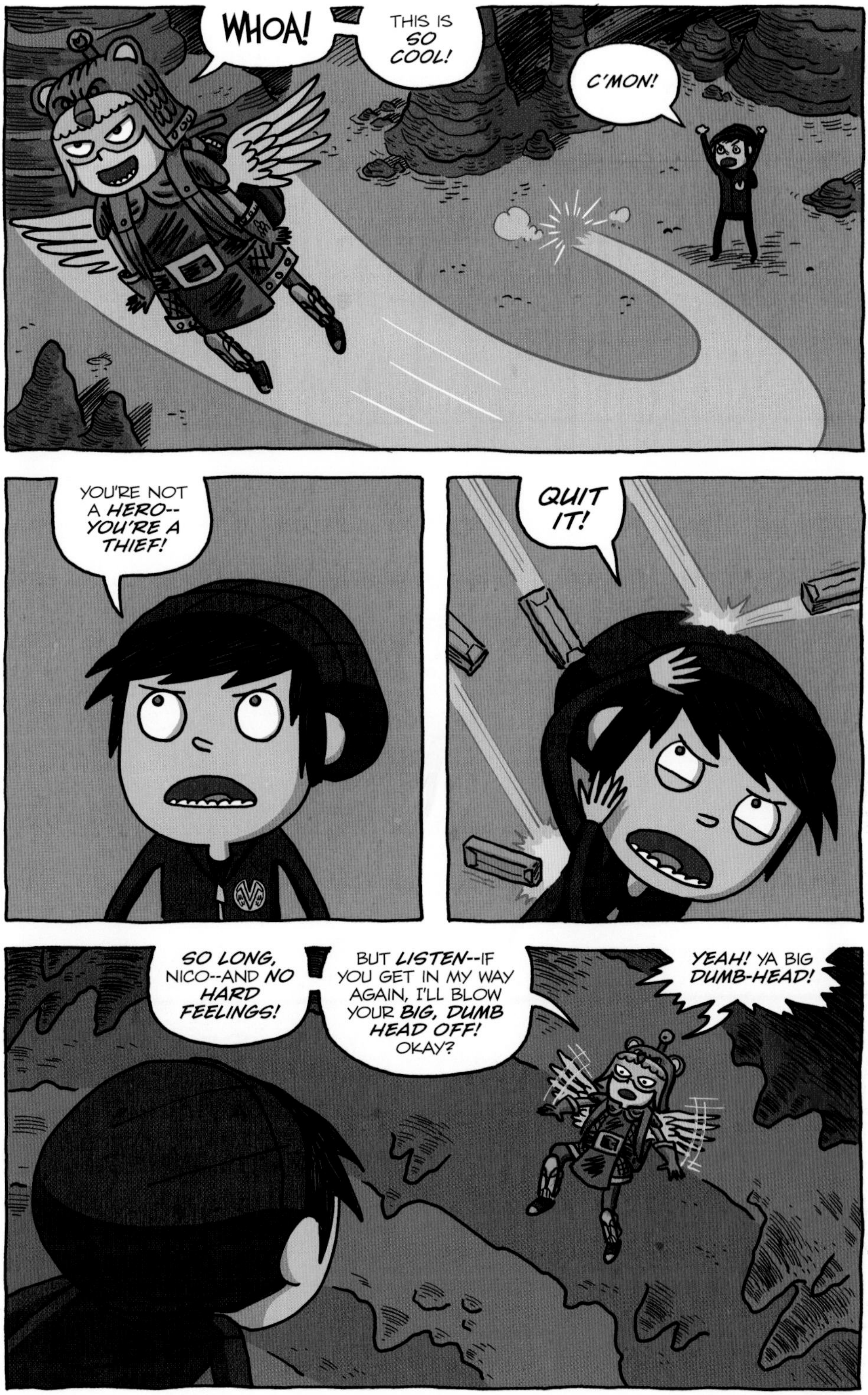
WHOA!
THIS IS SO COOL!
C'MON!
YOU'RE NOT A HERO-- YOU'RE A THIEF!
QUIT IT!
SO LONG, NICO--AND NO HARD FEELINGS!
BUT LISTEN--IF YOU GET IN MY WAY AGAIN, I'LL BLOW YOUR BIG, DUMB HEAD OFF! OKAY?
YEAH! YA BIG DUMB-HEAD!

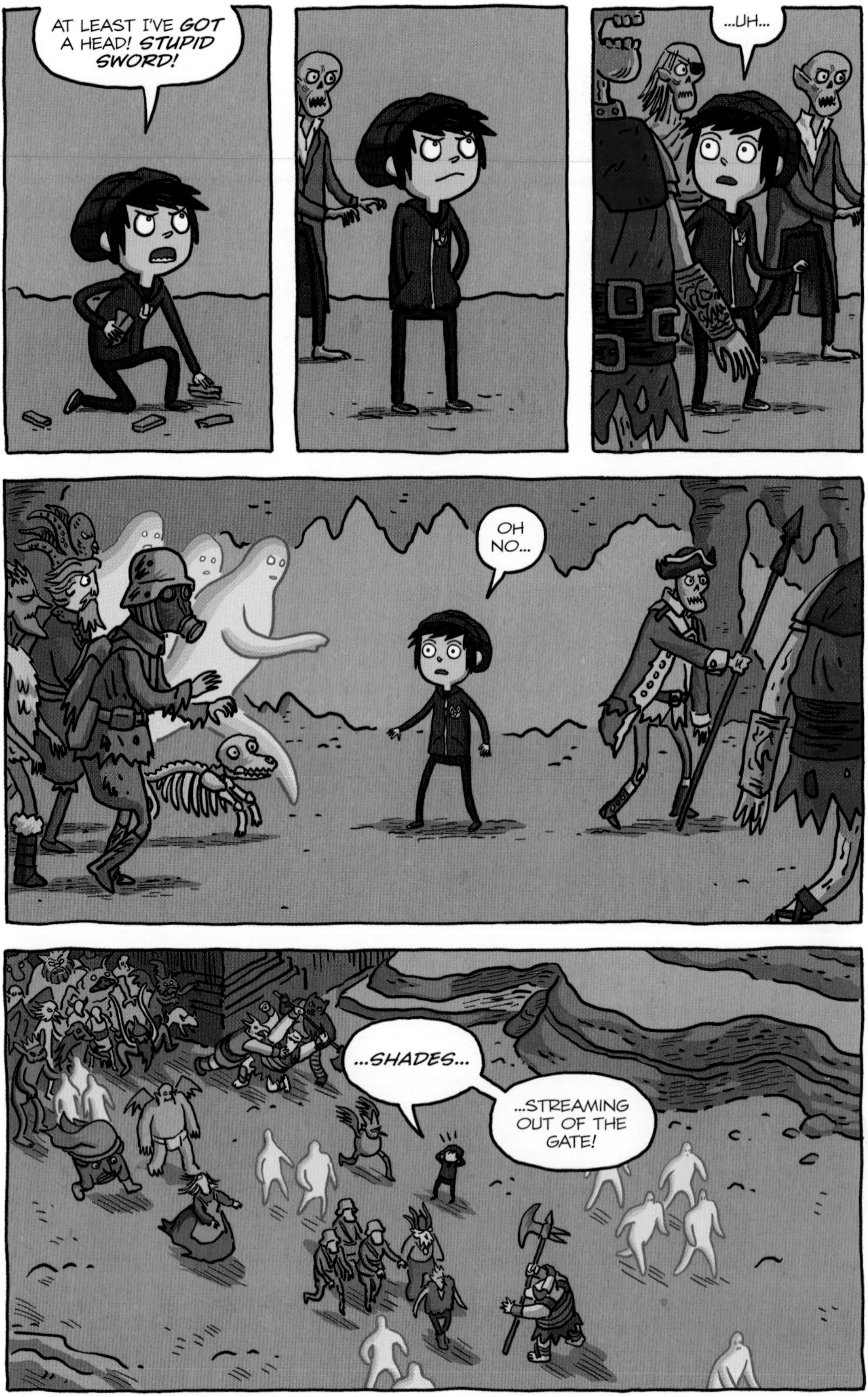
AT LEAST I'VE GOT A HEAD! STUPID SWORD!
...UH...
OH NO...
...SHADES...
...STREAMING OUT OF THE GATE!

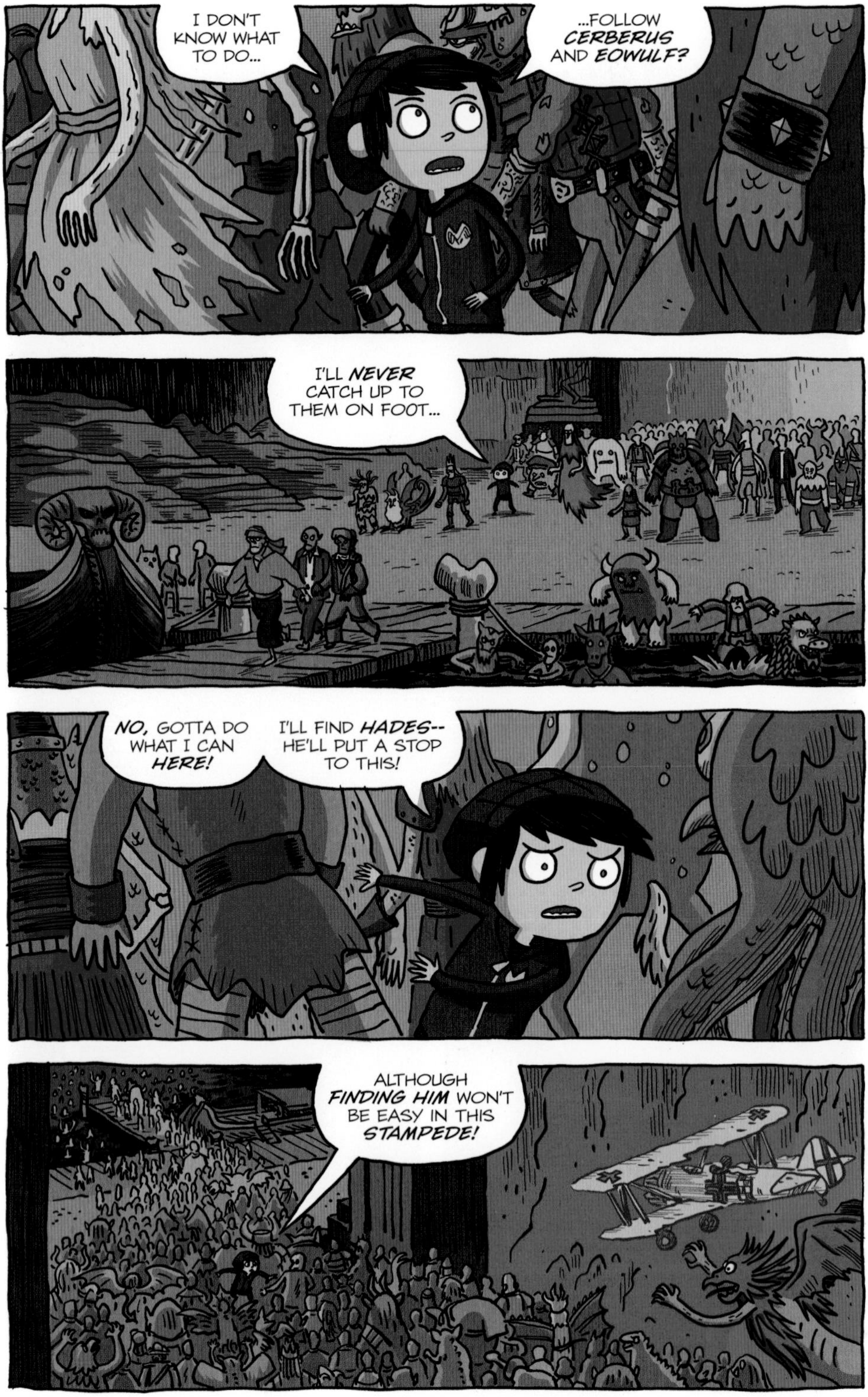
I DON'T KNOW WHAT TO DO...
...FOLLOW *CERBERUS* AND *EOWULF?*
I'LL *NEVER* CATCH UP TO THEM ON FOOT...
NO, GOTTA DO WHAT I CAN *HERE!*
I'LL FIND *HADES--* HE'LL PUT A STOP TO THIS!
ALTHOUGH *FINDING HIM* WON'T BE EASY IN THIS *STAMPEDE!*

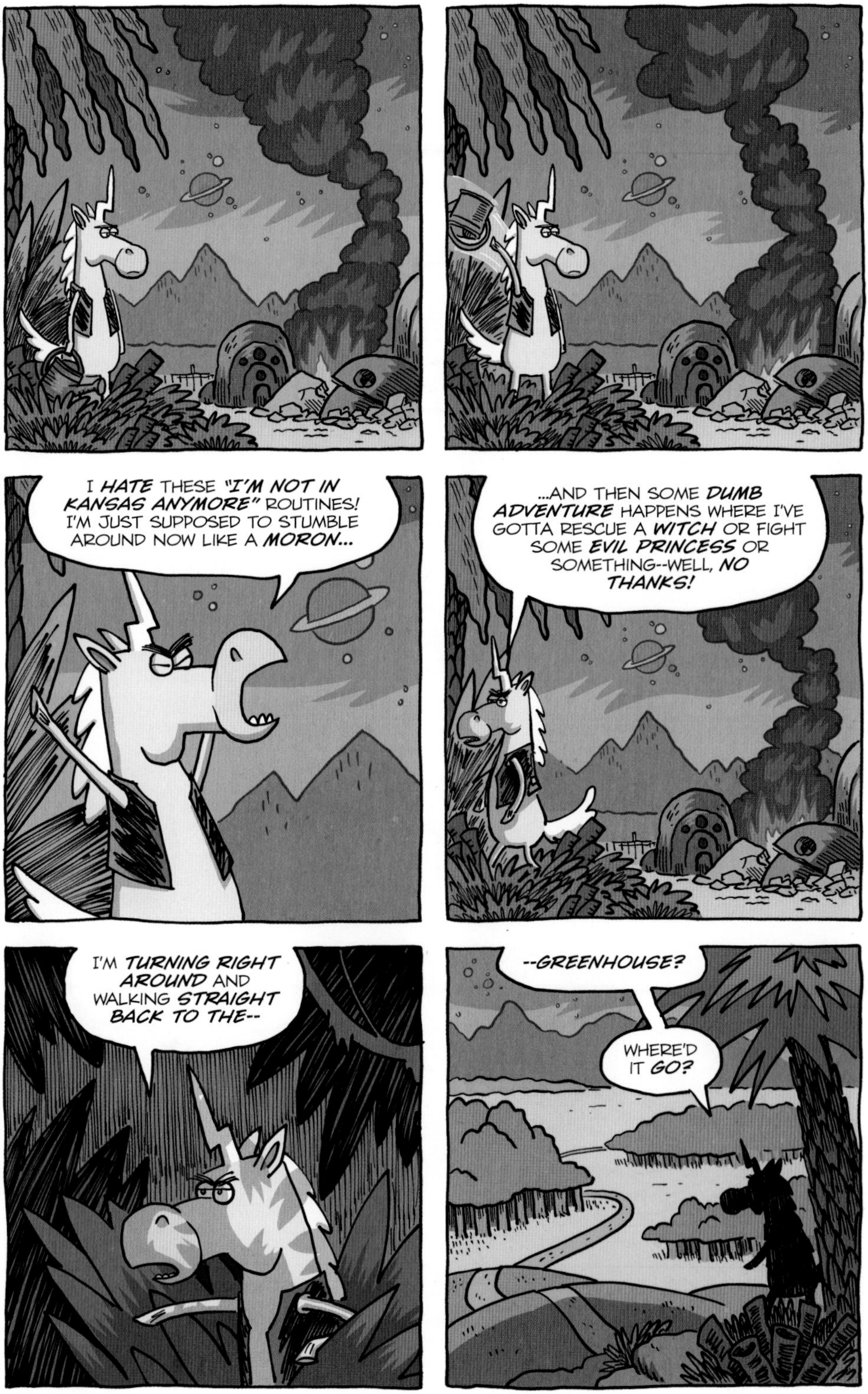
I HATE THESE "I'M NOT IN KANSAS ANYMORE" ROUTINES! I'M JUST SUPPOSED TO STUMBLE AROUND NOW LIKE A MORON...
...AND THEN SOME DUMB ADVENTURE HAPPENS WHERE I'VE GOTTA RESCUE A WITCH OR FIGHT SOME EVIL PRINCESS OR SOMETHING--WELL, NO THANKS!
I'M TURNING RIGHT AROUND AND WALKING STRAIGHT BACK TO THE--
--GREENHOUSE?
WHERE'D IT GO?

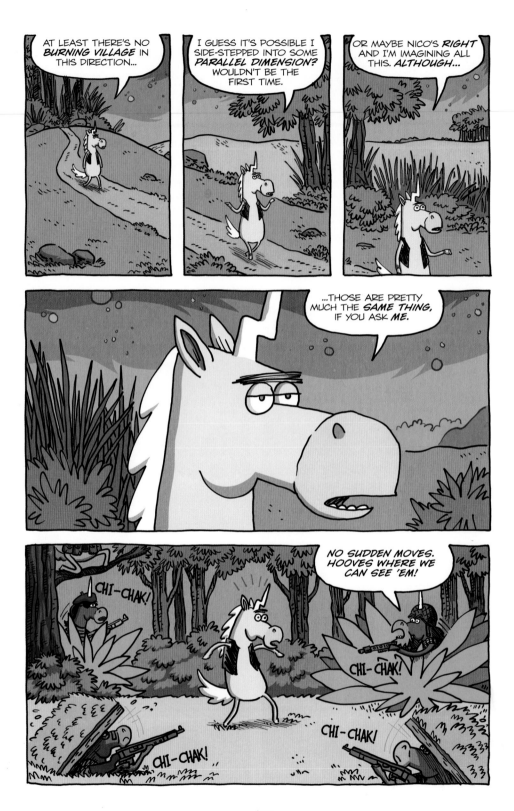

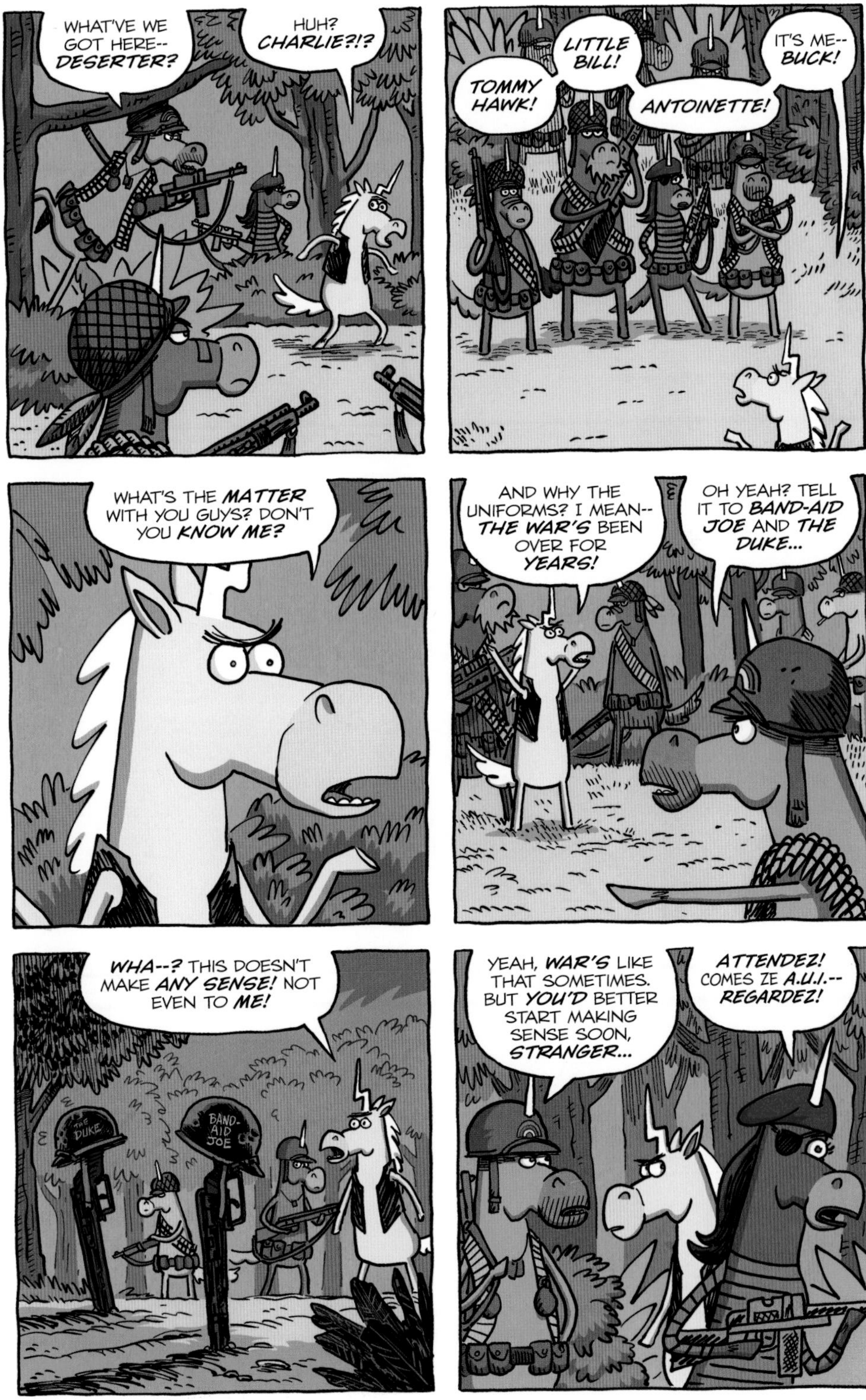
WHAT'VE WE GOT HERE-- DESERTER?
HUH? CHARLIE?!?
TOMMY HAWK!
LITTLE BILL!
ANTOINETTE!
IT'S ME-- BUCK!
WHAT'S THE MATTER WITH YOU GUYS? DON'T YOU KNOW ME?
AND WHY THE UNIFORMS? I MEAN-- THE WAR'S BEEN OVER FOR YEARS!
OH YEAH? TELL IT TO BAND-AID JOE AND THE DUKE...
WHA--? THIS DOESN'T MAKE ANY SENSE! NOT EVEN TO ME!
THE DUKE
BAND-AID JOE
YEAH, WAR'S LIKE THAT SOMETIMES. BUT YOU'D BETTER START MAKING SENSE SOON, STRANGER...
ATTENDEZ! COMES ZE A.U.I.-- REGARDEZ!

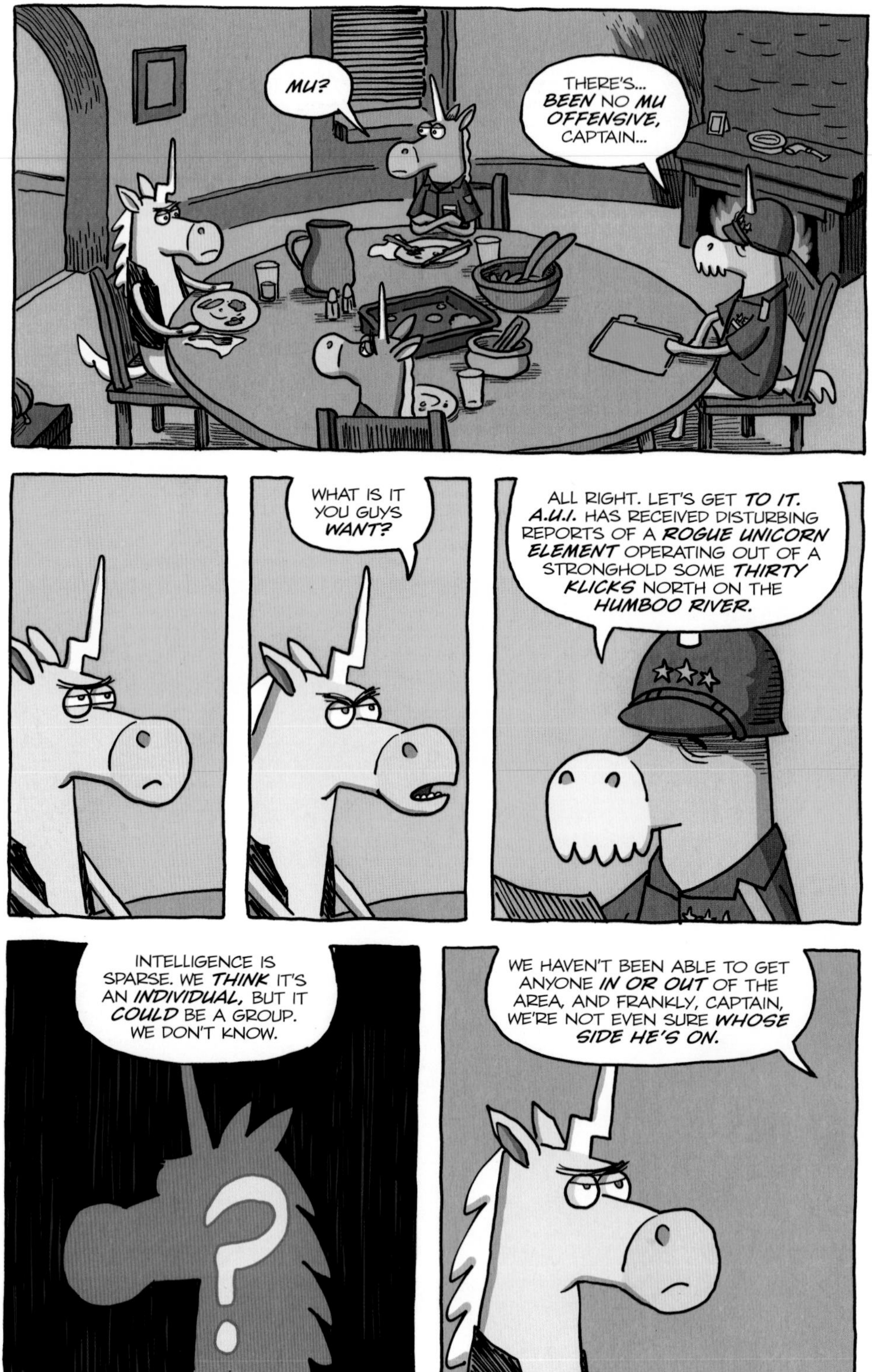
MU?
THERE'S... BEEN NO MU OFFENSIVE, CAPTAIN...
WHAT IS IT YOU GUYS WANT?
ALL RIGHT. LET'S GET TO IT. A.U.I. HAS RECEIVED DISTURBING REPORTS OF A ROGUE UNICORN ELEMENT OPERATING OUT OF A STRONGHOLD SOME THIRTY KLICKS NORTH ON THE HUMBOO RIVER.
INTELLIGENCE IS SPARSE. WE THINK IT'S AN INDIVIDUAL, BUT IT COULD BE A GROUP. WE DON'T KNOW.
WE HAVEN'T BEEN ABLE TO GET ANYONE IN OR OUT OF THE AREA, AND FRANKLY, CAPTAIN, WE'RE NOT EVEN SURE WHOSE SIDE HE'S ON.

108

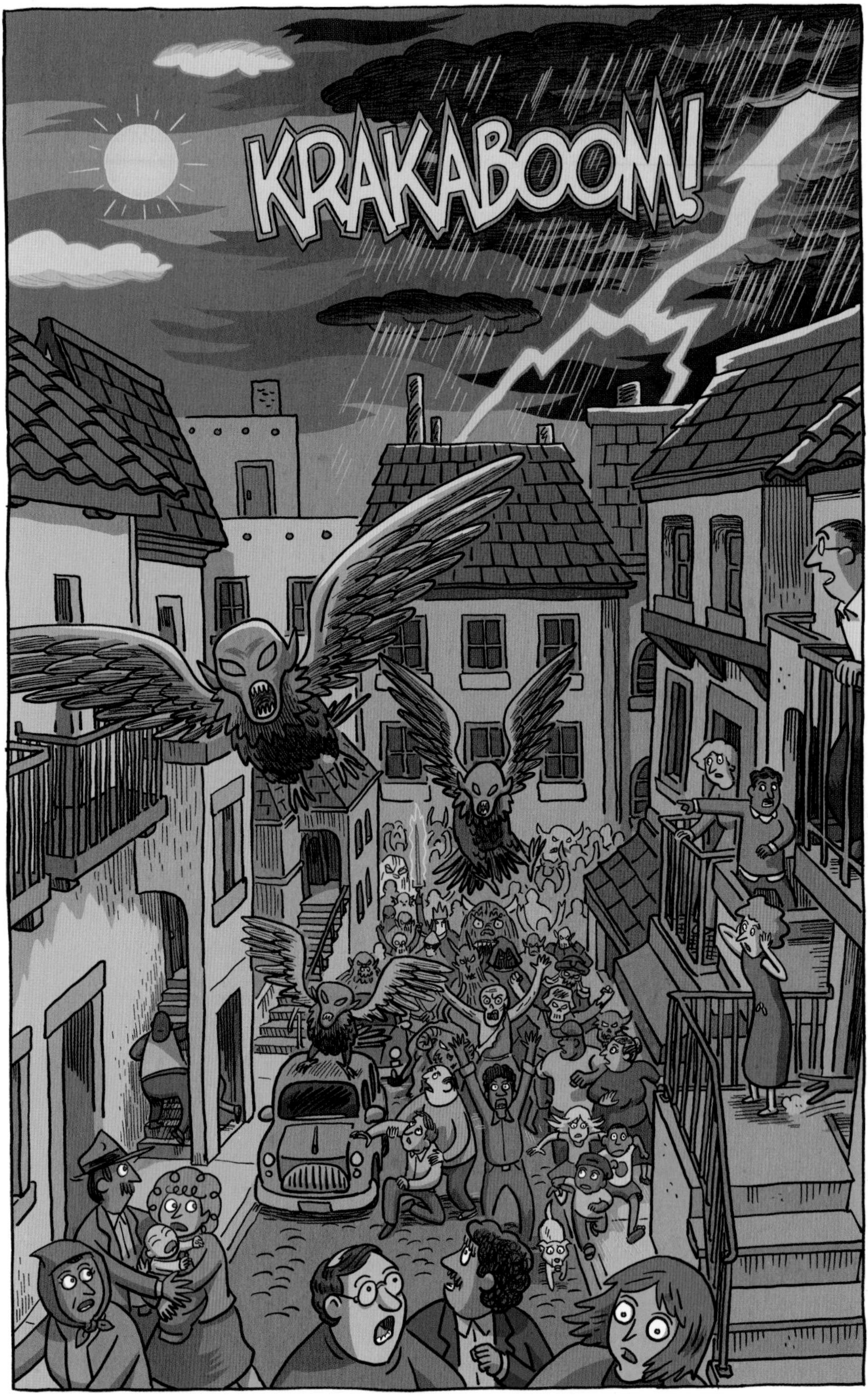
KRAKABOOM!

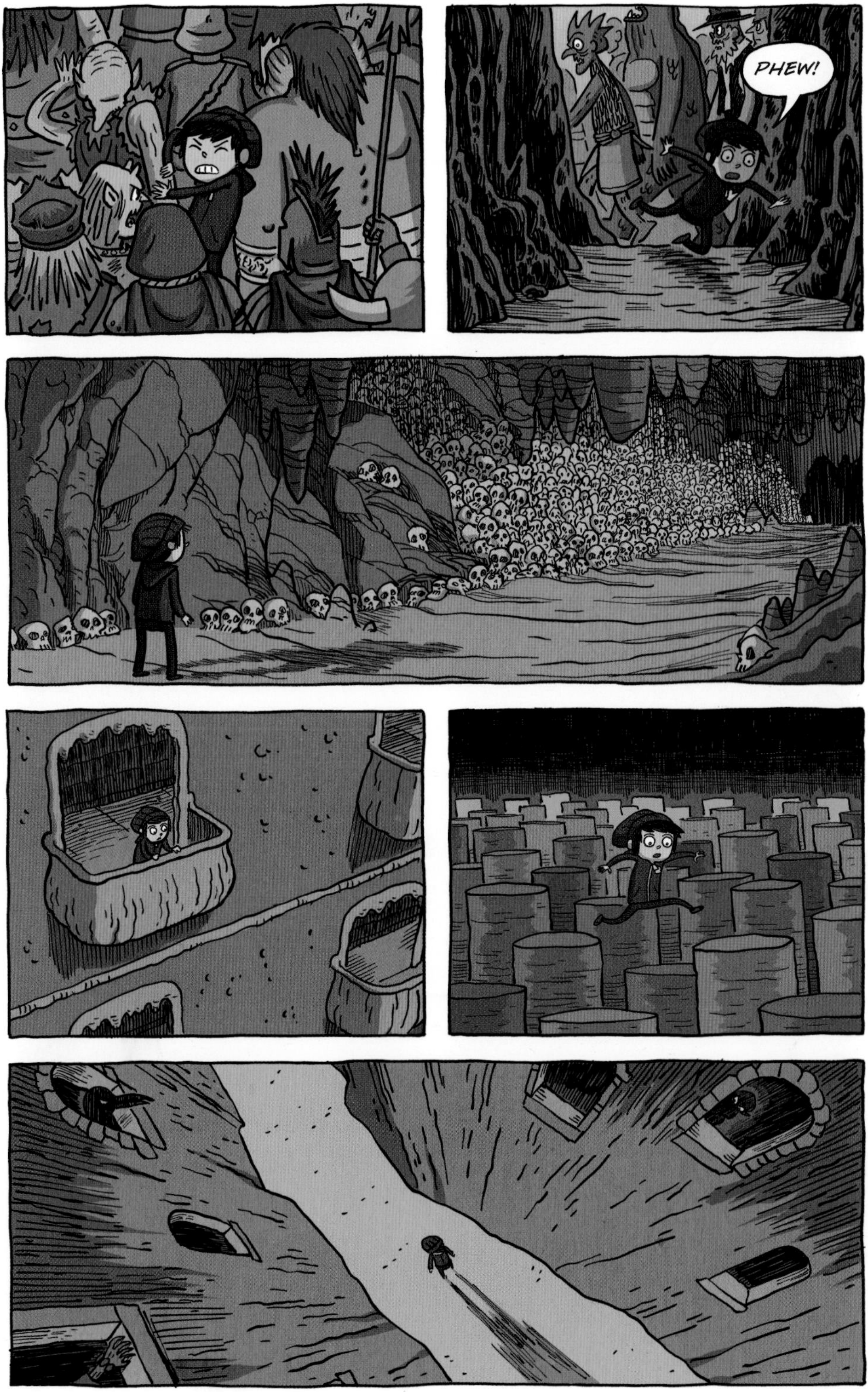
PHEW!

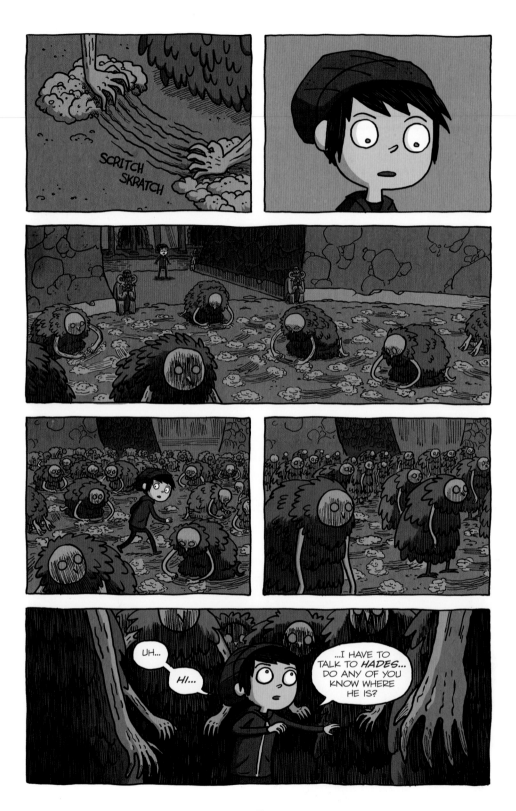

HEY! LEGGO!
WAIT!
STOP!

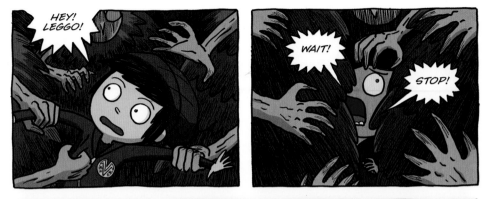

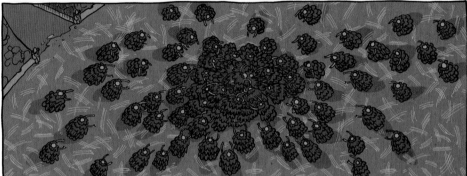

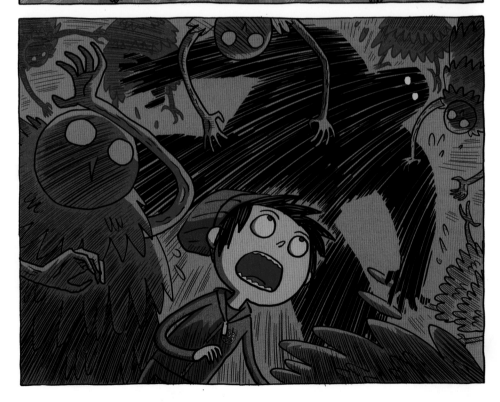

115

116

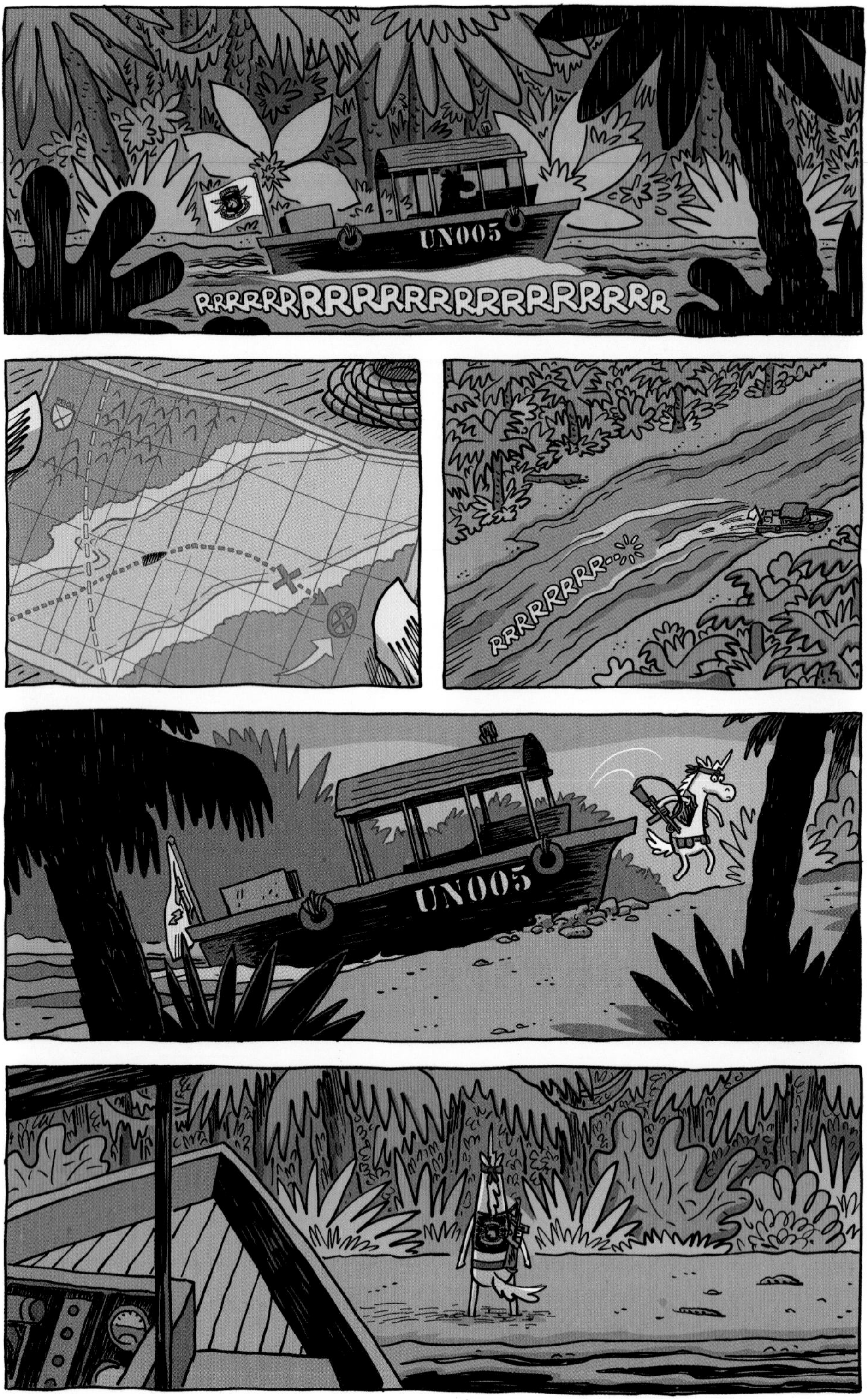
UN005
RRRRRRRRRRRRRRRRRRRRRRRRR
RRRRRRRR
UN005

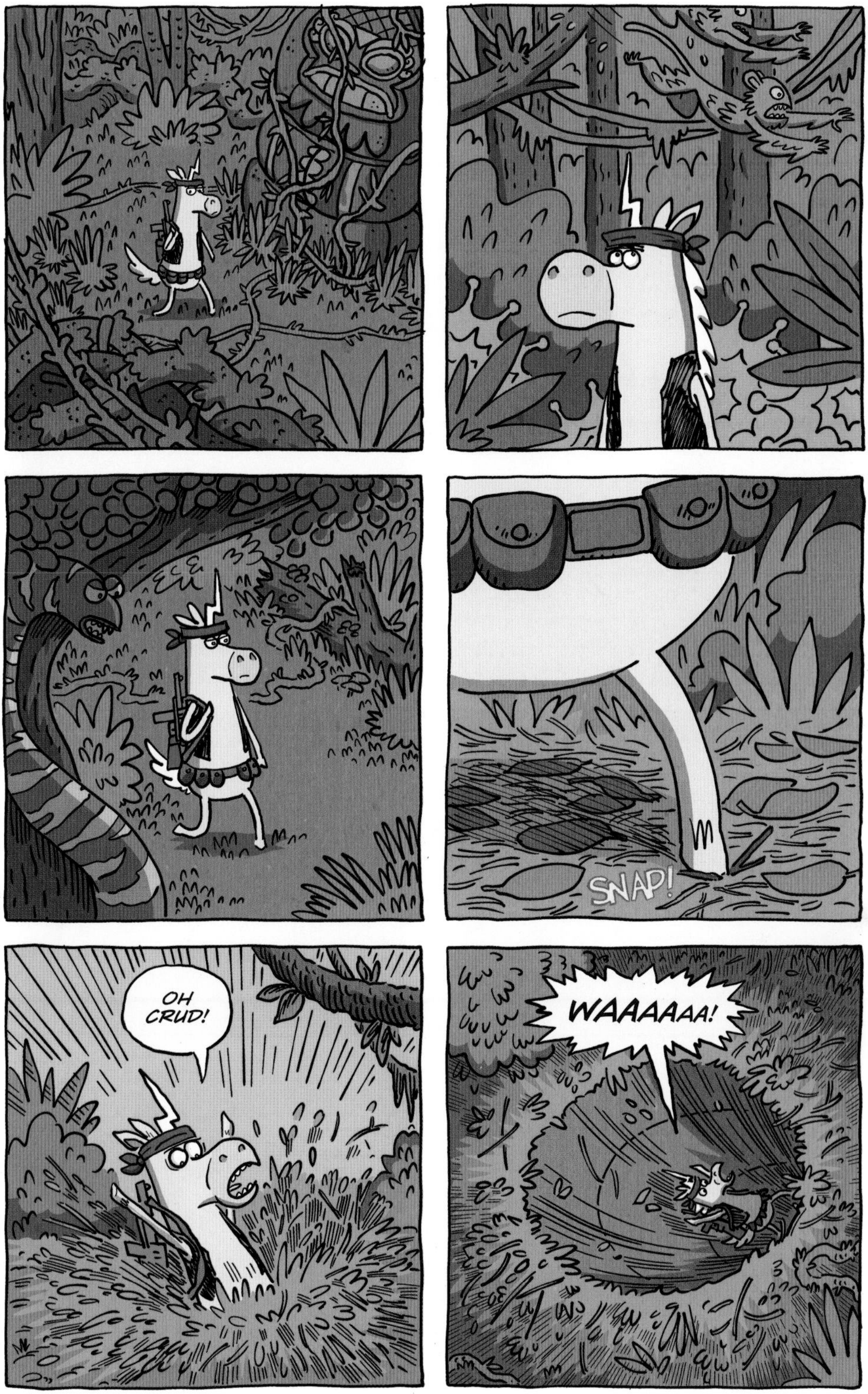
SNAP!
OH CRUD!
WAAAAAA!

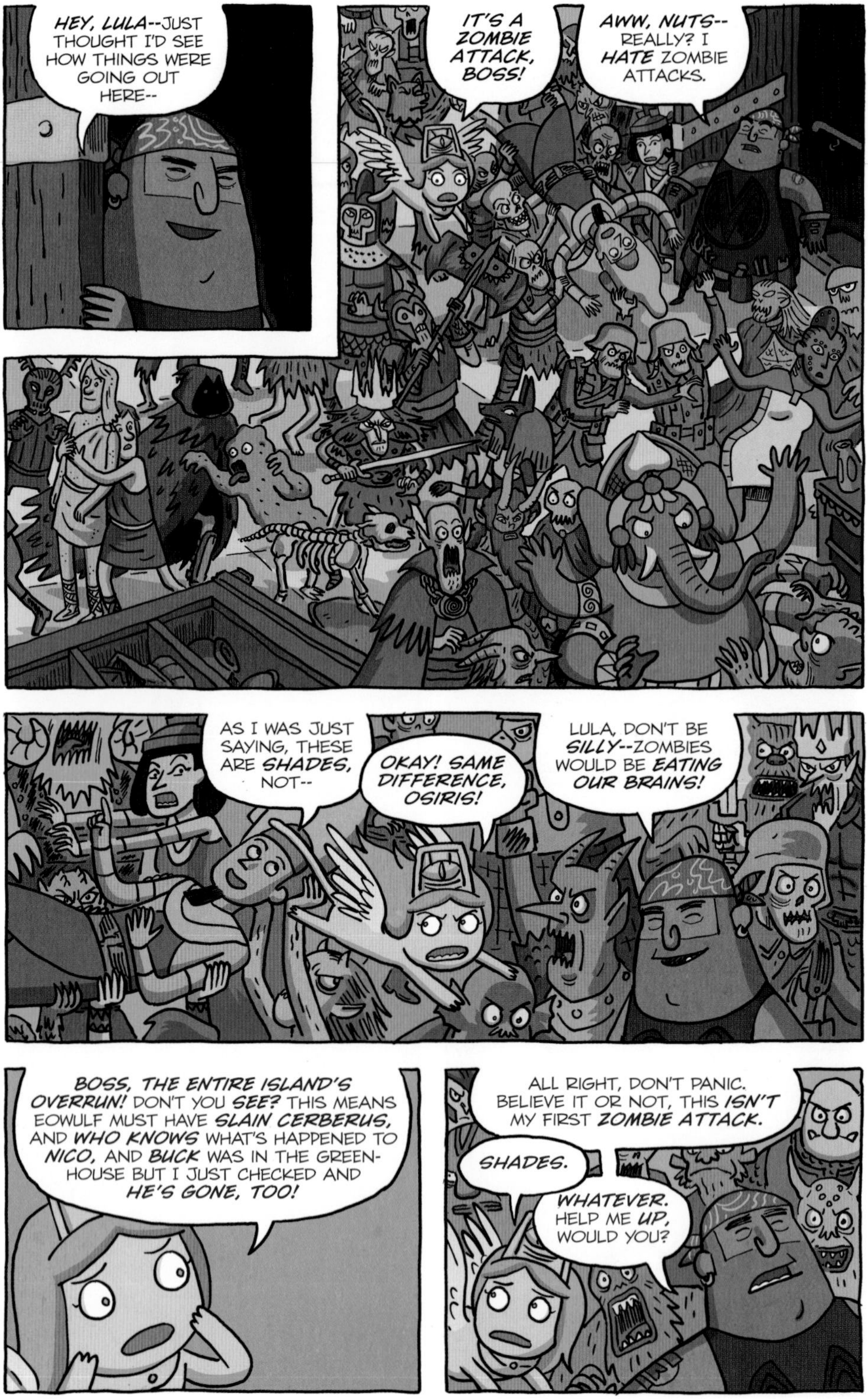
HEY, LULA--JUST THOUGHT I'D SEE HOW THINGS WERE GOING OUT HERE--
IT'S A ZOMBIE ATTACK, BOSS!
AWW, NUTS--REALLY? I HATE ZOMBIE ATTACKS.
AS I WAS JUST SAYING, THESE ARE SHADES, NOT--
OKAY! SAME DIFFERENCE, OSIRIS!
LULA, DON'T BE SILLY--ZOMBIES WOULD BE EATING OUR BRAINS!
BOSS, THE ENTIRE ISLAND'S OVERRUN! DON'T YOU SEE? THIS MEANS EOWULF MUST HAVE SLAIN CERBERUS, AND WHO KNOWS WHAT'S HAPPENED TO NICO, AND BUCK WAS IN THE GREEN-HOUSE BUT I JUST CHECKED AND HE'S GONE, TOO!
ALL RIGHT, DON'T PANIC. BELIEVE IT OR NOT, THIS ISN'T MY FIRST ZOMBIE ATTACK.
SHADES.
WHATEVER. HELP ME UP, WOULD YOU?

THANKS. IF NICO FOLLOWED EOWULF TO THE UNDERWORLD, I'M NOT SURE WHAT WE CAN DO--IT'S A *BIG PLACE* AND IT COULD TAKE A *LONG TIME* TO FIND HIM.

AND WE CAN'T JUST LEAVE THE SHOP CRAWLING WITH *ZOMBIES!*

SHADES.

WHATEVER!

NICO'S A *SMART KID*, THERE'S NO REASON TO ASSUME THE *WORST*. I'M MORE WORRIED ABOUT *BUCK.*

I LOOKED *EVERYWHERE* FOR HIM!

OKAY, SO MAYBE HE'S *NOT HERE.* MAYBE HE *CROSSED DIMENSIONS* FOR SOME REASON. I MEAN, THAT'S WHAT UNICORNS *DO*, RIGHT? MAYBE HE WAS TRYING TO *ESCAPE THE ZOMBIES.*

SHADES.

WHATEVER.

LIKE IT OR *NOT*, I THINK WE'RE JUST GOING TO HAVE TO *TRUST* THAT *NICO AND BUCK* WILL BE ALL RIGHT. YOU AND I HAVE GOTTA DO WHAT WE CAN *HERE*...

...IT'S NOT *JUST* THE SHOP--THE VILLAGERS MUST BE *TERRIFIED!*

I'M *WITH* YOU, BOSS!

125

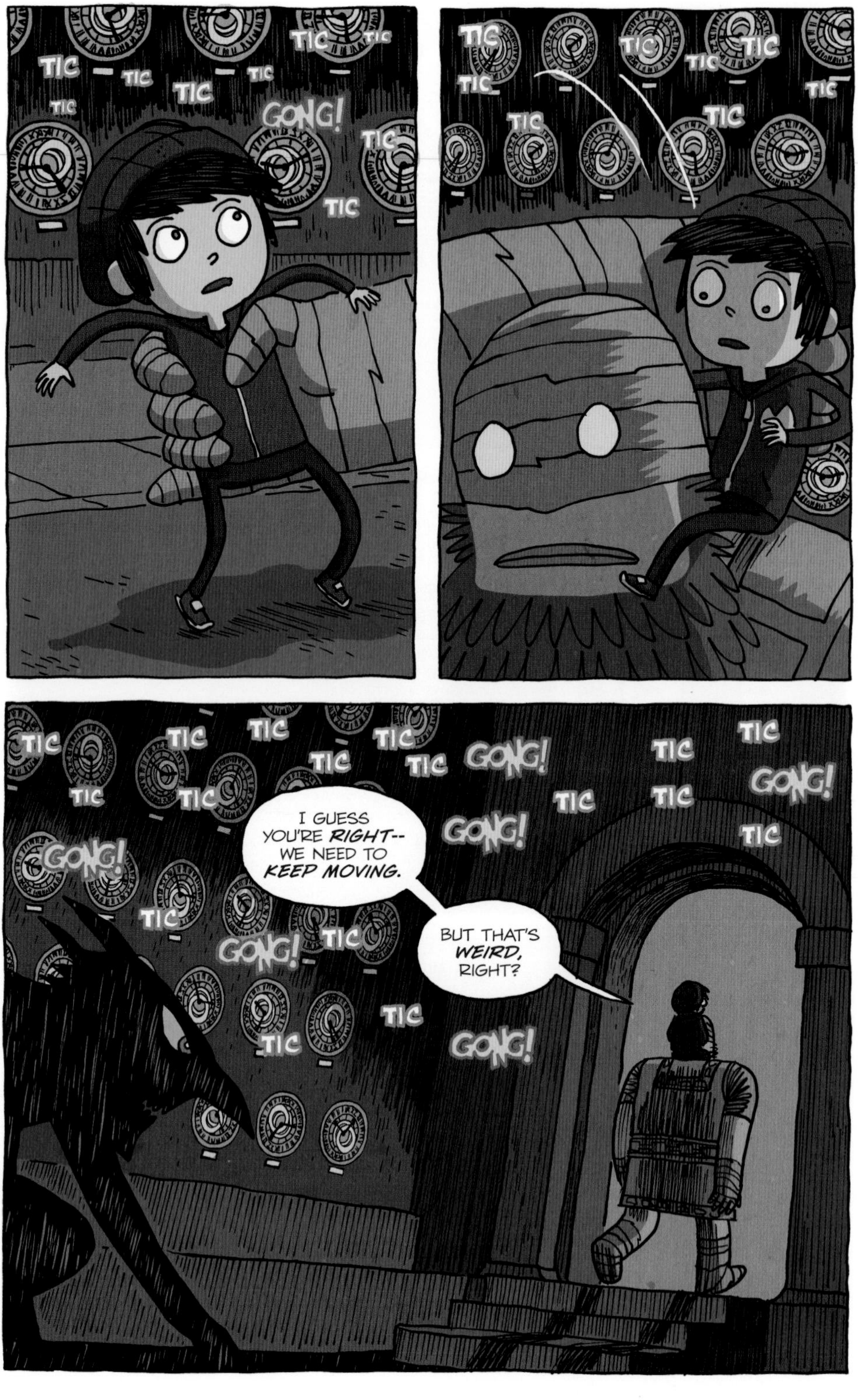
TIC
TIC
TIC
TIC
TIC
TIC
TIC
GONG!
TIC
TIC
TIC
TIC
TIC
TIC
TIC
TIC
TIC
TIC
TIC
TIC
TIC
TIC
TIC
TIC
TIC
TIC
GONG!
TIC
TIC
TIC
GONG!
GONG!
TIC
TIC
TIC
GONG!
I GUESS YOU'RE RIGHT-- WE NEED TO KEEP MOVING.
BUT THAT'S WEIRD, RIGHT?
TIC
GONG!
TIC
TIC
GONG!

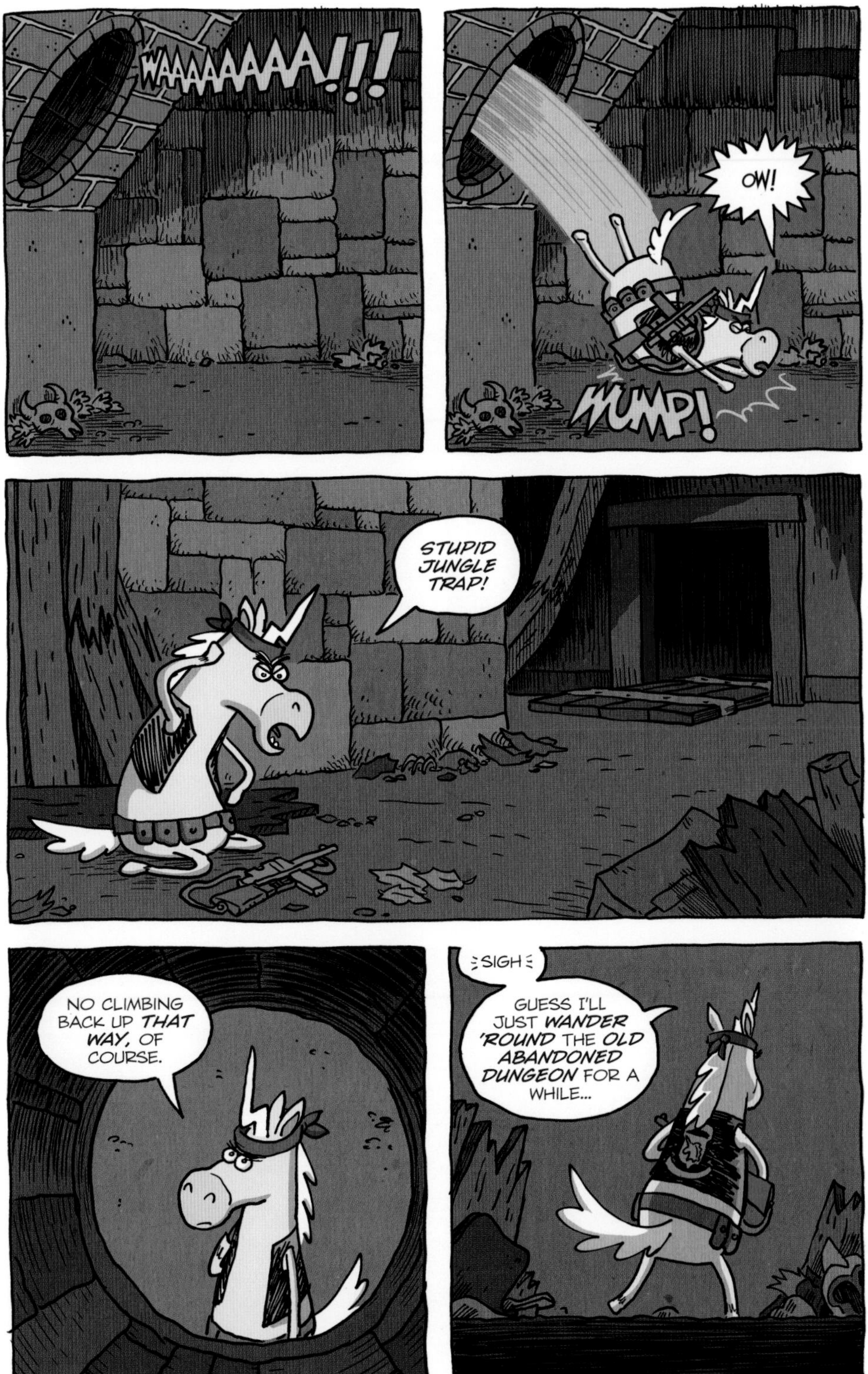
WAAAAAAAA!!!
OW!
WUMP!
STUPID JUNGLE TRAP!
NO CLIMBING BACK UP THAT WAY, OF COURSE.
SIGH
GUESS I'LL JUST WANDER 'ROUND THE OLD ABANDONED DUNGEON FOR A WHILE...

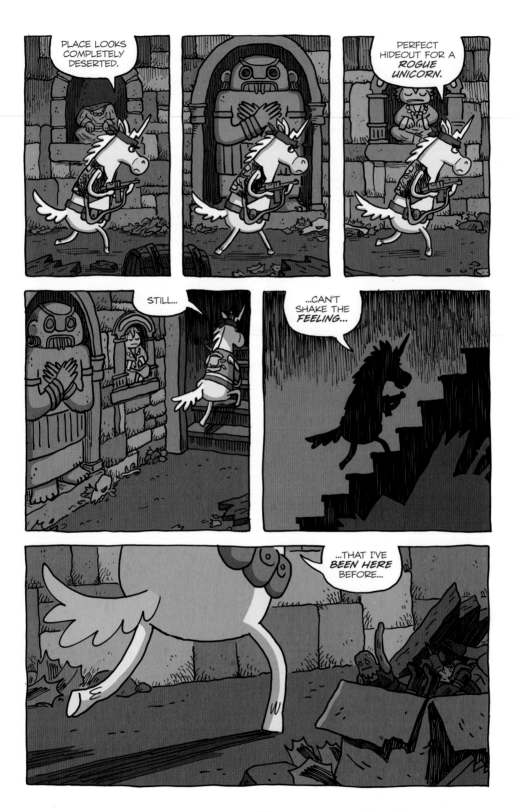

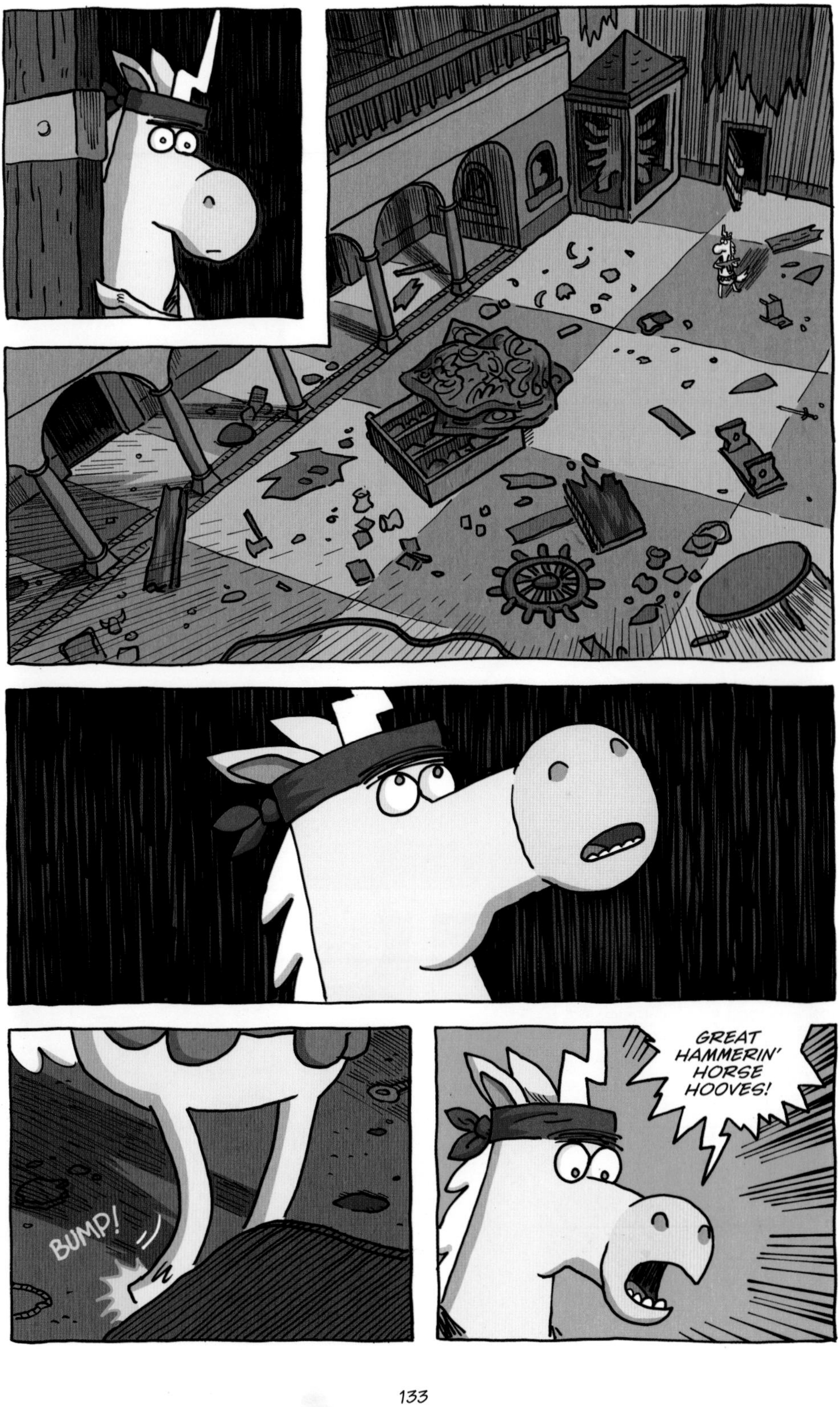
BUMP!
GREAT HAMMERIN' HORSE HOOVES!

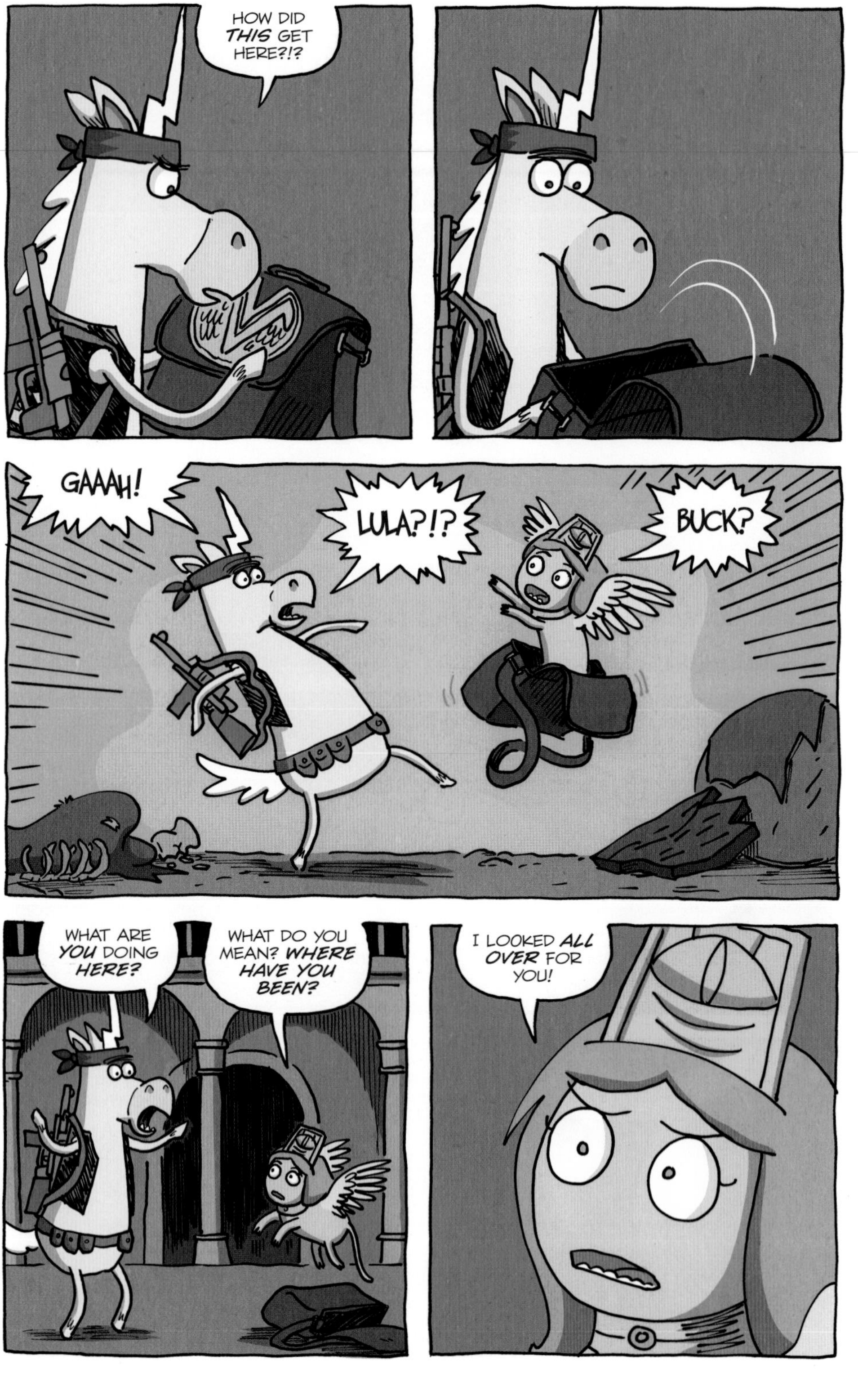
HOW DID *THIS* GET HERE?!?
GAAAH!
LULA?!?
BUCK?
WHAT ARE *YOU* DOING *HERE?*
WHAT DO YOU MEAN? *WHERE HAVE YOU BEEN?*
I LOOKED *ALL OVER* FOR YOU!

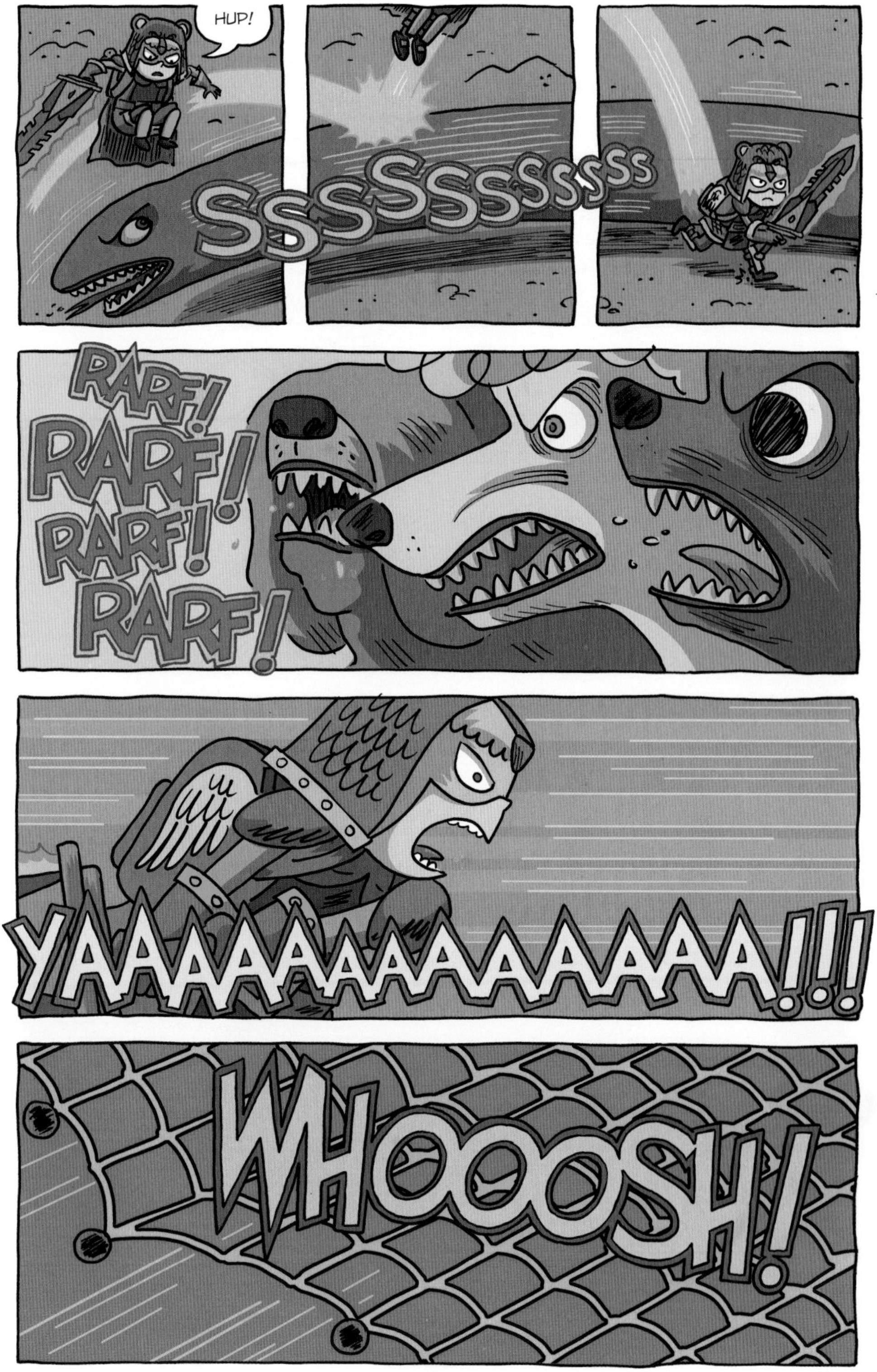
HUP!
SSSSSSSSSSSS
RARF! RARF! RARF! RARF!
YAAAAAAAAAAAAA!!!
WHOOOSH!

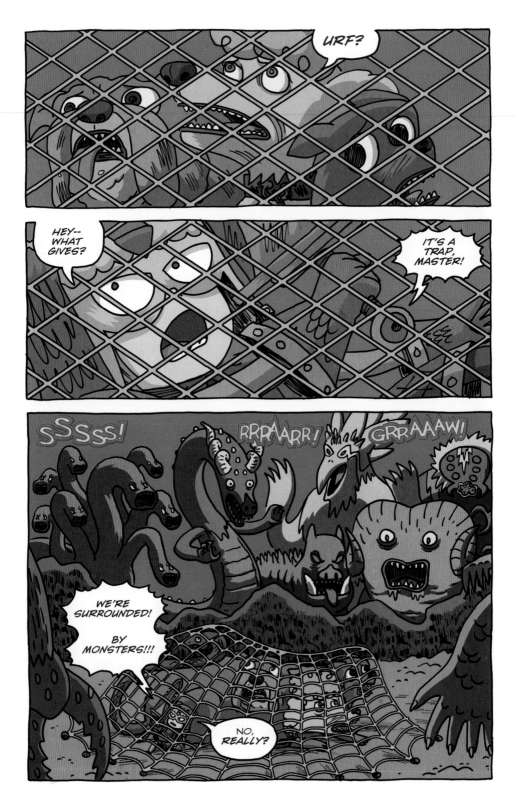

140

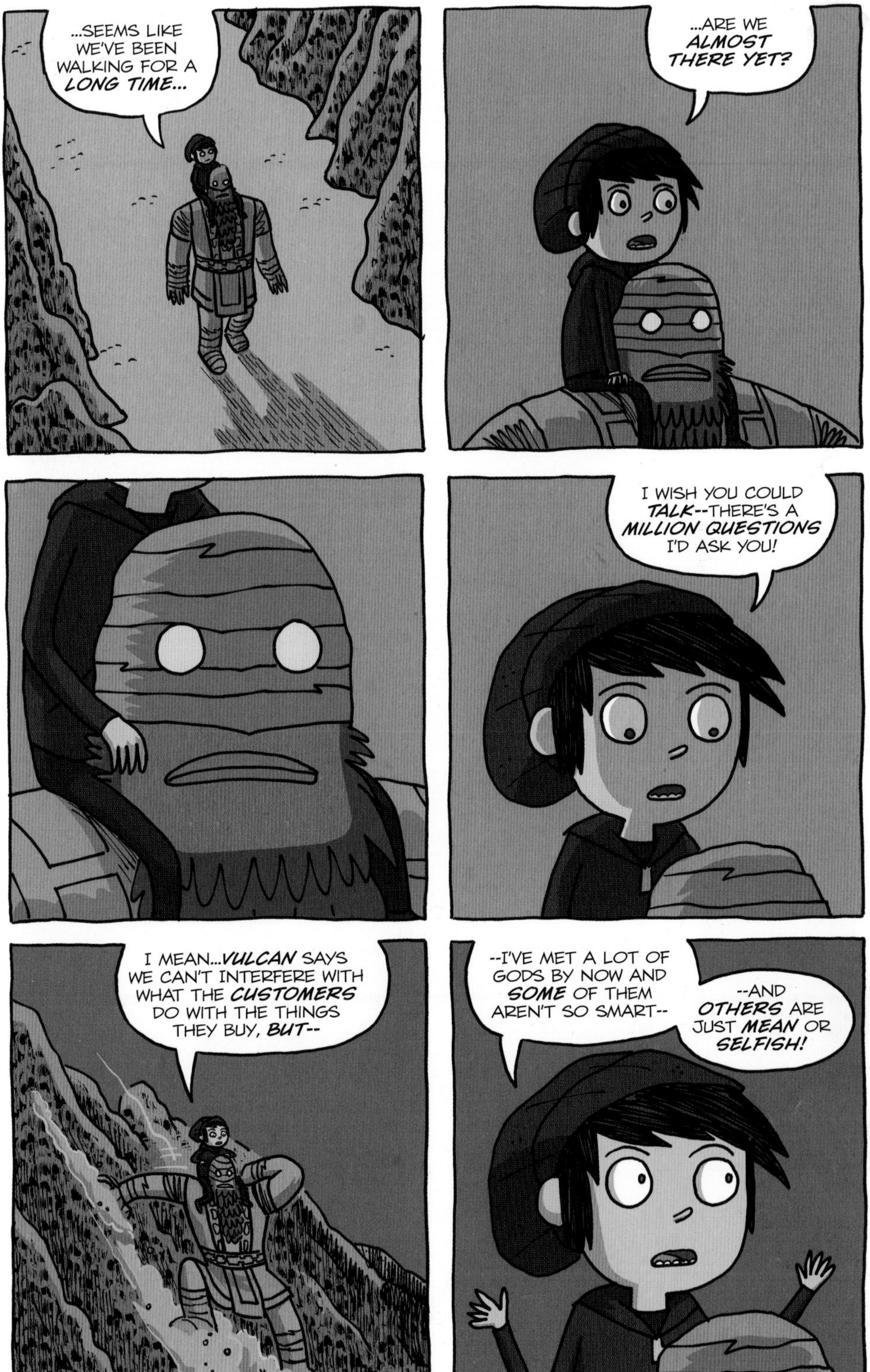
...SEEMS LIKE WE'VE BEEN WALKING FOR A *LONG TIME...*
...ARE WE *ALMOST THERE YET?*
I WISH YOU COULD *TALK*--THERE'S A *MILLION QUESTIONS* I'D ASK YOU!
I MEAN...*VULCAN* SAYS WE CAN'T INTERFERE WITH WHAT THE *CUSTOMERS* DO WITH THE THINGS THEY BUY, *BUT*--
--I'VE MET A LOT OF GODS BY NOW AND *SOME* OF THEM AREN'T SO SMART--
--AND *OTHERS* ARE JUST *MEAN* OR *SELFISH!*

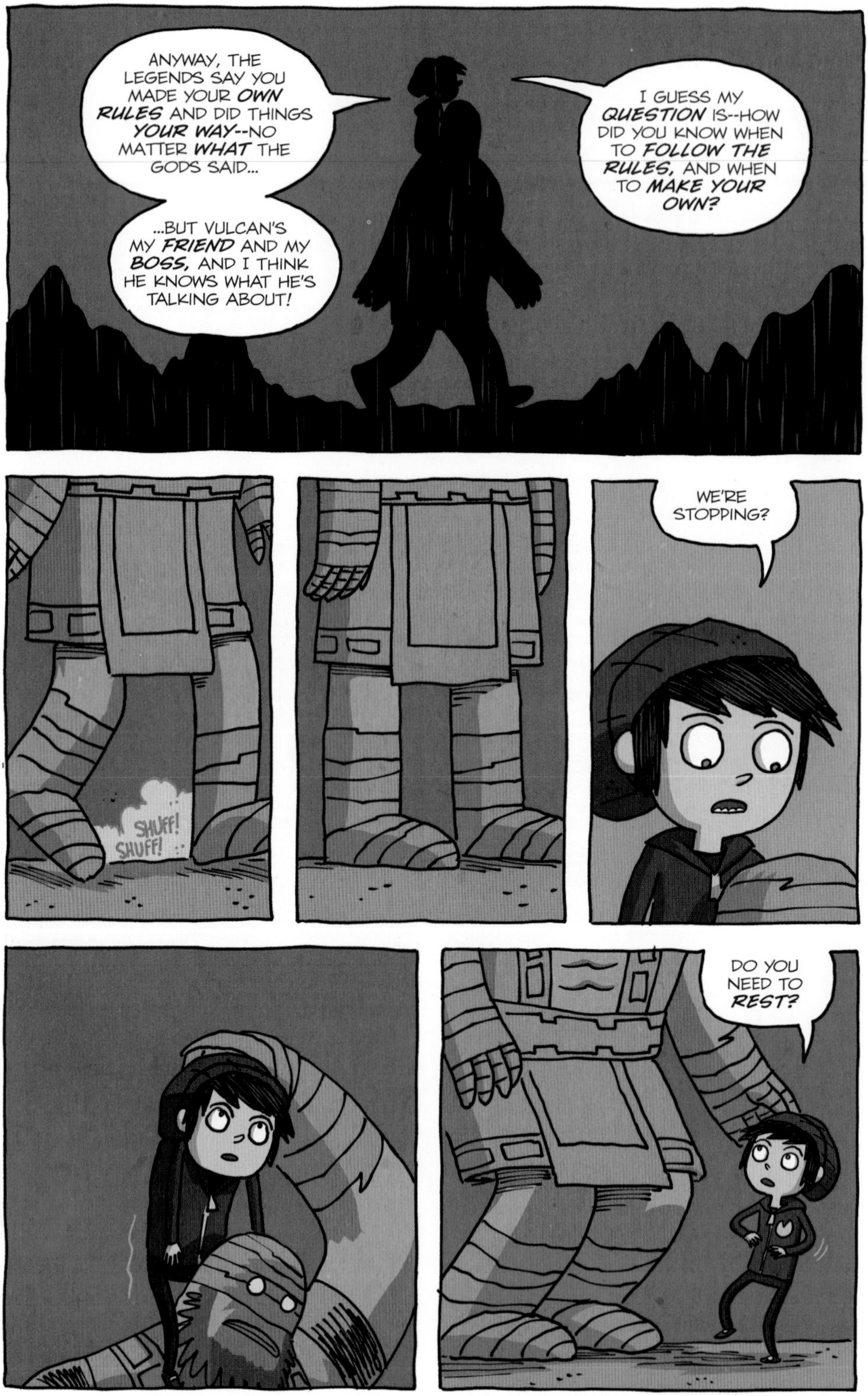
ANYWAY, THE LEGENDS SAY YOU MADE YOUR OWN RULES AND DID THINGS YOUR WAY--NO MATTER WHAT THE GODS SAID...
...BUT VULCAN'S MY FRIEND AND MY BOSS, AND I THINK HE KNOWS WHAT HE'S TALKING ABOUT!
I GUESS MY QUESTION IS--HOW DID YOU KNOW WHEN TO FOLLOW THE RULES, AND WHEN TO MAKE YOUR OWN?
SHUFF! SHUFF!
WE'RE STOPPING?
DO YOU NEED TO REST?

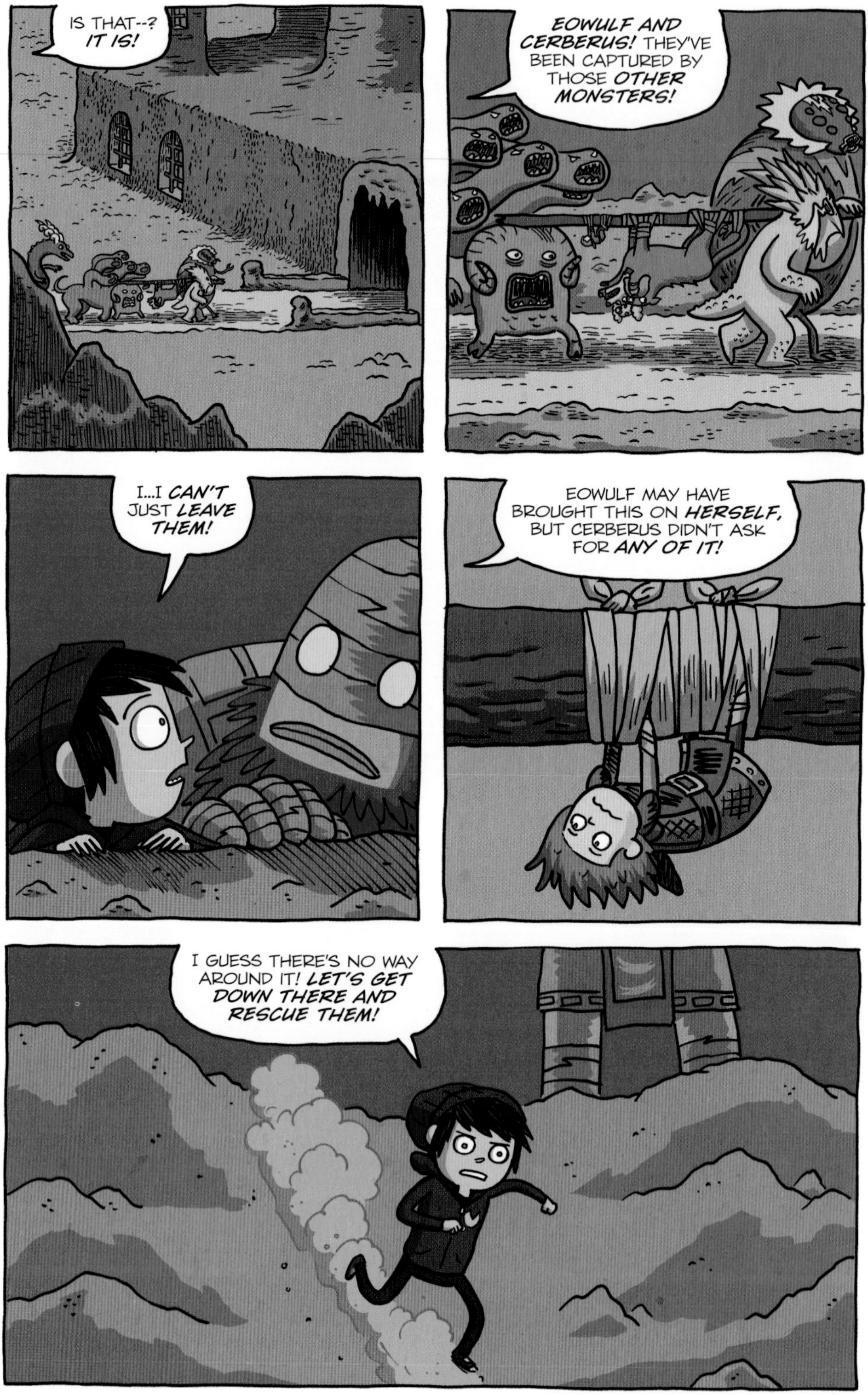
IS THAT--? IT IS!
EOWULF AND CERBERUS! THEY'VE BEEN CAPTURED BY THOSE OTHER MONSTERS!
I...I CAN'T JUST LEAVE THEM!
EOWULF MAY HAVE BROUGHT THIS ON HERSELF, BUT CERBERUS DIDN'T ASK FOR ANY OF IT!
I GUESS THERE'S NO WAY AROUND IT! LET'S GET DOWN THERE AND RESCUE THEM!

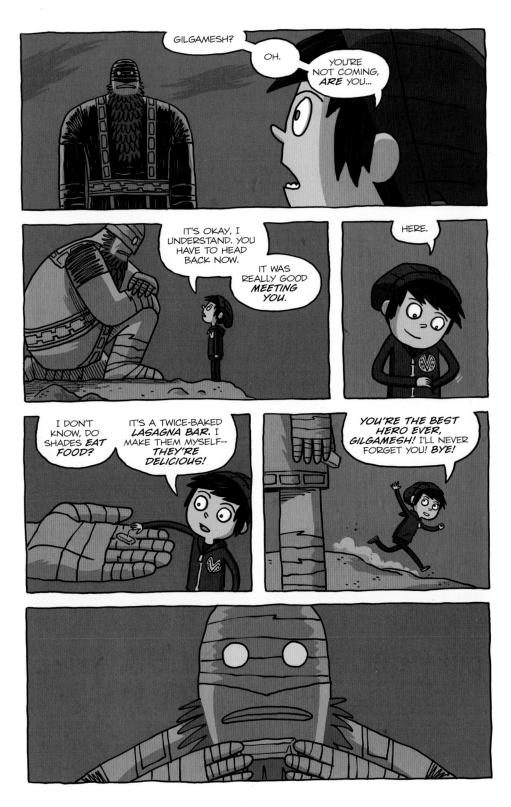

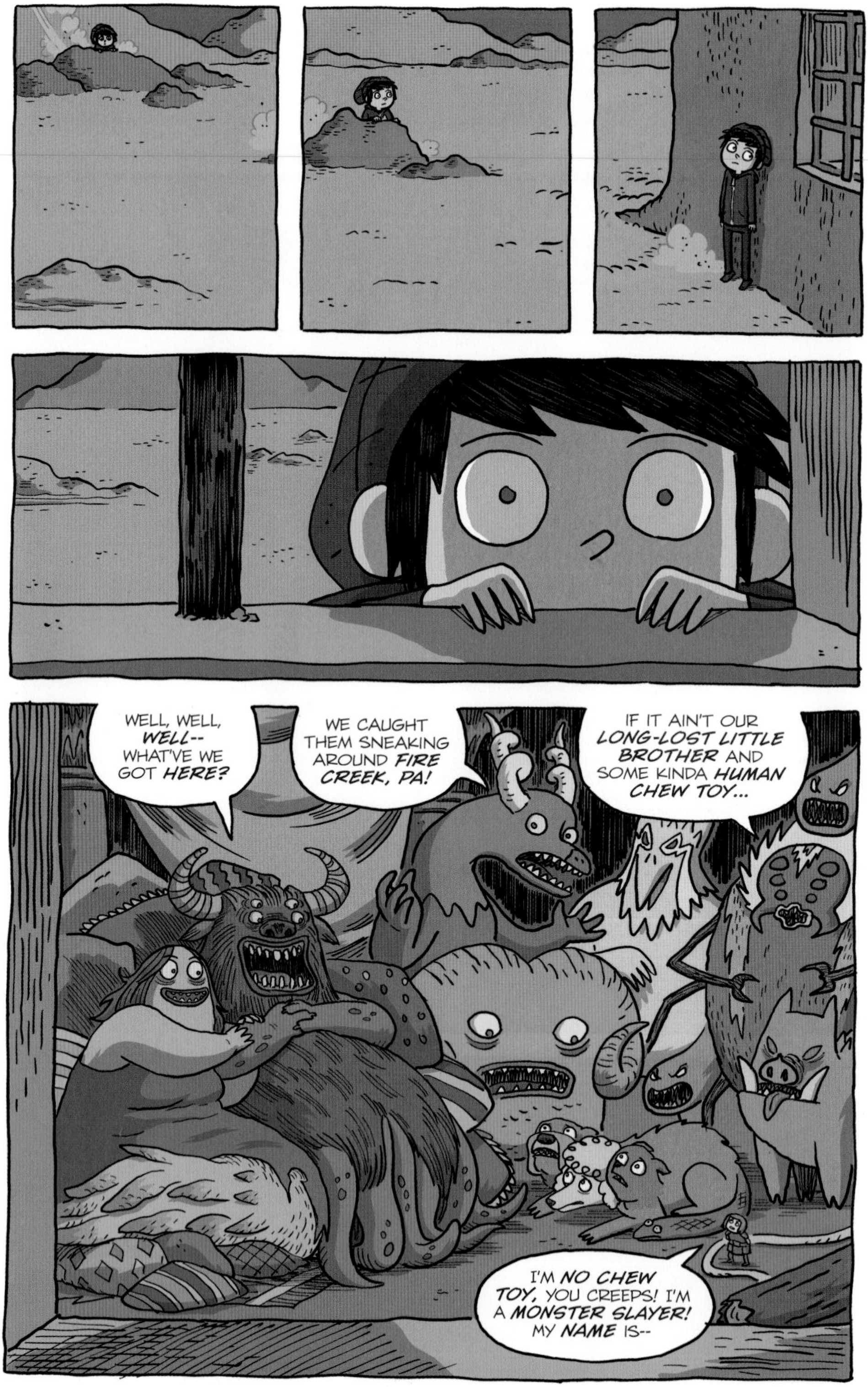
WELL, WELL, WELL-- WHAT'VE WE GOT HERE?
WE CAUGHT THEM SNEAKING AROUND FIRE CREEK, PA!
IF IT AIN'T OUR LONG-LOST LITTLE BROTHER AND SOME KINDA HUMAN CHEW TOY...
I'M NO CHEW TOY, YOU CREEPS! I'M A MONSTER SLAYER! MY NAME IS--

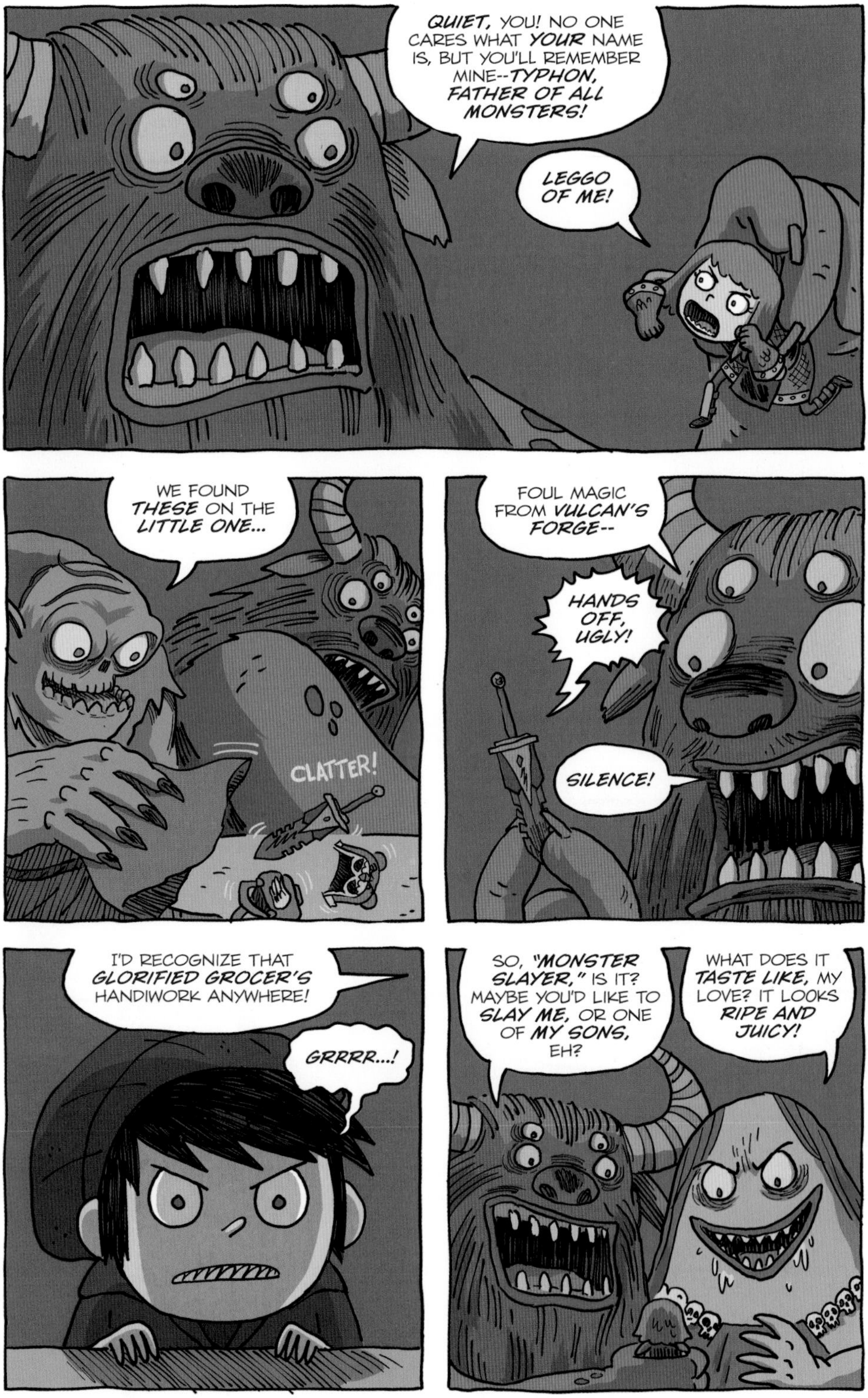
QUIET, YOU! NO ONE CARES WHAT YOUR NAME IS, BUT YOU'LL REMEMBER MINE--TYPHON, FATHER OF ALL MONSTERS!
LEGGO OF ME!
WE FOUND THESE ON THE LITTLE ONE...
CLATTER!
FOUL MAGIC FROM VULCAN'S FORGE--
HANDS OFF, UGLY!
SILENCE!
I'D RECOGNIZE THAT GLORIFIED GROCER'S HANDIWORK ANYWHERE!
GRRRR...!
SO, "MONSTER SLAYER," IS IT? MAYBE YOU'D LIKE TO SLAY ME, OR ONE OF MY SONS, EH?
WHAT DOES IT TASTE LIKE, MY LOVE? IT LOOKS RIPE AND JUICY!

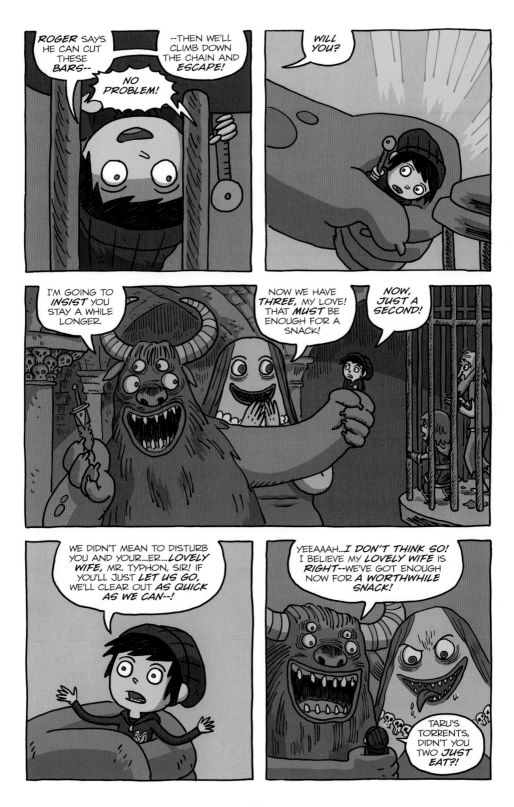

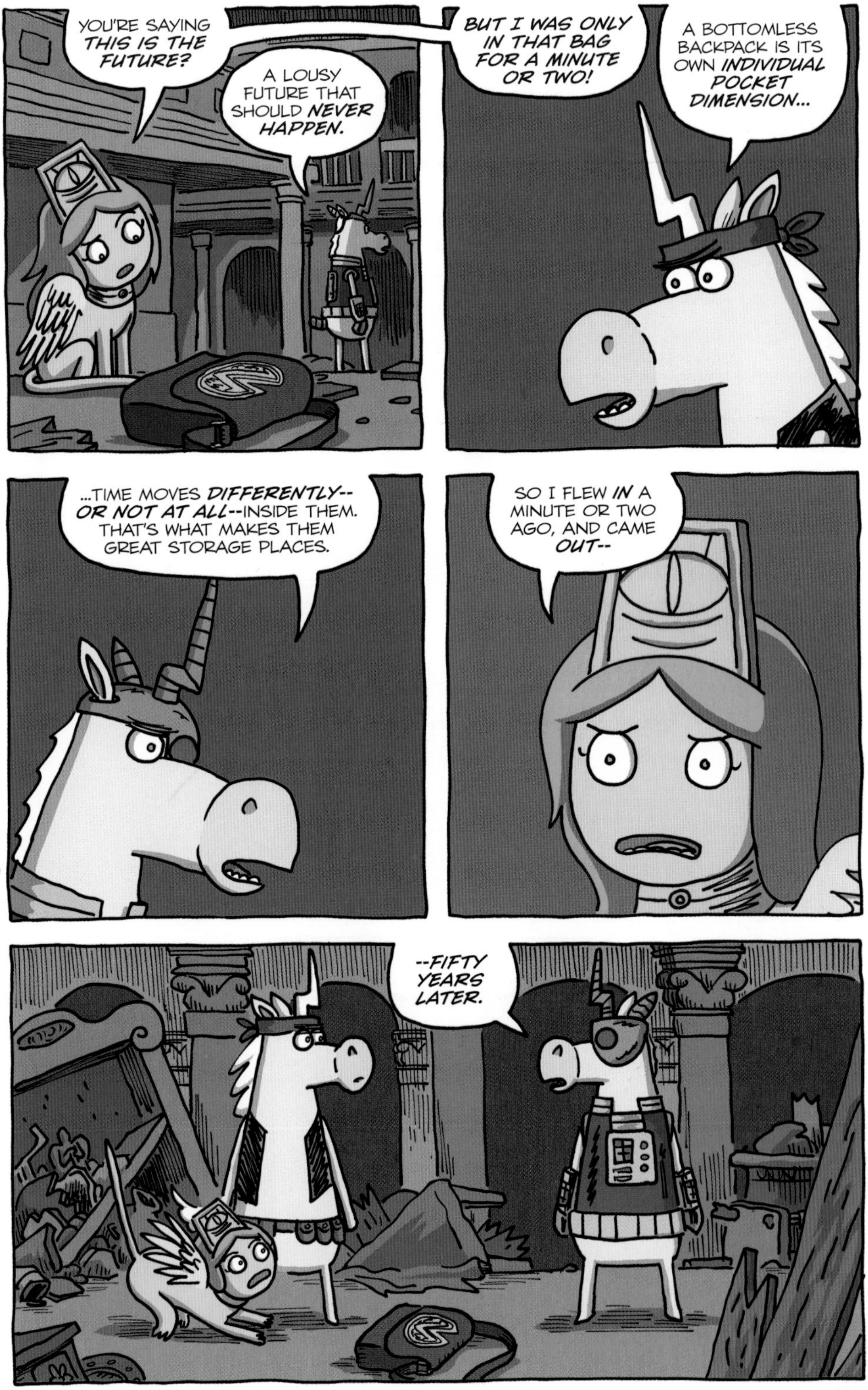
YOU'RE SAYING THIS IS THE FUTURE?
A LOUSY FUTURE THAT SHOULD NEVER HAPPEN.
BUT I WAS ONLY IN THAT BAG FOR A MINUTE OR TWO!
A BOTTOMLESS BACKPACK IS ITS OWN INDIVIDUAL POCKET DIMENSION...
...TIME MOVES DIFFERENTLY--OR NOT AT ALL--INSIDE THEM. THAT'S WHAT MAKES THEM GREAT STORAGE PLACES.
SO I FLEW IN A MINUTE OR TWO AGO, AND CAME OUT--
--FIFTY YEARS LATER.

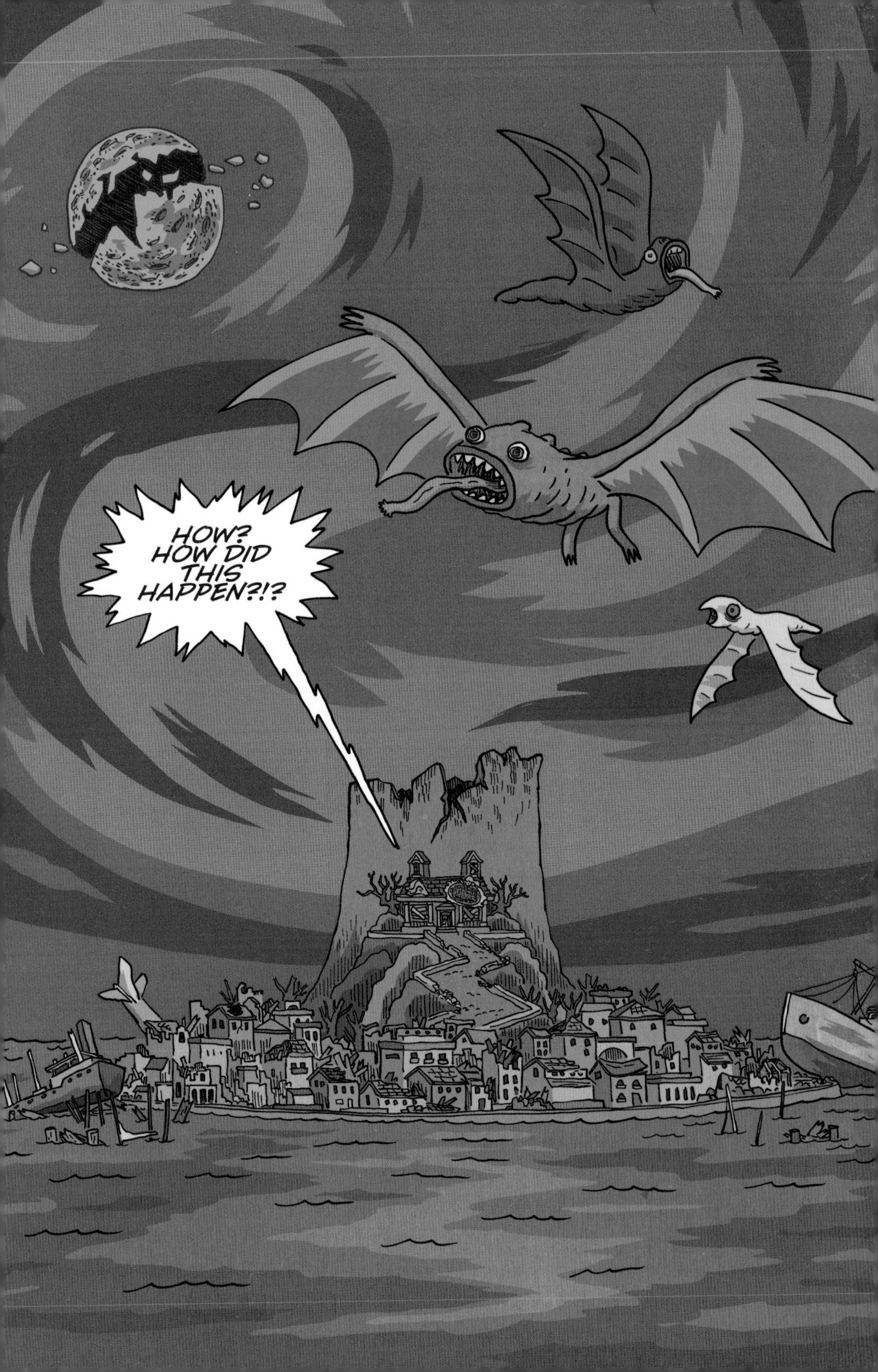
HOW? HOW DID THIS HAPPEN?!?

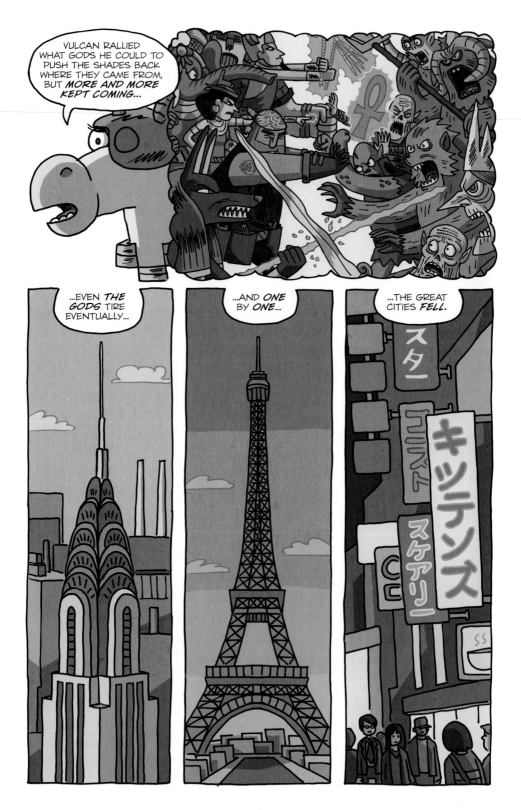

161

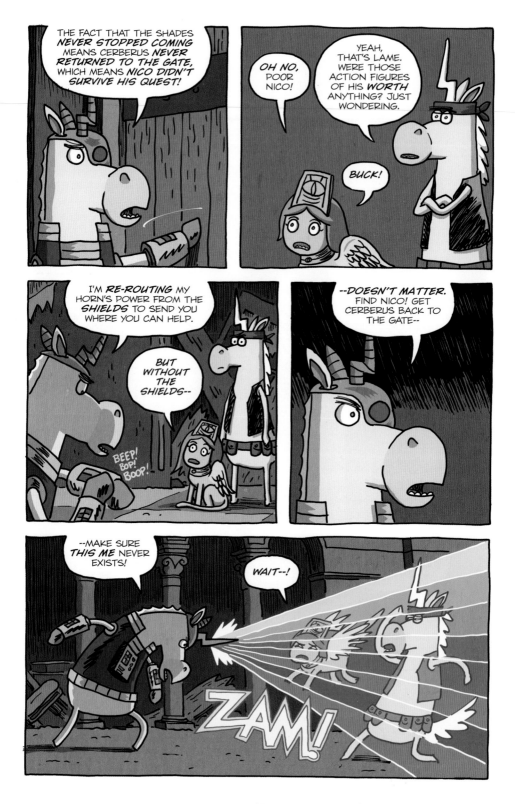

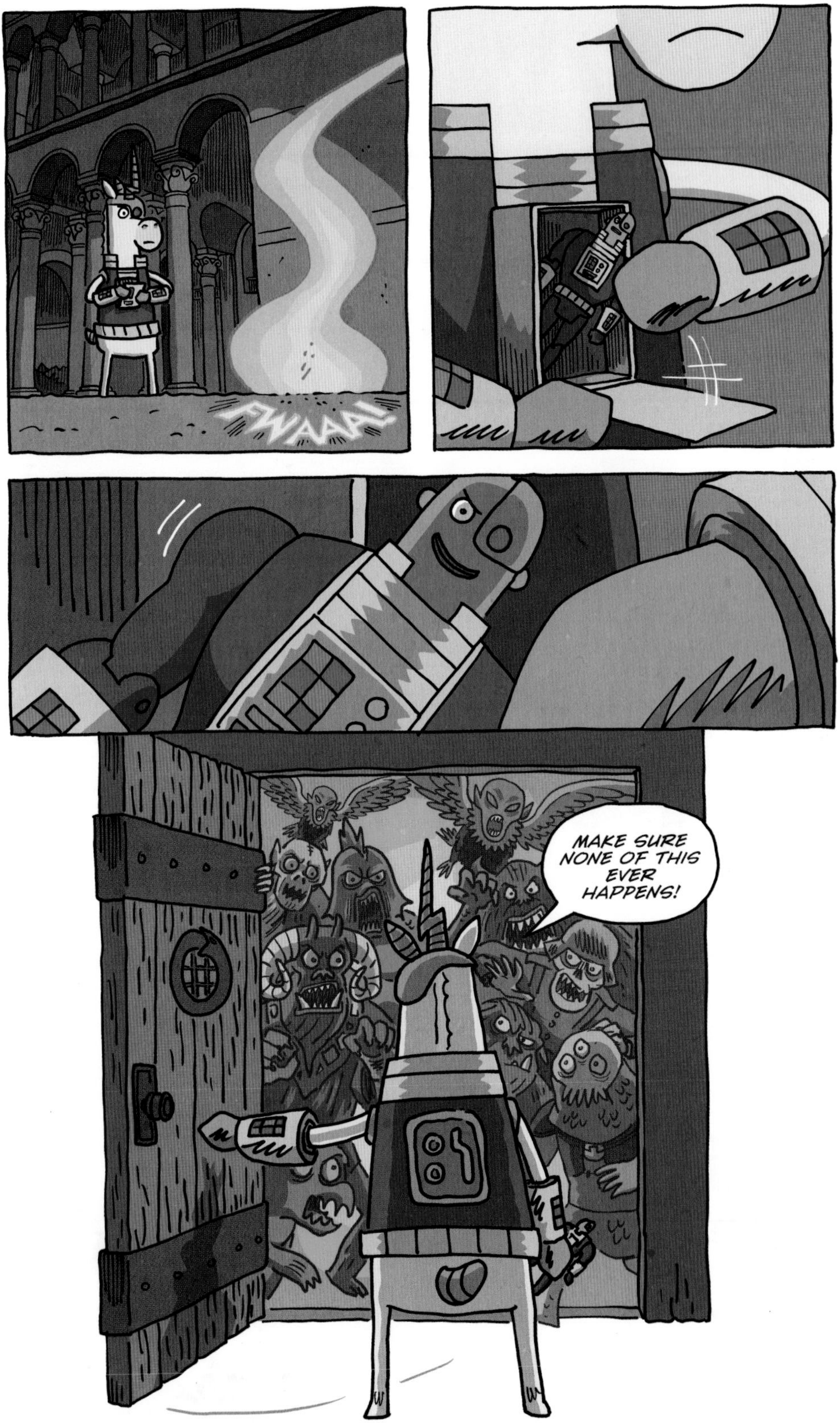
FWAAA!
MAKE SURE NONE OF THIS EVER HAPPENS!

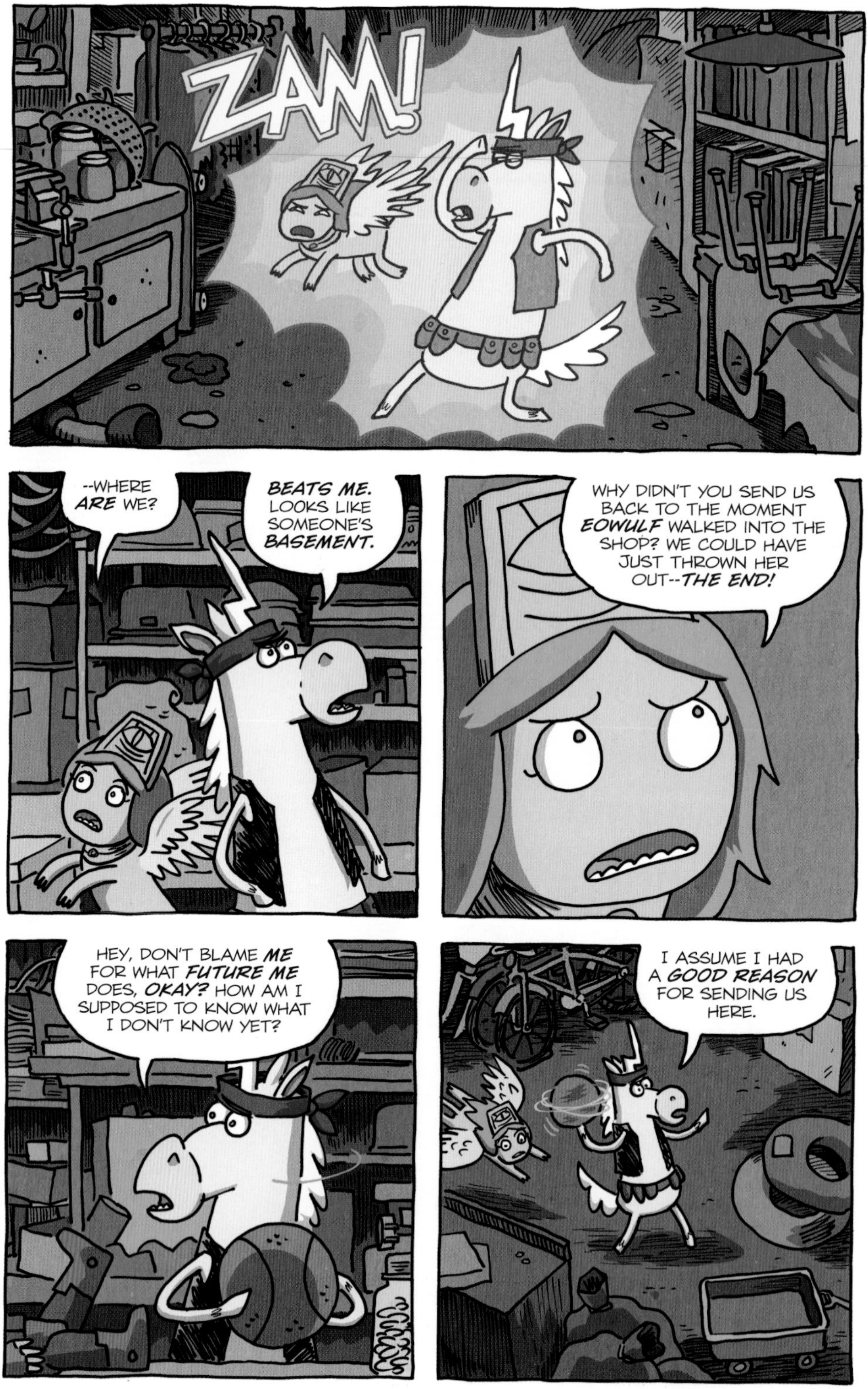
ZAM!
--WHERE ARE WE?
BEATS ME. LOOKS LIKE SOMEONE'S BASEMENT.
WHY DIDN'T YOU SEND US BACK TO THE MOMENT EOWULF WALKED INTO THE SHOP? WE COULD HAVE JUST THROWN HER OUT--THE END!
HEY, DON'T BLAME ME FOR WHAT FUTURE ME DOES, OKAY? HOW AM I SUPPOSED TO KNOW WHAT I DON'T KNOW YET?
I ASSUME I HAD A GOOD REASON FOR SENDING US HERE.

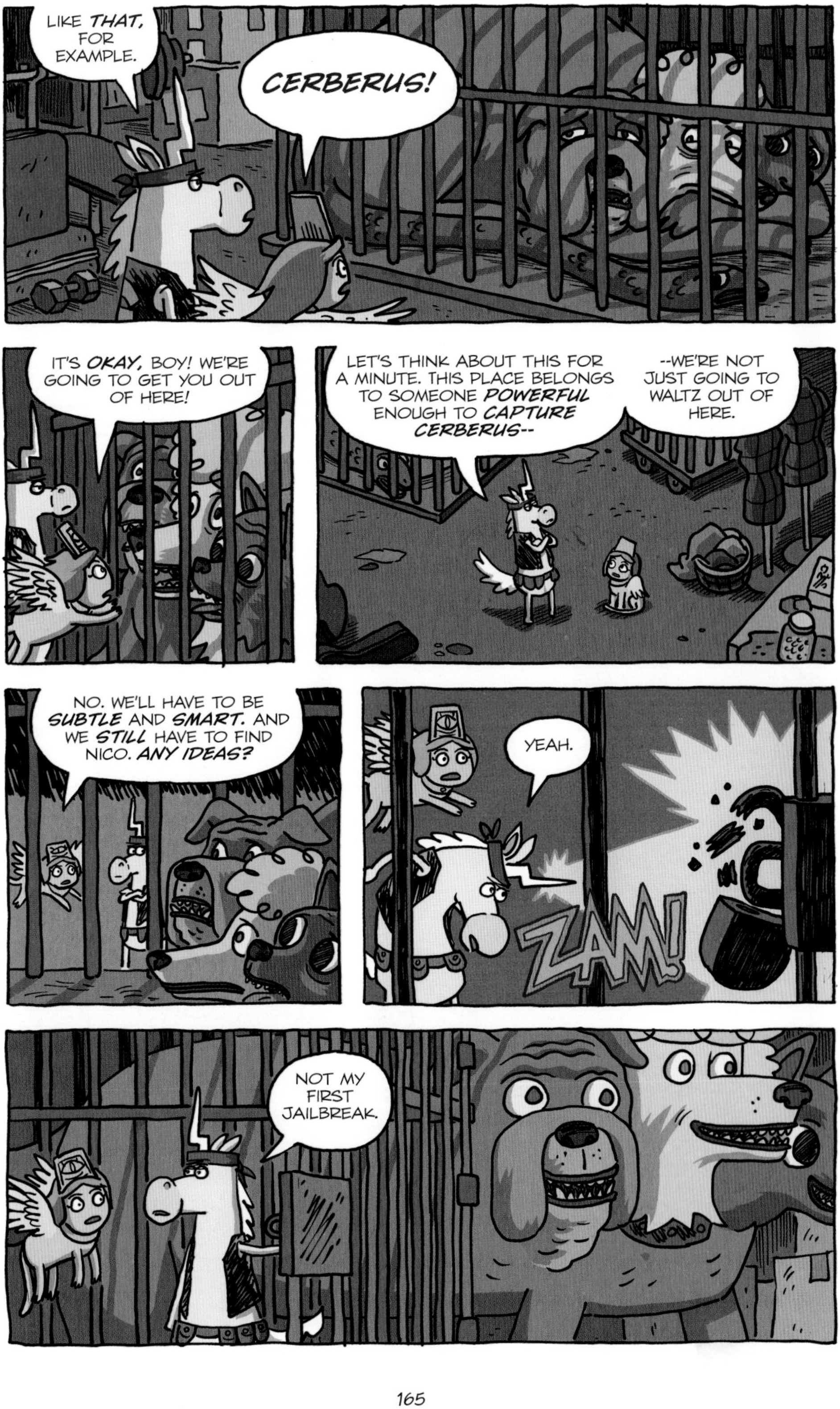
LIKE THAT, FOR EXAMPLE.
CERBERUS!
IT'S OKAY, BOY! WE'RE GOING TO GET YOU OUT OF HERE!
LET'S THINK ABOUT THIS FOR A MINUTE. THIS PLACE BELONGS TO SOMEONE POWERFUL ENOUGH TO CAPTURE CERBERUS--
--WE'RE NOT JUST GOING TO WALTZ OUT OF HERE.
NO. WE'LL HAVE TO BE SUBTLE AND SMART. AND WE STILL HAVE TO FIND NICO. ANY IDEAS?
YEAH.
ZAM!
NOT MY FIRST JAILBREAK.

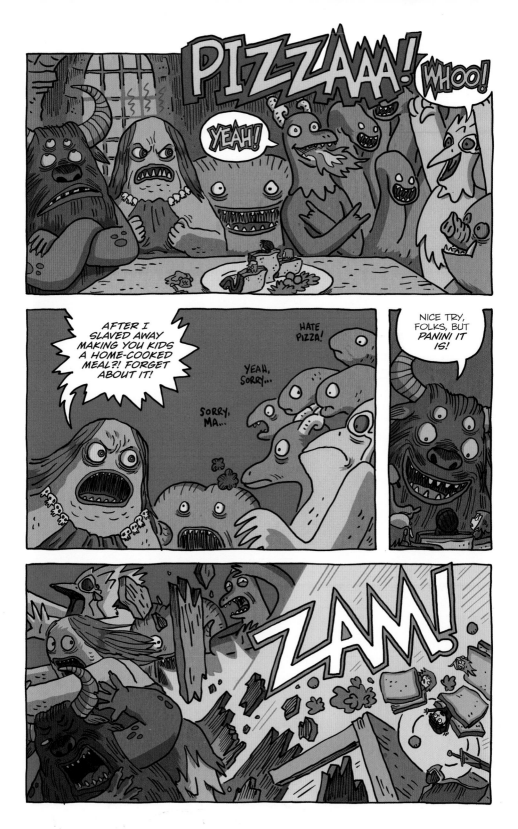

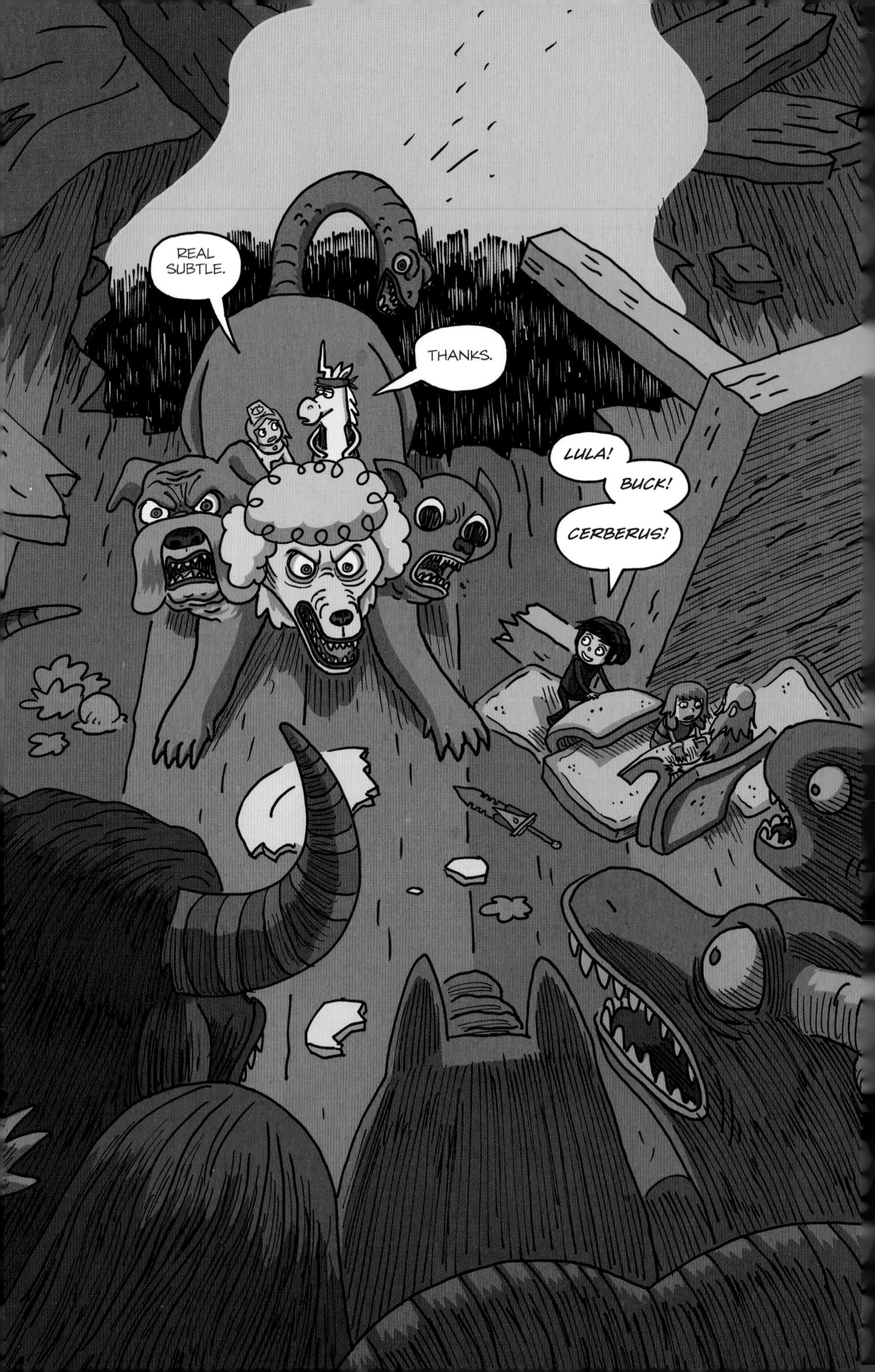
REAL SUBTLE.
THANKS.
LULA!
BUCK!
CERBERUS!

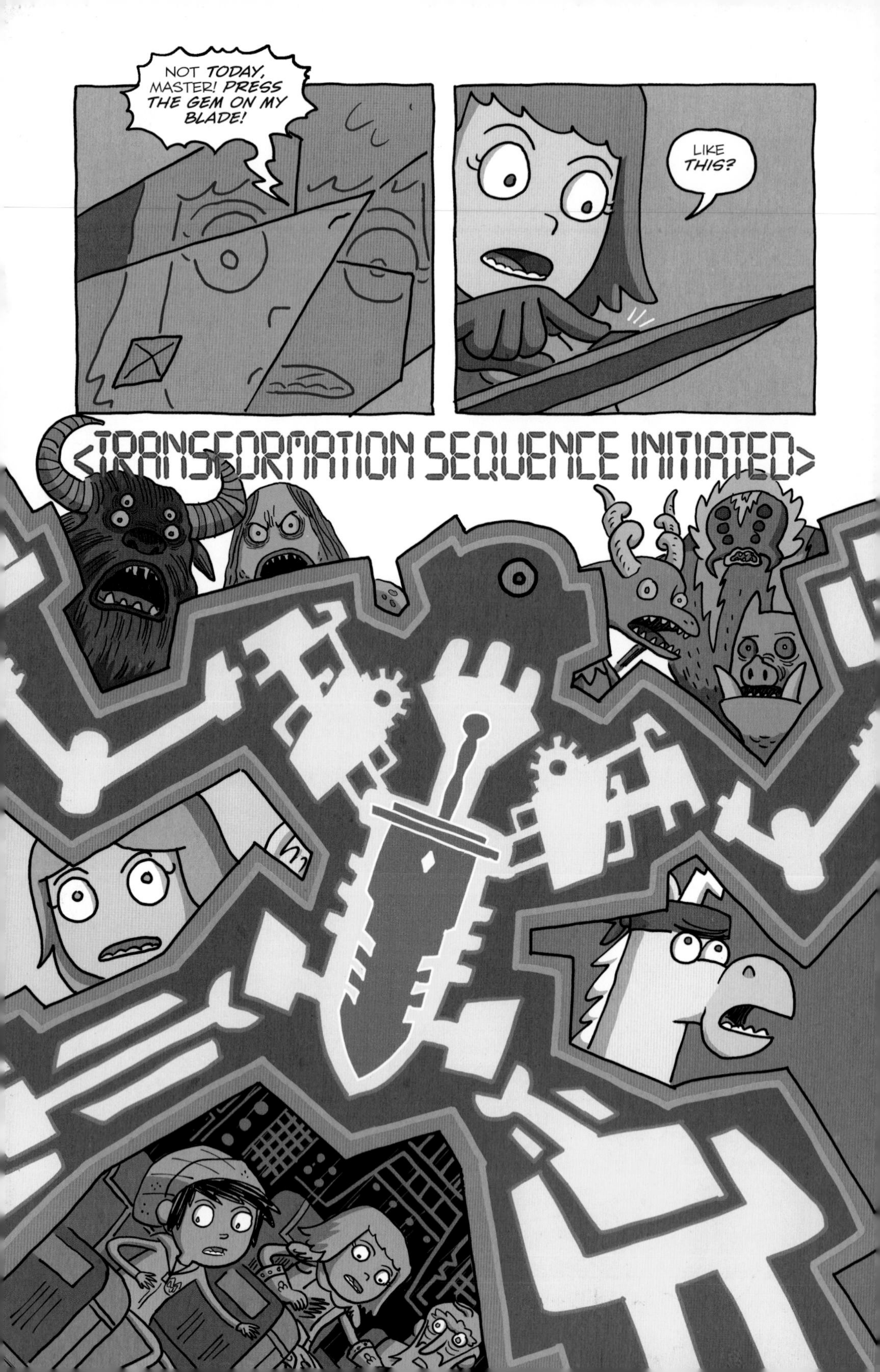
NOT TODAY, MASTER! PRESS THE GEM ON MY BLADE!
LIKE THIS?
<TRANSFORMATION SEQUENCE INITIATED>

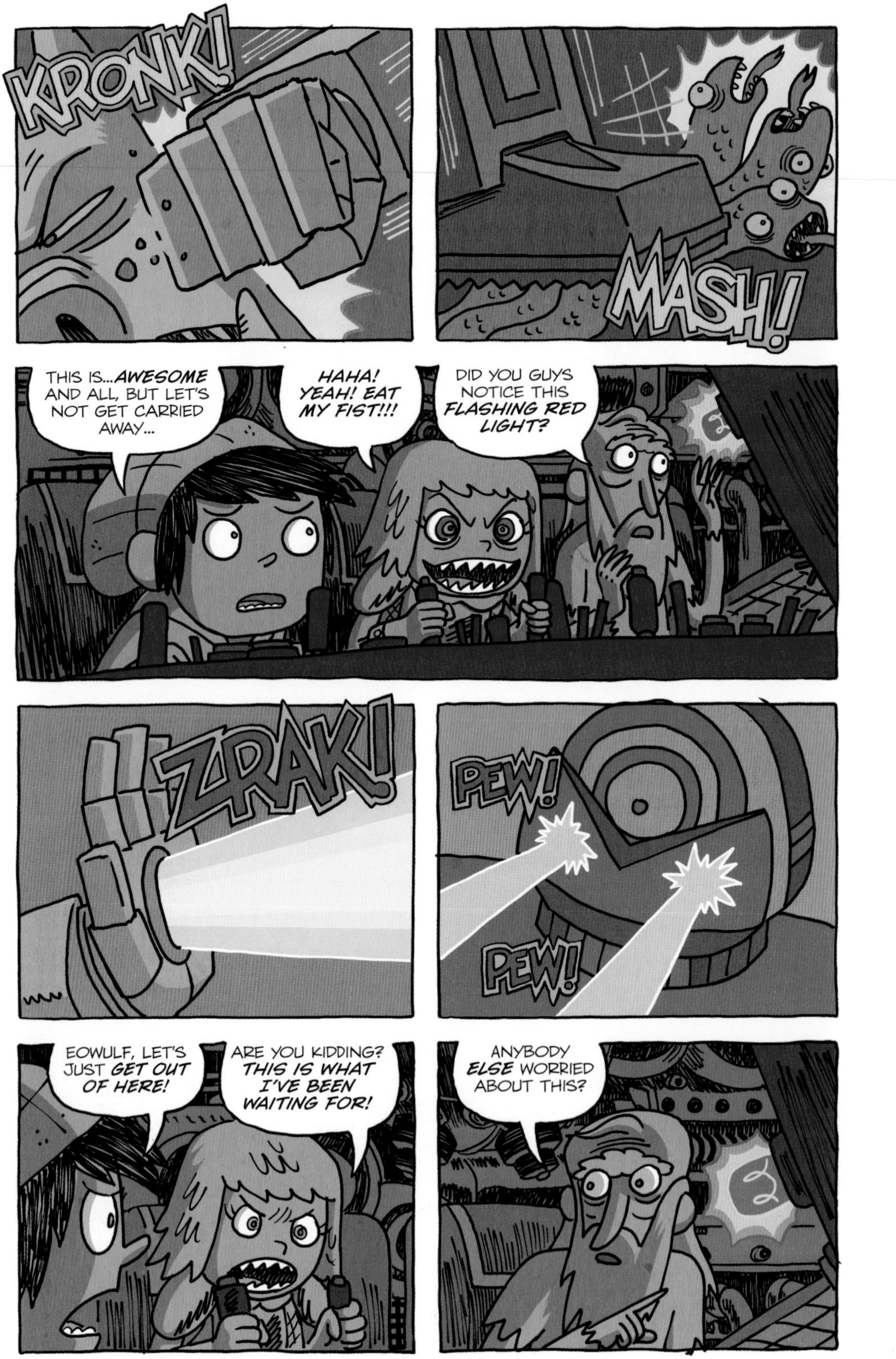
KRONK!
MASH!
THIS IS...AWESOME AND ALL, BUT LET'S NOT GET CARRIED AWAY...
HAHA! YEAH! EAT MY FIST!!!
DID YOU GUYS NOTICE THIS FLASHING RED LIGHT?
ZRAK!
PEW!
PEW!
EOWULF, LET'S JUST GET OUT OF HERE!
ARE YOU KIDDING? THIS IS WHAT I'VE BEEN WAITING FOR!
ANYBODY ELSE WORRIED ABOUT THIS?

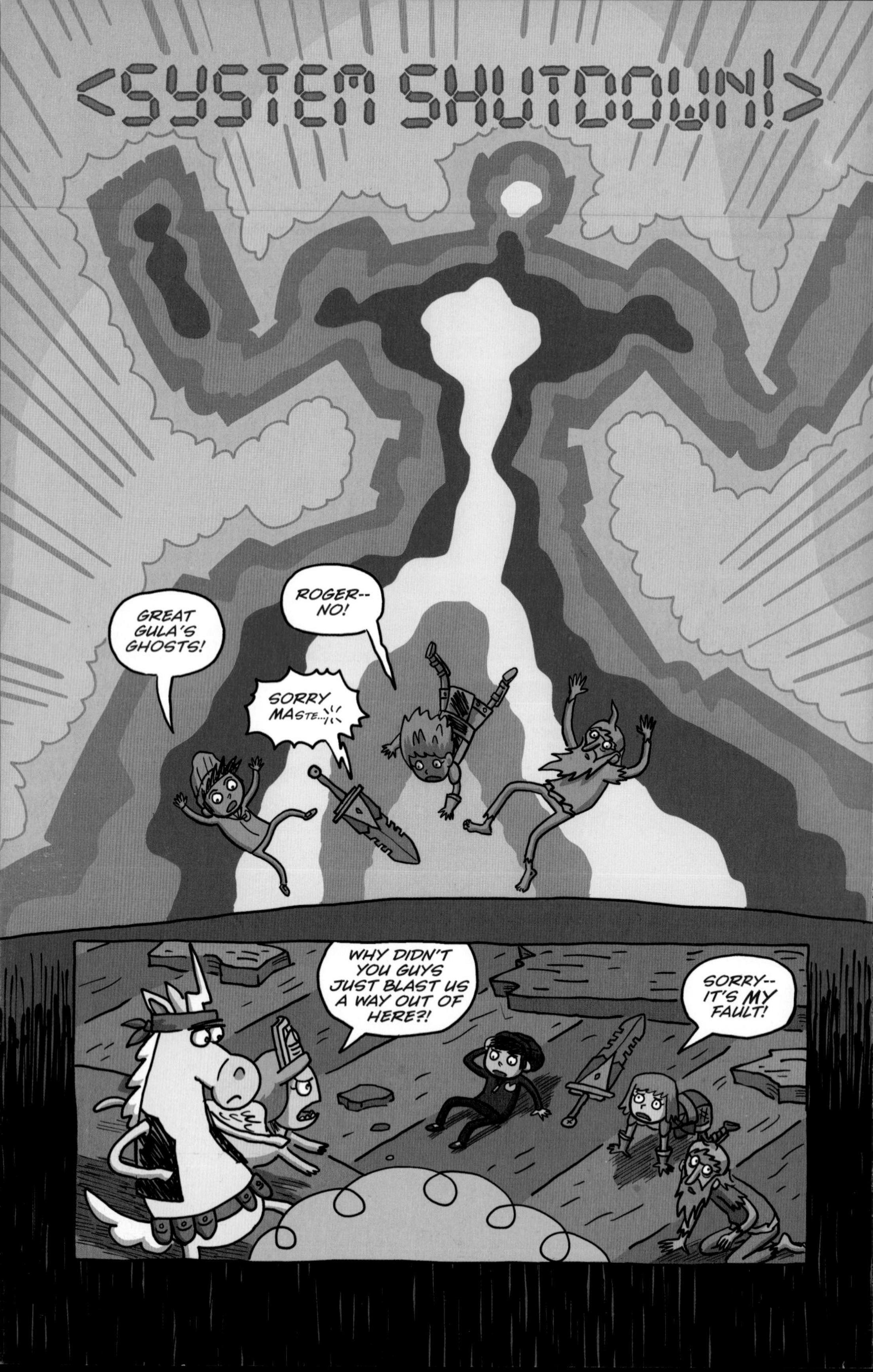
<SYSTEM SHUTDOWN!>
GREAT GULA'S GHOSTS!
ROGER-- NO!
SORRY MASTE...
WHY DIDN'T YOU GUYS JUST BLAST US A WAY OUT OF HERE?!
SORRY-- IT'S MY FAULT!

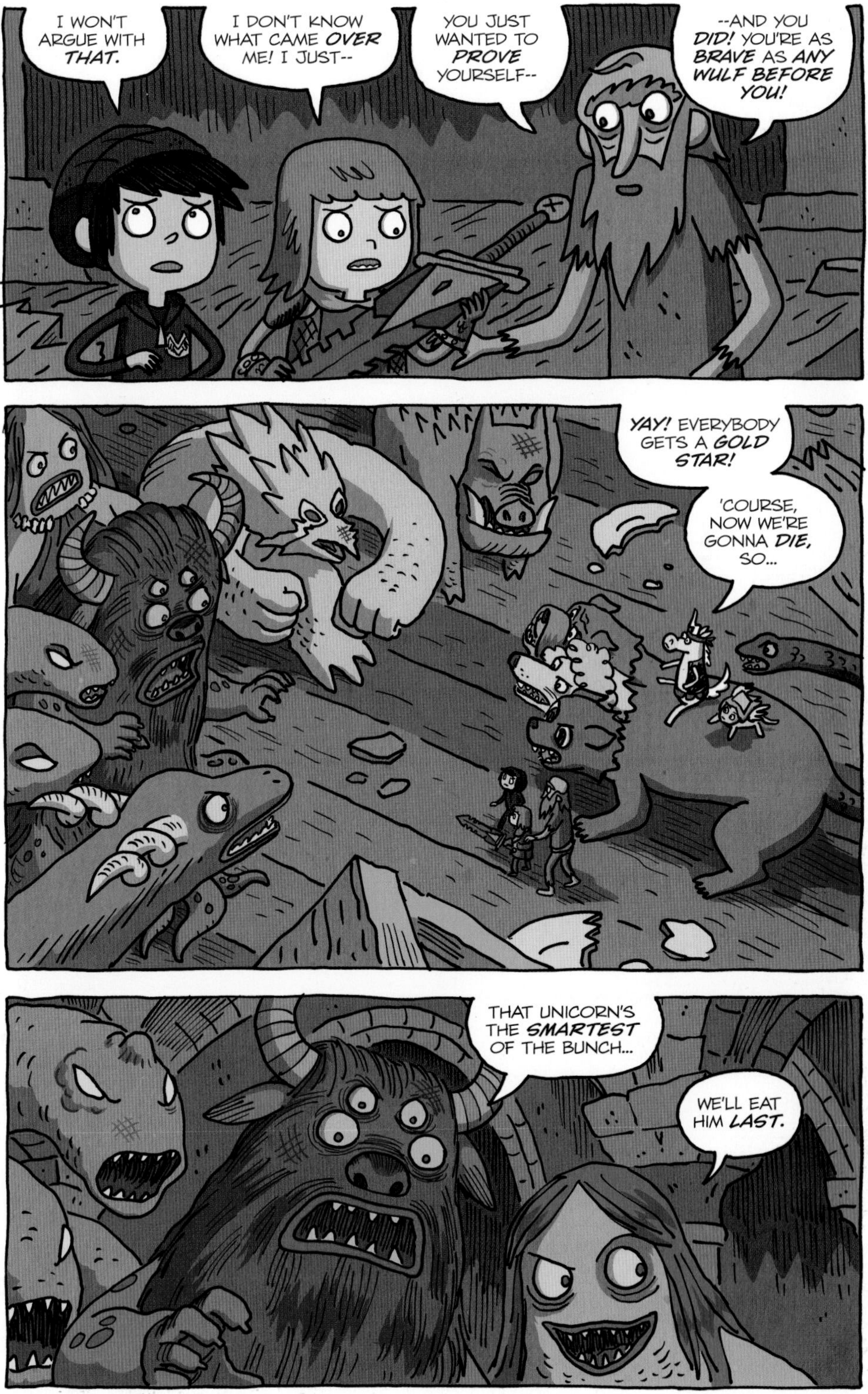
I WON'T ARGUE WITH *THAT.*
I DON'T KNOW WHAT CAME *OVER* ME! I JUST--
YOU JUST WANTED TO *PROVE* YOURSELF--
--AND YOU *DID!* YOU'RE AS *BRAVE* AS *ANY WULF BEFORE YOU!*
YAY! EVERYBODY GETS A *GOLD STAR!*
'COURSE, NOW WE'RE GONNA *DIE,* SO...
THAT UNICORN'S THE *SMARTEST* OF THE BUNCH...
WE'LL EAT HIM *LAST.*

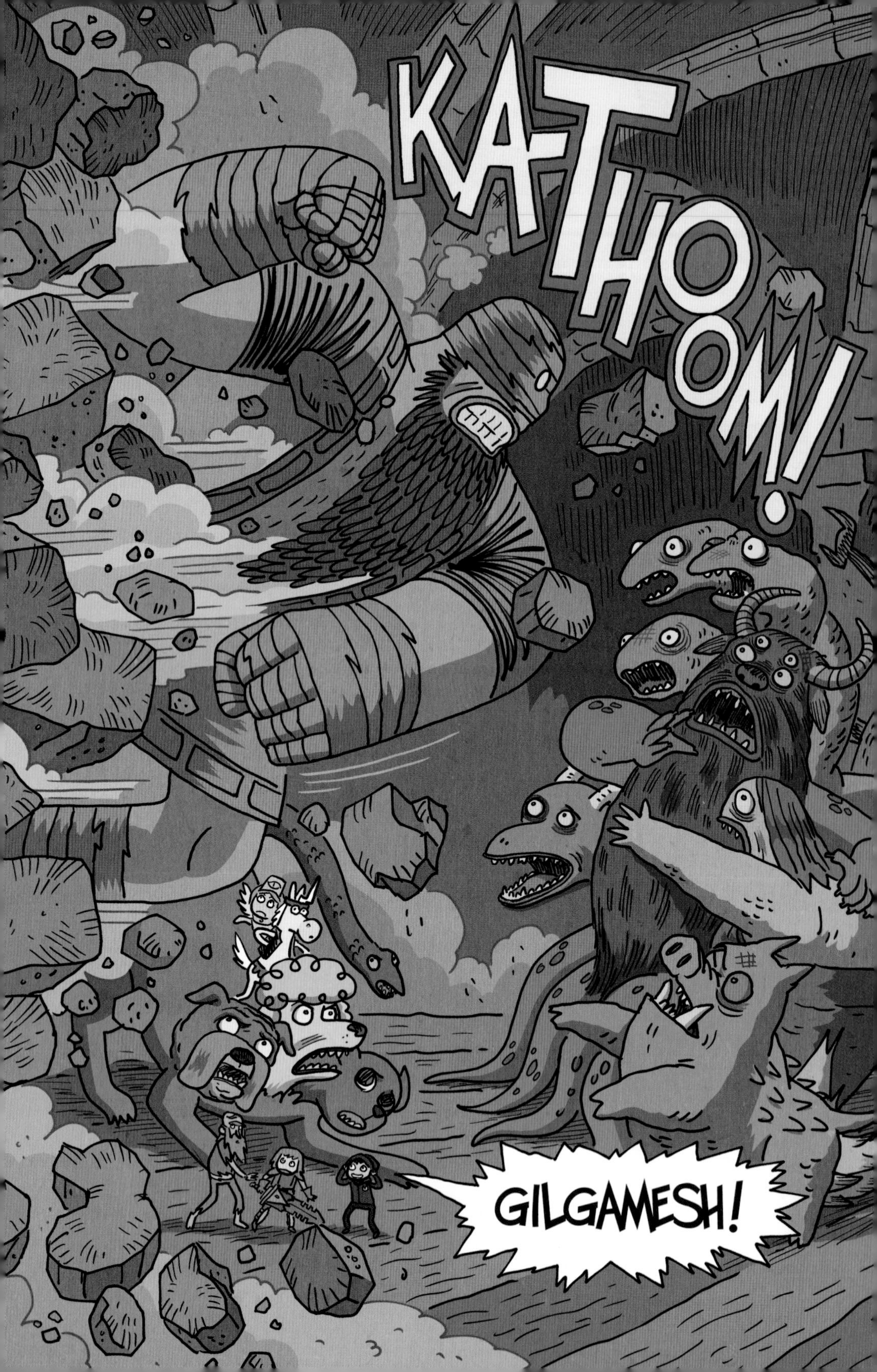
KATHOOM!
GILGAMESH!

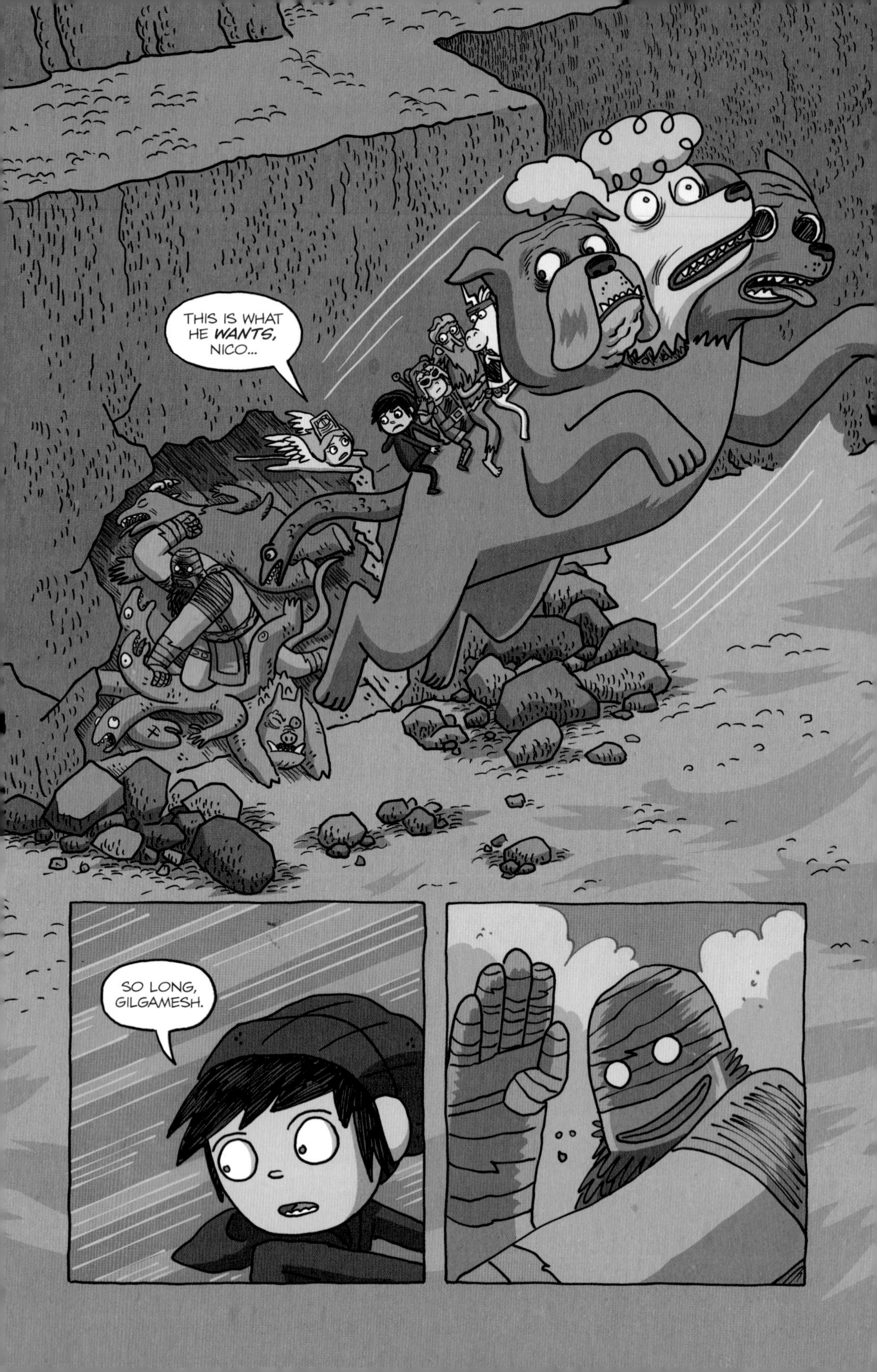
THIS IS WHAT HE *WANTS,* NICO...
SO LONG, GILGAMESH.

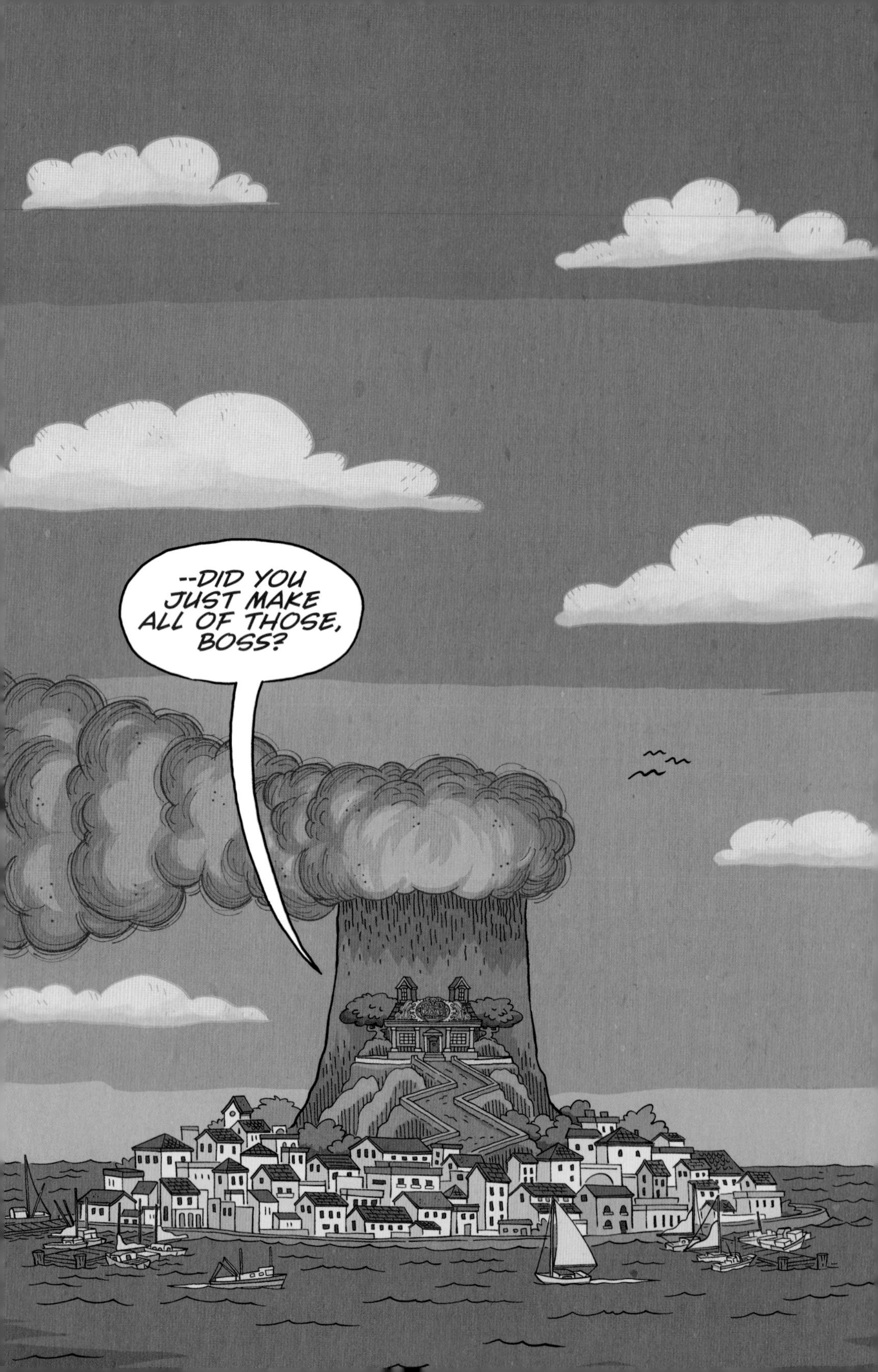
--DID YOU JUST MAKE ALL OF THOSE, BOSS?

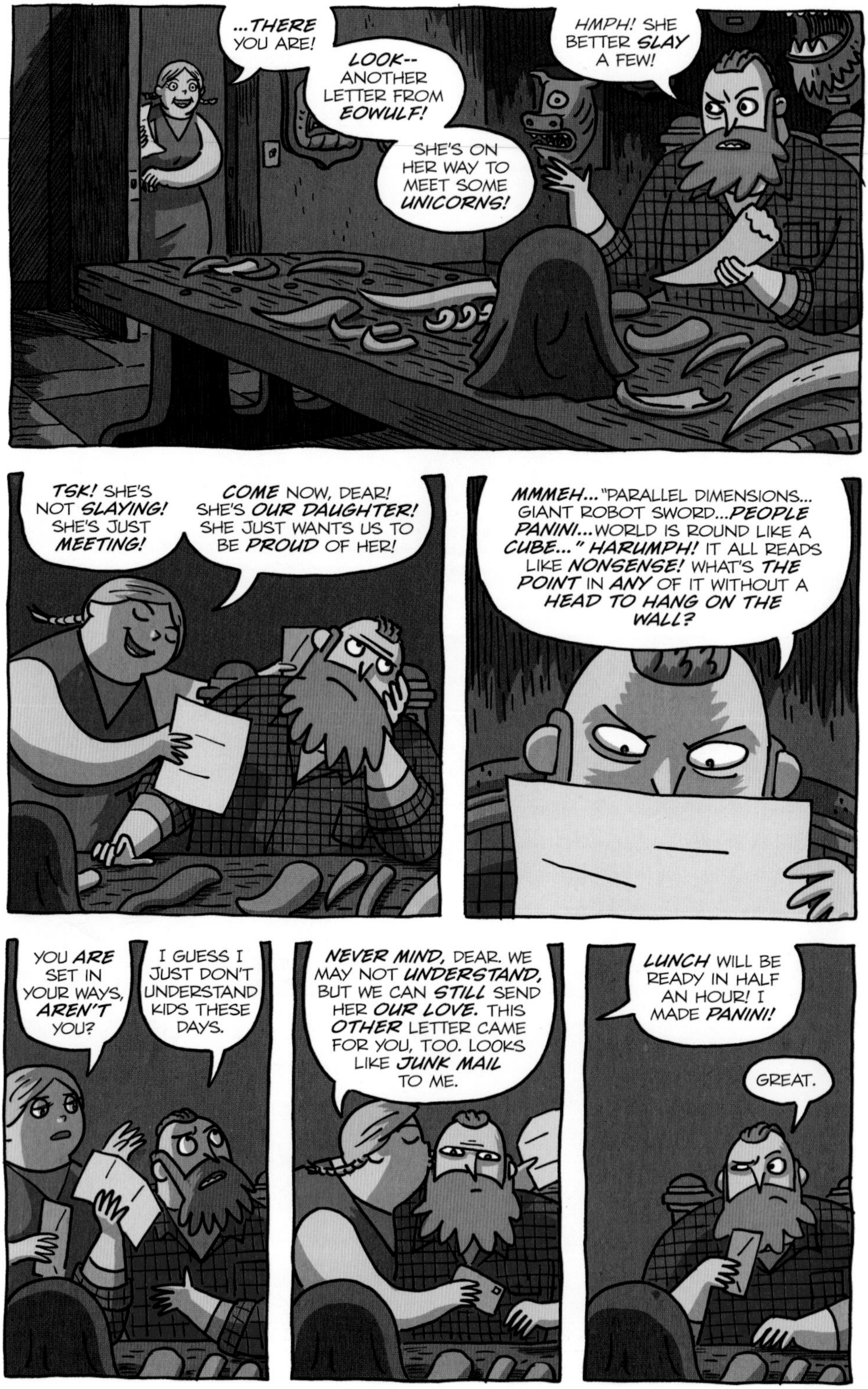
...THERE YOU ARE!
LOOK-- ANOTHER LETTER FROM EOWULF!
SHE'S ON HER WAY TO MEET SOME UNICORNS!
HMPH! SHE BETTER SLAY A FEW!
TSK! SHE'S NOT SLAYING! SHE'S JUST MEETING!
COME NOW, DEAR! SHE'S OUR DAUGHTER! SHE JUST WANTS US TO BE PROUD OF HER!
MMMEH... "PARALLEL DIMENSIONS... GIANT ROBOT SWORD...PEOPLE PANINI...WORLD IS ROUND LIKE A CUBE..." HARUMPH! IT ALL READS LIKE NONSENSE! WHAT'S THE POINT IN ANY OF IT WITHOUT A HEAD TO HANG ON THE WALL?
YOU ARE SET IN YOUR WAYS, AREN'T YOU?
I GUESS I JUST DON'T UNDERSTAND KIDS THESE DAYS.
NEVER MIND, DEAR. WE MAY NOT UNDERSTAND, BUT WE CAN STILL SEND HER OUR LOVE. THIS OTHER LETTER CAME FOR YOU, TOO. LOOKS LIKE JUNK MAIL TO ME.
LUNCH WILL BE READY IN HALF AN HOUR! I MADE PANINI!
GREAT.

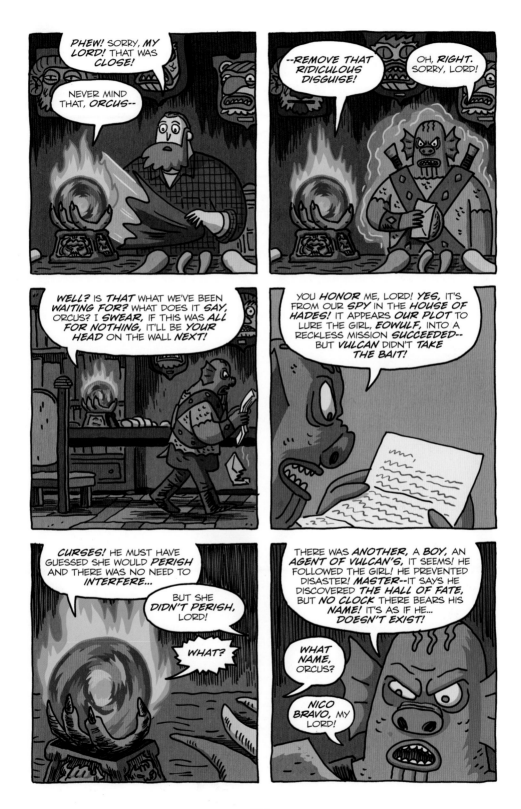

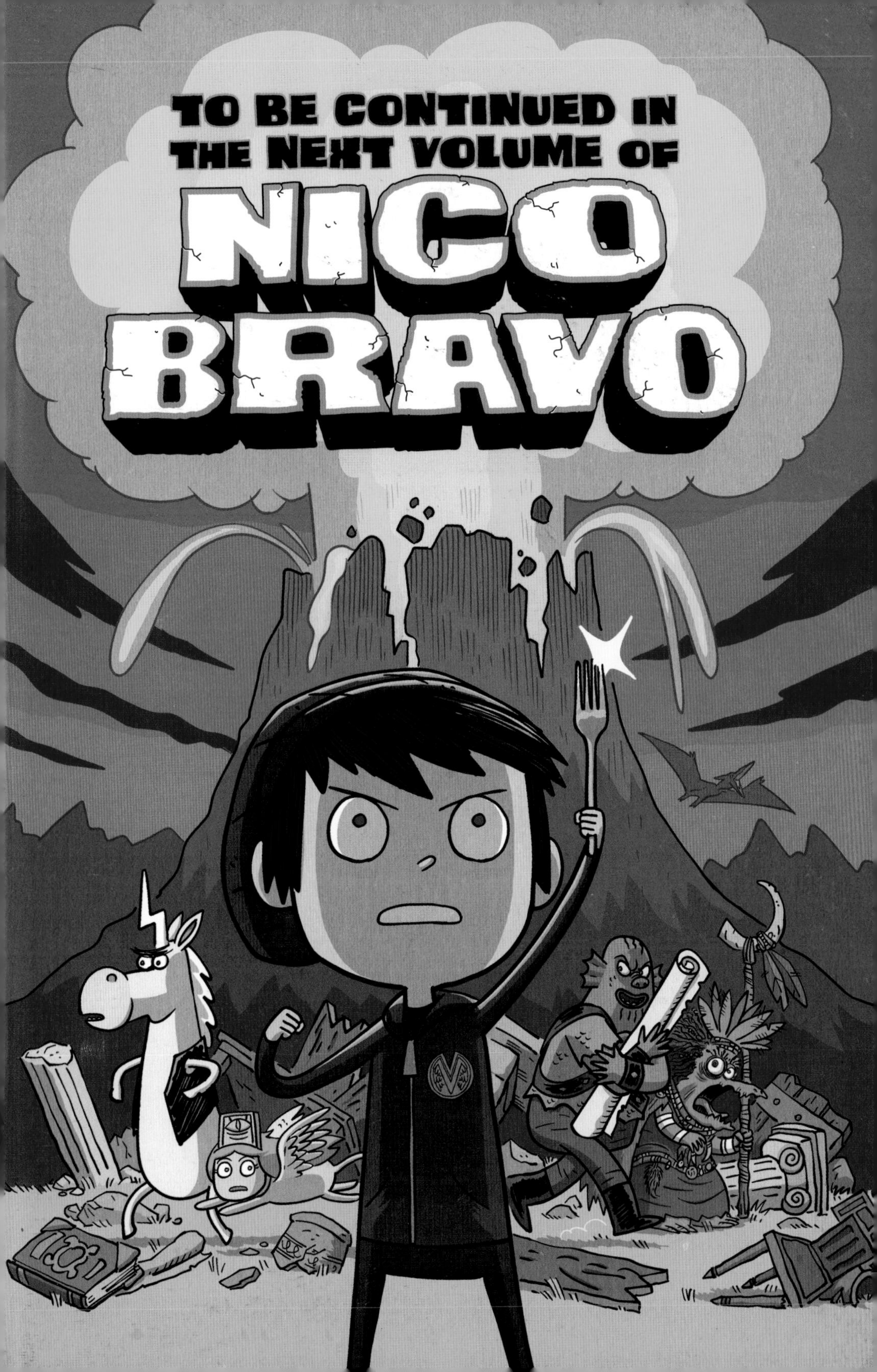
TO BE CONTINUED IN THE NEXT VOLUME OF
NICO BRAVO

THANK YOU

GIORGIA AND FRANK CAVALLARO; LISA NATOLI;
NICK ABADZIS; ANDREW ARNOLD; ROBYN CHAPMAN;
PETER DE SÈVE; SCOTT FRIEDLANDER; DEAN HASPIEL;
JOE INFURNARI; GEORGE O'CONNOR; JOAN REILLY;
BEN SHARPE; MARK SIEGEL; ED STECKLEY; STEVE BEHLING;
SARA VARON; KIARA VALDEZ; COLLEEN AF VENABLE;
THE BOUNCING SOULS FAMILY: GREG, SHANTI, PETE, BRYAN,
GEORGE, K8, MATTY, JANA, WIG, AND AUDREY;
AND CARYN WISEMAN AT ANDREA BROWN LITERARY AGENCY.